DORR TOWNSHIP LIBRARY (DOR)
3 1341 00067 1652
P9-CFJ-354

GOOD GIRLS GONE BAD

also by jillian medoff

Hunger Point

jillian medoff

wm William Morrow *An Imprint of* HarperCollins*Publishers*

Grateful acknowledgment is made to reprint the following excerpt from ONE ART by Elizabeth Bishop, selected and edited by Robert Giroux. Copyright © 1994 by Alice Methfessel. Reprinted by permission of Farrar, Strauss and Giroux, LLC.

This is a work of fiction. The characters, incidents, and dialogues are products of the author's imagination and are not to be construed as real. Any resemblance to actual persons, living or dead, is entirely coincidental.

Designed by Chris Welch

ISBN 0-06-621269-3

Printed in the U.S.A.

For Alice Martell and Dr. Nan Jones, who believe

author's note

The author is indebted to *Fundamental Concepts of Actuarial Science* by Charles L. Trowbridge (Monograph, Actuarial Education and Research Foundation, 1989) for all references to actuarial theory and practice. Any misinterpretation or misapplication of this material is my own.

Our sense of revenge is as exact as our mathematical faculty, and until both terms of the equation are satisfied, we cannot get over the sense of something left undone.

—Inazo Nitobe,
Bushido

When you write my epitaph,
you must say I was the loneliest person who ever lived.

—Elizabeth Bishop,
ONE ART: Letters, 1948

GOOD GIRLS GONE BAD

THE CONCEPT OF CREDIBILITY

PROLOGUE

I consider Tobias's back hair the key to our success as a couple. He has an awesome body: pectoral muscles like tectonic plates, ripped abs, massive shoulders, and lean, hard thighs shaped by prep school lacrosse. Other than his back hair and occasional impotence, my boyfriend, Tobias Teague, is absolutely perfect.

We lie together in his bed. Tobias stares at the ceiling. I reach out to touch his arm but he elbows me away, shielding himself with his hand.

"I'm sorry," I tell him but he's already standing and pulling up his boxers.

"It's not your fault," he replies as he pads to the bathroom. He's not facing my way so I can't be sure whether he's talking to me or reassuring himself.

He's told me before that it's not my fault but I know otherwise. I saw his erection strain his jeans the night we flipped past old concert footage of Jewel on VH1. "Jesus," Tobias said, squinting at the TV, "music sucked in the nineties." But he didn't change the channel. Nor did he take his eyes off her ass as she strummed her guitar and yodeled.

I watched him watch her, then casually mentioned that Jewel grew up in a converted bus in Alaska, hoping he'd understand that not every trailer-park girl ends up cleaning rooms at Days Inn with six kids to feed. Some of us, I wanted him to know, become famous pop stars who act and write verse.

But later in bed when I was slick with desire, silently screaming for Tobias to COME BACK ALREADY!, and he was in the bathroom telling me it's not my fault, so stop saying I'm fucking sorry all the time, I cursed Jewel's ass and wondered if I should learn how to yodel. Of course it's my fault. I don't have a guitar, or a tour manager, or a tight ass like Jewel's. If I did, I reasoned, we wouldn't have these problems. If I did, Tobias would be as hard as a rock.

Then I remembered his back hair. Tobias has light eyes, blond hair, and very fair skin, so I just assumed he had blond hair—or no hair—all over his body. But when he took off his shirt, I was surprised to see thick brown tufts on his shoulders and scraggly, moss-like patches down his spine. All that hair disgusted me at first, but now I use it to my advantage. When Tobias stands in the bathroom clutching his limp penis, and I'm alone in his bed naked and guilt-ridden, I picture his back hair and immediately feel better.

See, I tell myself. I may not get him hard. He may leave me in the end. But he looks and feels like a goddamn gorilla, and frankly, he's lucky I touch him at all.

Tobias doesn't return to bed, but I don't take it personally nor do I feel bad when he asks me to leave. His impotence may shame me, but his back hair gives me confidence I would otherwise lack. God knows where I'd be without it.

Tobias and I work together at Municipal Life Insurance in New York City. MuniLife is a monolithic institution on Twenty-third Street, and the building is a huge expanse that extends all the way from Madison Avenue to Park Avenue South. We're both actuaries, which means we create mathematical models to calculate how much a finger is worth if it's cut off on a meat slicer. With our training, we can determine the value of an enucleated eye, a severed leg, or an ear that's been ripped off in a freak skiing accident. If I study a man at the deli where I get my morning coffee, I'm able to mentally dismember him and determine the value of each of his body parts. No, it's not a glamorous skill but, as they say, it's a living.

Tobias's nickname is Tits, for Tobias Ingram Teague, but I don't call him this. I only hear the self-reference through the particleboard wall that separates our cubicles when he talks on the phone. I try not to listen but can't help myself. Once I overheard him telling a story that involved a girl with big breasts and a billy goat.

When I burst out laughing, Tobias rapped the receiver against the wall. "Great story, huh, Janey?" he said, to which I replied, "I don't know what you're talking about." I was curious how he got the goat in the cab, but didn't want to further incriminate myself nor did I want to break our invisible connection—me snickering on one side of the wall and he softly rapping on the other.

We've been seeing each other for three months and eleven days, which isn't long by most standards, but it's a lifetime if you're thirty-two years old and in the throes of your first real adult love. Or if the boyfriends who came before him thought a Whopper with fries was a big night out.

Tobias has been good to me so far. I say "so far" because I'm always prepared for his leaving. My mother left my father, Zack, and me when I was thirteen. She didn't write us a note or say good-bye. She just disappeared. "This should teach you a lesson," my dad said in a rare moment of self-disclosure. "Don't ever love nobody more'n they love you."

I try to remember this, but Tobias gives me presents, which he hides on my desk underneath stacks of spreadsheets—a picture frame, a baby cactus, a pair of dangly silver earrings. He calls me from his cubicle just to say hello, sends me inter-office E-mail, and pays for my lunch, a gesture the other boys—the Whopper boys—never thought to embrace.

Tobias senses I'm a late bloomer, which is why he wants to take our relationship slowly. Or this is what I tell myself when he refuses to take me to O'Malley's where he drinks with his friends. Maybe "refuses" is too strong. He says he isn't ready to take that step. I, on the other hand, wanted to move in with him the first time he kissed me. So maybe he's just being cautious. Maybe he knows that girls who bloom late have time to make up. Knowing myself, if our situation was reversed, I'd be cautious, too. In fact, if I were him, I'd get the hell out of Dodge.

I'm not unlovable, but I am insatiable. I come from Welter, New York, a factory town upstate where the Black and Wild Moose Rivers converge. Most of the boys from Welter worked summers in the paper mill (the "pulp" we called it), the primary source of income for all of Lewis County. Years before OSHA fined the pulp for safety violations, the boys stuck their hands into the antiquated machines to clean out hoods, change filters, or thread paper. As a result, they had palms thick with scar tissue and patches of flesh where the skin had burned off and didn't grow back. Some of the boys had stumps for fingers or no fingers at all, so my introduction to sex was fraught with the need to squirm away.

There were guys who came later, when I was a scholarship student at MIT. And there were guys after college and in graduate school, but not one of them touched me like Tobias. He caresses places guys rarely go—the nape of my neck, the underside of my arm, the inside of my ankle. His touch is gentle but insistent, and when he strokes me, I want to strip myself naked and spread myself open so he can explore every inch of my body. Because of this unfamiliar desire, I can't get enough of him. Of course I can't tell him this, so I spend an inordinate amount of time trying to hide how I feel.

"You want to go out for dinner?" he asks, calling on the phone from his cubicle. His voice is in stereo. I can hear him through the particleboard and through the receiver.

"I suppose," I say but silently scream, OF COURSE I'LL HAVE DINNER. WHAT ABOUT BREAKFAST? YOU BOOKED FOR BREAKFAST? Other times I say no to keep him at bay. Or I'll think about his back hair and laugh *ha ha ha* in superior disdain. These actions are small, but they give me leverage. They curb my desperation; help me hedge my hope. Sometimes I even convince myself he doesn't see through them.

I'm invisible to guys like Tobias, guys who speak to me as if I'm of no consequence, a cabdriver, for instance, or a suit salesman. They're often polite and sometimes charming, but only because I'm a substitute woman, a reasonable facsimile of the genuine article, someone to help pass the time until the pretty girls—the real girls—finally show up.

If a guy does seem interested in me, he usually believes in conspiracy theories and has a large science fiction collection. My guys are concerned about lunar power politics and whether or not it's ethical to terraform Mars to make it habitable for humans. This isn't to say these guys aren't nice. They're all very nice. But they're also as unmemorable and ordinary and invisible as I am, which means that when we're together, we cancel each other out.

Tobias has never mentioned Mars. Nor is he invisible. On the contrary, he's frequently too conspicuous. He's the guy who leaps into an elevator, bodychecks the closing doors, and clocks someone in the head with his squash racquet. He plays hockey in Municipal Life's marble lobby using an umbrella as a stick and a brown-bagged lunch as the puck. Once I saw him in the hall near the Xerox machine, putting golf balls into a small plastic cup. I often overhear other women discussing him; he seems to have dated every girl on our floor. In fact, the very first time he spoke to me, he was kissing someone else. We laugh about it now, although he laughs harder than I do.

That day I was returning to the office after lunch. I turned the corner, and there he was on Twenty-third Street, sandy-haired and broad-shouldered, a pinup boy for the J. Crew summer catalog. I had already decided that a guy like him, whose insouciant good looks suggested football games with the Kennedy clan, would never see a woman like me, scrawny and bookish, with a past I'd been hiding since the day I left home.

Tobias had a tall, lanky blonde pinned against the granite building, underneath the scaffolding. He and the blonde were kissing and they both had their eyes closed. I was mesmerized by his intensity, and how sweetly he cradled her head in his hands. As I watched, I wondered how some guys know exactly where to touch a woman and others can't stop obsessing about Mars.

Suddenly Tobias's eyes opened. "Hey, pretty girl," he said softly.

"Hey," the woman whispered back, her eyes still closed. But Tobias was looking my way. And we both knew his "Hey, pretty girl" wasn't meant for her. It was meant for me.

Why do you hide behind these goggles?" Tobias fingers my glasses. "You have such a pretty face." He's coaxed me into the stairwell in the MuniLife tower, which means I'll be late for a meeting with

Gretchen, my boss. The stairwell is small, which is surprising given the size of our building. I hang over the rail and look down, but all I can see in the meager light are square landings like the one I'm on and hundreds of steps leading to the ground floor.

Tobias moves behind me and slides his hands under my skirt. The stairwells are always locked, but Tobias got a key from one of the janitors. Tobias excels at getting people to do things for him, especially things they normally wouldn't. I should know. I'm in the stairwell with my skirt hiked up over my ass.

"I don't hide behind my glasses," I lie, pushing them up the bridge of my nose. My voice echoes down the deep stairwell. "My glasses," I repeat, louder this time so I can hear the words resound off the walls. I'm anxious, knowing Gretchen is looking for me, but I'm also excited to be alone with Tobias on company turf. I hold on to the rail and peer over, consider how many bones I could break if I jumped.

"Don't move," he says, reaching around my body to unbutton my blouse. His fingers move under my bra, over my breast, and against my nipple, which he rubs and rubs until my knees weaken. His touch persuades me to stay, convinces me Gretchen would find us amusing. "I want to have sex in the executive boardroom," he tells me. "Right on top of the mahogany table."

I wonder how this could happen, not our gaining entry into our company's sacred boardroom, but how Tobias could fuck me when he can never stay hard. When I try to visualize the two of us together, all I can see is Tobias kissing the tall, lanky blonde underneath the scaffolding on Park Avenue South. Like my guilt over his impotence, this image is a recurring problem for me. When I see him with the blonde, I imagine others just like her. But these women he takes to O'Malley's where they meet all his friends, to Maine where they brunch with his parents, and to churches where they stand at the altar in white wedding gowns. Because I see this so clearly, I can also imagine the end of our relationship, especially the very last day with its attendant Whopper-boy shrugs (his), hysterical crying (mine), desperate I'm sorrys (mine again), and complicated good-byes. Or no good-byes at all, just utter abandonment.

I tell myself that this won't happen, that we'll always be together, even if it's in a cold, damp stairwell with my skirt hiked up and my blouse wide open and Tobias behind me groaning in pleasure. But still, I pray. "Please God. Please let him always want me. And please, if he doesn't, let me die before finding out." So far I can say faith has been on my side.

We hear people on the other side of the door. I try to pull up my underwear, which is down at my knees, but Tobias is holding my arms and thrusting against me. "You're so hard!" I blurt out. Maybe I don't need a guitar, I consider. Maybe I have this Jewel thing all wrong.

The voices get closer. There's a jangle of keys.

Panicked, I imagine Gretchen in the doorway pointing to her leather-bound Palm Pilot. Horrified by my behavior, she sends me back to Welter, to my father and the pulp and the boys with no fingers. "What if they open the door?" I whisper, but I'm bucking against him and reaching behind to pull him in closer.

A key slides into the lock just as Tobias slides into me. "Put both hands on the rail," he commands, "and bend over." Behind me, he flips down my skirt and wraps his arms across my chest like ammunition belts. Then he nestles himself inside me as deep as he can, given the odd angle. "Don't move!" he repeats. Of course I comply and stand as still as a statue, that is, if I were a statue of a girl having sex doggy-style.

Whoever is on the other side of the door takes an awfully long time to open it. I hear more voices and laughter, then the fading of footsteps. Just when I think they're gone, the door swings open. A big man holding a key ring stands in the doorway, wearing a shirt that has "Eddie" stitched over his heart. "Excuse me?" he asks, but as he sizes us up, his lips curl into a smile. "You ain't supposed to be here."

I close my eyes and will myself invisible. I imagine a happy ending where my mother returns after her two-decade absence and my father breaks his silence and whoops with joy.

"I know, Eddie," I hear Tobias say, and for a second I think he's telling me he *knows* Eddie, that Eddie is the guy who gave him the key. "Janey dropped her ID down the stairwell. I was about to hike her over the rail so she could retrieve it, but we're having some difficulty."

"Son," Eddie says slowly, "you're on the twenty-fourth floor."

"No kidding!" Tobias breaks into his infectious frat-boy laugh, a laugh so chummy, it makes ordinary people do the most extraordinary things. I submit, as evidence, my current position.

"I'll be back in two minutes," Eddie tells him. "I suggest you find another place to—"

"Two minutes, no problem. We're already gone."

Eddie bends over to look into my eyes. "You all right, miss?" he asks, as if it has suddenly occurred to him that I might be in danger.

"Fine," I croak. "Just fine."

Eddie steps back. "Two minutes," he says. Then—although I can't be sure because it happens so fast—I swear I see Eddie give Tobias a "boys-will-be-boys" kind of wink. I can't see what Tobias is doing behind me, if he winks in return. I tell myself it's not possible, he'd never do that to me. Eddie's smile, however, suggests otherwise.

Once the door closes, Tobias picks up where he left off.

"Go slower," I moan, wanting to savor the unexpected pleasure of his erection.

But Tobias has only one goal in mind. He arches his back and pushes my head down. His grunts drown out the smacking sound my skull makes as it hits the railing. He comes quickly, finishes with a loud, drawn-out aaaahh, then shakes himself off, and pulls up his pants.

"That was great!" he sings as he buckles his belt. He kisses me and I taste cinnamon Tic Tacs. "I love you," he tells me. "Love you" echoes in my head like a call down a canyon.

I don't respond because I'm reeling. I touch my forehead where there's already a bump. He loves me, he said. Do I ask if he meant it? Do I say it back? "Did Eddie know?" I ask, which is not what I mean. I want to know if Eddie *knew*. If this was a setup, some grand master plan.

"I'm sure he got the picture." Tobias points to my Hanes for Her, which are still at my knees.

An hour later, after I've apologized to Gretchen for missing our meeting ("Something unexpected came up," I explained), I'm back at my desk. My phone rings. "That was great!" Tobias crows, his voice booming through the particleboard wall.

"People can hear you, Tobias!"

"You're the best," he whispers loudly, which again, I hear outside the receiver.

"No, you're the best. The best," I repeat, then hang up wondering about Big Eddie's wink and what else it will take to make Tobias stay hard.

"Tobias?" I whisper from my side of the wall. It's been two days since our stairwell session and I'm ready to tell him I love him.

"There's a party tonight at O'Malley's," he says.

"Really?" I squeal. "I'd love to go to O'Malley's."

"Bring your friend Alexandra. She's cute."

I'm confused. I don't have a friend named Alexandra. I'm about to point this out when I hear him hang up the phone.

As much as I believe in the inevitability of abandonment, I also believe in fate and serendipity and dreams that come true. Tonight I have an appointment with my eye doctor, who is near O'Malley's, give or take forty blocks. So overhearing Tobias is a sign telling me to seize the day, take a chance, live large. He's talking very loudly, I reason. He's wants me to surprise him. Guys love surprises, especially when they love you.

O'Malley's is packed by the time I arrive. My eyes are dilated, so I pick my way through the crowd carefully, blinking like mad to get the world into focus. Eventually I find the bathroom, where I sit in the stall. I hear the door open and see two pairs of high heels turn to the sink.

"How cool is it that Tits Teague showed up?" one girl says, snapping her gum.

I flush and step out, stand next to the girls. "Tits is here?" A tear slides down my cheek. "I'm not crying," I explain. "I just came from the eye doctor." Why I say this eludes me, but I'm sure it has something to do with the way the two women glare at my reflection.

The girl with the gum wears a velvet headband that pulls her hair back, exposing a forehead as smooth as an egg. "You know Tits?" she asks, still snapping away. She takes out her gum and sticks it on the mirror, right between my eyes. We both stare at my face. My oversize glasses and dilated pupils make me look like Mr. Magoo. Her friend, who is wearing a turtleneck embroidered with bluebirds, laughs.

"Did I say something funny?" I ask her.

"Not yet," Bird Girl informs me.

"How do you know Tobias?"

"We all went to prep school together. Did you go to Groton?"

"I went to Welter." I turn my head slightly and silently sniff. The pulp up in Welter has a smell—a mixture of sulfur, bleach, and factory exhaust—that is so thick, if you are south of the mill when the wind shifts, you can feel the air drip down your throat as you breathe. Even though I left home a hundred years ago, I worry that I still carry the smell, a stink as distinguishing as a Midwestern twang I can't seem to shake.

"How do *you* know Tobias?" Bird Girl asks.

Intuition tells me I should wipe my eyes and run. But I can't. This is my chance to live large. I throw back my shoulders and boldly announce that I am his girlfriend.

Bird Girl warms up. "Really? How did you meet?" When I tell her, she and her friend get excited. They ask me all kinds of questions: how serious we are, if I've met his parents, will I be attending the Groton reunion.

I relax a little, forgive my oversize pupils, consider asking them both to be bridesmaids. "We're not that serious," I say humbly. "But we're happy."

Bird Girl grabs my hand. "Come with me," she says. "I know where he is." As I'm led through the bar, I have a vision of Big Eddie and his split-second wink. I imagine him laughing with Tobias as they hoist a few pints and chuckle about women who like to have sex in the company stairwell.

But what I see in real life, outside my head, is infinitely worse. Bird Girl points out Tobias, who is leaning against a pool table kissing a tall, lanky blonde. I squint hard and even with my dilated eyes, I recognize the girl he had pinned against the Municipal Life building almost four months ago.

Suddenly the things that I see—the lanky blonde's head, Tobias's hand, the long cue stick resting on top of the table—start to grow fuzzy and refuse to hold shape. I wonder if something is wrong with my eyes, if the drops I was given are making me hallucinate. I blink blink blink, but Tobias is still there. The last thought I have before looking away is that I've imagined this so often, I've willed it to happen.

Bird Girl pats my arm in a comforting way, then asks, "How can you be Tobias's girlfriend if he's engaged to Debby Dupont?" She pauses. "They've been together since Groton. Do you not care or not know?"

"Both," I say and walk toward Tobias, who opens his eyes and freezes midkiss. His head swivels from me to the blonde, then over to his friends. Behind me, I hear Bird Girl gasp.

"Janey," he says finally, "why are you here?" His voice, harsh and accusatory, fills me with rage. I try to envision his back hair and resurrect my self-confidence, but I can't. Nor can I drift away unseen—I'm as present and imperiled as the day my mom left me.

"This is Debby." Tobias pushes the blonde forward so she's standing between us. "My fiancée."

"What does that mean?" My voice is loud, and people turn to look.

"It means we're getting married," Debby says sweetly, as though I'm retarded.

"I know what the word means. But who am I if you're his fiancée?"

Debby glances at Tobias but Tobias is watching his friends. He answers, not looking at me, not even seeing me. "You're the girl," he replies, "who I fuck on the side."

Everyone cracks up because no one believes him. Who would say such a thing? It's so absurd, even Debby chimes in. Some guy says, "Man, that's harsh," but still they keep laughing. When I hear Tobias laugh with them, I get in his face.

"I have herpes," I tell him, and turn to Debby. "You know what that means. It's the gift that keeps giving." Then I turn on my heel and storm out of the bar.

The story I just told isn't true. Well, it's true with the exception of two small points. First, Tobias has no back hair. His back is as smooth and as sleek as MuniLife's marble lobby. Second, I didn't have a snappy comeback that night in O'Malley's. When I say that Tobias could make me do things I normally wouldn't, I don't mean he could give a voice to my rage. I mean he could make me fall in love, and because he has no back hair, I had no leverage, so I kept right on falling.

What really happened is this: I raced out of the bar and started to cry. Tobias followed. "I wanted to tell you about Debby," he said, his voice sweeter than before. "But I didn't want to hurt you." He touched my shoulder. "Don't be mad."

I stared at him so hard I began to see double. His face grew distorted and his features blended together in such a way that he appeared to have none. In my memory of that moment, Tobias isn't a man, he's a shadow that dissolves as soon as I blink. Because of this, I can preserve the image I want: a boyish, sexy guy with clear blue eyes and ripped deltoids who hides dangly silver earrings underneath stacks of spreadsheets. Similarly, I'm sure that I spoke, but again memory fails me, and I can't say for sure what I said. I certainly hope, though, it had something to do with his erectile dysfunction.

I wish I could say there was a happy ending, but happy endings are hard to come by, especially for girls like me—trailer-park girls with oversize glasses and a genius for calculating the value of probable loss. I never spoke to Tobias again unless it was in monosyllabic responses (for which he seemed relieved) and soon I left MuniLife as unobtrusively as I had once arrived.

All of this happened more than two years ago, but for a long time after we stopped working together, I continued to keep track of Tobias's whereabouts. He lived in a brownstone in the Village. He still worked at Municipal Life. He left for the office at seven-thirty and took a cab to Twenty-third Street. When it was nice out, he walked. He bought his coffee, which he took light and sweet, at a diner on Sheridan Square. If he'd known how closely connected we were, he would've accused me of stalking. But I'm not a stalker. I'm a forecaster of futurity and a curator of history, both of which, like anything sacred, require constant attention and, sometimes, revision.

The practice of actuarial science has three different specialties—life, pension, and property/casualty. When Tobias and I were at Municipal Life, we were both on track to become life actuaries. Life actuaries have traditionally been interested in designing the perfect mathematical formula that graduates vast numbers of raw data to illustrate the force of mortality. My father asked me to explain this in normal people's words. So I said, "Dad, you're going to die. And I'm the person who can tell you when." That was the last time he asked about my work.

When I left MuniLife, I changed specialties. I'm now a property and casualty actuary. This means I study credibility, which has to do with interpreting claim experience when a subsection of a population exhibits a different claim experience from the whole. I know all about subpopulations, especially those populations living in weather-beaten trailers in foul-smelling towns. And I'm an expert at credibility; or rather I'm able to make up plausible details when the real story is too painful to tell. Graham, my boss, says I interpret these concepts too literally. But he's wrong. Without literal interpretation, language loses its meaning. Without it, we'd be nothing more than a pack of wild frat boys who call each other Tits and toss off "I love yous" like rubber lacrosse balls. I also think Graham would be less uptight if he slept with his own wife once in a while, but because he's a partner I keep those words to myself.

Actuaries understand that the impossibility of certainty is one of the facts with which all humans contend. The night I saw Tobias kissing Debby Dupont, I was reminded of this uncertainty. My mother abandoned me, the only guy I ever loved had betrayed me, and I was alone and crying on the sidewalk, thinking if only I were prettier or sexier or smelled less of pulp, my life would've turned out differently. The world, as I experienced it, was not a perfect place.

In many respects, the actuary's role is to help make the world, if not perfect, then a little less uncertain. That night at O'Malley's was a turning point for me. I realized that I had within me the power to change the course of my life. I could fix it so I'd never again be caught off guard. I'd never be laughed at. No one would ever leave me. Right there on the street, amid the wail of police sirens, I began to design the perfect model to express the only concept of which I was certain: the force of mortality—*my* mortality—the reckoning of which could deliver me from an imperfect, uncertain world. In normal people's words, I decided to kill myself.

As I trudged home, I considered the possibilities. My list, which was lengthy but comprehensive, included pills and guns, razors and ropes, and free-fall leaps down long, dark stairwells. I got into bed debating self-immolation, carbon monoxide, and injections of foreign substances into my bloodstream. Finally I slept clutching Tobias's dangly silver earrings and dreaming of Jewel in her Alaskan minibus, strumming her guitar and yodeling.

In retrospect, I believe it was the number of options that sustained me, not only that night, but in the days, then the months, then the years that would follow. But the force of mortality was a beacon for me, and I was never in doubt that I wanted to die. Eventually, I met the girls, and someone *did* die. The irony is—*ha ha ha*—it just wasn't me.

RANDOM VARIABLES

1

We met in Group, the girls and I. There were seven of us when we were with Dr. Hensen, then six when the Dream Weaver disappeared. The Weaver dropped out of sight right after we killed Tobias, so I figured she'd resurface once everything calmed down. But that was weeks ago and she still hasn't shown up.

I feel bad about Tobias, but his death was an accident and group therapy has taught me not to feel guilty about circumstances beyond my control. My feelings about the Weaver's disappearance, however, are much more personal and thus more distressing. When my mother left, I considered every conceivable explanation: kidnapping, drunk driver, a secret affair. But we never got a ransom call or found her body. Nor was there evidence she loved another man. "We had normal married problems," my dad told the sheriff. "But we loved each other." To which the sheriff replied, "Sometimes, Zack, disappearin' ain't got nothing to do with love."

I've harbored fantasies of my mother all my life. She's poolside at the Beverly Wilshire Hotel wearing black wraparound glasses and sipping piña coladas with Marcelo, her Pilates instructor. Or she shows up at my door wearing a sheer bathing suit and perky sun visor, having just sailed the world with a Greek fishing magnate. Since she left me nothing else, her legacy was my compulsive need to fantasize, even now, so many years after the fact.

When I'm in line in the deli, for instance, getting my morning coffee, I concoct elaborate scenarios with the handsome doctors, lawyers, and CEOs who cut in front of me. In my mind, I'm big-breasted and red-headed, and have a wicked, sexy smile. When I say, "I believe I was ahead of you," the D/L/CEO stutters at the sight of my beauty, asks for my phone number, and then we get married. Sometimes we have four kids, move to New Jersey, then retire in the Blue Ridge Mountains. Sometimes one of us tragically dies in a small commuter plane. But both of us understand that I am the love of his life, the woman against whom all others are measured.

In reality, I'm petite, with a boyish figure that would be very striking on someone taller, but because I'm so short I look like an underdeveloped teenager wearing her mother's ill-fitting clothing. Like many actuaries, I favor boxy brown suits and sensible pumps. I also have boxy brown hair and wear oversize glasses with very thick lenses that make my eyes look smaller than they really are. I don't wear contacts because sticking a plastic disk in my eye seems unnecessarily painful. I don't mind the idea of hurting myself. However, I'd rather do it with an impressive flourish that has the potential for media interest rather than hunched over my sink performing a mundane morning ritual.

Boxy brown suits and sensible pumps reflect the conservative nature of actuarial science. It is not, as a rule, a sexy profession. I design complex reserve models for workmen's compensation and other types of employee benefit plans at a Big Five accounting firm. This means I look at a company's claims history and develop financial paradigms that illustrate their future liability (i.e., how much they will pay out to policyholders over time).

When I was growing up in Welter, the pulp had no formal workers' comp plans, or rather, the plans they did have rarely paid out, so I think it's ironic that I'm designing them now. In Group, Dr. Hensen said he didn't think it was ironic at all, which was a signal for me that it was time to change the subject.

I like being an actuary. I work with statistical theory and laws of probability that are rational and judicious. When I apply these laws to a mathematical model, I step out of real time and space and move into a zone devoid of emotional entanglement. When I'm in this zone, I can lose myself completely, but don't indulge in fantasies in which mothers return and strangers propose. Nor do I shed any tears.

I don't know why the Weaver disappeared, but I'm sure it has to do with Tobias—the fact that we killed him, I mean. I also think it has to do with love, because when I met her, that's what she, like all the Group girls, was seeking. But most important, I think she left because of me, since I was the one who led us to Tobias in the first place.

So these are the facts: Tobias seduced me, and I fell in love. Tobias dumped me, and I met the girls. Tobias was killed, and the Dream Weaver went missing. Much of this, of course, is very upsetting, especially since I may have been spared guilt about Tobias's death, but I haven't been spared grief. To this end, I grieve the Weaver's disappearance the way I grieve my long-lost mother. I also grieve for Tobias, and will for the remaining forty-eight years of my life, plus or minus five years (rough 95 percent confidence interval with 2.96 standard deviations). This is assuming of course (the force of mortality being what it is) that I don't take matters into my own hands.

The girls and I call Suzanna the Dream Weaver because when it was her turn to share, she offered long dream sequences with entire casts of characters and fully realized plot points, all of which she seemed to be making up as she went along. I hate it when people recount their dreams in real life, but nothing compared to the agony of listening to the Weaver drone on in Group.

The Weaver has electric red hair that frizzes around her head, severely arched brows that give her a look of perpetual WOW, and green eyes that grow misty when she discusses Ginger, her beloved Pekingese. To digress, the Weaver and Ginger have a curious relationship. The Weaver is an emergency-room nurse at St. Vincent's and puts in endless hours of overtime to afford doggie day care. She also sneaks Ginger into the hospital on Bring Our Daughters to Work Day and dresses her in Baby Gap outfits that are so adorable, every time I see that fucking dog, I well up with tears triggered by my own baby lust. But what's worse than all this was how she gave Ginger star billing in all her made-up (and remarkably similar) dreams. In each of them, the Weaver and Ginger got caught in some sort of Lassielike predicament that Ginger resolved by using her cunning canine instincts.

One night in Group, about two months after we started, all seven of us were present (I use the term loosely) and listening to the Weaver's latest dream installation. In this episode, the Weaver and Ginger were on the beach when Ginger noticed a doctor from St. Vincent's doing a dead-man's float in the water. She immediately jumped in to save him, but as she paddled toward his billowing lab coat, the current suddenly shifted and swept her away. The Weaver tried to race in behind her but she couldn't move because her legs weren't legs—they were trees with thick roots that had consumed her body like a Venus's-flytrap. She screamed for help, but no one else was on the beach except a family of gypsies a hundred yards away.

As she rambled, the six of us waited, bored stiff, for Ginger to drag the doctor to shore, alert the gypsies, and rescue the Weaver from death by foliage. It was so predictable, the longer she spoke, the angrier I got. I wanted to scream, SHUT UP, SUZANNA! SHUT UP ALREADY! Instead, I waited politely until she was finished.

"Ginger was drifting in the wrong direction," the Weaver concluded. "I wanted to save her, but I was stuck in the sand. I was *becoming* a tree." She looked around the circle, her eyebrows arched, as if to say, CAN YOU BELIEVE IT?

"And the significance of this dream, Suzanna?" Dr. Hensen tilted her way. Although he had other poses, the head tilt was his favorite. Sometimes I found myself tilting with him, as if the Group room was a giant cruise ship and I was listing sideways from the pull of the tide.

"Wait a second, Suzanna," Laura broke in, removing her vintage cat's-eye glasses and twirling them on their long silver chain.

Here she goes, I thought, watching Laura shake out her curly black hair. Laura never missed an opportunity to offer her perspective, especially if she could make a reference to Proust. She's a freelance writer and extremely bright, but when we first met, it was hard to take her seriously. She wore a nose ring back then and tight leather pants. She was also a record-breaking gold-medalist in the one-night-stand Olympics, a title she defended with too many martinis. "For someone so smart, Laura," Bethany once remarked, "you sure are a slut."

"Suzanna?" Laura said again when the Weaver wouldn't respond. Laura knew that repeating someone's name when she wouldn't answer was a seemingly innocent way to get a rise out of her. I never do it myself, although I do have my own equally passive-aggressive tactics. But I'll get to those tactics eventually. This story isn't about only me.

"Let me get this straight," Laura continued. "Ginger's in the water and you're in a tree—excuse me, you *are* a tree—and a doctor is floating by and you want to save *Ginger*? You'd let an orthopedic surgeon who's asked you to dinner *three times* drift out to sea?"

"It's not an either-or situation," the Weaver snapped. "It's a *dream*."

"This is bullshit, Suzanna! Fred, you agree?" Fred was Dr. Hensen. At that point, though, I wasn't as startled by Laura's using Dr. Hensen's first name as I was amazed that someone was finally addressing the Weaver's unnerving relationship with her dog.

The Weaver also looked at Dr. Hensen, but he was scribbling on a chart. Although he could've been making valid therapeutic assessments, I suspected he was creating a grocery list. Natasha agreed with me, but I wasn't all that impressed with Natasha's observations since she was equally convinced that the air-conditioning unit leaked lethal chemicals into the Group room.

Natasha is a striking African-American woman with long braided hair who exudes a false air of serenity. The first time Group met, she sat quietly in her seat, nodding in sympathy as each of us explained why we'd come. She seemed to possess an inner peace I found very comforting. And then, of course, she spoke. "IcametoGroupbecauseIworry," she said in a breathless, squeaky voice that suggested a recent panic attack. "I just broke up with my boyfriend. We were together a year, then one day, completely out of the blue, he wanted a key to my apartment. At first I was happy to give him a key, but then he started acting really weird about it. He tried to appear nonchalant, but there was a calculating gleam in his eye, and he kept chuckling in this diabolical way. It was so obvious he was planning to use the key to sneak into my apartment while I was sleeping and hack me to death, so I reported him to the police. Long story short, he got all indignant, made me promise to see a shrink, and never called me again. Frankly, I'm lucky just to be alive!" Needless to say, Natasha is working on her free-floating anxiety, as well as her commitment issues.

Laura and the Weaver were still waiting for Dr. Hensen to speak. He glanced up from his paperwork but didn't say a word.

"Laura"—the Weaver straightened her shoulders—"you're hardly in a position to comment on my love for Ginger when you consider a relationship meaningful if some guy comes inside you!" She grinned in triumph, her tweaked eyebrows shouting GOT YOU!

You'd think at this point Dr. Hensen might have intervened, but as far as he was concerned, the Weaver could share what she wanted and it was up to us to express our exasperation. In theory, Group is a microcosm of real life, a safe environment where we can act out the anger, disappointment, and frustration that, for one reason or another, we are unable to express in day-to-day situations. Thus, it came as no surprise to me that three months passed before I worked up the courage to tell Bethany, the overgrown adolescent to my right, that my name was *Janey*, not *Jenny*. When I finally did confront her, she looked at me blankly. "I know your name, *Janey*. But I like *Jenny* better." (Bethany is a forty-year-old divorcée who still lives with her mother. Sometimes they wear matching T-shirts and toe rings. Enough said.)

The Weaver was basking in her tart comeback, but Laura wasn't easily foiled.

"You know what *I* think?" Laura tilted just like Dr. Hensen. This time, Group tilted with her. I think we all felt the ship changing course. "Oh, Su-zan-na," she said (sang, actually. We all heard the tune in our heads). "You know how in your dreams, you're completely helpless and Ginger always rescues you? Well, it's obvious you use Ginger to avoid intimacy. She can't help you because she's in the water. She's drifting away—get it? And you can't help her because you're a tree, an image that suggests you want to mature, but you're not ready." Laura sighed. "Poor you. Despite evidence to the contrary, Suzanna, Ginger is *not* a human being. And until you accept this, you'll never get a guy to marry you."

Foolishly, the Weaver asked why.

Laura smiled. "Because no man I know wants to share his bed, his pillow, and his mini reading light with a goddamn DOG." That said, she tilted to the left, the Weaver burst into tears, the rest of us snickered, and very soon after, the session concluded.

I raise this particular exchange for a couple of reasons. Not only was it the first time I could tell the girls apart (although I promptly forgot all their names as soon I got home), it also illustrates a pivotal moment in our collective history. When Group began, few of us could acknowledge our anger, much less express it appropriately. So even though Laura lashed out at the Weaver rather than the Weaver's behavior, she was finally articulating her true feelings. Granted, her execution wasn't perfect, but we appreciated her intent, and I think it was our first indication that Group was working.

Initially, we were all skeptical. Contending with the Weaver's doggie love, Laura's highbrow posturing, Natasha's irrational fears, and Bethany's arrested development was like facing a mental Mount Everest. Not to mention Valentine, an exceptionally large woman who was afraid of her own shadow, and Ivy, an exceptionally beautiful woman whose every body part had been subjected to surgical intervention of the cosmetic variety. And *I* wasn't exactly a paragon of mental wellness. I still continued to stroll over to the diner on Sheridan Square to watch Tobias order his morning coffee. I also maintained a detailed list of the ways I could die, which was expanded every time I failed to speak to Tobias and he in turn failed to beg my forgiveness. It wasn't until I was trailing Tobias up the street, weaving in and out of pedestrian traffic, that I realized I needed help. And while this was a positive step, it was completely antithetical to how I'd been conducting my life. Hard to imagine, but true: I've never been much of a joiner.

Dr. Hensen designed Group for single, divorced, widowed, or

otherwise unmarried and childless women between the ages of thirty-four and forty-five who had difficulty sustaining intimate relationships, or this was how he billed it in his *Village Voice* ad. He had a goatee, John Lennon glasses, and an ego wall, filled with his framed diplomas, above his shaggy head.

In our initial session, Dr. Hensen explained his belief that the years between thirty-four and forty-five were difficult for women. "Many women perceive this window as a race against nature. If they don't marry or have children, some believe they'll become . . . ah . . ."

"Spinsters?" Laura offered, peering over her glasses.

"No, uh . . ."

"I'm Laura. I realize this is our first session, but you really should learn our names, if only to be polite."

Dr. Hensen stroked his goatee. I could tell he was nervous. "Well, Laura, when women don't marry or have children, they often believe they become worthless."

"That's because our patriarchal society makes them feel that way."

Whatever the reason, he continued, many women in this age group have a difficult time dealing with their decreasing fertility, especially in a media-driven culture that projects so many conflicting messages about aging. He didn't tell us why he cared about these women, nor did he offer any solutions, but he did say this was the subject of his dissertation at Harvard. (Another digression: Dr. Hensen mentioned Harvard seven times in one session. From then on, at least once a month, I asked Dr. Hensen where he went to school. "I forgot," I'd say, staring at his diploma. My passive-aggressive tactics, to which I've already laid claim, tend to be more amusing to me than to anyone else but still I persist.)

Dr. Hensen continued to talk about true intimacy and Harvard and how anxiety about fertility often presents itself as feelings of desperation, but I stopped listening. I was studying Ivy, a rich socialite from Birmingham whose face was swaddled in scarves that hid bandages from a recent face-lift. "Ah tend to get cosmetic enhancements," she told us by way of self-description, "when Ah feel a little blue." In addition to a face-lift, Ivy had had Botox injections to smooth out her frown lines and several rounds of liposuction on what appeared to be long, lovely legs. By my estimation Ivy wasn't just blue—she was primed for long-term analysis.

"Look, Dr. Hensen," Laura was saying, "we know the issues we need to examine before we meet, mate, and breed. Most of us joined Group to learn ways to find husbands. So instead of revealing our secrets to seven perfect strangers, why don't we use these sessions as networking opportunities where we can multiply our chances of meeting eligible men?"

"Laura," Dr. Hensen replied, "since it is our first Group, I think it's best if I lead this evening." He was rather antagonistic, I thought, for a man who lacked the girth to fill out a suit.

I've heard that when someone takes off their shoes, the shoes will retain the essence of the wearer's personality. I didn't believe this until I walked into the Group room early one night. Dr. Hensen had kicked off his loafers and was padding around in his socks. His shoes were expertly polished, but I could see that their backs were broken where he stepped on them every morning and both heels were turned out with a touch of effeminate coyness. I must've had a weird expression on my face because Dr. Hensen asked if I was okay, but I was fascinated by how accurately his discarded loafers revealed him.

But in the beginning he wasn't so bad, and maybe we weren't either. All seven of us had coping mechanisms to protect us from intimacy and love, which we equated with pain and loss. The Weaver jettisoned human relationships for the company of a dog, Laura was sexually aggressive, Natasha obsessed over pending disaster, Bethany acted like a bratty adolescent, Valentine binged, Ivy was a plastic-surgery junkie, and I was the girl with death on her mind. But by listening to each other mess up our lives, put them back together, and mess them up again, we saw a method to our madness, which could be rechanneled once we understood its root causes.

Outside Group, we called ourselves Women Who Loved Too Much. We meant this ironically because we never talked about love. We didn't understand love as a measure of trust, intimacy, and fidelity. We understood obsession, we understood rage, and that was the language we spoke. We obsessed about why men didn't call us and why they wouldn't marry us. And we raged at the way they fucked us for sport, chased younger women, and left us after nineteen years of marriage for a stripper from the Bronx. (This was Bethany's ex-husband, which made it easier to forgive her for constantly calling me Jenny.)

Sometimes, though, I underestimated the girls. When that happened, I was reminded of my father telling me I was too smart for my own good and one day I was gonna get smacked for it. When we left Dr. Hensen after eighteen months, we tried to hold Group on our own. The Weaver came a few times, then dropped out. She said we were becoming too hostile and feared what we'd do next. At the time, I dismissed her, but seeing as how Tobias is dead, the Weaver is probably the most insightful of us all, despite her bogus doggie dreams. And now she haunts *my* dreams, which I suppose is karmic justice and the kind of smack my father meant.

But I'm getting ahead of myself. No story begins at the beginning, certainly not the story of how we met up with Tobias and lost the Dream Weaver to the Great Unknown. And to begin at my beginning—or the beginning of any Group girl—would take years of pain that I'd already suffered through. To make sense of all that's happened, then, I used my talent for designing financial models. I thought of Group as a series of continuums that I charted in my office. I plotted our relationships to men, to our families, and to each other. I also plotted our diminishing capacity for self-destruction, as well as our increasing capacity for self-awareness.

As I delved into this model, I studied the possibilities inherent in its wild fluctuations, overlapping symptoms, and three-dimensional structure. Eventually I saw that our story lay in Group, where each of us stepped into a scale model of a larger world and inched along its $x/y/z$ axes until we became the women we are now, which is very different from the women we were then.

This isn't to say that Group has cured me. Maybe there is no cure for the demons that possess us. I still find it hard to live in the world, to make peace with the fact that Tobias is gone. I still want to check out, to shred my wrists with a razor and rid myself of myself once and for all. But by trusting the girls, I've learned that however distressing it is to remember how Tobias duped me, I don't have to slip back into the madness that loving him inspired. If someone doesn't remember my name, I don't go blind with rage. Instead, I smile and tell them it's *Janey*, but people who love me call me *Jenny*. I can stand in line at the deli and say, "Excuse me, Mr. Doctor/Lawyer/CEO with your scrotal jowls and receding chin, I believe I was ahead of you." Sometimes I can even say this aloud.

And yet, sometimes, for no apparent reason, I can't stop myself from feeling Tobias's presence. Or from wishing things had worked out between us. Or from berating myself for feeling no guilt that the seven of us had a hand in his death. On days like this, when I'm caught up in Tobias, I believe that I, too, would be better off dead. It's easy to slide into the romance of suicide and very little can diffuse its magic. To fight the illusion—to remember it is an illusion—is no small feat. But because of Group, I have a way to protect myself. I can call the girls and one by one they'll appear—Laura and Natasha and Bethany and Valentine and the beautiful, long-legged Ivy. Hopefully the Weaver will return from wherever she went and she'll show up with everyone else.

We'll sit at a table in T.G.I. Friday's and once again I'll reveal my suicidal nature. We'll also discuss what we did to Tobias, and how we wish we could turn back the clock to our first year of Group, when he was still alive. But it was an accident, we'll agree, it wasn't our fault. And in the end, the girls will save me because they've agreed to always be there, to protect all my secrets, and to never betray me. I in turn will throw out my razors and promise to call when I'm desperate to use them. To honor this agreement is not a passive obligation but a deliberate display of love: a leap of faith, an act of will. A contract made among survivors, for better or for worse, in sickness or in health, in absentia or in person, no matter what you might say behind one another's backs.

2

I don't want her here," Laura says. I tilt toward the Weaver in sympathy, even though I don't want her here either. We've been together five weeks and I've heard enough doggie dreams to last the rest of my life.

Dr. Hensen asks Laura why.

"She's only shared twice in seven weeks." When Laura waves her glasses at me, I realize I am the she they are talking about. Embarrassed, I study Dr. Hensen's ego wall, wondering (not for the first time) if his diplomas are fakes.

"Five weeks," Valentine counters, standing up for me. "It's only been five."

"Regardless. She shouldn't be in Group unless she's willing to open up." Laura tilts toward me, which is my cue to speak, but her rejection has rendered me mute. I focus on her chin and marvel at how everyone is born with two eyes, a nose, and a mouth, yet still manages to look unique. How can so few features create so many different-looking people? There has to be a time, I reason, when the numbers catch up.

"If she's not ready to talk," Valentine says boldly, "she's not ready. We have to be patient."

"This isn't a twelve-step program," Laura barks. "This is *group therapy*. You're either in or you're out. We don't have time for anyone to square things with her Higher Power."

Valentine shifts in her seat, holding an arm across her chest as though it's a shield. She rarely calls attention to herself, especially if it means contradicting Laura. She's so soft-spoken, in fact, a lot of the time I forget she's in the room. Valentine is from Spanish peasant stock, which reveals itself in her massive thighs, pendulous breasts, and generous lap. And yet, regardless of how big she is physically (her square seat, for instance, is lost under the spread of her hips), she still seems somehow dwarfed by the rest of us.

"Valentine has a point," Dr. Hensen cuts in. "None of you is obligated to speak."

"Oh no," Bethany interjects, shaking a finger. "No way, Hensen. If no one speaks, then there's no Group. If there's no Group, I don't make progress. And if I don't make progress, I want my goddamn money back. Jenny, it's time for you to talk. We're on the clock here." Like Valentine, Bethany's a large woman, but she isn't fat as much as thick, and all her movements feel expansive and intrusive. Side by side, Bethany and Valentine are a mystery of proportion: How can two women of similar size have such dissimilar presences?

"I almost binged at a breakfast meeting," Valentine says, covering her mouth with her hand and speaking through her fingers. She sells cellular phones and other high-tech electronics, an unlikely job for someone so deferential. "They served muffins that were thick and moist and studded with nuts. They also had a fruit boat with blackberries and blueberries that were fat and ripe and as round as marbles. I put a marble—I mean, a berry—into my mouth, then spit it out. I didn't eat a thing." She waits for Group to praise her but no one does. "Or a muffin," she adds. "Not even a bite."

"That's great," Bethany says. "And we appreciate your vivid description of a fucking breakfast tray, but we're trying to focus on Jenny's big breakthrough. I hate to tell you this, Valentine, but you won't get us to like you best by pretending to be the nice one."

Valentine looks at her hands. "Her name is *Janey*," she whispers, but sounds as if she could be persuaded to change her mind if that's what Bethany wanted.

"That's what I said." Bethany eyes me again, daring me to contradict her.

Ivy snaps. "Ah swear, Bethany, what in hell is wrong with yew?"

Her words, which drip off her tongue like Tupelo honey, sound like, *"Ah swe-ah, Bethany. What innell is wrong with yew?"* I love listening to Ivy talk. My favorite expression is "He acted like some kind of varmint," which she uses to describe her estranged husband, Jackson. It always comes out *"He acted lahk some kinda var-mi-ent,"* but sounds so lyrical, the minute Ivy mentions that she saw Jackson, I ask how he acted just so she'll say *"lahk some kinda var-mi-ent."* "Yew and Laura are being shamefully rude and totally in-appropriate."

Both Laura and Bethany stiffen at Ivy's reproach, but neither responds. Like me, they're wary of Ivy because of her beauty (surgical intervention notwithstanding). It happens with women of my generation who are conditioned to defer to the prettiest girl, or the thinnest, or the one with the best accessories. When Ivy finally showed up without facial dressings in our third week of Group, we saw her flawless skin and elegant neck. She's also tall and regal and has gentle hands that flutter like wings when she gestures.

I often wonder how it feels to look in the mirror and see Ivy's face. This thought always leads to Tobias because Ivy is his type and everything I'm not—wide-eyed and lanky with sinewy arms from years of playing tennis. Before Group, I obsessed about Tobias flirting with a faceless woman. But now the woman has Ivy's face, which compels me to stare at her every chance I get.

Ivy turns to Valentine. "Ah think it's wonderful yew saw all that glorious food and didn't binge. Furthermore, if Janey isn't inclined to speak, there's no rule sayin' she must." She folds her arms across her chest. "Agree with me, Natasha," she adds, nodding in her direction.

"I had the TV on," Natasha blurts out, twirling a braid in her fingers. "The news guy was talking about a recent breakthrough in AIDS research and I looked up just as they showed a lab worker using a pipette to transfer blood from a test tube and I realized my hand was *resting on the set* and it occurred to me that it might be possible to get AIDS through the TV. So I spent the day researching the latest ways to contract AIDS, just to make sure that touching your TV while they showed HIV-tainted blood wasn't one of them."

"You blew off work because you were convinced you got AIDS through the TV?" Bethany asks. "*Through* the TV?"

"I know it sounds crazy, but at the time—"

"At the time it was still crazy!"

"Natasha," Dr. Hensen says kindly, "it wasn't crazy. I don't like the term 'crazy' and I'd prefer you didn't use it when referring to yourself."

"I didn't call myself crazy," Natasha points out. "Bethany did."

"I didn't say *she* was crazy," Bethany retorts. "I said *the idea* was crazy."

"As I said, Natasha," Dr. Hensen continues, "the idea wasn't crazy; it was an irrational thought rooted in anxiety. Perhaps you can tell us what you were thinking about just before it occurred to you that it might be possible to contract AIDS through the television set."

"We were talking about Janey, not Natasha," Laura cuts in, using her obnoxious little glasses to point at me again.

Dr. Hensen looks at me. "I want to focus for a minute on Natasha's anxiety," he says. "It may not be far removed from Janey's."

"How do you know Janey even *has* anxiety! She hasn't told us anything about herself except that she's an accountant, she makes a lot of money, and she has a boyfriend who won't commit."

"Back off, Laura," Ivy says. "Janey will talk when she's good'n'ready." She turns to Natasha. "Yew must go to work, honey. If yew lose your health coverage, you'll be up the proverbial creek." This is highly unlikely. Natasha is a graphic designer at *Ebony*, with a degree in fine arts from Yale. Her creativity tends to fuel her wild imaginings, all of which I consider a blessing. If you're saddled with compulsive thoughts, you might as well entertain your support group.

"What else is bothering you, Natasha?" Valentine asks gently.

"Nothing," Natasha says, starting to wheeze.

"It was a *TV set*, Natasha. You can't get *AIDS* through the *TV*!" Sighing heavily, Bethany adjusts her tiara-style headband, which would've been cute if she were dining with the prince of Monaco instead of participating in a neuroses round-robin. When her husband left her, Bethany received an enormous settlement. But money doesn't always translate into fashion sense, and Bethany shows up week after week in shiny pants suits, ball-gown skirts with bustles, and python-patterned hip huggers that are two sizes too small and two decades too young. It isn't just the outfits themselves that are so dreadful (although, thankfully, her wearing gauchos didn't herald their welcome return), the colors she combines can lacerate a cornea.

"I got scared," Natasha barks at Bethany. "The same way you get irritable bowel syndrome every time you confront your mother about moving out of your house!" Natasha may be obsessive, but she never backs down.

"Girls!" Laura peers over the top of her glasses. "We're talking about Janey." She looks at Dr. Hensen. "Let's try to stay on course here, Fred."

"Janey?" he asks. "Would you like to add anything?"

"*Add* anything? For God's sake, Fred, she hasn't *said* anything!"

I look from one girl to another, wishing someone would say something and cut the silence, which permeates the room like a wave of heat. I want to tell Laura that I'm not an *accountant*, I'm an *actuary*, and I'm tired of people always confusing the two. Then a thought strikes: *Maybe Ivy and Tobias already know each other. Maybe she told him about the nutty woman in Group with thick goggle glasses who never talks. "Such a sad, lonesome soul," Ivy must say. "Ah bet she doesn't have a friend in the world."*

"Janey?" Valentine says softly.

Everyone is waiting.

"You don't even *know* me," I spit at Ivy, which I know makes no sense, but I'm angry with her for being so beautiful. And I'm angry with Laura for making me talk and Bethany for being obnoxious and the Weaver for not being the girl the others like least. Then Valentine reaches over to squeeze my hand and something inside me shifts.

I swallow hard and will myself not to cry. Bethany is staring at me, her red lips set in what she probably thinks is an expression of concern, but looks more like she's fighting a bout of gas. And lo and behold, I start to laugh. At first it's a hollow giggle, but the laugh unravels in my chest, growing louder and more spasmodic as I try to suppress it. "I'm . . . so . . . sorry," I choke out. "Something struck me . . ." Talking only heightens my hysteria and I allow myself to surrender, the relief as blissful as it is unbearable. And all I can think as I laugh and laugh is, *Thank God I'm not crying in front of all these crazy girls.*

I live in a high-rise on the corner of Twenty-third Street and Second Avenue. Every morning on my way to the subway, I pass a residence for the deaf, a halfway house for the mentally ill, United Cerebral Palsy, and a school for the blind. Twenty-third Street is not a forgiving place, even for New York City.

When I walk down the street, I'm careful to make room for people sitting in wheelchairs or holding on to guide dogs. Once I grabbed the elbow of a teenage boy with viscid eyes and a long white cane to stop him from tumbling into the subway entrance. I led him down the steps, careful not to propel him too quickly in case he resented unsolicited help.

Down in the station, I zipped up his open backpack and directed him toward the turnstile. My sensible pumps clicked cadence with the tap of his cane as we made our way down the platform. I think I expected a "Thank you," because I sidled next to him as he waited for the subway, but he didn't acknowledge me. When the train came, he got on without any problem and took a seat near the door. Even though he ignored me, I felt as though we'd been uncommonly intimate, especially since his wallet had been sticking out of his unzipped backpack and when I pushed it deep into the pocket, I felt his pens and notebooks; nothing unusual, just things that were his. When the train started moving, I walked to the center of the car to give him space, just as I would a man I'd slept with, a man who, after fucking me, wouldn't hold my hand at the movies. But I felt slighted by the blind boy's behavior. Or rather, the same way I'd feel with the man I had sex with: pleased for having extended myself but also ashamed for wanting more.

Embarrassed to be laughing at absolutely nothing, I rush to the bathroom. I lock the door and hunt through the cabinets for Valium, a razor, a loofah, anything to ingest or rub against to take the edge off. Finding nothing, I vow never to return to Group.

When I reenter the room, Ivy is sharing. She looks up but doesn't stop talking. I apologize telepathically as I sit down. *It's okay if you love Tobias,* I tell her. *I loved him, too. I still love him, in fact.* "Janey, honey, yew okay?" she asks, breaking her sentence in midthought.

"I'm sorry," I say aloud. "I didn't mean to be nasty."

"We all get overwhelmed sometimes, honey. No need to apologize."

I clear my throat. "I don't speak much," I start to say.

"Then how the hell do you communicate?" This is from Bethany. "You write notes?"

I smiled—genuinely—for the first time. "I'm just not good in groups. I'm an actuary, not an accountant. An accountant audits a company's balance sheets to determine its value. They deal with assets and liabilities. An actuary deals with risk economics, mortality rates, that kind of thing. We determine what to do with a company's assets and liabilities based on the client's short- and long-term financial goals."

"Good to know," Bethany tells me, "in case I'm ever on *Jeopardy.*"

Laura shoots her a look. "And?" she prompts. "What about *you*?"

"I'm up for partner in a year, so I work very long hours. But I don't make a lot of money and never said I did." This isn't true. I make very good money, but don't like to discuss it. That was my father's legacy. When you talk about money, Zack always said, people think you're greedy. Especially, he added, when you make more than everyone else. Meaning him.

"And your family?"

"Well," I say quietly, "I don't have a mother and my father's not quite dead."

"He's alive?" Bethany catches herself. "Whoa, back up a second. We know you're an accountant—"

"An *actuary*. I just said I was an *actuary*. There's a difference."

"I realize that, Jenny. However, if I cared, I'd read the *Encyclopaedia Britannica*. We're here to focus on how you *feel* about being an *actuary*."

"Janey," Valentine pipes up. "Bethany means we can't help you if we don't know you."

"And more important," Bethany says, "you can't help me." Then she laughs, openmouthed, and with her tiara headband, caked blue eye shadow, magenta rouge, and pastel pants suit, she looks like an insane clown princess.

I study Dr. Hensen's diplomas. When I graduated from college, then grad school, I had my diplomas sent to my dad's house in Welter. I'm sure he threw them out because I haven't seen them since, but when I see other people's on display, I'm always saddened by their blatant appeal for attention. Look at me! Hensen's diplomas scream. Look! Look! Look! I'd applied to Harvard as an undergraduate but ended up at MIT on a full scholarship. I don't regret my decision; however, I think my initial resentment of Dr. Hensen had less to do with his passive approach to Group leading than his need to mention Harvard every single session.

"Janey?" Valentine prompts.

"Well, like I said the first day, I'm thirty-four . . ." I crack my knuckles. "But I lied about my boyfriend."

"He wants to marry you?" I know Valentine hopes we're moving in a more positive direction and I hate to disappoint her but I have no choice. "He doesn't exist." I pick at a run in my stockings until I make a hole. "I'm sorry I lied, but I felt pathetic not having anyone in my life. I don't even have a dog." I look at the Dream Weaver, who nods knowingly. "My father is in a chronic-care facility upstate. I say he's not quite dead because he's not really alive. He's had two strokes and will be dead soon." I pause, imagining Zack sneering, even in his atrophied state, at where I am and what I'm doing. "I joined Group because I sense that people—men, mostly—don't see me. I want to have children, but it's difficult to have them when you're invisible. I feel as if I'm running out of time. Well . . . that's all. Sorry I lied." I lift my briefcase into my lap. "So . . . uh . . . thanks for listening." I rise from my seat. "But I have to go now."

"Where are you going?" Bethany blurts out. Her voice is sweet, as though she has suddenly taken a liking to me. "That was great. And you have people in your life." She pauses. If music were playing, there would be a crescendo. "You have us." She smiles and her fiery red lipstick cracks. "Just because we're all crazy doesn't mean we don't see you—or care about you."

"Bethany," Dr. Hensen warns. "I don't like the word 'crazy.' "

"Okay, we're not crazy. We're perfectly normal people, sitting in a circle, talking about contracting a life-threatening virus through a standard household appliance."

"A television set isn't an appliance," Natasha cuts in. "It's an electronics device that can pick up all kinds of signals. You never know—"

Bethany ignores her. "I care about you, Jenny. And I have an accountant, so when tax time comes, I won't ask for advice. My ex-husband is a podiatrist, and at dinner parties there'd always be one whore at the table who couldn't resist showing him her corns. Hey, you should come over and eat Chinese with me and my mom. I'll invite my uncle Jake. He's an accountant, too."

I don't know what to say. Soon I'll learn that when Bethany realizes she's been obnoxious, she overcompensates with excessive kindness. But at this point, only five weeks into Group, she scares the hell out of me. If I were in line at the deli, she'd cut in front of me, then step on my foot for letting her do it.

I look from girl to girl, none of whom seemed surprised to see me standing. "When you start to open up," Valentine explains, "you sometimes want to run, but the idea is to stay and deal with your anxiety. That's how you get better." She points to my empty chair. "Tell us more. We're not here to judge you. We're here to help you."

I hesitate, then sit back down. There's a burst of spontaneous applause. Tears pool in my eyes. "I don't talk much," I say, my voice cracking like Bethany's Hell's A-Poppin' lipstick. "It's not that I don't want to, but like I said, people don't notice me." I twist a tissue. "It's hard for me to know how much to disclose and to whom. I get my signals all mixed up. Last week I told my doorman I haven't had sex in two years and now I have to avoid him every time I walk into my building. Then I come here and try to . . . you know . . . talk . . . but it's so hard for me to find my words." *I'm not really here,* I tell myself. *I'm not here at all.*

"Two years without sex?" the Dream Weaver pipes up. She looks at me, her eyebrows shouting OH BOY! "It's been two years since I even *kissed* a guy."

"Bullshit, Suzanna," Laura retorts. "Last week you said you kissed Dr. Neil."

"That was a *dream*, Laura. I said I kissed him *in a dream*!"

"I haven't gotten laid in three years," Bethany says. "You see me bitching?"

"You bitch all the time!" Laura yelps, which makes me laugh since I was thinking the same thing. "Every week we hear how horny you are. Like I need *that* mental picture."

"How long has it been since you had sex? Two hours?"

The rest of us tilt toward Laura, but she just cracks up. "You all think I'm too easy?" she asks. Group nods slowly, in unison.

"It's been two months for me," Natasha admits, glancing at the air-conditioning unit and sniffing. "And the last guy had a pulse but no power, if you get my drift." As the year wears on, impotent men, like distant fathers, will become a recurring theme. Most of us, having reached our sexual peaks, constantly fantasize about penises. Our forty-year-old male counterparts, on the other hand, are more concerned with receding hairlines, financial portfolios, and sleep deprivation.

"Ah haven't been intimate with anyone since Ah left Jackson," *who acts lahk some kinda var-mi-ent.* I want to believe Ivy, but I'd imagined her making love with Tobias so often, I can't help feeling that she's lying.

"You're up, Dr. Hensen," Laura says. "How long's it been for you?"

He clears his throat. "That's not relevant, Laura."

"We're all sharing," Laura says sweetly, twirling her glasses.

"Forget it."

"Fine. Ruin it for everyone." She turns to me. "Look, Janey, in here you're as significant as anyone else." She says this harshly, which I eventually realize is a sign of affection. "We all want a connection, we just express it differently. But we need you as much as you need us. You've got to share, and that doesn't mean we want a scholarly précis outlining what you do all day. We want to know who you've been sleeping with and why. And as long as you don't ramble or"—she looks at the Weaver—"bore us with convoluted dream sequences, we also want to hear your hopes, fears, and desires. If it's difficult to open up, we'll give you time." She waits a beat. "Time's up. You had sex two years ago? Who with?"

I shrug.

"We're gonna get it out of you eventually. Trust me."

"Okay," I say, knowing she won't. Tobias is mine. I'll never share him with anyone, even Ivy, who, if she *is* sleeping with him, has no idea how evil he can be.

"Janey," Dr. Hensen says, "in the coming week, you may start to get anxious. If it does happen, I hope you'll call someone for support or at least come back next week."

"That's up to Laura. She said she didn't want me here."

"Why are you listening to me?" Laura says. "Who the hell am I?"

"I'll think about it," I say slowly, hoping that someday she and I can be friends. I focus on her chin again, and get lost in my calculations of facial-feature variation and how long it will be before everyone on the planet looks exactly alike. Watching Bethany apply yet another coat of lipstick, I have a frightening image of whose face our grandchildren's great-grandchildren will have.

"What?" she squawks. "You're looking at me funny."

"I am not," I blurt out, immediately ceasing my mental calculations.

"You're jealous of my beauty," Bethany says without the slightest trace of irony. She adjusts her tiara and leans over. "Jenny, let me tell you something. I know this Group nonsense is wacky. But don't let Hensen fool you. Left to our own devices we're mad as fucking hatters, especially *that* one." She points to Natasha, reaches out to touch an invisible TV, jerks her hand back, and lets her head flop forward as if she's been killed.

The clown princess mime has spoken.

But Bethany isn't finished. "Just remember," she continues, "there are no nicer people than the clinically depressed." She tilts toward the girls, throws on her tangerine Pashmina shawl, and picks up her seashell-studded clutch. "Till next week," she crows, and my first attempt at sharing is over.

3

Group is held every Thursday night in an office suite in the East Sixties. There are other psychologists in the suite, but we rarely see them since we meet from seven to nine and the other doctors leave by six. Dr. Hensen has an office for his private patients, but he waits for us in the Group room, buzzing each of us in as we arrive. He always says hello, then pretends to study patient charts until all seven of us are assembled.

As we wait, the girls make idle yet intimate conversation. As much as I hate Group, I hate pre-Group even more. Every Thursday, I watch the girls compliment each other's hair, recount their weekly adventures, and become best friends for life, and will myself to say something clever. I even compose a list of pre-Group topics, which I tuck in my bag for easy reference.

- Clothing—Compliment Bethany's outfit, no matter what she's wearing. Say it with conviction.
- Feng shui—Casually mention you're a master of this ancient Chinese art. Explain that by moving around the furniture in a room, you can rechannel negative energy. Suggest rearranging the Group circle into an oval. Offer to move Bethany into the hall.
- Dr. Hensen—Ask if anyone knows why he chose to do his dissertation about unmarried hens. Mention your belief that he's gay. Make sure he's not in the room. If he returns unexpectedly, tell him the gay thing was Bethany's idea.
- Jobs—Ask the Weaver if it's difficult for nurses to acquire large quantities of pharmaceuticals. Tell her you have a friend writing an op-ed piece for the *Times*.

- Pashmina—Wonder aloud what to do with your overpriced, out-of-style, and unnecessary shawls. Suggest Bethany tie them together and wear them as a festive caftan.

By the time I pick a topic, formulate a sentence, and open my mouth, Dr. Hensen has cleared his throat, tilted his head, and said, "Shall we begin?" And I curse myself yet again for being so lame I can't even speak to a group of women who openly admit they are mental.

I often feel out of control during Group. I don't feel anxiety as much as overstimulation, as though I'm trying to unravel then retain too many mathematical concepts. Although I'm finally able to tell the girls apart, it's still impossible to keep track of their jobs, family members, ex-boyfriends, and ex-husbands. Eventually I decide that the best defense is a good offense. No matter who's sharing, the minute she stops I interject, "Well I, for one, am humbled by your courage. Who agrees?" This works fine until the night Laura flings her glasses at me across the Group circle.

"How can you be *humbled* by Valentine's courage?" she shouts. "She just said she was so afraid of Margot, she hid from her in the ladies' room." I have to admit I'm stumped, especially since I have no idea who Margot is or why Valentine fears her (full disclosure: I can barely remember Valentine).

It takes a while to match the girls with their issues, but it takes even longer to feel comfortable sharing without being prompted. Group started in June, but it's August before I can speak without Laura waving her glasses in my face. Once I get a momentum going, though, I start to coast. In September, I admit that I carry a lot of anger behind my mousy exterior, and by the end of the month, I'm talking about Welter and the pulp and my father's two strokes. Finally, in October, four months after our first session, I tell the girls about my mom's disappearance.

I can see that the girls are pleased with each confession, and every week for three or four months is a mini Group triumph. But I leave out a lot. I don't tell the girls, for instance, that I have silent conversations with Audrey, the twenty-three-year-old doe-eyed junior actuary in my practice, who sits outside my office. She's pretty. She's sweet. She's totally unblemished. All it takes is a fifteen-second exchange with her and I spend the entire day questioning every choice I ever made.

"Hi," she said the other morning. "I'm going downstairs. Do you want some coffee?"

"No thanks," I told her, wondering why I was wearing a wool suit during an Indian summer. Rivulets of perspiration ran down my back.

"You sure? How about a yogurt? Yogurt helps prevent wrinkles."

"Actually"—I reached into my wallet—"I'll have a black coffee." *What the hell do you know about wrinkles, Audrey? You don't have a single line on your face. I, on the other hand, resemble a fossil with hair. God help me, I can't stand to look at you. And yet, I can't stop.*

"Do I have something in my teeth?" Audrey gave me a toothy grin, picked at an invisible poppyseed, then said, "Hey, Janey, can I ask you something? My friends and I were debating if you'd be more successful if you were married."

"I wouldn't know, Audrey. I'm not married."

"We didn't mean *you* as in *you*. We meant women in general."

"Well, since you put it that way . . ." I fought the urge to smack her perfect face. "I still wouldn't know. I'm not married." *Look, you dope, I* chose *not to marry, okay? I* want *to be single and barren. I realize most women my age are complaining about the cost of a private school education instead of their glandular disorders and irreversible skin damage, but I'm just as happy with my choices, Audrey. Can't you see how fucking happy I am?*

My conversations with Audrey aren't the only things I keep from the girls. I also fail to mention my high-pitched anxiety, my suicide ideation, my tragic affair with Tobias, and the silent but exhilarating moments I have with random strangers—like the one I had at the deli near my office one rainy Tuesday morning.

I was about to order coffee when I noticed a Doctor/Lawyer/CEO with no neck ahead of me, a guy who must have been a linebacker in college. I liked the way his silver hair curled around the edge of his collar, and the authority he commanded by rapping his ring when he chose his croissant. I asked where he got his ring (since it looks like a Super Bowl ring, I said coyly). Then bragged that I was a big-shot actuary as well as a carefree, spontaneous gal who could go from the boardroom to Bermuda with only a change of underwear and the ability to transform my double-breasted jacket into a sarong. WATCH ME! I shouted, demonstrating my powers of clothing origami while he shook two sugars into his coffee. TAKE ME TO BERMUDA! I CAN'T BEAR ANOTHER WEEKEND ALONE.

I was so deep in thought I jumped when the counter guy barked, "Lady! Pretty lady with big glasses. Toasted poppy today or no?" I glanced up at the D/L/CEO. Something in his eyes suggested disdain and I began to obsess that I'd thought aloud, or worse, during my mental displacement, I actually took off my jacket, wrapped it around my waist, then put it back on. I exited the deli quickly, and it wasn't until I was out on the street and all the way down the block that I realized I'd left my coffee and toasted poppy on the deli man's counter.

Why tell the girls any of this? I argue. What can they possibly say that will stifle my jealousy of Audrey or enable me to speak to the next D/L/CEO I stand behind in the deli? Everyone has silent thoughts, irrational insecurities, and private sorrows. If I started talking about mine, I'd have to go backward, and that's a place I refuse to travel with anyone else.

Two days before Halloween, Laura invites me to get a drink at T.G.I. Friday's after Group. I'm surprised, since she usually ignores me and when she does speak to me, it's only to point out that it's my turn to share.

When I get to the restaurant, Laura, Valentine, and Ivy are already seated at a table in the back. It's strange to see the girls in real life. They don't seem to belong anywhere except the Group room. Ivy spots me and waves but Laura eyes me suspiciously.

"We ordered," she says. "I didn't think you were coming."

"Where else would I go?" I sit down next to Valentine, who tries to scoot over but can't manage because of her size. For many reasons this saddens me. I've never been this close to her before and realize she has glamorous features—lustrous black hair, smoldering black eyes, and sexy red lips. Her weight, however, gives her the bloated look of someone on cortisone. Her cheeks are puffy, which makes her eyes appear smaller than they really are, and the distended skin diminishes her otherwise delicate bone structure. But there's no mistaking the fact that she looks like Rita Hayworth (or rather, Rita Hayworth's heavier and shyer younger sister).

"You're so pretty," I blurt out, surprising myself with my candor.

"Oh, please." Valentine bends her head, hiding her face behind a curtain of hair, which only serves to make her look mysterious. She separates a roll into four pieces, puts one in her mouth, chews and swallows, then dabs at her lips. Her mannerisms are deliberately restrained, as if to prove she doesn't enjoy eating. "Anyway, men don't make passes at *chicas* with big asses. Laura, what were you saying?"

"I said, if all these guys are asking her out, she's got to know *something* about men. I've seen the guys. And we're talking men with jobs and lab coats and real estate!"

"When did yew see these guys?" Ivy asks.

Laura sips her wine. "I went to a benefit cocktail party for St. Vincent's."

Valentine is amazed. "She invited you to a work function?"

"I invited myself," Laura explains. "She mentioned it and I asked if I could tag along. Of course she said no, but I went anyway. I'm a magazine writer. I can get invited anywhere. And I'm telling you—these guys fall all over her. It's got to be the hair. Men *love* red hair."

Ivy shakes her head. "It's cause she's all dreamy and helpless and dog-lovin'. Men need to be needed. The Weaver's their damsel in distress."

Waitin fer her Prince Var-mi-ent. I wonder if Ivy's speaking to Jackson. He finally moved out of their apartment and her face is unnaturally blotchy, as if she just had a laser peel.

"I can't believe you showed up at the Weaver's cocktail party," Valentine clucks. "Laura, that's so inappropriate!"

"Are you talking about Suzanna?" I ask, struck by Laura's

audacity. I can't believe she's talking about a Group girl outside Group. Don't we have rules about this sort of thing?

"Of course I'm talking about Suzanna," Laura replies. "Who else among us has access to eligible doctors?" She stares at me. "What's your problem, Chatty Kathy?"

"I don't think it's right to discuss her when she's not here."

"That's interesting. Just last week she said she wished you'd drop out of Group because you never talk."

"I do so talk!"

"Don't listen to her, Janey," Valentine assures me. "The Weaver never goes out with us." She sweeps her hair off her face with a flourish, and I realize that Valentine may seem ungainly at first, but when she's not conscious of her size, she's actually very graceful. "Laura's just playing with you."

I look at Laura, then at Valentine, not sure who to believe. "Do you go out after Group every week?"

Laura nods. "And to fabulous cocktail parties!" She smiles broadly, a mad glint in her eye. At first I think this is her way of apologizing for teasing me, then realize she's smiling at our waiter, a gawky teenager wearing a button that says "Hi. I'm NICK. Ask me all about our Rib Ranchero."

Just as I open my mouth to ask Nick about the ribs (because his button tells me to), I notice that Laura's blouse is unbuttoned, revealing the curve of her breasts. I lean over to tell her when she yawns and presses her breasts together with her upper arms, giving Nick a shot of her cleavage, which is as long and as deep as the crack of an ass.

"Excuse me," she asks, watching him put down her salad, "is this chicken salad breast meat or thigh?" Then she fishes out a piece of lettuce that has somehow gotten lodged in her cleavage and reaches into her shirt to adjust her bra. Instead of a discreet tug on the strap, though, Laura takes her breast out of its cup and holds it in her palm before slipping it back in. Then she buttons her blouse, peers at Nick over her cat's-eye glasses, and tells him she'd like to order more wine. "What do you suggest?"

I, of course, am reeling. *She held her boob!* Nick's eyes haven't left Laura's tits. I glance at the other girls but they're pretending not to notice. Valentine is hunched over her plate as if Nick might snatch it away and Ivy is studying her lips in a hand mirror. *She held her boob! She held her boob in T.G.I. Friday's.*

"Nick?" Laura says. "I asked what wines you have."

He blinks a few times and closes his mouth. "Lady, this is T.G.I. Friday's, you know? It's not like we have a wine cellar or anything. I mean, our menus are plastic."

She takes his arm. "Then bring me another chardonnay, would you?" She says this breathlessly, as if she's not ordering wine but having an orgasm for the camera.

"Chardonnay, yeah, sure, no problem." He scribbles on his pad, then glances at her chest.

Laura nudges him. "Why don't you ask the other girls if they'd like a drink?"

"Sure. Anyone? Drink? Anyone? Breasts?"

Valentine and Ivy tell him they're fine. He's turning to leave when Laura calls out, "You forgot someone!" She points to me.

"Sorry," Nick says. "I didn't see you sitting there!"

"I'm here," I sing out cheerfully, embarrassed that the girls have finally borne witness to my infamous invisibility. "I'll have a glass of merlot and a turkey club with no mayonnaise." I look around the table. "I hate mayonnaise," I explain.

When he is gone, Laura snaps, "Were you just going to sit there? Janey, you have to stick up for yourself. Otherwise, you'll never meet anyone."

"Like that waiter?" Ivy asks. "Laura, yew could've given birth to that boy."

"Can I help it if he was gawking?"

Valentine and Ivy catch my eye and smile, which makes me glow with sudden camaraderie. A few minutes later, Laura asks if this happens a lot, men not seeing me. "You talked about it in Group, but I thought you were being melodramatic." She squints at me. "You're hair's a little drab for your coloring. Have you ever considered red?"

I touch my head. "Maybe I don't expose myself in public!" *You boob-holding, Proust-spouting, nose-ring-wearing slut!*

Laura's quiet for a second. She plays with the chain attached to her glasses. "It's a compulsive reaction. I'm sorry if I embarrassed you, but I'm aware that I do it and I'm trying to stop. You're not the only one who feels men don't see her anymore."

No one says anything for a long time. Unable to bear the silence, I look up. "Ever hear of feng shui?" I ask. "I happen to be a master of the art."

Confession: Last summer, at his diner on Sheridan Square, I overheard Tobias tell the guy behind the counter that he was moving around the corner. To find out where, I called the Groton alumni office and told the secretary I was with the Yale Development Fund. "We lost Tobias Teague's new address when our system crashed," I said. "Computer virus. But we want to send him a plaque thanking him for his $100,000 donation." I also intimated he has much more to give. "I believe it's from his accident." I lowered my voice in a conspiratorial whisper. "He fell backward off a jet ski and the motor blew off his genitalia. It was quite the tragedy. But now he has more money than God."

Confession: Tobias lives on Bank Street in a turn-of-the-century, two-story brownstone, which is close to my apartment, more or less (full disclosure: more, not less). I have never—I repeat—never stood on his street and peered into his window. I may have passed his window when I happened to be in the area but I did not loiter. That would be wrong.

On Monday morning, the week after my first night out with the girls, my assistant, Audrey, knocks on my door. "Janey," she says firmly, "I need to talk to you."

I rise from my seat. *What happened to my ass? It's jiggling like a Jell-O mold. Feel my ass, Audrey! Feel my ass!* "What's wrong?" I usher her into my office and close the door.

"I have a personal problem."

You're twenty-three years old, Audrey. What kind of problems could you have? I've lost all the elasticity in my ass. That is a problem. And speaking of asses, yours is hanging out of your skirt. This is an accounting firm. Cover yourself, for God's sake. "How can I help you? Cute skirt, by the way."

"I need someone to talk to." Audrey crosses her legs. "Why are you wearing sunglasses?"

"I can't find my regular glasses. And I have a conference call in ten minutes. What's up?" With the door closed and the blinds drawn, my office is very dark. And with my sunglasses on and Audrey cast in shadows, she's not nearly as pretty as she is in daylight. Her hair looks greasy and her face has a dark sienna tint. Although I complain about my glasses all the time, I actually love them. My big glasses—especially my sunglasses—are my magic shield. People can see me, but they can't really *see me.* Behind my glasses, I'm not even there.

"You look really groovy in those sunglasses," Audrey observes.

"Groovy? Did that word come back?"

Audrey shakes her stupid head. "It's retro. I mean, from your generation."

"I wasn't even born yet when people said 'groovy.' " I swivel toward my computer and type "Audrey is a dope," which glows in my dark office. The screen's turned away from her, so I type "I hate my Jell-O ass," hoping she'll leave. "Audrey, I'm busy right now, but if you came back later . . ." I study the screen as if analyzing a spreadsheet. "I'd ask you to help me with this proposal, but it's not billable time." I type "I hate my Jell-O ass" a few more times.

"I need advice, and I thought since you're so polished and professional and everything, maybe you could help me."

Polished and professional? Moi? I whip off my sunglasses. "What do you need?" I chew on the tip of my glasses like the corporate mogul I am. "Is this about work?"

"Kind of. I've been seeing Jon since college, but I met this other guy, Frank, who works in tax. Frank's really cute and sends me E-mails every day asking me to have drinks with him . . ."

I stop listening and study Audrey's hair, which, with my sunglasses off, hardly looks greasy. On the contrary, it's lush and full and frames her heart-shaped face. I put my sunglasses back on and return to my computer.

"So what do you think I should do?" she asks finally.

I hesitate since I missed half her story. "I'm not sure you'll like what I have to say, but to be frank—*ha ha ha*—I think you should spend some time on your own. Relationships are important, but if you're so conflicted, it may make sense to stop obsessing about Jeff—"

"Jon."

"—Jon or Frank or whoever else comes along and start figuring out who *you* are and what *you* want. Then you'll be in a position to make intelligent choices. Audrey, there's nothing wrong with being alone. It's actually very empowering." *I hate that word. It's a Dr. Hensen word.* "I mean, it's very validating." *I hate that word, too.* "It feels groovy," I conclude.

Audrey considers this. "You're right. I should spend time on my own. I don't want to be single forever, like, I don't want to end up alone in my thirties, but for now maybe it's best to work on myself." She stands up and thanks me. "I knew I could come to you."

"Don't mention it." *And don't hug me, for God's sake.* Then I do what any self-respecting, single woman in her thirties would do—I call Ivy and ask for the name of a good plastic surgeon.

In Group a few weeks later, Laura tells us she went out with a guy she met on the Internet. I'm happy to see the girls (all of whom are single and way past thirty). In fact, ever since I started going to post-Group at T.G.I. Friday's, I feel more comfortable speaking. I contribute regularly to Group sessions and introduce new topics to pre-Group discussions. It shouldn't amaze me how much mileage I get from Audrey considering that everything she says involves my age, weight, or marital status, but whenever I bring her up, everyone sympathizes.

"How was the date?" I ask, hoping Laura had sex so I can experience a vicarious thrill.

"Don't break out the taffeta and pearls yet," Laura cautions. "But I liked him a lot. There was a moment, too, when we were kissing when it felt right, like maybe this time—"

"If yew just met him, honey," Ivy pipes up, "why were yew kissin' him?"

"Sorry I'm late!" Bethany rushes into the room and plops into her chair. "My mother kept me on the phone for over an hour. Then I couldn't get a cab and—"

"How can your mother keep you on the phone if you live together?" Natasha asks.

"*Hello?* My *cell* phone." She waves her phone in Natasha's face. (Thanks to Valentine's generosity, all seven of us each have one. I privately refer to us as Group-on-the-Go—a movable crisis hot line with no roaming fees or hidden costs.)

Ivy interrupts them. "Ah believe Laura was sharin', ladies."

"Bethany," Dr. Hensen repeats, smiling weakly at Ivy, "Laura was sharing."

"Whatever, Hensen." Bethany never calls him "Doctor." In fact, she doesn't address him at all except to say that he's missing the point. Bethany's father left when she was ten, and her mother tainted all men for her, painting the entire gender as weak, stupid, and worthless. "All I had to say before I was so *rudely* interrupted"—she glares at Natasha—"is that my mother drives me crazy." She looks at Dr. Hensen. "Was that so disruptive?"

"We had a few drinks," Laura continues, "and he said some nice things. Then he kissed me good night." She takes off her glasses. "I really thought he'd call, but it's been two weeks already. Why do women have to wait for men to call? It's so unfair. I hate this waiting! I hate it!"

"Why are you waiting?" Dr. Hensen asks. "Men like it when women call."

"I want *him* to call *me*, Fred. I know I'm overreacting, but it happens *every time*." With that, Laura starts to cry, which is particularly jarring because I well up, too.

"Sometimes," Dr. Hensen says slowly, "you can react to a certain situation because it triggers historic rage. From what you've said about your family, Laura, it appears you didn't have a safe environment for expressing anger. Your father was a tyrant, your mother very passive, so rather than get angry, you buried your feelings. Now that you're an adult, a situation in which you feel slighted by a man's bad behavior may tap into that childhood anger. Feelings eventually find a way to seep out. In fact, the longer you go without giving them a forum, the more intense they can become."

I'm amazed by how intelligent Dr. Hensen sounds. I think Laura is, too, because she asks him how to distinguish between normal anger and overreactive anger. "It's trial and error," he replies. "You have to practice." Then he looks at me and I feel my face grow hot.

"Laura?" Valentine asks. "Did something else happen?"

"I slept with him," she whispers. "He kept saying I was pretty and I convinced myself that the more he said it, the more he meant it. But he won't call. I knew it as soon as he left my apartment. He should call, though. I deserve a mercy call."

"Laura," Dr. Hensen says, "I think you jump into bed so quickly because you're afraid to let a man get to know you. When he doesn't call, you're upset, but I think you're also relieved."

Suddenly Natasha grabs my arm. "I left my stove on!" she yelps in my ear. "I have to get home before the whole place blows up!" She bolts from her chair.

Bethany winces when Natasha slams the door. "What's wrong with her?"

"Bladder problems," I reply.

"This guy will call you," the Weaver is telling Laura. "It's only been two weeks."

"Suzanna," Dr. Hensen says, "we're concerned about how Laura feels regardless of whether or not this guy calls. It's about her, not him."

Bethany takes out her cell phone. "Mom?" she screeches. "What's the name of Uncle Jake's urologist? Natasha from Group has a bladder problem."

"Bethany!" I elbow her ribs. "We're in the middle of Group."

"I know, but I *love* this phone." She snaps it shut and turns to Laura. "Continue."

Laura shrugs. "Maybe Fred's right. Maybe I do rush to have sex to avoid intimacy." She blinks back a tear. "Still, it would be nice if this guy called."

"But we all know he won't," Valentine says sadly. "It's the cow and the milk thing. Why drink the milk when the cow's free? Or is it why eat the cow when the milk's in a carton?"

"It's why buy the cow when yew can milk it fer free. And it means yew shouldn't live with a guy before yew get married."

"It can be applied here, too, Ivy," Valentine says. "Why buy a girl dinner when you know she's a sure thing?"

"Or why call the cow when yew already drunk all her milk?"

"Excuse me, ladies," Bethany hisses, "but the cow is in the room with us. Let's be a little sensitive, shall we?"

Laura turns to me. "I don't know what to do."

"There's nothing to do," I say, "except remember how bad you feel now. Next time, maybe you'll do something different, like—"

"Go back to the barn alone," Bethany cuts in.

"—get to know a man before you have sex. That way, you can decide how you feel about him and if you want to sleep with him."

"That's the problem," Laura explains. "I never know *how* I feel. I have a void where I should have feelings. I don't know how to *be* with men. I don't act, I react."

"I do, too," Valentine admits. The rest of us agree, even the Weaver, who has more men than she knows what to do with.

"And that void," Dr. Hensen crows, "is why you're all here." He looks so triumphant, I fear he may break into a full body wave.

"That's the best you got?" Bethany sneers. "I could've learned that on *Oprah*." She opens her phone again. "Ma, I'll be home in twenty minutes. Order me chicken and broccoli. No, no soup . . . Nope . . . *Ma, I don't want any fucking soup.* Why don't you listen . . . yeah . . . I guess . . . okay, won ton's good. Lots of noodles." She looks up. "You were saying?"

Dr. Hensen narrows his eyes. "Next week, I'd like to explore the void you all claim to have. Understanding where it came from can help you develop more self-confidence, as well as a better sense of your own needs and desires. This, in turn, will enable you to have lasting intimate relationships. But for now"—he glances at Bethany—"it appears our time is up."

4

"My name is Laura and I'm an alcoholic." Laura turns to me and winks.

The Alcoholics Anonymous group responds in unison. "Welcome, Laura."

"My name is Natasha Anderson. I work at *Ebony* and I'm extremely conscientious and financially secure—Laura, *stop* pinching me—I'm also an alcoholic. Could I get some air? I'm gonna hack up a lung with all the dust in this room." Natasha puts her head between her knees and her braids fall forward.

"First names only, please," the meeting leader says, cracking a window. "Anyone else here for the first time?"

Bethany raises her hand. "My name is Bethany and I'm thirty-nine, I'm divorced, I love shopping, and my favorite food is Chinese. I'm looking for an honest man who likes long walks in the park, and won't mind living with my mother if we get married—"

Laura kicks her. "Say it!"

Bethany rolls her eyes. "I'm also an alcoholic."

It's my turn. "My name is Janey," I say. "And I'm an actuary."

"Is that like an accountant?" I swear I hear someone ask.

"A lot of people confuse the two—"

This time Bethany kicks me. "No one cares, Jenny. We're here to meet men. Stick to the *plan*!"

I rub my knee and glare at Bethany. "My name is Janey. And I'm an alcoholic."

As the meeting starts, I canvass the room. I can't believe Laura dragged us down here. "I did a piece for a woman at *Vogue* who met her husband at AA," she explained, trying to convince us to accompany her to a church in the East Village. "He's gorgeous, rich—"

Bethany snorted. "And a drunk."

"A *recovering* drunk," Laura pointed out. "Men in AA are *recovering,* which means they won't take you to seedy bars and ply you with martinis to get you naked."

"I thought you liked that kind of man," Natasha said.

"I'm *recovering* from that kind of man. We'll meet all sorts of interesting guys at AA, guys who *want* to discuss their feelings, who *understand* what it takes to be in a relationship."

But as Lloyd, the opening speaker, gives his twenty-minute qualification, I begin to have doubts. Apparently Lloyd was a surgeon who drank while he operated, beat his wife, and lost his medical license. He was living in a cardboard box on Avenue C when he finally realized he needed help. Apparently Lloyd isn't much of a joiner, either.

"You'd think drinking a quart of vodka at ten A.M. might've tipped him off," I whisper to Laura, who snaps, "Don't be so judgmental."

I'm not being judgmental, I think indignantly as I survey the stifling room. *I just don't want to live with a man in a cardboard box.* I listen intently as the alcoholics confess to urinating in public, driving drunk, and blacking out. I can't figure out what I'm doing here until Laura nudges me. "Check that guy out. He seems like your type."

My type? He has a long braided beard and wears dirty jeans and a leather vest without a shirt. On his forearm he has an eagle tattoo, and on his bicep he has a heart. Inside the heart, "Roseanne and Damien 4-Ever" is written in script.

"He's a biker!"

"So what? I swear, Janey. You are *so* picky."

When I look at Damien, he tips his leather cap as if to say, "Howde-doo, ma'am. Want a ride on my hog?" *Maybe I am too picky.* I study his tattoo. *At least he's not afraid to admit he's in a relationship.* I sigh, push my glasses up, and smile. Damien smiles back.

"Look at you, girlie girl!" Laura yelps.

"Fuck off," I tell her, still smiling.

After the serenity prayer, while everyone gets coffee and hugs, I sidle up to Natasha and Bethany, who are congratulating Lloyd on his sobriety.

"You are very brave," Bethany says. "Do you still live in a box?" She bats her eyelashes, which are so thick with mascara they stick to her brows. But Lloyd has his sights set on Natasha.

"You're a painter?" he asks her, tucking a cigarette between his lips.

"It's more of a hobby. I actually make my living as a graphic designer."

"But still," Lloyd presses her. "You're an artist. I always admire creative people."

"She's *very* creative," Bethany agrees. "And very proud of her African-American heritage." For all of her foibles, Group is teaching Bethany to rise to the occasion, which makes me ashamed I told her she should run with the bulls in Pamplona when she showed up earlier wearing toreador pants and a red blouse with diaphanous sleeves.

"You have to give Natasha credit," Bethany continues. "She grew up in a *ghetto*. Her parents were *illiterate*. She studied in her stairwell with a *flashlight*. But she went to Yale. Yale! What do you think of that, Lloyd?"

"I think that's amazing." He gazes at Natasha. "It must've been so hard for you to overcome your tragic background."

"I grew up on Park Avenue," she snaps. "My mother's a gynecologist and my father's a heart surgeon. They were hardly illiterate. They were just busy people with busy practices. So what if they traveled for weeks at a time and left me alone. I learned how to be independent and self-sufficient. Sure, I was afraid of serial killers sneaking into the house and bludgeoning me to death with baseball bats, but what child isn't? Besides, my parents always came home if I needed them. Once they flew all the way from Katmandu because I thought I was having an appendicitis attack. It turned out to be gas, but they came, Lloyd. You can't say they didn't care." She glances at the coffee urn. "I wonder if I could get herbal tea. Caffeine makes me way too wired."

Lloyd takes a giant step backward, then scurries away.

Bethany watches him go. "My mother says men like women who are mysterious, Natasha. Next time, save something for the second date."

"Why did you make up that story about my parents? All that does is perpetuate stereotypes about black people."

"I was *trying* to be helpful. I want you to meet someone nice."

Natasha looks skeptical. "He lived in a box!"

Bethany pats her shoulder. "And you're out of your mind," she says solemnly, leading Natasha away. "At our age, we have to make certain compromises. But if you don't like Lloyd, we'll find someone else."

I feel a tap on my shoulder. I turn to see Damien of "Roseanne and Damien" lurking behind me. "My name's Damien."

I point to his bicep. "I can see that. Where's Roseanne?"

"With Dutch. We split up when I got sober. Is this your first meeting?"

I nod, taking in his large frame and bare chest. *Okay, so there's a ring in his nipple. He seems friendly enough. We can tool around on his Harley. I'll wear leather. I'll get a tattoo. I'll throw out my boxy brown suits and sensible pumps. I want to feel the wind whip through my hair. I want to get married in a field with goats and little girls holding daisies. I want to attend Hell's Angels rallies. Who needs a D/L/CEO? The times, they are a-changing.*

But when Damien leans close to me, I get a whiff of pot. "You want to go outside and smoke a fattie?" he asks. His breath is so thick, my eyes water.

I take two steps back. "I have to find my sponsor."

Laura yanks on my arm. "We're out of here," she says, disgusted. "These guys have to be sober for a *whole year* before they can have a relationship? It's an AA thing."

I look into Damien's glassy eyes. "Is that true?" I ask. He stares at me as if he has no idea who I am. So much for the wind beneath my wings.

Bethany and Natasha are waiting by the exit, arm in arm.

"When did you two become such good friends?" Laura asks.

"When we decided this was a bad idea," Natasha says.

"And that you're too bossy," Bethany adds. "You're a know-it-all, and everyone's sick of it. Especially Valentine and"—she raises an eyebrow at me—"Jenny."

Laura looks at me. "Why didn't you say something?"

Bethany's red clown lips part in delight. "Because Jenny barely speaks."

"I do so speak!"

"Can we go?" Natasha asks. "The dust in this room is eating away the soft tissue in my bronchial passages."

"We're going." Laura surveys the room. "Maybe this AA thing wasn't the best idea, but if you think I'm too bossy, Janey, just say so." I open my mouth to deny this, but Laura's already out the door. She glances back one more time. "God, I could use a drink. Who wants to come with?"

We can't get to the bar fast enough.

Although our AA outing doesn't yield any potential husbands, I'm even more determined to meet a man. A few days later, I tape an "On Deadline" sign to my office door, close my blinds, and study the personal ads in the *Voice*. One catches my eye, especially when I imagine spending my summer in a beach house in East Hampton.

Summer of Love—*Let me be the center of your life! Devilishly handsome, extremely successful entrepreneur (45, looks 25) seeks stunning, slim (height proportional to weight), buxom woman 21–27 for fun in the Hamptons. Must be athletic, independent, and ready to bear and raise my children. No fatties! Will answer responses only if they include full-length photo, preferably one of you wearing revealing attire that shows off your boobies. Box 2020.*

I turn to my computer and type my response:

Dear Moon-Doggie—*Look no further! I'm a successful executive seeking summertime romance with a much older man. I play the harp, speak five languages, have lived all over the world, and am a world-class gymnast. I've enclosed a picture of myself lounging poolside. Although I've aged a bit since this shot was taken, I just turned thirty, so my eggs are ripe for harvesting. Love and kisses, Gidget (212) 555-4203.*

In deference to his request for a full-length photo of revealing attire, I attach a picture of myself at eleven, standing by the Lewis County Municipal Pool in a polka-dot bathing suit and sunglasses with heart-shaped lenses. Then I put the envelope in the mail and wait for his call.

In Group on Thursday, Ivy discusses Jackson, her ex-husband, which isn't surprising. If she's not talking about the var-mi-ent, she's lifting her skirt and grabbing her thighs to show us the area she's targeting for her next liposuction.

"Jackson wants to try again," Ivy says. "Go to counselin' and such, but Ah think it's best we leave our bad memories behind. Ah just can't forgive him for kissin' that blond deb he had clerkin' in his office last spring. Ah came by to surprise him with supper and he had Ole Miss hiked up on his desk. Yew know what's weird? Him kissin' her didn't bother me—Ah mean, it bothered me, Ah'd be lyin' if Ah said otherwise—but what really hurt was my realization that there were girls out there, younger'n me and more beautiful, who Jackson might desire. It was awful seein' him with Ole Miss, but it was more awful seein' myself as an older version of her."

"Was this when your preoccupation with plastic surgery started?" Dr. Hensen asks.

"Gosh, no. Mama gave me a nose job for mah sweet sixteen." Ivy sighs. "Poor Mama."

"What's wrong with your mother?"

"She's dead!"

Dr. Hensen flipped through the charts in his lap. "That's right," he says softly.

"Jesus, Fred," Laura snaps. "Get it together."

"Exactly how many procedures have you had?" Dr. Hensen asks Ivy, who mumbles a reply. "How many?" Hensen repeats.

"Eleven. Not countin' a tummy tuck back in ninety-nine. It was a millennium thing."

We're all a little awestruck, I guess, since no one says anything. We do tilt, however, and give Ivy the once-over. "Why don't you count the tummy tuck?" Dr. Hensen wants to know.

"It was a revision. Ah don't count the revisions."

"Ivy?" Hensen asks in his therapeutic voice, which is a song-like baritone. "What does cosmetic surgery give you?"

"A better body? More opportunities to meet men? Ah don't understand the question."

"What he means, Ivy," Laura interrupts, "is how do you feel when you have surgery? Why do you keep doing it? He's looking for the relationship between you—Ivy Halliwell from Wherever, Alabama—and the act of having a doctor carve up your otherwise healthy body."

"Well, Mama always said that the first thing to go is a woman's looks. She had two face-lifts—not countin' revisions—before she passed. Ah'm just tryin' to look good, is all."

"Okay," Laura says. "But how do you feel before and after?"

"Well, the time leadin' up to the procedure is mah favorite part cause Ah have somethin' good to wait for. Then after, Ah don't feel much of anything. Sometimes Ah feel a little let down, but my doctor says that's normal—"

"So what you're saying," Laura cuts in again, "is that you're more interested in the act of surgery itself than the results. Maybe you're bored. Did you ever consider getting a job?"

"Mah only skill is a whup-ass backhand. Who would want to hire me?"

"Who wouldn't? You're personable and smart and have lots of common sense."

"You could try temping," Valentine suggests. "That way you don't have to make a commitment. We hire temps in my office all the time, but Margot is there and . . . well . . . we all know how she is."

"Yes, we do," I say triumphantly. I know who Margot is. I also know why Valentine despises her. A while back, Margot set up Valentine on a blind date. Afterward she said, "Don't be upset if he doesn't call you. He's not attracted to full-figured women. You didn't eat in front of him, did you?" Valentine can't recount the story without bursting into tears.

"Honey," Ivy says, "while Ah appreciate your kind offer of havin' me temp in your office—which Ah am considerin', thank yew, Laura, for the tip—if Ah saw that Margot Ah'd give her a piece of my mind!"

"She's not so bad," Valentine murmurs.

"I can't believe you're defending her," Laura says. "She's absolutely awful! Next time she says something nasty to you, she'll have to answer to us."

Dr. Hensen looks amused. "Meaning what?"

"Don't patronize me!" Laura snaps. "You have no idea what you're dealing with."

"I think I do," he replies, holding her gaze. "I know much more than you think."

"Is that a threat?"

Dr. Hensen shakes his head. "It's a promise."

"This is so wrong," I tell Laura on the phone four nights later. "I can't go out with a guy I met through a *personal ad*!"

"Oh please, Janey. You liked this guy when he called, right? You said he sounded very friendly. You don't have to marry him. You're just having dinner. What's the harm in that?"

"The harm," I retort, discarding another blouse, "is that I don't know how to date. I sit across from a man, decide on an appetizer, then immediately wonder how he'll look at our wedding. By the time we have dessert, I'm a divorcée stuck with three kids in a house I can't afford and he's a deadbeat dad living with a hooker and spending his child-support payments on crack." I rip off my skirt. "And I don't have a goddamn thing to wear."

Everything about this evening feels wrong: the awkward first phone call when Lenny said he was charmed by my note; my rambling discussion of financial modeling systems; the stilted way he asked if I wanted to meet; and finally, his sign-off. "I've never been out with a world-class gymnast before," he said, which left me petrified he'd ask to see a round-off.

By the time the doorman buzzes, I've worked myself into a Natasha-size frenzy. *What if Lenny really is handsome? I'm just an average-looking woman with a Jell-O ass, an A cup, and rotting eggs in my womb. What if he sees me and leaves?*

When I get to the lobby, I freeze. Parked in the street is a battered brown van with "Bagel Land" stenciled on the side. Standing next to the van is a barrel-chested bald guy who looks like the Michelin man. *That can't be him! Please, God,* I beg, searching for my devilishly handsome entrepreneur, *don't let this be him. He's barely five feet tall!*

Just as I turn to run upstairs, the guy waddles into the lobby. "Janey? I'm Lenny." I stiffen as he hugs me. He waves at the van. "Do you mind riding with me so I can find a spot?"

"That's your van?" I choke out.

"Sure is! Your door is tricky, so get in on my side and inch over." Sadly, I get inside, kicking away empty bags and discarded napkins. "I had a hell of a time getting here. I live over in Jersey. Took me two hours."

"Bagel Land is your business?"

"Yepper!" He thumps the dashboard. "Just opened my second store in Morristown." He tries to start the van, but the engine fails. "Needs to warm up a bit." He appraises me from the corner of his eye. "You look different from what I expected."

"What did you expect?" *Don't judge me, you blockheaded, neckless bagel-store owner.* "Someone taller?"

He shrugs as the van finally starts. "Hard to say."

We drive around the block a few times but can't find a spot. Lenny's a nervous driver. He won't accelerate past twenty and rides the brake with a leaden foot. After a while, I begin to get nauseated. "Why don't you pull into a lot?" I ask, rolling down the window.

"That'll cost a fortune!" he exclaims. "I have an idea. Let's just keep driving. We can eat in the car." He reaches behind him and pulls out a bag of bagels. "I've got cream cheese and lox spread. You like lox spread, Janey?"

I nod, wishing I could open my door and fall out. We aren't going fast. I'd barely get bruised. "So where's your beach house?"

"What beach house?" Suddenly Lenny slams on the brakes and flings out his arm, catching me across my A cups. "Whoops! Sorry about that. I need a caffeine jolt." He jumps out of the van, which he keeps running so the engine won't die, then raps on my window. "Cream and sugar?"

"Just black."

I'm about to slip into his seat and drive myself home when he returns holding two coffees and a bear claw. "You wanted cream and sugar, right?"

I nod and take the cup out of his hand.

As we drive up Park, Lenny hands me a bag of bagels. "Watch the cinnamon raisin," he warns, pulling down his lower lip to reveal a gap in his teeth. "Hard crusts." I take an onion bagel from the bag and bite into it, trying not to cry as we speed through the streets.

"These bagels are good," I say in an effort to make conversation. *Compliment him*, Laura said. *Ask questions about his life. Appear interested and urbane, witty and warm.* "I was thinking of opening a deli, Lenny. How do you find the bagel game?"

He proceeds to tell me about the plans he has for Bagel Land's expansion, the new manager he hopes isn't stealing, and the seven-part juicer he purchased for the Morristown store. As he talks, I study his square head. *He's not so bad. So he lives in Jersey and he's missing a tooth. I'd be lucky to have a guy who owns his own business.* I squint at him in the passing streetlights, imagining us working side by side, wearing aprons, cutting lox for all our customers. I reach for another bagel.

"Try the poppy," he says. "They're my best."

See? He's so friendly, and we'd never go hungry. "Did you get a lot of responses to your ad?" *Poor Lenny*, I think, envisioning the other women's horror upon meeting him. I feel morally superior to them because I'm able to appreciate the kind heart inside the portly body.

"Maybe a hundred. I've been on twelve dates so far, but most gals want to jump right into marriage. I'm very picky, though. I need someone who brings as much to the table as I do."

Twelve dates already? And they're ready to marry him? I give him another once-over. "You have lox spread on your cheek, Lenny." *Has the world gone mad?*

He wipes his face with the back of his hand, which he proceeds to lick with canine exuberance. "What languages do you speak?" he asks. "I love gals who speak languages. It was the reason I answered your ad."

"I know some Spanish, I guess . . ."

"Say something in Spanish! Say, 'This night is great.' "

"*El noche esta* . . . I don't know . . . *grande* . . . no, *marveloso* . . . no, *el noche esta groovy.*"

"*El noche esta groovy,*" Lenny repeats. "Ha! They have slang, too."

I catch his eye in the streetlight. He smiles at me so sweetly I let myself melt. "I'm having a nice time, too, Lenny." *Wanna see a round-off, Big Guy?*

Lenny stops short again and I fly forward. He taps the window. "Here we are!"

We're back at my building. Lenny's studying me intently, gearing up for a good night kiss. I try to forgive his rubbery lips, missing tooth, and fishy breath. *One kiss is only fair. He did feed me.* I close my eyes and lean toward him. But he isn't trying to kiss me I realize, when I feel him reach over me and kick open my door. He doesn't even shake my hand. But he does give me a dozen Bagel Land bagels with handy freezer bags.

"*El noche esta groovy,*" he says as I get out. "I'll call you." And he drives off, leaving me to clutch my bagels and watch his big, square head jerk back and forth as he sputters all the way down the street.

After Lenny leaves, I spend an hour crying. Not because I like him, but because the evening has been such a waste. I'm bloated from carbohydrates, nauseated from exhaust fumes, and still alone. I consider calling Laura, but decide not to. She's just a Group girl, someone who sits in the same stupid chair every week, talking about the same stupid problems. Therapy, like trolling for men, is turning out to be more trouble than it's worth.

Group was resurrecting ghosts. It started the night Bethany

explained why she was afraid to ask her mother to move out. "My mom's lived with me since Peter left," she said in moment of rare vulnerability. "I know we should live separately, but I've never been alone before and I'm not sure I could stand it." Then she ran a finger through her frosted hair, a gesture that tweaked my breathing. It was my own mother's gesture: hands flat, fingers spread, a rake through the bangs like a long-toothed comb. I hadn't seen my mother do it for decades, but from that moment on, every time I notice a long, tapered finger brush a golden strand of hair, my chest constricts in pain, the ache lingering like a sore muscle I haven't exercised in a while.

I work hard to forget my mother. I don't bring her up in Group. I steer conversations away from my childhood. I don't enter card stores on Mother's Day. I can go about my business, not paying much attention, but just as I find a rhythm with the world, a tall blonde steps out of a bookstore and my mom is as present as the day she left me. Or I'll be in a meeting with a client and a thin woman in a sundress appears in the corner of my eye. The next thing I know, the client's voice has grown dim and I'm drifting, wishing I were alone in my office or at home in my bed so I could go through the process of forgetting again.

The night my mother turned up missing, my father got on the phone and marshaled his troops. He moved into action with such precision it seemed as if he'd known all along that she was planning to go. The boys from the pulp helped him with flyers and drove from town to town showing her picture. He went out with the sheriff when his men combed the woods and sat in the boat when they dragged the Wild Moose River. I went out on the boat with him once. I wore an orange life preserver over my wool sweater, and cupped my hand in the black water until it grew numb. But I didn't peer over the side because I knew we wouldn't find her at the bottom. She wasn't dead; she was gone. When I was thirteen, I wanted to believe there was a difference.

I was sad when my mother left, but I was also secretly excited for her. I was sure she was alive and well and living somewhere far away from Welter. And she wasn't working double shifts at the pulp. She was drinking Bombay martinis, eating pâté, learning to speak French. I didn't begrudge my mother her new life, unlike my father, who became silent and hard, like settled concrete. In fact, I vowed to follow her, to get out of Welter and leave my bad memories behind.

But not fearing her dead exacted its own price, which was having her return to me in my dreams. I'd feel her hovering over my bed as I slept, not a person but a presence with long blond hair that brushed against my face. I'd lift up my arms to touch her, but just as she leaned over to kiss me, I'd stir in a panic, then curse myself for waking too soon. Eventually, my memory of what my mother looked like began to fade. In my mind, she wasn't the woman in the few pictures I had, but the woman of my adolescent dreams: shapeless, faceless, easily lost.

When I started Group, my mother returned as if I'd summoned her simply by invoking her name. The harder I tried to forget her, the more frequently she appeared. Eventually I surrendered, and let her come to me in my sleep. Her presence is warm and comforting and fills me with joy, much like I imagine having a husband would feel. But when I wake up in the morning, I'm always alone, the dream—like the husband—just another illusion.

A few weeks after my date with Lenny, I'm taking my usual Saturday constitutional down Bank Street when I bump into the Weaver who's out walking Ginger. "You live on Twenty-third Street, don't you?" The Weaver asks, holding Ginger out for a kiss.

I nod. "Do you live around here?"

"There." She points to a brownstone, two doors down from Tobias's. "St. Vincent's is nearby." She squints at me. "You come here a lot, don't you?"

"Why do you ask?"

"I can see the street from my window. And sometimes I see you—or the woman I thought was you—loitering in front of this apartment. Do you know someone who lives here?"

"I don't *loiter*," I snap, realizing that if the Weaver could see me, then Tobias could see me, too. *Is he watching me right now, talking with crazy Suzanna and the dog she has dressed in a painter's smock and purple beret? Does he think we're friends?*

"I was sure it was you." She glances at Tobias's brownstone.

"Don't look at that window!"

"Why? Who lives there?"

"I gotta go, Suzanna. See you in Group." I scratch Ginger's neck, then quickly dash off before Tobias can open the door and ask me why I've been loitering in front of his apartment for two and a half years without ringing the bell.

THE PRINCIPLE OF UTILITARIANISM

5

Actuaries study financial security systems. Underlying these systems is the philosophic principle of utilitarianism, which is roughly stated as "the greatest good for the greatest number over the longest period of time." This good can be called happiness, pleasure, or utility, but its basic goal is maximization.

I wasn't able to see how utility maximization related to Group until our eighth month together. Up till then, we were in a constant state of negotiation. We grappled with when to let down our guard, which parts of our lives to share, and how to give feedback without being hurtful. And we continued to discover each other's flaws, which made us simultaneously sympathetic and irritated. Why doesn't Valentine ever stand up for herself? Why can't Ivy see her own beauty? Why can't Natasha hear how demented she sounds? Then something happened in that month, some ephemeral, unspoken understanding whereby we realized that if not for each other, then who?

Confession: On Sundays, I comb the *New York Times* style section for Tobias's wedding announcement. I also count the number of first-time brides thirty-five and older and calculate my chances for finding a husband. By comparing the number of brides over thirty-five to my demographic target group (gainfully employed men aged thirty-three to forty-five), I realize that I'm more likely to be tapped for a Congressional appointment than to ever find Mr. Right.

Confession: I call Tobias once a week just to hear him say, "Hello? Hello? Hello?" Okay, twice a week. Three times if there are no first-time brides over thirty-five on Sunday.

Confession: I call Tobias at Municipal Life using the handy Shirt Pocket Micro Voice Disguiser I bought from the *Soldier of Fortune* catalog. I leave a message on his voice mail from the chairman's office, saying the black-tie dinner that evening for all senior executives was changed to a costume party. I suggest he go as a bunny.

It's February when Bethany announces she has a blind date. "My mother says I should go," she tells us, "but I'm nervous. What if something bad happens to me?"

"What could happen to you?" Dr. Hensen asks.

"You know perfectly well, Fred," Laura snaps. "It's brutal out there."

Over Christmas, she'd gone out with an aspiring actor whose face was as weathered as Southwestern clay. She really liked him, she told us, until they slept together. "You'd be perfect," he whispered during their postcoital glow, "if I could combine your intellect with a stripper's body." Laura appraised his reptilian tongue and the doughnut of scalp where he should've had hair, then generously noted, "All things being equal, Siddartha"—né Sheldon Green of Great Neck—"three more inches on your dick wouldn't suck."

"I have an idea!" Laura shouts. "We'll all go on the date with Bethany."

"Bethany should go by herself," Dr. Hensen says emphatically.

"We'll sit at the bar and won't say a word. We'll just be there for moral support."

While they argue, Bethany peers into a compact. "*Bethany* speaks," she says, puckering her lips. "And *Bethany* doesn't want to go. So don't talk about *Bethany* as if she isn't here."

Dr. Hensen apologizes. "But I think you should meet this man. It's an opportunity to hone your dating skills and could be fun. If nothing else, you may meet a new friend."

Laura snorts. "Let's be realistic. You can eat lo mein and watch reruns of the *Golden Girls* with your mother. Or you can meet a guy, have a few drinks, and possibly have sex."

"Fine. I'll go." Bethany throws on a cape that's festooned with gold tassels. It seems better suited as a window treatment, which I fear it may be.

"Who set you up with this guy anyway?" Laura wants to know.

"My mom," Bethany says sheepishly. "He's the son of her Weight Watcher's lecturer."

"Your *mother*? Girls, looks like we got ourselves a date!"

Five nights later, I haul myself to a sports bar on the Upper West Side for our grand rendezvous. I don't see the girls, so I perch myself on a stool near the front windows where I can easily spot them when they arrive.

"Great legs," I hear a man say, but I'm too self-conscious to look up.

"Oh," I murmur, sliding my skirt above my knee. "They're nothing special. You must say that to everyone. Do you?" Oh so casually, I swivel on my stool to get a good look at his face. I catch his eye and flash a come-hither smile just as he starts to massage the thigh of a pretty redhead wearing a sparkly tube top.

"Do I what?" he asks me, nuzzling the woman's neck.

"Do you . . . canoe?" I reply and whip back around, feeling like the world's biggest goat. *How could I think he was talking to me? Am I the twenty-year-old starlet with big breasts? No, I'm the sad, sick cow who will die alone in her bed.*

Why wait? I ask myself and pull out my list of suicide strategies.

My Death List
By Janey Fabre

- Gentlemen Prefer Blondes—Have affair with much-loved politician (not mandatory). Put Jackie Gleason's *For Lovers Only* on the hi-fi. Swallow a bottle of Seconal. Chase with vodka. Call Tobias to say good-bye. Tell him you're HIV positive and suggest he get tested. Crawl into bed. Close eyes. Become icon.

- Farewell to Arms—Write good-bye note to Tobias in minimalist prose. Tell him his three-year-old son, Gunther, wants to live with his father. Mention Gunther will be calling to arrange moving in as soon as he's released from the burn unit. Get gun. Blow brains out.
- The Socratic Method—Send letter to the North American Man/Boy Love Association from Tobias offering to host their next meeting at his house. Acquire large supply of hemlock. Drink.
- Highway Robbery—Download child pornography. Write note: "Janey, I ran away with Arthur. He's only thirteen, but we love each other. Don't try to look for me. Your faithless husband, Tobias Teague." Purchase fake AK-47. Rent car. Put Tobias's note and child porn on passenger seat. Drive to New Jersey Turnpike. Hit the accelerator. When cops stop you, step away from car. Scream, "The pedophile left me! He lives on Bank Street in New York City." Whip out gun. Aim at cops. Pretend to pull trigger. They will riddle your body with bullets.
- The Bronx Bomber—Make three hundred copies of a skeleton key with a tag on each that says: "Fifty-dollar reward if you return this key to Tobias Teague, Bank Street, NYC, 212-555-5059." Distribute keys all over the South Bronx. Withdraw $80,000 from your 401(k) account. Befriend crack dealer. Give him $40,000 to show up at Tobias's office, demanding the drugs Tobias stole. Then give him another $40,000 to shove you out a window.

Laura taps my shoulder. "What's that?" She snatches the paper away and quickly scans it. "Know what I think? Suicide ideation is mental masturbation. It's like your math models. The more intricate the details, the better it feels. I bet if you shared this in Group, you could diffuse your obsession."

"I share as much as I feel is appropriate."

"You share selectively. And not-telling," she adds, "is the same thing as lying."

I crane my neck to see behind her. "Where's everyone else?"

"On their way. The Weaver's coming, too, if you can believe

that. She got Ginger a sitter. There they are! Hey, girlie girls! We're reviewing Janey's suicide list."

Ivy pulls up a stool. "We walked right by yew." She wiggles her fingers. "Give it here. That kind of thinkin' is perverse and destructive. Once you get started, yew can't never stop."

"Like Botox injections?" I ask, but she's already turned to Laura.

"Guess what! Ah got mahself a temp job. Ah'm just answerin' the phones now, but Ah'm gonna learn Windows." She hugs Laura. "Ah'm so happy, and it's all because of yew."

Laura glances at me. *See?* Her expression says. *I may be bossy, but I know what I'm talking about.*

"Beginner's luck," I tell her.

Where's Bethany?" Natasha whines, pressing her face against the window. "They should be here already. Something's wrong. I can feel it."

Laura holds up her martini. "Have another drink, Chicken Little. They're probably still at Bethany's house, putting her mother in restraints for the night."

Valentine eyes a bowl of pretzels on the bar. "Is Barbara that bad?"

"A total nut job. I don't think Peter left Bethany as much as he left Barbara."

"I thought she cooked and cleaned." Valentine inches the pretzel bowl closer to her.

"Are you kidding? All Barbara does is shop for Bethany's wacky outfits." Laura casually moves the pretzel bowl away, but not before Valentine grabs a fistful.

"You said you loved her outfits!"

"I also said your bingeing seemed under control." Laura smacks Valentine's hand until she drops the pretzels.

Valentine's eyes narrow, but instead of responding, she orders a club soda and turns away. At the other end of the bar, the Weaver is holding court with three banker types. Laura slides off her stool. "I'm going back there. She can't take all of them home."

"She won't take *any* of them home," Ivy reminds her. "That's why they keep askin' her out."

Laura shakes her head. "It's the red hair. Men *love* red hair."

At that moment, Natasha cries, "Thar she blows!"

The six of us rush to the window.

"He's cute!" Natasha screeches.

"He's *really* cute," Laura agrees.

"He's young."

"He's *really* young,"

Natasha presses her face against the glass again. "What the hell is Bethany wearing? She looks like she's going to a prom. Oh, God!" She jumps back. "They're coming in."

We scramble for our places but Bethany doesn't appear.

"Natasha," Laura orders. "Look out the window and tell us what's happening."

"That window's so dirty."

"Two minutes ago you were practically licking it!"

Ivy gets up and peers out the door. "They walked right by us. They're all the ways up the road. Maybe she wanted to be alone with him after all."

Laura disagrees. "Something's wrong." She takes out her cell phone and calls Bethany. "She's not picking up." Laura's lips are pursed in concern as she frantically redials.

Suddenly I feel a hand on my thigh. I look up to see a familiar face smiling at me. "I do canoe," he says. "Do you?"

"Say what what?" I reply and motion for him to sit down.

Gosh, Bob. I *love* hearing people's dreams. See her?" I point to the Weaver, who has a man's jacket wrapped around her shoulders. "She tells me her dreams all the time."

"Are you high?" Laura asks me, then turns to Bob, my new boyfriend. "Did Janey tell you how much she loves square dancing?"

Bob shakes his head.

"Well," Laura confides, "when they let her out of the home, she always makes me take her square dancing. And—what's your name again?"

I push her away. "It's Bob. And you should be trying to call Bethany, not interrupting other people's conversations."

Laura ignores me. "Bob, I'll tell you something you probably already know. It's hard to find a square dance in New York City. So we take Janey to Grand Central, throw some hay on the floor, and do-si-do awhile. Bob, are you wearing a toupee because your face is so ugly?"

"The home?" Bob asks, tugging his hair.

"Laura, stop it!"

She just laughs. "She also has a thing for deformed men—really ugly men with tiny penises. So I'm not surprised she likes you, Bob, since you're the ugliest man I've ever seen."

Bob stands up. "You're crazy," he mutters and walks away stiffly.

"Why did you do that?" I shriek. "He's the first person to notice me in years! You are so selfish. Does it bother you so much when someone else gets attention? Are you that jealous a person?" I light one of her cigarettes but inhale too quickly and start to choke. Laura reaches out to pat my back. "Don't touch me," I manage, coughing hard. "Don't you *dare* touch me."

Laura waits until I compose myself. Then she says, "I'm sorry you feel that way. But ten minutes ago, I saw Bob take a number from a tall redhead."

"Was she really young and wearing a sparkly tube top?"

Laura nods. "She kissed him good-bye, on the mouth." She pauses. "With her tongue."

Tears well up in my eyes. "Laura, I didn't mean—" But her cell phone interrupts me. "Who is it?" I ask, but she keeps saying, "Uh-huh, uh-huh," then snaps the phone shut.

"That was Bethany," she barks. "It's a Code Blue. Round up the girls. Let's *go*!"

We find Bethany sitting on the curb in front of a movie theater. Under her cape, she's wearing a sleeveless pink dress with a tight bodice and a full skirt. She's been crying and her face is streaked with mascara. The tears of a clown, I think sadly. "Bethany, what's wrong?"

She won't answer. Laura tries to get her to stand, but she won't budge, so all six of us sit down beside her in a line on the curb. Valentine hands her some pretzels. "You're gonna freeze to death out here," she says. "We were waiting for you inside the bar. Why didn't you come in?"

Bethany hangs her head. "The guy wanted to go to the movies."

"WHAT DID SHE SAY?" Natasha calls from the end.

"SHE SAID THE GUY WANTED TO GO TO THE MOVIES!" Laura yells.

"WHY DID HE WANT TO GO TO THE MOVIES?" Natasha calls back.

"Because he wanted to ditch me," Bethany murmurs.

"WHY?" Natasha calls.

"BECAUSE HE WANTED TO DITCH HER!" Laura screams.

"This is ridiculous." I stand and pull Bethany up with me. "Tell us what happened."

"The minute I opened the door," Bethany says as we gather around, "I could tell he was disappointed—like it's my fault I'm not five-ten and a hundred pounds. Then my mother showed up with her boobs hanging out. She kept saying, 'Isn't she beautiful, Douglas? Isn't she beautiful?' Finally we left and I told him I wanted to go to the bar like we planned, but he wanted to go to the movies." She starts to cry again. "I thought he . . . wanted to go to the movies . . . so he wouldn't have to look at me, but . . . this is so embarrassing . . . the movie was his getaway plan."

"What are you talking about?" Natasha holds out a tissue.

Bethany blows her nose. "He bought the tickets, we found our seats, and he . . . he . . . he . . ."

"What did he do, Bethany? Did he hit you? Did he force you to have sex with him? Did he force you to have sex with his friends? Did he—"

"He got up from his seat and never came back!" Bethany tries to compose herself, but can't. She wails so hard, I'm positive she's going into convulsions. I open my cell phone in case we need an ambulance.

"Are you okay?" I ask, poised to dial.

Bethany hiccups. "It was just so *humiliating*. I looked everywhere. I had the manager check the men's room, but he was gone. I feel like such a loser."

"He's the loser," Natasha snaps.

"No, he was a young, handsome guy. I'm the forty-year-old sow with bat wings."

"What are bat wings?" Laura asks.

Bethany flaps. Her underarm fat swings. "These are bat wings. And if you think that's bad, wait till you see my thighs when I run."

"He was rude," I blurt out. "No one has the right to treat you like that."

"Thanks, Jenny. I didn't think you cared."

"We all care, Bethany," Valentine says, holding out more pretzels. I look at her face. Could she be storing snack food in her cheeks? "Come on. Let us take you home."

We take two cabs up to West End Avenue. When we get to Bethany's building, she won't go inside. "Whatever you do," she pleads, "don't tell my mother what happened." The six of us promise. But the second we get to her door, Bethany calls, "Mommy? Where are you? That stupid guy left me in the movie!" And she rushes to Barbara, who stands, arms wide, waiting to receive her.

What did you do to make this boy run off?" is Barbara's first question. She stands in the living room with her hands on her hips. Bethany wasn't kidding about her breasts. They hang like deflated balloons underneath her sheer nightgown. *The horror*, I think. *The horror*.

"I didn't do anything, Mommy." Bethany's voice is as small as a child's.

"She didn't," Natasha cuts in. "This guy was a total jerk.

Bethany did nothing wrong." She tugs a lock of Barbara's hair. "That's a hell of a lot of hair spray."

Barbara looks Natasha up and down. "Who the hell are you?"

"I'm nobody, actually, but I'm pretty sure that the fluorocarbons in hair spray will eat your brain if you use too much—not to mention what you're doing to the ozone."

Barbara stares at Natasha and I stare at Barbara. Her mascara is caked on thick, her eye shadow glitters, and she has a line of foundation where her jaw meets her neck. It's like seeing an older, harder version of Bethany. She turns away and clomps to the phone in her high-heeled mules. "I'm gonna call Sandy and give her a piece of my mind. What kind of son did she raise?"

"Mom, don't!" Bethany appeals to us. "Would one of you say something?"

"A little pomade will give her the same hold without any environmental toxins," Natasha offers.

"Maybe Bethany should be the one to call this guy," Laura says. "Don't you think it would be better if she stood up for herself?"

"At this point I don't know what to think. Here." Barbara hands the phone to Bethany. "Call."

"I didn't mean now. I meant in a day or two."

"Who are all of you?" Barbara asks suddenly.

"We're her friends," Ivy tells her, which makes Bethany smile.

"Yeah, they're my friends."

"Well, Bethany, it's late and this evening has been very upsetting for me, so please tell your friends to go." Barbara sighs. "You looked so beautiful. Like a little princess."

As Bethany ushers us out, Barbara calls, "Do you always travel in a pack like this?"

Natasha gives her the evil eye. "We do now."

Did you see that?" Laura crows on the sidewalk. "Did you see that?"

"We saw that," Valentine agrees, holding a bag of Doritos.

"Where did those come from?"

"The kitchen."

"Give it here." Laura grabs the bag. "Valentine, you're a roving buffet."

"I always eat when I'm nervous." She tries to reach into the Doritos bag, but Laura won't let her. Defeated, Valentine skulks away.

Ivy nibbles a chip. "Ah'll tell yew what. It's no wonder Bethany acts how she does. Her mother is crazy as a loon. As a loon!"

"That's what I've been trying to tell you," Laura says. "We have to convince Bethany to move her mother out of that apartment."

"Ginger!" the Weaver cries. "I forgot Ginger!" She starts to run, then turns back. "I know you girls don't like me—"

"That's not true, Suzanna," Valentine says. "We like you a lot. We want to get to know you better."

"Well, I thought tonight was great. I mean, it was awful about Bethany, but still, it was great." She looks at Laura. "I'm just very lonely," she says, and skips down the street.

"Suzanna!" Laura calls, but the Weaver has already turned the corner. "I guess that was a breakthrough, huh? Maybe we should talk her into getting rid of Ginger."

"One thing at a time." I pause. "I'm sorry for calling you selfish. I didn't mean it. I was just so happy a guy noticed me. It's been a long time."

"There will be lots of guys, Janey. You have to learn to trust me."

My eyes fill. "I've never had a friend like you before."

Laura waves at the girls. "And now you have six. Six hormonally wrecked, penis-obsessed, youth-challenged hens. We're a premenopausal pussy posse! All for one and one for all." She reaches out to hug me, using the strength of her embrace to promise that she'll protect me from the Bobs of the world, that she cares about me, too, that I'm not alone anymore.

6

United Cerebral Palsy of New York City is on Twenty-third Street, between Lexington and Park. Sometimes I pass the back of the building just as the buses pull into the driveway, and I'll stay to help the drivers roll the wheelchairs onto the sidewalk. I've seen enough telethons to know what a palsied body looks like, but television doesn't capture the person trapped inside—the blueness of their eyes, the texture of their skin, their body's unique sounds and smells.

My father had his first stroke when I was working at Municipal Life. It was a mild stroke, he claimed he was fine, but I took a few weeks off and went back to Welter. He didn't talk much, but I didn't care. Seeing him unable to clasp a cup in his hand made me flush with a daughterly love I'd never felt before. I cleaned up his spills, made his favorite grilled-cheese sandwiches with burnt bacon, and took him for short walks in the woods.

He returned to the pulp soon after. But a year later a second stroke left him partially paralyzed, and he was forced to stop working and take disability. I called Aunt Honey, my mother's sister, who lived in the next town over. She agreed to help, but Zack refused. With no other recourse, I asked Willy and Rufus, his lifelong pals, to help me move a hospital bed into the trailer and I hired a nurse to stay with him when I couldn't be there.

"I have to work," I explained. "And you need the help. I'm not Mom. I won't just leave you." He lay in the new bed, glaring at me, saying nothing. In the weeks that followed, he continued to ignore me. If I asked him a question, he closed his eyes. If I touched him, he flinched. He wouldn't respond, no matter what I said or how loudly I spoke.

My father worked at his silence as stubbornly as he'd once worked to find my mother. Over time his silence became the language we both adopted. And in the end it was what finally pushed me away. Silence between a father and his daughter is not quiet. Father-daughter silence is the loudest, most lonely sound in the world.

The last time I saw Zack, I tried to lift him out of his bed. He lay there immobile, thick and heavy, like a fallen tree. I slipped my hand under his back and told him to raise his good shoulder, but he wouldn't budge. Willy and Rufus knocked and my dad's eyes fluttered open. He waved them in with his good arm and offered beer in his garbled speech. I stood there, my hand still trapped between his body and the bed, and I suddenly understood how my mother felt living with him: sweaty and exhausted, ignored and alone.

My anger came fast. "You made her leave! It's all your fault. And you know what else? I hate you, too!"

Willy whistled. "Jane," he said quietly, "you're treading on thin ice."

I ran out of the trailer. My shame was as thick as the stink of the pulp but I never went back. I couldn't, not even six months later when Willy and Rufus moved him into a chronic-care facility. I agreed to pay his bills but refused to see him.

When I pass the UCP building and I see the people in wheelchairs, I ache for my father. I'm embarrassed about the way I left him; that I'd even left him at all. His body is broken, my spirit is palsied, and like all those afflicted, we long for a cure. Or, if not a cure, then something resembling justice.

The girls and I decide to convince Bethany that her mother should move out. Two weeks after we meet Barbara, Laura casually mentions that her apartment is being fumigated. "Can I stay at your place tonight, Bethany?" she asks. "Or will your mother get annoyed?"

"I pay the rent," Bethany answers indignantly. "Of course you can stay."

After Group, Laura and I take the subway to her apartment in the East Village so she can get a change of clothes. I sit at her desk because she doesn't have a couch. Nor does she have a table. All she has is a futon, a computer, and hundreds of books in floor-to-ceiling shelves. The starkness surprises me. Given Laura's sexual activity, I figured she'd have an intimate boudoir. When I say this, she rolls her eyes. "I'm a writer," she tells me. "Not a hooker."

While she packs a bag, I rifle through her drawers. "Don't you have any pictures of your family?" I say this as though I have hundreds, but in fact I have only one, of my mom and dad at the state fair. I took the picture myself and accidentally cut off their feet. Because of this my mother appears stunted and freakish even though she was five-nine. She also looks distracted, as if she'd rather be somewhere else. But maybe I see her this way because that's how I felt when I was with her. We'd lie in my bed together, arm to arm, leg to leg, but her hundred-yard stare made her seem out of reach. My father is standing next to her, his big hand resting on her shoulder, and she's either pulling him toward her or pushing him away, I really can't tell. When I look at the picture now, my dad seems to be hanging on to her as though he's afraid she might flee. But again, maybe it's a trick of the mind—a few months after the shot was taken, my mother left for good.

"I don't like my family," Laura is saying. "And stop going through my drawers!"

"What's wrong with your family? Laura!" I gasp. "You have guns!"

"They're antiques. My father gave them to me for protection when I moved to New York but they haven't worked since 1903, which shows you how bright he is. And nothing's *wrong* with my family other than their heft. People in Montana eat a lot of beef. Collectively they weigh about a ton and a half. Hey, Janey? JANEY?"

"What?" I'm focused on the guns. She has three. Finally, a stroke of good fortune.

"I told Bethany I'd be there by ten." Laura puts on her coat. "You ready?"

"Absolutely," I say and rise from her desk, hoping she doesn't notice the bulge in my pocket.

When we get up to Bethany's, Valentine is waiting in the lobby, holding a sleeping bag.

"She doesn't suspect anything, does she?" Laura asks. When Valentine shakes her head, Laura turns to the doorman. "Please ring 25J. Bethany's expecting me."

Bethany might be expecting Laura, but she certainly isn't expecting Valentine. Or me. Nor is she expecting Natasha, who shows up as we step into the elevator.

"What are all of you doing here?" Bethany exclaims when she opens the door.

"My apartment's being painted," I reply.

"My mother and father are visiting from Spain," Valentine says.

Bethany turns to Natasha. "Why are you here?"

"I'm afraid of the dark. You know that."

"I guess it's okay. But we have to be quiet." Bethany glances at Barbara's bedroom door. "My mother will have a conniption if we wake her up."

Just as she says this, the doorman buzzes from the lobby. "A Miss Ivy is here with her luggage. Should I send her up?"

"Ivy's downstairs!" Bethany shrieks. "What the hell is going on?"

Laura shrugs. Ivy knocks. This is turning out to be better than we expected.

Ivy has a steamer trunk, a carry-on, and a large cosmetics case, all of which the doorman moves into the foyer. "Bethany, Ah can't stand bein' alone in mah big ole apartment. Ah heard Laura say she was comin', so Ah thought yew wouldn't mind if Ah came, too. Ah brought mah own linens." She pulls a sheet from her trunk. "Natasha, help me blow up this air mattress."

Natasha cringes. "I don't *blow into* polyethylene."

"Ah'll pop a stitch if Ah do it mahself. Yew got any wine, Bethany, honey?" Ivy pulls out Brie and crackers from her trunk. "A merlot will go real nice with these snacks."

"My mom's gonna kill me!" Bethany yelps in panic. "How long are you staying?"

"Ah'm not sure," Ivy says, slicing the Brie. "Long enough for me to feel okay bein' alone."

"That could take years!" The buzzer rings again. This time the doorman announces the Weaver. Bethany shrieks again. "She brought Ginger! The Weaver brought Ginger."

"Well, let her up," Laura crows. "The more the merrier."

The Weaver arrives with a futon, which she wheels into the apartment on a handcart. Ginger sits on top, wearing a plaid nightshirt and a hat with a white pom-pom. "Ginger doesn't like to sleep on the floor," the Weaver explains, parking the handcart against the hall closet.

"Suzanna?" Bethany asks through clenched teeth. "Why is Ginger here?"

"I couldn't leave Ginger alone, could I? That would make her so unhappy."

"But why are you here?"

"I didn't want to be without Ginger."

"What *the hell* is going on?" We all turn to see Barbara standing in the doorway of her bedroom wearing a short kimono that rises above the tops of her fleshy thighs. "Who are all these people and why are they lying on the floor of my house?"

"They needed a place to stay for the night," Bethany says meekly.

"Well, it might be more than a night," Laura says. "I might need an extra day or two."

"Ah'm packed for two weeks!" Ivy holds out her hand. "Cheese cracker, Barbie?"

Barbara points at Bethany. "How do you expect me to get any sleep with all these people camped out in my living room? Get in this bedroom now! I want a word with you in private."

"Ma, I'm not a baby." At first Bethany's voice is weak, but it gets stronger. "I'm a grown woman and these are my friends. They needed a place to stay and I said okay."

"You didn't even ask me. When will you learn consideration? No wonder Peter left!"

Bethany's eyes widen. She looks at Laura who nods. "Mom, Peter and I had lots of problems. It wasn't just my fault. And I am considerate. I let you live here, don't I?"

Barbara cocks her hip. "What's that supposed to mean, Bethany Joy? You begged me to move in here. You said you were lonely, you cried every night. How dare you!"

"I'm not lonely anymore. I have friends."

"So this is how it's gonna be? Well, I'm your mother and if your friends don't leave right now, I'm moving out! And you'll have to live with that decision for the rest of your life."

"Excellent," Laura says. "We'll help you pack."

Later, all seven of us lie in the dark. No one speaks. I know Bethany's doing the right thing, but being motherless myself, I can't imagine what it feels like to have one, then cast her aside. "Bethany?" I whisper. "You okay? Why are you breathing so hard?"

"It's me," Natasha says. "I'm having a panic attack."

Laura asks Bethany how she's doing.

"Do you really think she'll leave?" Bethany asks quietly.

"She might." Laura pauses. "Your middle name is Joy?"

"I know, ironic, huh?" Bethany sniffles. "What if she never forgives me?"

"She's your mother," I tell her. "She'll forgive you." I understand the gravity of the mother-daughter bond. There is only you and she. You have exactly each other. Take one away and both of you lose. I wonder if my own mother realized this when she decided to go; if she feels my absence now, wherever she is.

There's a long silence. Finally Bethany whispers, "But who will love me like she does? Who'll be there for me?"

"I will," I reply, unsure if she's even talking to me.

"Me, too," says Ivy. Then all the girls echo, "Me, too, me, too," our voices rising in a solemn promise, a kind of prayer.

During pre-Group two weeks later, I tell Ivy I have a cocktail party at the 21 Club in May. "It's an actuarial thing and I have to make an appearance. What should I wear?"

"A cocktail dress. Short, simple, and elegant. Ah have about ten if yew want to borrow one."

"Are most actuaries men?" Laura asks.

Before I can reply, the clock strikes seven. Dr. Hensen clears his throat. "I want to mention how nice it is to see this Group come together. I sense you are spending a lot of time with each other, which is a great way to practice your relationship skills."

"Oh, admit it, Fred," Laura says. "You're still curious about Bethany's date."

"I'm just surprised that no one wants to share with me what happened."

"Nothing happened. Bethany met the guy, then hooked up with us. We took her home, said hello to her mom, then we left. That's all there is to tell. You were the one who said nothing could go wrong."

"I'm not suggesting anything went wrong. I'm just interested in your observations." He turns to Bethany. "Are you going to see him again?"

"You asked me that already. And I said no. Do you know how much has happened since then? I have a completely different life."

Dr. Hensen tilts her way. "What do you mean by a completely different life?"

"This is really boring. Can't someone else share? Valentine, what's going on with that bitch in your office whose name I can't remember?"

"Her name's Margot!" I shout.

Bethany flinches. "This isn't a game show, Jenny. Calm down. Valentine, you go."

"Well, she did say something . . ." Valentine trails off. "Forget it, it's too embarrassing."

"Tough shit. You have to talk." None of us blinks at Laura's harsh tone. It's April. We've been together ten months. No one gets out unscathed.

Valentine appeals to me, but I can only shrug. "It's out of my hands."

"Fine," she says, realizing we're not going to let her off the hook. "There was a sales meeting today. All the big bosses were there. Margot looked me over a few times and said, 'I wanted to wear a pants suit but Jeremy said it would be inappropriate.' Then she added, 'I didn't realize they made such nice pants in your size. I've always been meaning to ask you where you shopped. My great-aunt is the size of a barn and never knows where to go.' "

The room is silent.

"She really said that. She said 'the size of a barn.' " Valentine looks around the circle. "How come no one's speaking?"

"Because we're in shock," Laura explains. "What did you say back?"

Valentine looks at her hands.

"Valentine, you have to stick up for yourself! Normal people don't talk to each other like that. God, I despise that woman. We need to teach her a lesson!"

"What kind of lesson?" Dr. Hensen asks in alarm.

"She can't say shit like that and get away with it." Laura addresses the rest of us. "Does everyone agree?"

"I also agree, but it should come from Valentine, not you." Dr. Hensen tilts toward Valentine, who's still studying her hands. "Did you binge?"

"Anger and bingeing do not have a direct causal relationship, Fred. She might not binge for days until something else triggers the need for release."

"That shows how much you know, Laura," Valentine blurts out. "You don't know. You don't know anything! I ate a salami sandwich and a bag of Mint Milanos and three soft pretzels."

"You were angry," Dr. Hensen points out.

"And an apple and a pizza and a hunk of Cheddar cheese and two bags of peanuts!"

"Valentine, honey," Ivy cuts in. "Yew don't have to recount—"

"And three Dove Bars. Three! See, Laura? See? You don't know what you're talking about. *Estoy como una vaca! Estoy tan gorda como uno vaca. Me doy asco. Estoy harta de la vida y me quiero morir!*"

"You were angry," Hensen repeats, stroking his goatee, obviously not fluent in the romance languages.

"No, cariño," Bethany says suddenly. *"No digas eso. Tu no estás como una vaca. Tu eres muy guapa."* Shocked, the six of us stare at her. It's like seeing your three-year-old suddenly belt out Puccini. "What are all of you looking at? Valentine said she was a pig and I said she wasn't."

Valentine continues to moan in Spanish. It kills me to hear her sound so distraught. I take a deep breath. "Valentine, I told you I fantasize about suicide, but I never said why, mostly because I know it'll sound simple and stupid. But it is kind of simple, and I guess it's also kind of stupid." I pause.

"Keep going, Janey," Dr. Hensen prompts.

"Basically, I fantasize about suicide because it seems much easier to disappear than to deal with the constant embarrassment of being alive and alone. The other night, a handsome guy standing behind me in the deli smiled at me. So I smiled back *very* seductively and inched closer to him. At the same time, a stunning woman appeared holding a little boy. The kid looked at me, pointed to the woman, and said, 'She's my mom!' almost as if he knew I was flirting with his dad. Everyone laughed—I laughed, too—but I felt guilty and foolish. I started thinking lonely peoples' thoughts: 'I'm not anyone's mother. I don't have a family. I'm alone on a Saturday night checking out someone else's husband,' which only made me feel more distant and depressed. By the time I paid for my turkey burger, I couldn't stand being in my own body. 'I don't have to do this anymore,' I kept reminding myself. 'I don't even have to be here.' And I started to imagine all the ways I could make that happen."

Valentine's eyes are glassy. "The death list?" she asks.

I nod. "I've always existed half in my life and half out, knowing I can end it whenever I want. But Group has taught me that half-living isn't living in any real sense. It's just a means of avoiding horrible feelings. It's similar, I suppose, to what happens when you binge. Everything else falls away. But when I talk about these thoughts, I feel much more grounded, more connected to the world. I can't check out as easily. So maybe you and I could help each other, Valentine. Maybe if we keep talking, we'll find a reason to . . . I don't know . . . stay."

"I guess," is all she says.

"Janey," Dr. Hensen asks, "did you have a chance to say goodbye to your mother?"

"What does she have to do with this?"

"What you said to Valentine sounded like something you might've told your mother, given the opportunity. I was wondering what the two of you discussed the last time you saw her."

"I didn't say anything. She left when I was still in school. Why are you focusing on me? Valentine's sharing!"

"Calm down," Laura says. "Fred was just asking a question."

"Well, stop it!" I'm close to hysterics. "Stop asking so many fucking questions!"

"We can focus on Valentine if you're uncomfortable," Dr. Hensen says, but he continues to watch me in a way that's so intimate I have to avert my eyes. I feel naked and transparent, not in a sexual way, but metaphysically, as though he can see beyond my body and into my consciousness. It dawns on me that his questions are only beginning.

We settle it in post-Group at T.G.I. Friday's. Margot will not get away with insulting Valentine. It's up to the pussy posse to teach her a lesson. All for one, and one for all. We outline a plan and then we shake hands. In a matter of weeks, revenge will be ours.

7

The girls and I scheme all through the following week. We have a standing conference call at noon every day, so it's weird when I check in on Tuesday and I'm alone on the line. I wait fifteen minutes but no one else clicks in, so I decide to go out for lunch. When I get back to the office, my door is closed and all the lights are off.

"What's going on?" I ask Audrey.

"Maybe it's a power failure."

"But the lights are on out here." I peer into her cubicle. "And your computer's working."

She raises her hands as if bewildered by it all. Watching her, I feel an acute sense of loss, although it's not her looks that bother me. It's the way she moves: lazy and insouciant, with the absence of worry. I don't envy Audrey's girlness as much as I miss my own.

"Janey?" she asks. "If you're my mentor, how come we never do things together?"

"Like getting our nails done?"

She claps. "I'd love that! But I meant more professional things, like going to lunch. My friend Lainey who's upstairs in Accounting has already been out twice with her mentor, and you and I haven't even gone once."

I shake my head, amazed by my stupidity. In a lapse of sanity, I agreed to register with her for our company's mentoring program. If I were a different person, I could be a good mentor. I would take Audrey to lunch, advise her about her actuarial exams, teach her how to network. But I'm cranky and exhausted, and at that moment all I have to say about life as an actuary is, "Kid, be something else."

"Audrey, I'll tell you what. There's a cocktail party at the Twenty-one Club for the American Society of Actuaries. Why don't you come as my guest and I'll introduce you around?"

"That would be great! Lainey's letting me borrow a dress for her brother's bar mitzvah on Saturday so she has it upstairs. I'll go get it."

"The party's not until the end of May, Audrey. That's five weeks away."

"I won't be able to do any work until you tell me if it looks okay." Audrey jumps up. "Oh, thank you, Janey. Thank you, thank you, thank you!"

Oh my God, she's hugging me. I'm being suffocated by Tommy Girl perfume. Help! I wrench myself away, lunge into my office, and flip on the light.

Valentine, Laura, Ivy, Natasha, Bethany, and the Weaver jump up. "Surprise!"

I'm so startled, I don't move.

Laura blows a horn in my ear. "I bet you thought we forgot your birthday."

"Your assistant helped us plan," Valentine says. "My God, she's skinny."

"And young," Ivy pipes up. "So young it breaks mah heart just to look at her."

My office is filled with streamers and balloons. "This is unbelievable," I say, truly taken aback. There's a sheet cake on my credenza with "Happy 25th Birthday" written in blue frosting. "You actually remembered." I swipe the *H* with my finger. "I only mentioned it once."

Laura laughs. "*Once?* All we've been hearing for months is 'I'm turning thirty-five. Do I look thirty-five? I can't believe I'm thirty-five.' "

"I wasn't that bad."

Ivy touches her face. "Believe yew me, honey. We all understand."

"Thank you," I tell them. "This means a lot to me."

"You're welcome." Laura props her feet on my desk. "Okay, party's over. It's time to get down to business. We're all set for next week. I made a one o'clock reservation at Balthazer. Valentine has Margot's schedule and she promised to find out her shoe size." She glances at Valentine. "You don't have to do anything else. Just invite her to lunch and make sure she shows up on time."

"You're okay with this?" I ask Valentine.

"She's fine." Laura's about to say something else when Audrey appears in the doorway wearing a short, strapless dress. She holds out her arms and twirls. "Do you like it?"

Valentine gives her the once-over. "Have some cake," she says, cutting her a slab.

Audrey looks at the cake on the table. Then she looks at me. She's stupefied. "You're only twenty-five, Janey? I thought you were way older—"

Ivy pats Audrey's arm. "Honey, we're all twenty-five in spirit."

"I'm only twenty-three, but sometimes I feel twenty-five. I don't mind getting older."

"Is that so?" Bethany retorts. "Come back in ten years when your tits are sagging, your legs look like cottage cheese, and your crotch smells like swamp. Then we'll talk."

"Bethany!" I pull Audrey away from her. "Show me the dress."

She twirls again, this time more slowly. "What do you think?"

What do I think? If I could fill out a dress like that, I'd have it surgically attached to my body. Then I'd cab over to Municipal Life and dance the Watusi on Tobias's desk. *Hey, jackass,* I'd say. *How's the impotence problem working out?*

"Know what I think, Audrey? That dress needs a jacket."

I bet Valentine chickens out," Bethany says as she and I walk into Bloomingdale's. "She's such a wimp." We take the elevator to the lingerie department. "After we look at the bras," she continues, "I can help you find a cocktail dress."

I take one look at her pleather pants and "YOU SUCK" T-shirt and politely decline.

"Valentine's not a wimp anymore. She's changed a lot." I hold up a red teddy. "What about this?"

Bethany shakes her head. “It’s not really you.” She holds up a bra. “Do you like this?”

“I don’t need any bras.”

“It’s for me, you dope.” She turns to a saleslady. “Miss! Do you have this in a thirty-eight E? “Oh, miss!” Bethany calls loudly, but the woman won’t respond. “Fine, I’ll just try this one.” She slips on the bra over her shirt. “Hook me,” she instructs, turning around.

“Bethany, why don’t you use a dressing room? I don’t mind waiting.”

“Hook me.”

Grudgingly I hook the bra, which barely closes. “Jenny, why do you think the Weaver is so obsessed with her dog?”

“She’s just lonely, I guess.”

“She’s crazy.”

I look at her wearing a bra over her shirt. “She’s no more crazy than the rest of us. Bethany, please. Go into the dressing room.”

“I’m trying to make a point. That woman is pretending she doesn’t see me.”

“Maybe she really doesn’t. She’s on the phone.”

“Oh, she sees me all right.” Bethany waves her arms over her head. “I can read her name tag from here. It says”—she squints—“ ‘Candice.’ Look at her now!” A blonde wearing stiletto heels and a fur holds up a robe for Candice’s appraisal. “If I’m embarrassing you”—Bethany wriggles into a pair of panties, which she pulls up over her pants—“you don’t have to stay. Candice is obviously too busy to help a fat old cow so I’ll just help myself. Here.” She hands me a demi-cut bra in pale lavender. “Try this on.”

I watch Candice fawn over the elegant blonde. “Give it here,” I say, all at once feeling reckless and giddy, caught up in the thrill of my own invisibility. I whirl around. “I’ve never done anything like this before! Hook me, Bethany.”

She picks up a pair of lavender panties. “These go with the bra.”

I pull them on over my jeans and the sheer material tears. Both of us howl.

“Was that yours?” Bethany squats. “Or mine?” Her underwear/outerwear rips in half. I laugh so hard, I snort, especially when she produces a thong. "Would Candice approve?" She pulls it on and does three deep lunges, then spots a silk slip. "I love this!"

"It's totally you. Try it on."

Bethany puts the slip on over the bra and panty set, which is over her pleather pants and T-shirt, then plops into a chair and lights a cigarette. It's at this point that Candice jets across the room.

"There's no smoking in here!" she snaps, giving Bethany an evil look. "I'm with another client, but I'll be happy to help you when I'm finished. And *please*"—Candice draws the word out into three long syllables—"retire to a dressing room to try on foundation garments."

When Candice walks away, I pull on a lacy camisole. "Is it me?"

Bethany claps. "It's so you, it's more than you!"

"What do we do now?"

Bethany hands me my jacket, which I put on over my new camisole, which is over my lavender demi-bra and pantie set, which is over my T-shirt and jeans. She smiles. "We leave."

"What if the tags set off the alarm?"

"We run."

So we did. And imagine my surprise when we race outside in our stolen lingerie and see Tobias Teague strolling up Lexington Avenue, close enough to reach out and touch.

Forgetting that years have elapsed, I raise my hand to wave. "OhmyGod, Tobias—" Then I remember my outfit. I pull Bethany back into the store and whip off the lingerie.

"We have to get out of here!" she yells.

She tries to fight me off, but I'm too strong. I grab her by the lapel and drag her through the cosmetics department. "Just a sec. I need makeup. I suddenly feel very naked."

"But we're gonna get caught!" Bethany keeps peering over her shoulder as I maniacally apply eye shadow from a Mac tester. "I'm leaving, Jenny. I swear to God, I'm leaving you."

Tobias is in front of the Clinique counter, fifteen feet away. He cranes his neck, looking for me. "Janey? It's Tits Teague! I just saw you on the street. Where did you go?"

I crouch down in the aisle.

"She's right here!" Bethany shouts, but I pinch her bat wing and push her forward. I can't face Tobias. Not wearing aubergine eye shadow.

"We have to go, Bethany." I try to move her toward the door, but she won't budge. "Now!"

"But he's cute, Jenny. And he knows you."

"Close your coat and keep walking."

"Did you see a woman run in here?" Tobias asks a cosmetologist.

"I see a lot of women." She holds up a mirror. "Can I interest you in a moisturizer?"

Tobias squints at his face. "My skin is dry, isn't it?" He turns around. "Janey? It's Tobias. Where are you?"

He's an aisle away and closing in fast. I grab Bethany's hand and we've almost made it to the street when Tobias spots us. He picks up his pace and we pick up ours. Just as I lunge for the front door, I hear him behind us. "Janey! I knew it was you."

I pull Bethany out the door and scream, "Run for your life!"

There are few places more crowded than midtown Manhattan on a Saturday afternoon. But I sprint down the street, weaving and bobbing, dragging Bethany with me.

"My . . . feet . . . hurt," she pants. "And . . . you . . . stole . . . that . . . eye shadow tester."

"I'll . . . take . . . it . . . back."

"Good . . . it's . . . an . . . ugly . . . color."

Bethany starts to lag. I pull her arm and try to keep us moving. I refuse to slow down until we're safely on Thirty-fourth Street.

"What . . . is . . . your . . . problem?" Bethany gasps. "We just ran twenty-five blocks." She pulls the slip over her head, unhooks the bra, and steps out of the panties. "And I ruined my new foundation garments." She throws everything into a garbage can.

I keep turning around, unable to shake the feeling that Tobias is behind us.

"Who was that guy there?" Bethany asks.

"What guy?" I can't believe he looks the same. Most men his age have sagging jowls and soft bellies. But Tobias has a square jaw, an athlete's body, and every strand of his thick, sandy hair.

"Don't play games, Jenny. My corns are killing me. Who was that guy?"

"Back there? I made a mistake. I thought he was somebody else." I take a deep breath. "Well, okay then. That was fun. What's next?"

Margot!" Laura waves. "We're over here!" It's Friday at one and we're seated in Balthazar, on Spring Street. Our table is decorated with streamers left over from my birthday celebration ten days ago. All seven of us are assembled. Our plan is in motion.

Margot barrels through the crowded dining room, using her briefcase to push people out of her way. "I almost didn't make it," she says when she finally reaches us. "But Valentine insisted and I hate to miss a party."

"We're so happy to meet yew," Ivy pipes up. "So very, very happy."

"Take it down a notch, Ivy," Laura whispers.

"These are my friends." Valentine's voice quivers. "We're celebrating Janey's birthday."

"There's cake for dessert," Natasha says, "but I don't eat refined sugar or food coloring or artificial additives or anything else that might cause cancer."

"Well, I love cake." Margot surveys the table. "Would someone please tell me how Valentine found all these friends? I never thought of her as a people person. Although big women *do* tend to be jolly, right?"

I almost tell her to go fuck herself, but that's not the plan. The plan is to get Margot to lunch, then up to Saks Fifth Avenue. The plan is to act friendly, successful, and smart. No doggie dreams, no boob holding. The plan, we agreed, is to try to act like normal people.

But first I have to stop Natasha from dipping all her silverware in her water glass. "I can't stop," she says. "Cleaning calms my nerves. Give me your spoon. I'll sterilize it for you."

"I don't need my spoon sterilized, Natasha."

"What about lockjaw?"

"What about it?" I turn to Margot. "Most of us met Valentine at my wedding. In fact, my husband Fred introduced Valentine to her boyfriend."

"*Fred?*" Laura cries. "Your husband *Fred*?"

"Valentine has a *boyfriend*?" Margot's voice is as shrill as Laura's. "A *boyfriend*?"

"Men fall all over her everywhere we go," I say. "But she only has eyes for one very gorgeous billionaire star athlete."

"A billionaire? I thought rich ones only went for skinny Minnies."

Bethany leans forward. "I'm going to kick you so hard, you'll never walk again."

"What? I can't hear you. It's so noisy in this place."

"We should order," Laura suggests loudly. "I have an appointment at four, but I want to stop at Saks first."

"What's happenin' at Saks?" Ivy asks, right on cue.

"Major shoe sale," Laura replies, also on cue. "Two-for-one Calvin Klein boots. If anyone else wears size nine, we can get both get a pair for half price."

"I wear size nine!" Margot exclaims.

"Want to go?" Laura asks.

"Definitely! We can share a cab."

"Sounds great." Laura glances at her watch. "We should order. Margot, lunch is my treat. It's Ivy's birthday and we're celebrating."

Margot looks confused. "I thought it was Janey's birthday."

"It's both their birthdays!" the Weaver says. "They're twins!"

Margot squints at Ivy, then at me. "Really? You don't have an accent, Janey."

"Ah don't have an accent, neither," Ivy drawls, smiling broadly.

As soon as Laura and Margot drive off, the girls and I race to a pay phone. I whip out my Shirt Pocket Micro Voice Disguiser and pick up the phone.

Valentine grabs my arm. "Wait a second. I feel funny about this."

"Let's reflect. As soon as Margot brought up how jolly you were, you emptied two breadbaskets. Then you scarfed my fries when she mentioned—again—how surprising it was to see you with friends. She also pointed out that your skin doesn't wrinkle because it has to cover such a large mass, and you polished off Laura's trout, Ivy's pasta, and Natasha's Caesar salad." I hold the phone toward her. "Well?"

"I'll call myself."

"Is this the designer shoe department?" she asks the sales clerk at Saks. "This is Special Agent Freddy Hensen, FBI badge number 230303394903. I want to report that a known shoplifter has escaped our custody and is en route to your store. Her name is Margot Dreiser and she's a white female, age thirty-nine, with blond hair and blue eyes. She is charged with grand larceny, and generally targets upscale department stores in the middle of the day. Be aware that she is armed—I repeat—armed and dangerous. If you see her, detain her until we arrive with reinforcements. Do you copy?" After a beat, Valentine hangs up. "Now we wait."

Laura's call comes at three-thirty. "Mission accomplished," she says and fills us in on the details. "I tried to be nice at first so she wouldn't get suspicious. I even told her that I know a lot of eligible men if she is interested. You should've seen how fast she nodded. I thought her head would snap off her neck."

"And?" I prompt.

"And nothing. She's pathetic and desperate. She could've been any one of us. But then she wanted to know all about Valentine's boyfriend." Laura pauses. "Thanks, Janey. I had to rack my brain for believable details about a nonexistent billionaire star athlete. Anyway, Margot leans over and says, 'There's really no boyfriend, is there?' and I wanted to shove her out of the cab, which by the way, was thirteen bucks plus the three hundred dollars I shelled out for lunch. We *had* to eat in Soho, didn't we?"

"It was *your* idea, Laura," I said. "We'll pay you back. Finish the story."

By the time they got to Saks, Laura and Margot were carrying on like old friends. They strolled through the shoe department and no one stopped them until Laura spotted a beefy security guard near the escalator and maneuvered Margot into his line of vision.

"Excuse me, miss," he said, grabbing her elbow. "Is your name Margot Dreiser?"

Startled, she tried to pull away but his grip was too tight. "How do you know my name?"

"I'm with security," he said sharply. "And I need to ask you a few questions, if you don't mind."

"Of course I mind!" Margot wrenched her arm away and stood her ground. "You can't just come up and *grab* someone. This is America, for God's sake!" She lowered her voice when she realized that other shoppers were gawking. "We have rules in this country. Tell me how you know my name."

"That's not important." The guard asked permission to unzip Margot's briefcase.

She shrugged. "Go ahead. I have nothing to hide."

He reached inside, pulled out Laura's antique pistol, and held it up. "Do you have a permit for this, Ms. Dreiser?" The crowd gasped.

"It was like watching a cop show," Laura says, laughing, "especially when I got a whiff of urine." Margot had peed in her pants! She kept screaming, 'That's not my gun. I don't know how it got in there, I swear!' The guard started to lead her away, and she grabbed me. 'Don't leave me, Laura! It's not my gun. Where are you going, Laura? Laura? Laura, Laura, Laura.' She was so annoying, I almost smacked her."

"Ma'am, do you know this woman?" the guard asked Laura, who looked first at Margot and then back at him.

"I've never seen her before in my life," she replied and stepped onto the escalator.

How was your week, Valentine?" Bethany asks slyly in Group a week later. "Any problems from Margot?"

"She said something about a mix-up at Saks. She hasn't spoken to me since."

"What's this?" Dr. Hensen asks.

"Valentine fixed up the situation with that awful woman in her office," Ivy tells him.

"What did you do?"

"She took her to lunch," Laura cuts in. "It's no big deal."

"Actually it's a very big deal. Valentine, what happened?"

Laura doesn't give Valentine the chance to respond. "She told Margot to stay away from her, and by God, Margot listened. That, Fred, is the whole story." She turns to the Weaver. "How's Jason? You guys still hot and heavy?"

Three sessions ago, the Weaver announced that she'd started dating a brilliant D/L/CEO. Jason is a D, a neurosurgeon at St. Vincent's. None of us has met him yet, but according to the Weaver, he's a real dog person.

"I finally got up the nerve to introduce him to Ginger. And he treats her as if she's his very own child." We don't know whether to applaud or groan, but the Weaver's eyes are done up like a diva's and her arched brows scream I'M GETTING LAID, which makes everyone feel celebratory. "I told my mom," she adds, "but she was drunk and didn't recognize my voice. She did recognize Ginger, though—"

"Is this in a dream?" Laura interrupts.

"No, this was real life. My mother's an alcoholic. I never had friends growing up because she was always passed out on the couch. The kids made fun of me. I still have emotional scars."

"Well," Laura says after taking this in, "you reached out. That has to count for something." The rest of us whoop in agreement.

The Weaver's happiness seems to steer all of us in a positive direction. Ivy is still temping. "It's wonderful," she drawls. "Ah used to wait all day for Jackson to come home, but now Ah don't think about him ever." She pauses. "Well, just not as much." Bethany continues to live apart from her mother, and after weeks of debate, I decide to lobby for partner.

When I announce my plans, Dr. Hensen sits up and beams. He looks so proud, I wonder if he's in love with me. The thought makes me giddy. I want to climb into his lap and stroke his goatee. We can move to Woodstock where he'll stoke the fire, I'll can preserves, and the girls will visit on Thanksgiving with sweet potato pie. Is it considered unethical if I'm only one seventh his patient?

"Janey?" I hear him ask. "Congratulations."

"Congratulations to you, too, Fred," I say dreamily, tasting his name on my tongue.

"You're the one who decided to lobby for partner."

"It hasn't happened yet, Fred." He'll make such a good husband despite what they say about psychiatrists. And I'll be such an undemanding wife. All I want him to do is buy a new pair of loafers.

"You made a decision. That's a tremendous step. In fact"—he surveys the room—"you're all making great progress. You should be proud of yourselves. I know I'm proud of you."

"You're patronizing us again. I'd watch my tone."

"Laura!" I snap. "He's trying to be nice."

"So marry him, Janey."

Marry him? I glance at Fred and bat my eyelashes.

Despite her attitude toward Fred, even Laura is changing. The following Thursday, she shows up with her hair pulled back in a swinging ponytail. She can't stop smiling. "I went out on a date," she says, all giddy and girlie. "And I didn't let the guy kiss me good night!"

"You sure you didn't sleep with him?" Bethany asks.

"Nope. We went to dinner and"—Laura turns to Valentine—"I did what you said. I kept asking myself if I liked him instead of focusing on what he thought of me."

I want to point out that this was my husband Fred's, not Valentine's, suggestion, but I don't want to deflate Laura's infectious excitement.

"And you know what?" She claps. "He's a real estate mogul, his name's Steve, he's kind of handsome—if you go for the aging surfer look—and he's single."

Fred looks pleased. "Are you going to see him again?"

"God, no. He's *heinous*. He's spoiled and self-absorbed and boring. He was one of the worst dates I ever had. Isn't that amazing?"

Ivy's skeptical. "A month from now, are yew gonna tell us that yew sucked his viper in the backseat of a taxicab?"

"I didn't even *see* his viper! I said good-bye and went home alone."

We all cheer until Fred says, "Laura, I think it's wonderful you didn't sleep with him. Although most people would consider that a *bad* date."

"Back off, Hensen," Bethany warns him. "Don't ruin this moment."

"Ah agree," Ivy says. "Dr. Hensen, yew are out of line."

He tries to backpedal. "I don't mean to sound discouraging."

Laura, however, doesn't seem the least bit disturbed. She gives my husband Fred a long, measured look. "If I were you," she says calmly, "I'd watch my step."

8

I heard you're taking Audrey to a cocktail party." My boss, Graham, stands in my doorway. He's a tall, distinguished man in his early fifties with salt-and-pepper hair and piercing green eyes. I wonder if I'd still consider him handsome if he didn't pull in close to a million a year.

"You're the fourth person to mention it this morning. Did she hold a press conference?"

"She's young. She still finds those things exciting. I actually stopped by to see if you're finished with the Kimberly-Clarke proposal."

"What do you think?" *Want to have sex with me, Graham? I'd love to have sex with you. Then again, I haven't had sex in such a long time, I'd probably fuck anyone with a pulse.*

"I think you already sent it over and you're waiting for them to sign off."

"If you think that, then you'd be right." *Actually, Graham, I don't know if I can have sex. I haven't used that area in so long it's probably rife with shrubbery.*

"I knew I could count on you. And it's great that you're mentoring Audrey. You make a wonderful role model." He chuckles. "Janey, you're blushing!"

"Blushing? Who's blushing?"

On Thursday night, Laura interrupts me as I'm sharing. "I have an observation." She tilts my way. "Janey seems to have tremendous difficulty discussing her mother. Every time we bring her up, she freaks out."

"Shut up, Laura." I'm annoyed that she cut in just as I'm revealing how jealous I am of Audrey. "I don't want to change places with her. I just want more out of my life than what I have now." I canvass the girls for a reaction.

"Fascinating." Bethany picks her teeth with a paper clip. "But I'm interested in the way you change the subject every time we bring up your mother."

"Bethany, you're just feeling superior because you resolved one issue in your life. Telling your mother to move out doesn't mean you're cured."

"You told your mother to move out?" Dr. Hensen is stunned. "Why didn't you say something?"

"To whom?" Laura asks. "All of us know."

"*I* didn't know," Dr. Hensen shoots back.

"I told my mom to move out months ago." Bethany smiles. "Now you know."

He clears his throat. "Excuse me, ladies, but before we continue, I'd like to say something. I'm concerned that the seven of you are angry with me. I suspect my gender is threatening to you in some way. I think, though, if you can confide in me, we can build a relationship, which will ultimately help you to trust other men."

"I thought the idea was to build relationships with each other," Natasha says. "I mean, no offense, but does everything we do have to be brought in here?"

"Of course not. I just sense some resentment, that's all."

"Don't worry, Dr. Hensen," I tell him. "We don't resent you. And if it'll make you happy, we'll include you more. We didn't realize you felt so left out."

"Thank you, Janey. But you don't have to take care of me."

"Then what do you want?"

"Who cares what he wants?" Laura exclaims. "Fred, if you're upset because we like to talk to each other more than to you, you should reevaluate your reasons for starting Group."

"Laura, he's just being nice."

"You keep saying that! His job is more than just being nice. And why do you always take care of him, Janey? Did you take care of your dad after your mom left?"

"No, my father was fine."

"But who took care of you?" Valentine asks.

The unexpected question makes my eyes water. "I . . . I can't talk about this."

"Why?" Ivy asks softly. "What are yew feelin'?"

"Please. Someone else talk."

Only the Weaver speaks up. "I had the weirdest dream last night," she begins and I hear an audible groan from the girls. "Ginger doesn't want me touching her."

For the first time ever, I'm happy to hunker down and listen to a dream about Ginger even if it's two hours long. "Is this in the dream or in real life?"

"*In the dream, Janey*. Jason and I were driving around with Ginger and she kept pushing Jason's hands off the wheel. Then *she* was driving the car! Instead of being anxious, I was relieved to have the dog drive. It was remarkable, actually, her sense of direction." The Weaver glances up, but no one says a word.

Dr. Hensen tilts her way. "What do you think this dream signifies, Suzanna?"

"Fred!" Laura yelps. "Janey is unable to talk about the most traumatic experience in her life and you want to analyze Suzanna's *dream* about her *dog*? Where are your priorities?"

"Laura," he says sharply, "I believe Suzanna is communicating with Janey vis-à-vis her dream. Perhaps Suzanna is saying that Janey's jealousy of Audrey is just misplaced anxiety about her own life, but once she makes some final decisions, such as whether or not to lobby for partner, she'll get some relief."

"So why doesn't she say it vis-à-vis her real-live waking life and not vis-à-vis her doggie dream life? And you're still talking about Janey's job. We're totally past that."

"I was also going to say that Janey may feel responsible for her mother's leaving." Dr. Hensen is still tilted. My own neck aches from tilting with him. "Do you?" I shake my head. "But when you're a child," he presses, "even if you're told it's not your fault, you may still believe it is, especially when you're feeling her absence."

"I shut down as a child. I didn't feel much of anything." I don't want to tell the girls how badly dislocated I am. I've always had trouble recalling specific events of my childhood, but didn't realize until now that I can barely conjure up memories. "I wanted my mother to be proud of me. She wasn't much of a student. She didn't even finish eleventh grade, but when I studied, she used to lie in bed with me and stroke my hair. She was all I ever wanted to be. And it wasn't because she was smart or beautiful or uniquely talented—she wasn't any of those things. In fact, she got pregnant with me when she was in high school—"

Dr. Hensen cuts me off. "Do you feel that if she hadn't had you, she might've lived a different life?"

"I used to. I saw her as this girl who dropped out of school, worked in a factory, and lived in a trailer. But as I grew older, I realized there was more to her life than I could account for. Like, I never doubted how deeply my father loved her. After she left, he spent a year trying to find her but when he couldn't, he just gave up. He used to lie in their bed staring at nothing, as if waiting for her to appear and tell him it was time to get dressed. Once I found him with his head in their tiny closet, sniffing her dresses. So there had to be more to her life than I understood if she had the guts to leave, and maybe there was more to my father if he was able to harbor that kind of love, and once she was gone, that kind of grief."

"It must be awful not knowing what happened to her," Laura says.

"What's awful is not knowing why."

"Why she left Welter?" Dr. Hensen asks. "Or why she left you?"

"Me," I say quietly. "Why she left me."

Dr. Hensen pauses. "Janey, recently you told Valentine you thought about suicide because you have feelings of shame or anger. You said that was *why*, but it's actually *when*. The *why* is what brought you to Group, and I suspect it's wholly connected to your mother's disappearance."

"Maybe, Dr. Hensen. All I ever wanted was for someone to love me the way my father loved my mother. In fact, I joined Group thinking I'd learn how to meet men. But we've been together for almost a year and I'm still alone."

Laura sits up. "See, Fred? I *told* you the *first day* we were all here to meet men!"

Dr. Hensen smiles. "First you have to learn how to be with yourselves, Laura. That's the goal of this Group. You're most important. The men come later."

"It's not just the man thing," I say, relieved that no one has noticed I've steered the conversation away from my mother. "It's the whole baby thing."

"Babies will come, too," Dr. Hensen tells me, "when you're ready. Janey, you've done excellent work in here. Look at how much you've learned about yourself. But what I think isn't as important as what you think. So let me ask this: Is being without a man worth dying for?"

"It's certainly not a reason to live," I reply.

Confession: I can tell Group when I think about suicide. I can even admit it's probably a bad idea. But what I can't do is stop the fantasies—the planning and plotting and endless desire. I stroll down Twenty-third Street with Laura's gun in my hand. The pistol is small and fits in my palm but it's heavier than it looks and proves I mean business. I can whip it out, shove it in my mouth, and pull the trigger. One shot to the head, simple and clean. One shot to the head and I'm gone.

During the night, I dream that my mother and I are shopping at the Hostess cakes outlet in Welter. The store is closed now, but years ago my mother stopped there every Friday afternoon to buy smashed cupcakes, stale coffee rings, and mismarked loaves of bread. She loved the coffee rings, not the cake but the nuts, and she'd pick them off the top, leaving only the pitted pastry. In the dream, she's sitting in the cab of my father's truck and I hand her box after box of coffee rings through the open window. The boxes are white with a black expiration date stamped in the corner. "Here's more nuts," I say. "Have as many as you want." I'm tremendously anxious, as though I know something terrible is about to happen.

I wake up in a cold sweat, struck by an incident that happened about a year before she left. My father was slamming the kitchen-cabinet doors. I walked in just as he pulled one off its hinges. *"Sally,"* he said, as if her name was a slur, "other people like the goddamn nuts, too." I'd never seen him so angry. I could practically taste his rage. My mother didn't respond, and I thought the whole thing was forgotten. But the following Friday, she returned from Hostess with five coffee rings.

"I got these for Daddy. Wasn't that nice of me?" She spoke deliberately, in a small, tight voice that terrified me. She took each of the coffee rings out of their white boxes, picked off all the nuts, and lined them up on the table. When I looked at her, I expected to see anger but instead saw resignation. Her mouth was slack, her eyes empty, her cheeks hollow.

I wish I could say that when my father came home, they had a fight, a huge blowout that rocked the house with broken plates and smashed windows and a black eye. If there had been a fight, there would've also been an aftermath, with tears and apologies and all kinds of promises. But when my father came home, he pretended not to see the five nutless pastries lined up on the table. He also pretended that my mother wasn't sitting, unconcerned, on the couch and that I wasn't pacing in front of the TV. He made himself a hamburger. He set himself a place. He pushed the coffee rings aside. He didn't say a word.

You said your name was Jane?"

"Jane," I repeat, looking up at the man next to me. He's six feet tall, has Tobias-blue eyes, and from what I can tell, an awesome body. He is not, in my experience, a typical actuary. And yet here he is, mingling at the 21 Club, stabbing cheese cubes with the rest of us. "So where do you work?" I ask. *Do you want children? Do you want me? Do you want children with me?*

"KPMG. Before that, I was at Price Waterhouse before it was PWC/Kwasha/Microsoft/IBM/Viacom." He laughs at his joke, which is lame because he is, after all, an actuary, and I laugh with him because he has a penis and because if my calculations are correct, he's smack in the middle of my demographic target group. "I'm Jerry Dresher," he says, extending his hand.

"Janey Fabre."

"You said your name was Jane."

"*You* said my name was Jane." I'm on my third glass of chardonnay and feeling flirty.

"But you didn't correct me."

"That's right." He has a very sexy grin, I decide. And no wedding ring. As far as I'm concerned, Jerry Dresher is ripe for the picking.

"Excuse me," he says as he leans over to grab a carrot stick. I can't be sure, but I'm almost positive he's brushing my breast with his arm. When Jerry leans over again, I lean, too, so there'll be no doubt in his mind that I do, in fact, have breasts (or at least the semblance of a pair). The tray is huge, and filled with every conceivable vegetable that can be sliced, diced, and dipped. He leans once more, so this time I lift the tray off the table and hand it to him. "Crudité?" I ask.

"Don't mind if I do." He takes the tray from me, grabs a handful of cucumber, and taps the guy next to him. "Crudité?" he asks, winking at me.

HOW CUTE ARE YOU? I scream (silently).

"In college I dated a woman who looked exactly like you. You both look like—"

"*Marilyn Monroe!*" I exclaim, covering my mouth so I don't shoot cheese bits all over his face. "People tell me that all the time."

He smiles. "You're actually much prettier."

"And sexier. And let's not forget"—I'm reeling from the wine—"*bigger boobs.*" I push my glasses, then take them off, vowing to get contact lenses. "I only need these for reading," I say in a total non sequitur. I smile at him, only this time his face is blurry, which is fine since the big brown mole next to his nose detracts from his ever-increasing good looks. "Do you go to these parties often?"

"Never. Actuaries don't make the best cocktail party conversation unless you're really fascinated by the time value of money."

"The time value of money can be very intriguing."

"How so?"

I don't have a snappy retort, so we stand in an awkward silence. Finally I ask, "Have you heard of feng shui?"

"Feng . . ." Jerry trails off, then looks up at a tall woman who's bounding toward us.

GO AWAY, GIANTESS! I shout. HE'S MINE.

But my mental telepathy isn't working because the giantess squeals, "Thank God you're here," and flings her arms around my neck.

"Hello, Audrey," I groan, extricating myself. "You made it." She's wearing the strapless dress she'd modeled in my office, which hugs every inch of her body. As I look her over, I feel myself fade. I take another sip of wine and consider leaving. It's only a matter of minutes before I'll be as interesting to Jerry as the fake trees lined up behind the buffet table.

"I'm Audrey. Janey's my mentor."

"Is that right?" Jerry's looking at me, but I can't make out his expression. Why? Because I'm not wearing my goddamn glasses. He turns back to Audrey, taking in, I'm sure, her big breasts, perfect legs, and unlined face. He asks Audrey all kinds of questions, where she went to college, if she's taken her exams, if she wants to fuck him. Feeling like a hag, I stab a jumbo shrimp, which when I bring it to my mouth turns out to be a discarded napkin wrapped around a half-eaten cheese cube.

"I'd like a beer," Jerry says. "Can I get you something? Jane—eee?"

Facial reconstruction, I think. *And a pair of breast implants.* I shake my head.

"Audrey?" Jerry asks. He gazes into her eyes. I bet he wishes they were alone so he could hike her up against the wall and wrap her legs around his waist.

"I'd like some wine." She puts her hand on Jerry's arm, then spots someone else. "Excuse me, but there are so many other people here to talk to. I'll come back soon."

"You sure you don't want anything?" Jerry asks me.

Liposuction, perhaps? I shrug. "I guess I'll have another glass of wine."

"It's amazing," Jerry says suddenly.

"What's amazing?" *Audrey's ass? Her tits? The way her dress barely covers her crotch?*

"Every time I meet a young woman, I immediately calculate the age difference between us. Do you realize I'm closer to being dead than I am to twenty-three?"

"She's cute," I say, gesturing toward Audrey, who's greeting a senior partner from our firm. *Note to self: Remind Audrey that business associates don't hug.*

"You're her mentor?" Jerry cracks a wry smile. "Tell her to put on a jacket."

We talk for the next half hour. I drink two more glasses of wine, during which I learn that Jerry is forty-two, lives alone, and was married before, when he was in his twenties. "It didn't take," he tells me. "I wasn't ready."

"But you'd like to get married again, of course?" I press. My voice rises with desperation as I immediately relinquish my status as an independent, career-minded woman.

"I like my freedom. If I were to get married again, it would take a very special woman." His slow, sexy smile makes my heart race. I feel tingly and girlish and decide I should stay drunk all the time. Jerry and I can lounge in my bed, wear silk dressing gowns, drink mimosas, and count the brides over thirty-five in the *New York Times. Note to self: Buy silk dressing gowns.*

Just as he leans over to kiss me, I hear someone shout, "Jenny? Jenny? Jenny, we're over here!"

"Is that woman calling you?" Jerry asks.

"I didn't see any woman."

"She's at the buffet." He laughs. "Maybe you should put on your glasses."

"I only need glasses for reading." But I put them on and look across the room. I groan when I see Bethany waving a jumbo shrimp at me. Laura and Ivy are bobbing among the fake trees. Natasha, the Weaver, and Valentine are attacking the cheese tray. I hear a bark. I can't believe it. The Weaver brought Ginger!

"Do you know those women?"

"Maybe." I turn back to the bar and suck down my wine.

"JENNY!" Bethany screams as she crosses the room.

"I thought your name was Jane."

"Listen, Jerry. Regardless of what happens in the next ten minutes, I want you to know I'm a very normal person. I work hard, I eat right, I exercise—well, I don't exercise as often as I should, actually I don't exercise at all—but I do pay my bills before any interest accrual. I also think you're very nice and would love to have a drink with you sometime."

"Why are you telling me this?"

I watch the girls make their way through the crowded restaurant. Bethany pushes anyone in her path. Natasha sniffs the air. Valentine holds a fistful of cheese cubes. Laura's breasts fall out of her dress. The Weaver strokes Ginger, who's wearing a strapless doggie-size evening gown and a name tag that says "HELLO. My Name Is Virginia." And Ivy's her long-legged, beautiful self, which immediately makes me feel short, skinny, and ugly. *Note to self: Resolve issues with Ivy's beauty. Consult therapist?*

The Weaver reaches me first. She pushes Ginger in my face. "Give Ginger a kiss. She hates cocktail parties."

I look at Jerry. He doesn't even flinch.

Jenny met a guy," Bethany tells Dr. Hensen. "Actually, we all met Jenny's guy." She cracks up.

"Is that so?" Dr. Hensen tilts my way. "Where did you meet him?"

"At a cocktail party at the Twenty-one Club," the Weaver says. "They don't allow dogs there."

"You took Ginger to the Twenty-one Club?" he asks.

"I told the maître'd she was my service dog."

"What's a service dog?"

"Why are you asking so many questions?"

Dr. Hensen shifts his weight. "So all of you showed up at Janey's party? Janey, how did that make you feel?"

"She was too drunk to talk."

"I wasn't drunk, Bethany. I was angry. You'd be angry, too."

"We just wanted to meet some guys, Jenny. You said most accountants are men, so Laura suggested we show up."

"I'M AN ACTUARY! AND MY NAME IS JANEY."

"Have an attack, why don't you?" Bethany mutters.

Dr. Hensen strokes his goatee. "It's great that you're able to tell the girls how angry you are. Have you heard from this mystery man?"

"NO, I HAVEN'T!"

Dr. Hensen blinks and continues to stroke his face.

"That guy acted like he was in love with you," Valentine says.

"He shore did," Ivy agrees. "Ah woulda bet money he woulda called yew, Janey, honey."

"I can't believe he didn't call either," Laura tells me. "He was all over you."

"They were kissing," Natasha explains to Dr. Hensen.

I start to cry. "I can't believe it myself. I really thought he liked me. I just don't understand it." I blow my nose. "We had so much fun. Why didn't he call me?"

"You can always call him," Dr. Hensen says. "There's nothing wrong with a woman calling a man in this day and age."

"God, Fred," Laura sneers. "You are so lame."

Dr. Hensen *is* lame. I could never marry him! He says the most obvious things. I *know* I can call Jerry. In fact, I *did* call Jerry, but I'm not gonna tell that to stupid Dr. Hensen. It was so humiliating. Jerry acted flirtatious and coy, but when I asked if he wanted to get a drink, he told me he'd be out of town for a while. "I'll call you," he said, rushing me off the phone.

"Ah know it doesn't feel better to hear it," Ivy says, "but his not calling is no reflection on yew. Ah just hope you don't stay angry with us for showin' up where we weren't welcome."

"You guys would've come up at some point. I can't hide you forever."

"Then let's make a deal," Laura suggests. "We agree never again to show up uninvited if you agree to answer any question we have. And to tell us the truth—the entire truth."

"Fine," I say indignantly. "I always tell the truth. What do you want to know?"

"Where's my gun?" Laura asks.

"In my coat pocket. I took it from your apartment the night we all went to Bethany's. You had three, so I didn't think you'd miss one."

"Do you think I'm stupid? When I looked in my drawer for our hit on Margot, there were only two and no one had been in that drawer but you. Why do you even want that gun? I told you it doesn't work." She holds out her hand. "Give it back. Now."

"Your hit on Margot?" Dr. Hensen asks.

I walk across the circle and slam the gun into Laura's palm. "Happy? Can we move on?"

This time Bethany speaks up. "One more thing." She looks at Laura. They both turn to me. "Jenny," she asks, *"who the hell is Tobias?"*

ECONOMICS OF RISK

9

Actuaries are trained to calculate risk. As a life actuary, I learned that risk is sorted into homogeneous classifications to determine values for the probability of death. For insurance purposes, sorting people into classes is based on equal measures of statistical sampling and human psychology.

When human beings are faced with decisions concerning mortality, they can be expected to act—or select—based on their perception of their own best interests and to select against any system that limits this perception. In most instances, selection and antiselection refer to risk aversion (i.e., purchasing life insurance as a hedge against risk). However, they also refer to risk acceptance, where the inverse is equally true (i.e., taking one's own life rather than risking what that life might bring). Before I got to Municipal Life, I might not have had the language to articulate this idea, but I certainly understood its implications.

I was thirteen when my mother tried to kill herself. As I've said, I don't retain many memories of my childhood or adolescence. But that day was significant for reasons that weren't directly related to my mother or to the fact that she attempted to take her own life. That day, I fell in love with complex problem solving. Because of this, whatever joy I feel when I lose myself in financial models will always be inextricably linked to my mother's bid for self-destruction.

My math teacher, Mr. Alonzo, asked me to stay after class. I often stayed to help him grade papers or talk about math, so his request wasn't unusual. I'd stick around for an hour or two, which meant missing the bus home, but I didn't mind the walk, nor did I mind the attention. Other than Mr. Alonzo, there weren't many adults interested in my otherwise unremarkable seventh-grade life.

When the other kids filed out of the room, Mr. Alonzo suggested I try a few problem sets. There was a solemn quality to his request, which made me anxious. I was a nervous child, just as I am a nervous adult. I responded to other people's moods as if they were my fault, my mother's most of all. It's a habit I have yet to grow out of.

He handed me a booklet. "These are college level," he said, "but I know you can do them. Apply the equations we talked about. The answer is in the question. Let it reveal itself. Ready?" He clicked his silver stopwatch. "Begin."

I studied the page. I looked and I looked and I looked but couldn't see the answer. The question was long and convoluted and I had no idea where to start. I drifted, wondering why my father wouldn't move out of Welter when he knew it would make my mother happy. "It's so simple, Dad," I'd say. "Let's just pack up and leave."

"Give it a rest, Janey. We're not moving. Where do you get these ridiculous ideas? Your mother's bored. She'll get over it."

The way my father denied my mother's mood swings was as baffling as the moods themselves. Sometimes she was bitter and angry. An hour later, she'd be tearful and apologetic. Later still, she was excited and talkative. There was never a clear reason for how she was feeling, no pattern at all to how she behaved. The way she expelled emotional energy left us both drained and exhausted. For me, it was like walking through an electrical storm. I can only imagine what it was like for her.

I stared at the page until the numbers grew blurry. I tapped the desk with my pencil. Just as I was about to give up, I had an idea. I stopped thinking about my mother and my stubborn, stubborn father and started to work the equation. I lost my anxiety. I lost Mr. Alonzo. I lost the very essence of time. What I found was a process that even now, more than two decades later, still fills me with a feeling of power and purpose. The pieces clicked. I solved for x. The sensation was as exhilarating as flying.

I practically ran the four miles home. The two-lane highway

was long and twisted and the sun was hot on my back. I always liked the winter best, when the woods were bare and silent, but it was late September and the trees were still choked with the vines and ferns of summer. As I skipped along, I could hear the Black River in the distance, but couldn't see it from the road. The sound of the rushing water made me feel even giddier.

I stayed close to the woods, where tangles of wild grapevines scratched my bare arms and legs. I rested on the stump of an old tree and loosened a clump of mud from the waffles of my sneakers. I breathed through my mouth so the stink of the pulp wouldn't filter into my nose, and found a walking stick to use for my last mile home. As I turned the corner, my enthusiasm waned. The break in the trees fifty yards ahead led to my house, where I knew my mom would be waiting.

I cringed when I stepped inside the trailer. It wasn't old, but it was dirty and run-down. The wood veneer on the walls was chipped and the fluorescent panel lights in the living room had burned out, which made the room dark and ominous. The worst part, though, was the kitchen. There was a four-burner stove with used pots on top, a tiny gas oven caked with dried food, and a sink filled with empty cereal bowls. The cheap wood cabinets were flooded with ants; two of them were missing doors. The refrigerator leaked. There were crumbs everywhere.

No one was home. My father was working swing shift, so he wouldn't be back till ten-thirty. I figured my mother was at her friend Ellie's where she picked at stale coffee rings and complained about Welter.

As I put down my books, I heard a voice. "That you, Monkey?" Behind me, my mother was sitting in my father's big chair. I heard her but couldn't see her until she snapped on the light and came into focus. Her thin face was pale and chalky and her eyes were heavy. She took painkillers for a bad back, which left her drowsy and glazed and slightly off balance. I liked her best this way. I could talk to her without worrying that I'd set her off.

I didn't question my mother's moods because I didn't have anything to compare them to. I thought everyone's mother was unpredictable, all of their reactions slightly off-kilter. The smallest thing would ignite her—a torn blouse, a missing fork, my spending five minutes too long in the shower. She'd reach in through the curtain, shut off the water, and leave me standing with a soapy head, bewildered and embarrassed.

Now that I'm thirty-five and have some perspective, I realize that I'm less lonely living on my own than I ever was living with my mother. When she yelled at me, her eyes were distracted, as though she was speaking to someone else far off in the distance. She also seemed disconnected from her anger, which seized her without warning, as if it came from a place inside her but also separate from her. It was very confusing to watch. I didn't understand that a person could be present and absent at the very same time.

My father ignored her, but I couldn't. I wanted to be simultaneously smothered by her and left all alone. I never knew if my own actions—if my very presence—contributed to her erratic behavior, so I was obedient and meek, afraid to call attention to myself or take up too much room. But I couldn't escape her and she couldn't escape me. I was her only daughter, her focal point, her veritable extension, and I became the receptacle for her every emotion. If she was enraged, I'd want to scream. If she was sad, I'd want to cry. I absorbed my mother's feelings through my skin, exhaling every breath she took as though we shared a single set of lungs, the same beating heart. We lived together amid her impulses and emotions while my father lived apart from us and alone although he occupied the same space.

Given my family's dynamics, I find it surprising that it took me until age thirteen to discover math and to feel within me its perfect order and symmetry. But when I did, it was like getting a glimpse of a rare and unified world that had always eluded me. I wanted to share this feeling with her, the sensation that everything could finally work out. "Something good happened at school, Mom," I told her. I wondered if she'd been sitting in that chair all day.

"I'm tired." She smacked her lips, which were so dry I could hear them pulling apart.

I wiped a glass and filled it with water. "If you drink this," I said in my most parental tone, "you'll feel better." What I really meant was, *Why is your mouth so dry all the time? Why can't you produce saliva like other mothers? Why don't you ask me what happened today?*

I went to the farthest corner of the trailer, where a blanket hung on a rope to separate my bed from the rest of the room. I lay down and stared at the patch of wall where I'd taken a knife and carved my initials in the fake wood paneling. I heard her stumble toward me but didn't turn over.

"I can see you, Monkey." She was peeking through the blanket. Her words were slurred. She'd called me Monkey ever since I was a baby. She said I used to wrap my arms and legs around her and cling like a little chimp. But I didn't remember those days and knew she didn't either.

She lay down beside me, curled her body into mine, and ran her fingers through my hair, pulling each strand through her nails as if she was sifting sand at the beach. As we breathed together, I lost myself in a recurring fantasy in which we were on a raft adrift in the ocean, breathing the fresh air of a tropical paradise.

"Let's run away together, Monkey." Her voice dragged like a record played at too low a speed. "Let's get out of this place."

I waited a long time before speaking, loving the feel of her hands on my head. Finally, I said, "Mr. Alonzo says if I take a test, I can go to an advanced math program in Syracuse. That means we can move—"

I stopped when I heard her soft, steady snore. I wanted to tell her my plan, but couldn't bring myself to wake her. Her full, upturned lips were pressed together, making her look childlike. The mole underneath her left eye made her seem vulnerable. She had a scar on her chin from a long-ago fall. Everything about her face broke my heart. Feeling the need to protect her, I wrapped our arms around each other, then eventually I, too, fell asleep.

It was dark out when I woke up, but my father still wasn't home. "Mom!" I tried to disentangle myself from the web of her arms. "Mom, wake up." But no matter how hard I shook, she wouldn't budge.

Trapped under her body, I considered my options. I knew I should call someone. If I didn't, she might not wake up this time. The other times it was my father who found her unconscious on the couch, on the floor, in the tub. But those times were accidents, he said. What he meant was, those times didn't count. Even when she was cut up and bleeding and sent to the state hospital, my father still called them accidents. But how many accidents would it take before he called it something else, something like self-destruction or escape or even revenge? Even I knew you were allowed only a certain number of accidents before you were carried away and never brought back.

On the other hand, I also understood loyalty. I knew I should nod when she complained that her back hurt; promise not to tell my father when she was late home from Ellie's; agree that every time she was rushed away, it was only an accident. And therein lay my conflict. If I didn't call for help, my mother could finally get out of Welter. So which betrayal was worse—making sure she lived or letting her die? I picked up the phone and called 911, but even today, the question still haunts me.

When I started Group, I hoarded a litany of secrets that I felt were very risk intensive: the truth about my mother, my relationship with my silent father, Tobias's betrayal. Sharing these secrets was, in my estimation, taking a risk too high to gamble on. But the girls got me talking and, eventually, my perception of risk started to shift. I began to realize that the potential for self-destruction lay not in confession but in the not-telling.

I never told my mother about Mr. Alonzo and the math problems. She killed herself before I had a chance, seven months after she passed out in my bed, which is just as well. I doubt she would've been able to revel in my personal triumph. Maybe I don't give her enough credit. Maybe it would've thrilled her to know I found something of my own to care about. And maybe, too, I overstate the joy of discovering math to offset the horror of my mother's suicide. But memory is very complicated. When faced with tragedy, the human mind takes compensatory measures to process the unthinkable. I say this not to exonerate myself from telling lies about her death but to illustrate one method of self-preservation. Shifting the relative significance of events was how I stayed sane. My father, on the other hand and true to form, pretended the day had never happened, that, in fact, I'd never had a mother at all.

Her funeral was in the morning. He went to work the same afternoon. Her sister, Aunt Honey, asked how he could do such a thing.

"What else is there to do?" my dad replied and got into his truck and drove to the pulp.

The only time he talked to me was when he returned from work and told me to go to sleep. "It's been a hard day, Janey. And there are harder days to come. She was a good woman. I know you'll miss her."

I didn't know how to respond, being only thirteen and half-orphaned, and my father didn't press me. But later, when I tried to talk about her, he said he wasn't up to it.

"You understand," he insisted, wanting me to see that it was over and done with, that she'd made her decision and now she was gone. What more, he implied, was there to say? We talked about school and the pulp, shrinking the world to small, everyday topics to distract us from those larger and more unpredictable. I think if we had allowed the magnitude of our situation to filter into our consciousnesses, the cumulative effect would've snapped us in half. Compensatory measures, after all.

As the years passed, my father grew even more distant. We spoke to each other in tight, clipped sentences, or rather, he spoke to me that way and I responded in kind. Sometimes I stared at him across the breakfast table. He was a big man with big features, a hardworking boy from hardworking stock. He had ruddy cheeks, a thick nose that had been broken in two places from football, and a thatch of brown hair that curled around his ears when it grew too long. He was only thirty-five (the age I am now) when my mother left us, and still looked from a distance like the kid on the field who scored a winning touchdown. But his eyes gave him away. Behind his glasses, they were red-ringed and cloudy. In them, I saw immeasurable sorrow and unspannable distance.

In high school, I spent my free time alone although I was aware that other people gossiped about my tragic family. It was a strange paradox—being so utterly visible to be talked about and at the same time so invisible I was never talked to. When I turned sixteen, my dad's buddies taught me to drive. I got a job at the pulp during the summer, where I worked in accounting and helped manage the books. I bought a beat-up car, which I drove to math classes at Syracuse University. I applied to college, and when MIT offered me a scholarship, I moved to Massachusetts. That was a compensation of sorts, too. I wasn't able to escape with my mother but I no longer had to live with my father.

Once, Valentine described her relationship with food. "If I get upset," she explained, "I shove food in my mouth, but I'm never actually conscious of eating. It's only after the fact when I'm totally stuffed that I realize how far I've gone. Then I panic, wanting to relive the lost time. If I could just restart the clock, I know I'd never take that first bite."

When she said this, I thought of my father. I wasn't aware we were drifting apart, that I didn't know him and he didn't know me. It's only now, so many years later, that I wish I could retrieve those mornings at breakfast and ask him what he was thinking, if he missed my mother, if he loved me even a tenth as much as he had loved her.

In Group I work hard to forget my dad and my mom. But Group isn't a place for forgetting. The point of the process is to dig deep and remember, then confess your memories until it hurts, because it hurts. I try to evade the girls' incessant probing, their need to know me like my father never did, like my mother never would. Talk about your mother, Janey, they say. Do you miss her? What was it like growing up without her? What do you feel when you think of her?

I can't tell them this: When she lay in my bed and stroked my hair, my mother could reduce the world to one perfect sensation. My memory of being thirteen will be forever linked to the feel of her hands on my head, the smell of her skin, the very breath of her. Unfortunately, it's a distant memory, like a scene I saw once in a movie that only seems partially real. What lingers instead is the metallic smell of gas, the squeal of a siren, the sight of an EMT lifting her into his arms, the interminable echo of my father's silence.

So I tell them this: My mother was not afraid to take risks. She considered her options, made a choice she felt was in her best interests, and decided to go. But her leaving for good was an accident. She got carried away, and once she was gone, she couldn't come back.

All of which, in a manner of speaking, is true.

10

Lately I've been thinking that if the girls and I had stayed with Dr. Hensen, we never would've killed Tobias. Laura says I'm wrong. As far as she's concerned, our plan was to teach Tobias humility. We had no idea he'd get hurt, and would've gone after him regardless of whose ass warmed the big leather chair. The fact that we outgrew Dr. Hensen is a completely separate issue.

But still, I wonder.

In retrospect, the dissolution of our relationship with Dr. Hensen was inevitable. With the exception of the Weaver, none of us had found men, but we had found each other. And for girls like us, girls who have to explain time after time why we're not married, girls who are transparent to waiters and salesclerks, we now had community, and this boon of unexpected, seven-sided love taught us more about intimacy than any sexual relationship ever could. We were ready to move on, which meant leaving Dr. Hensen behind.

Dr. Hensen disagreed. He told us we were moving too quickly, acting impulsively, leaving him out of important decisions. Looking back, he might have been right, but there were seven of us and only one of him, and his caution was lost in our collective momentum.

As time passed, he seemed overwhelmed by the Group he'd assembled, as if it had never dawned on him that seven grown women with varying types and degrees of neuroses might finally learn to express some hostility. He tried to referee when we bickered, but his "Ladies, please!" always sounded as pathetic as it was ineffectual.

Normally I would've been filled with lust for him, still unable at that point in my therapeutic growth to distinguish pity from desire, but I became resentful of the way he lost control. He talked intelligently about a woman's need to express anger, but when any of us actually did, especially toward him, the poor guy forgot all he learned at Harvard about transference and countertransference and stroked his goatee in nervous confusion.

Thus, when we began our second year together, the seven of us bounding toward what we considered mental health, we decided—at Laura's insistence—that Dr. Hensen was holding us back from realizing our true potential. I agreed with Laura but never banked on how difficult it would be to say good-bye to him, nor did I foresee the way things would get out of hand once we had.

Our relationship with Dr. Hensen really begins to fracture a few months after Bethany's mother moves out. He won't let the issue rest.

"I know it was a while ago, Bethany," he says, "but I'm still curious how you managed to ask her to leave. That must have been so difficult."

"I didn't do it alone." Bethany waves at the rest of us. "Everyone helped me."

"They encouraged you? Gave you advice? That sort of thing?"

"No, they slept over." She proceeds to tell him how we arrived at her apartment one at a time. "Ivy had a whole set of luggage." She laughs. "And a huge wheel of Brie. Remember the Brie, Ivy? It was so great. '*Cheese cracker, Barbie?*' Remember that?"

Dr. Hensen looks confused. "You invited them over knowing your mother would get angry? Were you trying to provoke her?"

Bethany shakes her head. "They didn't tell me they were coming. That was the beauty of it. I never would've asked my mother to move out if they hadn't stepped in."

"But weren't you mad that you were duped? Didn't it bother you that they planned the entire thing without telling you?"

"No," Bethany says slowly. "I don't see it that way—"

"But," Dr. Hensen presses, "no one asked your permission.

They just barged into your home, planning to deceive you. Didn't you feel betrayed?"

"I don't know. They wanted to help me, I guess."

"But there are ways of helping that aren't so outright—"

"Shut up, Hensen! Stop right there!"

Thinking the outburst came from Laura, I turn to her, but she's staring at Valentine. "You just told Fred to shut up," she says, amazed.

"Excuse me?" Dr. Hensen says, equally shocked and so flustered he knocks his charts off his lap.

Valentine rubs her thighs. "While it might have been wrong to mislead Bethany, it wasn't quite the betrayal you're suggesting. We saw her in an unhealthy situation, and decided to take action to help her out of it, which, I might add, you were incapable of doing."

Dr. Hensen's fingers flutter against his chin. "Therapy is a process . . . uh . . ."

"My name's Valentine."

"Of course it is. You can't expect change to occur overnight."

"It was hardly overnight." She shifts her weight in her chair. "Bethany, we planned that evening because we care about you and wanted to help. You know that, right?" The Group tilts not toward Bethany but toward Valentine, waiting to see what she'll say next. "Do you understand? And do you forgive us?"

Bethany nods, her lipstick-ringed mouth still pursed in an *o* of surprise.

"Good." Valentine turns back to Dr. Hensen. "Going further, if we tell you something, please don't twist it around. We're supposed to be in this together, right? We have to know we can trust you. Now," she addresses the rest of us. "Who wants to share?"

It's weird to see Valentine assert herself, but not as weird as seeing myself. I'm changing in ways that both excite and frighten me. During a morning deli visit, there's a slightly stooped yet disarmingly handsome D/L/CEO ahead of me in line. Actually, he was standing beside me until I glanced at the clock, and when I turned back, I was staring at the back of his head.

I realize this is one of those pivotal moments I've been working toward. I can use what I've learned in Group to announce myself or remain forever invisible in the presence of men. My mental debate is preempted when the guy behind the counter points at the D/L/CEO and says, "Mister! You don't cut off pretty lady. Go to end of line or I'll throw you out."

The D/L/CEO turns to me, his hand still resting on the pastry case. His fingers leave a perfect set of prints on the glass. "I'm sorry," he says, "I didn't see you there."

How could you not see me? I screech. *I'm here! I exist! I noticed you the second you walked through the door.* Which is true. I even indulge in an elaborate fantasy in which he taps my shoulder and says, "Don't I know you from somewhere?" As it turns out, we both attended MIT. His name is Dylan, he played lacrosse, and he always wanted to talk to me in class but never had the nerve. He asks if I want to go somewhere else for breakfast. I hesitate at first, but then say yes, so we leave the deli, elope, move to Palm Beach, and grow old together. Over the years, his back curves like a question mark, making his stoop more pronounced. But I pat his hump tenderly as we shuffle with our walkers to early bird specials for roast chicken and Chilean sea bass.

Okay, maybe I backed up as Dylan circled the deli and—full disclosure—allowed him entry into the long line of people waiting to pay. And maybe I did it because I planned to talk to him, a plan I'd been practicing with the girls for weeks. "Hi," I was supposed to say. "You look familiar. Do you work around here?" And he was supposed to respond with a lascivious grin, if not a marriage proposal.

So Dylan's claim not to notice me pisses me off, especially when he knows I granted him access into the line. Instead of saying something seductive that will compel him to invite me to his beach house in Quogue, I snarl like a feral she-wolf. "I'm *here*, for Christ's sake. Are you *fucking* blind?" To which the deli man, always poised for a fight adds, "Get out of my deli, mister. You don't upset my beautiful customers. Out!"

When I recount the story in Group, though, I don't feel victorious. On the contrary—I feel a sense of doom.

"Why?" Laura asks. "You finally stuck up for yourself."

"True," I say, looking at Dr. Hensen, wanting to ask what was happening to me because I didn't recognize myself anymore. Or rather, I was coming into focus and the woman I was seeing was nothing like the woman I'd imagined. "But I didn't get a date either."

"That'll come," Dr. Hensen promises. "But you have to let the pendulum swing a little left of center until it finds a happy medium."

"But if this new behavior continues, someone could wind up dead."

Laura holds my gaze, lovingly, the same way Dylan had in my fantasy. "Maybe, but at least it won't be you." Then she looks at Dr. Hensen. And she laughs.

During the next few weeks, I become afraid for Dr. Hensen. Not because any of us will physically harm him, but because we're wearing him down. In the beginning, he was always in the Group room before we arrived, perched in his chair and ready to roll. But in late August, our fifteenth-month mark, Hensen shows up ten, sometimes twenty minutes late. For three weeks in a row, the seven of us stand outside on the street, debating whether or not to leave. When he finally races toward us, he apologizes profusely, fumbles with his keys, then scrambles into his chair like a boy late for dinner. He tries to compose himself, but too often, his tie is unknotted or his shirttail hangs out, which only exacerbates our annoyance.

"You're late," Laura snaps.

"And time is money," Bethany chimes in.

I always smile at him kindly, ask where he went to school in some roundabout way, and tell him his tardiness is completely understandable. Something about the way the chair dwarfs his skinny frame reminds me of my father lying in his hospital bed. Both men seem bewildered—Dr. Hensen having lost the power of language and Zack betrayed by his once-sturdy body—and I am touched by this bewilderment. Women are repeatedly warned that we'll lose our looks, so we spend our lives preparing for our inevitable obsolescence. But men are encouraged to believe they'll become more valuable as they get older. Knowing this makes me want to protect Dr. Hensen the same way I want Zack to die and his misery to end, not because I don't love him, but because in my own way, I do.

It also saddens me to see Dr. Hensen deteriorate. During Group, he makes comments but quickly pulls back, as if testing our mood before plunging in. He and Laura never address each other anymore. She doesn't agree or disagree with him; she simply negates his presence. Watching this noninteraction worries me. I'm afraid Hensen will get so frustrated he'll start to cry and the girls and I will have to console him. Or worse, he'll give up on us and disband Group altogether, leaving us to negotiate our sanity by ourselves.

On the other hand, if fears are actually wishes, maybe I truly want him gone. And if I do, I'm not alone. The girls and I meet every week at T.G.I. Friday's for post-Group summits, and have started to kick around the idea of leaving Dr. Hensen for good.

Laura is the most adamant. She says he lost whatever enthusiasm he once had for helping us. I can see her point, but I'm afraid if we don't have him around, we'll lose objectivity.

"Dr. Hensen may be pathetic," I say when we're all reassembled at the restaurant, "but he isn't invested in himself. He's not gunning for his own time to share."

Laura shakes her head. "Have you forgotten how upset he gets when we won't tell him something?"

Bethany snorts. "He's an idiot. I've said that from the beginning."

"In mah experience," Ivy breaks in, "most men are idiots. Look at how stupid they behave when they go on blind dates." A week ago, Ivy was set up with an old family friend who showed up at the Four Seasons stinking drunk. "You want to fuck me?" he asked an hour later, slurping an oyster. To which Ivy replied, "While your offer is temptin', Junior, Ah believe that Ah'll pass."

"Ah feel so violated," she continues. "Ah know that's dramatic but that's how Ah feel. Like he tore off my shirt and looked at mah boobs without mah permission."

"Ivy," Laura interrupts. "Let's stay focused."

Valentine squares her shoulders. "I have a problem."

"Have you been bingeing again?" Laura asks.

"No, I have a problem with you." She flips her hair off her shoulders. "I'm not comfortable with you being the new Group leader."

Laura laughs. "Who said anything about me being the leader? If you want, we'll crown you queen of the fucking Maypole. Jesus, Valentine. Ever since our hit on Margot, you've become so aggressive."

"And what's wrong with that? My sales have gone up fifty percent this quarter."

"You're just not very nice."

"Where did being nice ever get me?"

We continue to argue about whether or not we should stay with Dr. Hensen. But it's obvious that one way or another—I glance at Valentine who glares at Laura who rolls her eyes at the Weaver who babbles to Ivy who disagrees with Bethany who teases Natasha—something is bound to happen.

Janey," Dr. Hensen says in September, "you still haven't told us about Tobias." He tilts toward me. "You seem ready to share."

I jerk my head up, surprised that he remembers. It's been four months since Bethany asked about him.

"She shared," Laura cuts in. "She slept with him and he didn't call her again. What else is there to know? It happens to everyone at some point." Laura's covering for me. She knows the whole story but I've asked her not to tell. Some things, I explained, are just too private.

"It hasn't happened to me," the Weaver pipes up. "Guys always call me."

"Excuse me, Suzanna. I forgot you're God's gift to men."

"Why do you think I'm ready to share?" I ask Dr. Hensen.

"As your therapist, I'm trained to hear what is said, but also what's unsaid."

"Are you implying I don't tell the truth?"

"You said it yourself. You came into Group with a suitcase of stories, which we've watched you unpack as the year progressed—"

"Nice metaphor, Fred," Laura says. "But why don't you back off?"

"—and I suspect that you continue to hide behind these half-truths to protect yourself. But you'll never have the intimate relationship you desire if you don't allow yourself to become vulnerable. And to do that, you have to start telling the entire truth, in here, where you are safe." He pauses. "Now tell us, Janey. What happened with Tobias?"

"She *told* us."

"Shut up, Laura," Valentine says. "We want to hear." "To hear" echoes in the room. Feeling overheated, I remove my jacket.

"Have you been in contact with him?" Dr. Hensen's voice sounds hollow, as if we're inside a tunnel. The light in the room grows fuzzy. I keep hearing "in contact, in contact." Why is the echo so loud?

An embarrassing confession: I had sex with Tobias after finding out about Debby Dupont. He called me one night from a bar. It was late and he was drunk. "I liked you, Janey," he said, slurring and spitting. "I still like you." He told me he broke up with Debby and asked if he could come over. Maybe he wants me back, I'd thought as I told him yes. I wanted to see him so badly. I figured I had nothing to lose.

He lay naked on top of me. He stank of beer and cigarettes. My legs were spread wide. He was as hard as a rock, grinding deeper and deeper inside me until I couldn't tell where he ended and I began. He fucked me without touching me. I tried to move with him but couldn't find a rhythm. I wanted to tell him to stop, that he was in far too deep. As I strained under his weight, I realized that sometimes the having can be more painful than the wanting.

Tobias left my apartment in the middle of the night while I was asleep. The next day I overheard him through the particleboard talking to Debby. He never spoke to me again.

How could I be so stupid? I hate myself! I hate myself!

I can see Laura rise from her chair and move toward me, but it's like having a spotlight in my eyes and I have to shield my face with my hand. I keep hearing a woman screaming as though she's being beaten. I wonder why no one is helping her. It takes me a few seconds to realize that I'm the one making that noise. It's me screaming out loud.

I fall into Laura's arms. The noises slowly subside. I feel an odd yet buoyant sense of calm. "Tobias," I say.

"Tobias what?"

"He used me. I was so stupid. I hate myself."

"Don't hate yourself," she whispers. "Hate him."

Moments pass.

I hear Dr. Hensen's voice. "Janey? Are you all right?"

I'm holding my breath. "I'm fine." The air rushes out as if I've been punctured. "What happened?"

Dr. Hensen holds out his hands as if beckoning me. "You were telling us about Tobias. You were very angry."

"I don't remember speaking." I can't stop shaking.

"Sometimes the body experiences a memory the mind can't articulate."

As Dr. Hensen says this, I look at the floor, feeling the warmth of his eyes on my skin. "You have new shoes!" I exclaim, amazed to see he's wearing brand-new loafers. The buoyant sensation returns, leaving me clearheaded and calm and safer than I've felt in a very long time.

Laura says I'm having separation anxiety. I insist it's a psychotic break and decide to see Dr. Hensen privately. I procrastinate for a few weeks, but in November I finally make an appointment.

There's something ominous about being alone with Dr. Hensen. In the Group circle, I feel protected by the other girls, but in his office, with just the two of us and a couple of plants, I feel overly exposed, as though my body's filling every inch of the room.

"We haven't spent much time alone, Janey," Dr. Hensen begins.

"We *never* spent time alone, Dr. Hensen." I try to laugh but it sounds more mental than cheerful. "Have you been avoiding me?"

"It's funny you should say that. Usually I see patients once a month outside the Group setting, but after the first few meetings with your Group, I changed my approach. You got along so well, I thought it best to let each of you decide if you wanted to see me alone."

"Has anyone else come to see you?" I lift my head but avert my eyes.

"Yes."

"Are you going to tell me who?"

He smiles. "Why are you so uncomfortable? We've known each other a long time now."

"But we don't really *know* each other, do we?" I rise from my chair and stretch. "You mind if I sit on the couch?" I move to a sofa near the window, at the far end of the room. At first I sit, then kick up my heels and recline. "This is better," I say.

Dr. Hensen's chair is positioned behind me. "I can't see your face."

"This is better," I repeat. "Where were we? I think you were going to tell me who comes to see you privately."

"Why is that so important?"

"Because it's part of the reason I'm here." I curl on my side and face the wall, carving my initials with an imaginary knife. "I'm worried about you."

"Ah," he replies. "Are you sure it's me you're worried about?"

"I'm not worried about myself, if that's what you mean."

"I meant you were worried about your mother, or rather the impact her abandonment has had on you."

I shake my head in disbelief. "Why are you always bringing up my mother?"

"Because you never do."

"Let's start again. Dr. Hensen, Group is falling apart and I don't think you see it."

I can hear him shuffling papers behind me. "Could you be more specific?"

"The girls hate you," I blurt out, grateful that I can't see his face and he can't see mine. "How can you be so blind? You let Laura act like she's in charge and Bethany talk to you like you're an idiot. Why don't you stick up for yourself?"

When he doesn't answer, I'm afraid I've offended him.

"Why don't *you*?" he finally asks.

"Forget about me for a second. I'm here to help you."

"Then why won't you look at me?"

I peer over the arm of the couch. "I'm looking at you." Dr. Hensen holds my gaze. I blink first.

"I appreciate your concern, but you don't have to worry. Part of the process is allowing Group to find its own rhythm. My job isn't to force that rhythm, but to allow it to rise and fall in accordance with the temperament of its members. There are always some personalities that are stronger than others, which can sway the Group in a particular direction, but it's up to Group, not me, to work that out. I am concerned, however, that you feel it isn't working for you."

"I didn't say it's not working for me!" I shout. "I'm saying it's not working for *you*. Forget it." I lie back down. "You're not listening."

"I'm always listening. Janey, you've experienced terrible tragedy. At some point, you have to revisit these tragedies and realize you weren't responsible for them, which could release you from the shame and the anger you carry. But I can't force you to examine your past until you're ready to take that risk. In the meantime, you need to take care of yourself. My relationship with the Group will run its course. I'm not worried and you shouldn't be either."

I'm struck by a thought. "You know we want to leave you, don't you?"

"Of course. I also know you're as conflicted about leaving as you are about staying."

"Then why aren't you doing something to stop it?"

When he answers, his disembodied voice is soft and sweet. I feel it caress me, like the brush of hair against a thirteen-year-old cheek. "The pendulum swings one way. But it always swings back. Just remember that I will not abandon you or anyone else. I'll be here when you're all ready to work." He gets up from his chair, sits beside me on the couch, and stares into my eyes. *Oh my God. He's going to kiss me!* "Look at me, Janey," he insists.

"I don't think that's a good idea."

"Trust me. Sit up. That's right. Now open your eyes."

I do as he asks but brace myself, ready to pounce should his shaggy face come too close. "I want you to promise that you'll call if you ever feel like hurting yourself. Even if you're absolutely, positively sure you no longer want to live and you've got a razor blade in your hand, you must pick up the phone and call me."

I nod, still waiting for him to lunge.

"I need you to say it out loud. I'm giving you my home phone number. I want you to use it if you find yourself in trouble. Promise me you will."

"I promise," I tell him, annoyed when I realize he's *not* gonna kiss me. *What? I'm not attractive enough? Do I smell?* "Why are you making this so difficult?" I ask.

"I thought I was making it easier. I'm giving you permission to leave."

This makes my eyes fill with tears. "You're supposed to be stupid, Dr. Hensen," I say.

"Sorry to disappoint," is his reply.

The following Thursday, he's in the Group room early, perched in his chair, looking fit and relaxed. I arrive first and he says hello, but makes no mention of my private visit. Slowly the other girls arrive. Dr. Hensen greets each one warmly, then settles in.

"Even though Suzanna's not here yet, I'd like to begin. Lately I've been sensing resentment toward me." He pauses. "I also suspect you're planning to leave."

"Janey!" Laura snaps. "You told him."

"I didn't tell him anything." I glare at Hensen, who I can't believe has betrayed me. *I hate you, Dr. Hensen. I'll hate you forever. And I didn't want to kiss you either.*

"Here we go again!" Bethany exclaims, snapping her gum. "Hensen, you deal with your problems on your own time or next week you'll have to pay us."

Just as he's about to respond, the Weaver rushes into the Group room wearing her hospital scrub suit and holding a bouquet of roses. "Sorry I'm late," she says, her long red hair flying all over her face. "The ER was backed up, then I couldn't get a cab."

"Who are the flowers from? Your boyfriend?"

"Yes, Laura. They're from Jason. They're 'I'm sorry' roses."

"Ah know about those," Ivy cuts in. "Jackson used to bring me roses. 'Specially when he was fuckin' Ole Miss."

That var-mi-ent. I glare at Dr. Hensen.

"So what happened?" Laura asks the Weaver.

"Nothing much. Typical Jason bullshit. You know."

"Obviously I don't know, which is why I'm asking."

"I don't feel like talking about it." The Weaver pulls her hair into a ponytail. "A few nights ago I had this dream." Laura groans, but she continues. "In the dream, I was kissing Jason, but it wasn't Jason, it was another guy. We were lying in a boat and the boat was drifting and—"

"Ginger grabbed the rope and pulled you back to shore," Bethany says.

"Ginger wasn't in the dream."

"She wasn't?" Dr. Hensen is geared up and ready to do full therapeutic battle. He looks like a dope. *A lot of guys want to kiss me. And despite what you may think, I wear very effective antiperspirant. I smell like a fucking rose.*

"No, if you must know, it was a sex dream—"

"And Ginger wasn't in it?" Laura asks.

The Weaver shivers. "That's just wrong, Laura. Don't even joke that way. Anyway, I was kissing this guy—"

"What guy?" Laura interrupts. "Have you kissed him in real life?"

"He's just a guy, okay? So in the dream, I knew that sleeping with him would be great. He knew exactly where to touch me. I enjoy having sex with Jason, but it's not . . . I don't know . . . *passionate.*"

"Do yew want to break up with Jason?" Ivy asks.

The Weaver shrugs. "We've talked about marriage, which is something I've never done before. On the other hand, I don't feel for Jason what I felt for this other guy."

"*What* other guy?" Laura demands, knowing (as we all do) that the guy in the Weaver's dream is actually a guy in real life.

"I don't recommend your leaving Jason," Dr. Hensen breaks in. "Suzanna, relationships change over time. Passion is supplanted by comfort and familiarity and—"

"How would you know if she's comfortable with Jason?" Laura snaps. "She hasn't mentioned him in weeks. Furthermore, how could you possibly know what it feels like to be a forty-year-old woman who's never been married, has no prospects, but faces a very real biological deadline? Most of us have only a few years left before our fertility is over. How the fuck could you possibly understand that?"

"Obviously, Laura, I can't, but—"

"That's right. You can't. So don't try and act as though you're one of us when you're not."

"Would you like to talk about your father, Laura?"

"What the fuck does he have to do with this?"

"You said your father was very controlling. Perhaps my advising Suzanna on what to do about her boyfriend is stirring up feelings for you that are reminiscent of him?"

"You're kidding, right? I know you can't be serious because if you are, you're the biggest moron I ever met. I'm stirred up because the only way Suzanna will admit she's been sleeping around behind Jason's back is to blather on about some bullshit dream. Furthermore, you continue to discuss her damn dog as though it's a person. This is ridiculous." Laura gets up from her seat and puts on her coat. "I'm leaving."

"Then we'll see you next week," Dr. Hensen replies. Instead of tilting, his head falls forward, as if it's too heavy for his neck to support.

"I mean I'm quitting."

Bethany hops up. "I'm quitting, too."

Natasha rises, too. So does Valentine, Ivy, the Weaver, and, finally, me.

"You're leaving, Janey?" Dr. Hensen asks, still studying the floor as if he might find the answer in the multicolored carpet.

"I'm sorry." I follow the other girls out and stand at the door. "It didn't have to be this way."

"Yes," he says firmly. He stares at the circle of empty chairs. "It did."

11

Our first Thursday-night Group session without Dr. Hensen gets off to an inauspicious start when Natasha arrives at T.G.I. Friday's wearing a surgical face mask. No one mentions it until we're all settled, then Laura asks politely if something is wrong.

"I had to take the bus," she replies through the mask, leaving a wet imprint of her mouth. Her black eyes peer over the top, like a raccoon's. "I can't stand all the nasty fumes."

"Yew all knotted up about leavin' Dr. Hensen?" Ivy drawls.

Laura glances at Valentine, who's buttering her third roll. "No more anxious than anyone else," she says, wrenching the roll out of Valentine's hands.

"I was eating that!"

"Food is not your friend." Laura cracks her knuckles. "Well, now that we're on our own, I think it would be a good exercise for us to share something we've never told each other before, something we weren't comfortable saying in front of Fred."

"I thought we agreed," Valentine cuts in, "that you wouldn't be leading Group."

"I was just making a suggestion. If you want to lead, go right ahead." She waves. "Lead."

"We need to establish ground rules. First of all, each of us should be allotted twenty minutes, which we should time on a stopwatch."

"Ah hate to be disagreeable, honey," Ivy says, "but Ah don't want yew watchin' the clock while Ah speak. It's hard enough to tell yew mah troubles in the short time Ah have allotted."

"Let me finish. I also think we should share everything that's going on, so what happened with Dr. Hensen doesn't happen again."

Laura puts her hands on the table. "Our leader has spoken. Girls?"

"If ya'll wanna time each other, Ah'm not comin' back."

"Okay," Valentine concedes. "But what about sharing everything? Bethany?"

"Whatever. Can we order?" She waves at the waiter, but Valentine grabs her hand.

"We can't eat until Group is over."

"No snacks?" Bethany crows. "We can't just sit here for two hours without snacks."

"We can sit as long as we want." I point to the waiters gathered by the kitchen door. No one has approached us since the busboy gave us bread and water ten minutes ago.

"Fine." Laura looks at Valentine, who's once again dipping into the breadbasket. "Obviously four rolls don't count as snacks. Girls?"

"No snacks," Ivy says.

"No snacks," Valentine repeats. "No phone calls, no missing sessions, and everyone stays until the two hours are over." She looks around the table.

"Agreed," Ivy says.

"Agreed," the Weaver repeats.

"If we have to decide everything this way," Bethany whines, "let's just go back to Hensen."

Laura whips around. "That's not an option." She turns to Valentine. "Do you like the idea of telling each other something new? Just for our first session?"

"I approve. Girls?" Everyone agrees except me. "You're overruled, Janey."

"Obviously," I mutter. "But can we begin the secret-sharer game next week?"

"No," Valentine and Laura say in unison.

After a bathroom break, Valentine asks who wants to go first. "Laura, you seemed adamant about leaving Dr. Hensen. Was he bringing up issues that felt too close? Your father, for instance?" Her chair squeaks as she leans into Laura's personal space.

Laura jerks back. "The idea, Val-en-tine, is to choose the secret yourself."

"So he *was* getting too close. Maybe you need to expose your breasts to complete strangers because when you were a child, you didn't get enough attention from your father."

"Valentine," Bethany warns, "you're not playing the game right."

"Well, it could be true. If she discussed her relationship with her father, maybe she wouldn't spread her legs every time she meets a guy."

We shift nervously toward Laura, who's wiping her glasses with the hem of her blouse. "You seem to forget that I haven't slept with anyone in quite a while. But I'll talk about my father if you tell us why you eat so much. You use your weight to avoid intimacy. If you're fat, which you are, you can attribute rejection to your size rather than something else."

"Like what?" Valentine asks, opening her hand and dropping what must have been her seventy-fifth roll.

"It used to be your eager-to-please disposition, which probably came across as desperation. But now it's because you're a bitch."

"Laura," Natasha says, her voice muffled through her face mask. "That wasn't nice."

"She asked for it."

"Laura, you are such a—"

"Ah have a secret," Ivy interrupts. "Remember when Ah missed Group a while back? Well, Ah had me some liposuction. Nothing dramatic, just some work around my lateral thighs."

Valentine looks her over. "Why? Your body is perfect."

"Because it was Tuesday?" I suggest.

Bethany laughs. "No. Because it was raining."

Ivy glares at us. "Actually, Jackson served me divorce papers. He found himself a new girlfriend who isn't much older than Ole Miss. Ah would've told ya'll sooner but Ah couldn't bear talking about it. But Ah'm happy ya'll find me so entertainin'." She turns to Natasha, who's spraying the table with 409 cleaner. "What's yours?"

"My phone's being tapped."

"That's not a secret," Bethany says. "That's a delusion."

"I have a secret," the Weaver says slyly. She pauses. "Jason and I broke up."

"When?" Laura asks.

"A month and a half ago."

"Why didn't you tell us? We wasted an entire session on him. In fact, we left Fred because of that discussion."

The Weaver shrinks in her seat. "We were leaving Dr. Hensen anyway. And I was embarrassed. You were all so happy I found someone, I didn't want to disappoint you. I was afraid if I told you we broke up, you'd feel like we weren't making progress."

"We don't want you to stay with someone you don't love, Suzanna," I tell her. "Jesus, give us some credit."

"I broke up with Jason because he made me crazy, not because I didn't love him. He was *always* in my space. I couldn't stand spending so much time with him. The only person I can do that with is Ginger."

"For God's sake, Suzanna," Laura says. "Ginger isn't a person. She eats from a bowl on the floor, pees outside, and chases cars. She's a dog, and you use her to avoid relationships."

"Maybe I do, but I'm entitled to break up with Jason for any reason I want."

Laura studies her face. "Just admit you met someone else."

"Yeah, Suzanna," I belt out. "Admit you fucked someone behind Jason's back."

"You only asked for one secret!" Her eyes fill with tears. "You are so mean, Janey."

"Sorry," I say blithely. "I'm just surprised." Actually, I'm furious. I know I'm being a hypocrite, but finding out she lied makes me feel out of control, as if there are countless other secrets she's still hiding. I don't trust the Weaver, and I don't want her to talk anymore. I turn to Bethany. "You go."

"Six months ago I got a dog. I thought it would help me meet someone. I know it's pathetic, but it seems to work for Suzanna—"

"It's not pathetic," I tell her. "I considered doing the same thing."

"Is that your secret?" Laura wants to know.

"Yes," I say firmly, but she shakes her head.

"Tell us something sacred. Tell us why you won't talk about your mother."

I turn to Bethany again. "Don't look at her," Laura says. "She can't help you."

I suddenly realize that if Group is ever going to work, I have to do it right. The jig, as I understand it, is up. "I can't talk about my mom because I miss her too much. She said she was going to come back for me, but she never did."

"Do you have any idea where she might be?"

I must have an expression of sheer agony on my face because this is the last question Laura asks.

Our Thursday-night sessions continue without much drama until December, when the Weaver shows up in tears. We immediately think something has happened to Ginger, but she shakes her head. "It was a guy." A tear dribbles down her pale cheek. "He clicked off the phone and never came back."

"Wait a second," Laura says. "Start over. You broke up with Jason and met this guy."

"No, you were right. I met this guy before I broke up with Jason. And it wasn't like I broke up with Jason because of the guy. I met him while I was walking Ginger—"

"I knew that dog helped you meet men!" Bethany exclaims. "Why isn't mine working? I walk it, I feed it, I sing to it, but that smelly beast has done nothing for me. I can't figure out what I'm doing wrong."

"Suzanna's sharing," Valentine says. "So you were out walking Ginger . . ."

"And he invited me out for coffee. Then he kissed me. I mean, he *kissed* me, long and hard and he sucked my lips and licked my tongue and it went on for hours—"

"We get the picture," Valentine says. "And?"

"He never called me. Who kisses someone like that and doesn't call?"

"Practically every guy I've ever gone out with," Laura says.

"Well, you're a slut," Bethany points out. "Guys don't call sluts back."

Valentine's annoyed. "Give Suzanna a chance to tell her story."

"She's taking forever."

"Damn it, Bethany, shut up! Suzanna, don't pay attention to her. Keep going."

The Weaver hesitates, then says, "I wanted to kiss him again. So I called him. And while we're talking, he said he had another call and clicked off. But he never came back on the line."

"Did you call him back?" I ask.

"Three times." She hides her face behind her long red hair. "I know it's nothing to you guys since you've been fucked over so many times, but this has never happened to me. I've never liked anyone so much, and I don't know how to handle it."

"First of all," Laura says calmly, "you may want to consider a more tactful way of making your point in the future; however, the fact that we've been hurt before has no bearing on what happens to you. Pain, as we all know, is relative."

The Weaver's muffled sobs sound like dog yaps. "Why did he do it, Laura?"

Laura pulls the Weaver's hair out of her face. "I don't know. But I think that a lot of the time men do things to hide their own insecurities, not because they don't like you."

"Maybe he *didn't* like her," Valentine suggests. "Maybe he just wasn't interested."

Laura takes off her glasses. "That's mighty sensitive. Valentine, your newly found confidence is making everyone tense."

"Is that true?" She looks at Ivy. "Do I make you tense?"

"Well, honey, yew do seem a little rough around the edges lately."

"Do I make you tense, too, Janey?"

"Remember when Group started and we were all afraid of Bethany because she was so abrasive?"

"I was not," Bethany says indignantly.

"You were abrasive and you were scary, but now you're just you." I put my hand on Valentine's shoulder. "You're our new Bethany."

"That's not true. I've changed, that's all, and everyone else is jealous. I'm self-assured and strong and I'm not afraid to assert myself when I'm being taken advantage of—"

"Can I *please* finish?" the Weaver squeaks. "This guy seemed to like me *a lot.* He showed up with a bouquet of flowers and a toy for Ginger. We had drinks and dinner and—" She looks at Laura. "You know what?" Her voice is quiet. "I didn't just kiss him."

"I didn't think so," Laura replies.

"He said he would call me."

"Of course he did." Laura puts her arms around the Weaver. "I hate to see you so upset." Her voice rises. "And I hate men who have sex and then never call again!"

I agree. "But we don't have to take it. We can do something about it." I wave around the table. "Bring on the pussy posse."

Valentine's skeptical. "What are we gonna do? Make prank calls? Toilet-paper his house? We're grown women. Let's drop it."

"I have a great idea!" Bethany exclaims. "We'll get the phone company to disconnect his service. Or cancel his credit cards. Or have his mail forwarded to Tokyo."

"You've obviously considered revenge before," I say dryly.

"Jenny, my husband left me for a younger woman. His *People* magazines are *still* routed through Japan. He gets them six months late and completely dog-eared." Bethany cracks up. "The Japanese are *obsessed* with *People.*"

"No," Laura says. "We should do something more sophisticated. What if we find out where he works, break into his office, and send E-mails from his computer announcing Ku Klux Klan meetings at his house—"

"Or send pornography to everyone in his company," I interject. "Or a manifesto about why he believes the Holocaust never happened."

Natasha is studying the ceiling. "What's the likelihood of those beams dislodging and crashing on our heads?"

"Yew know what Ah'd do?" Ivy tells us, her accent as thick as Mississippi mud. "Ah'd git me a big ole butcher knife and plunge it into his heart till he bled like a stuck pig."

This shuts us up.

"Jesus, Ivy," Bethany says finally. "It didn't even happen to you."

The Weaver pleads with us. "We shouldn't do anything. Valentine's right. He's probably just not interested in me. Let's forget it ever happened."

"Okay," Laura says, glancing at Ivy, Bethany, and me. "We'll forget it."

The way Laura explains it, avenging the Weaver's honor makes perfect sense. "Haven't we learned anything in Group? We're significant, we're visible, we're strong, vital women. So to prove this, not to the world, but to ourselves, we need to shake things up, wreak a little havoc. Let's choose one guy whose behavior was truly heinous and unforgivable and show him that his actions have consequences."

Bethany warms to the idea immediately. "I choose Peter."

Laura shakes her head. "Ex-husbands are too easy. Pick someone who'd never expect it."

"I'm not comfortable with this," the Weaver says. "I'm not comfortable at all."

"You seemed pretty comfortable when we went after Margot," Laura points out. "In fact, if I recall, you were the one who came up with the idea of putting the gun in her bag."

"I'm not comfortable either," Valentine pipes up.

"We're doing it. Case closed. You're either in or you're out."

Valentine glares at Laura. "Sometimes I really don't like you."

"You're not the first person to say that. Suzanna, you in or out?"

"I haven't decided. But I don't want it to be my guy. It has to be someone else."

"Fine," Laura says. "Next week, everyone bring a list of possible candidates."

And so it began. As an actuarial case study, it makes a compelling argument for risk avoidance. Assume you have a population—in this case, seven mildly neurotic but basically unthreatening women—grouped together based on their lack of intimacy skills. The harm they could inflict appears to be negligible. But an actuary considers anomalies when she calculates the value of uncertainty. And in some situations violence is committed, not by the most hardened and callous criminals, but by sensitive people harboring unexpressed hurt. Uprisings like our collective rage happen because girls like us, girls who have suffered dishonesty and injustice and basic bad behavior, now have a plan for reprisal. And it is this feeling of strength, this sense of righteousness, this taste of power that makes danger possible.

"So who's it gonna be?" I ask Laura on Saturday. It's almost Christmas and we've been meeting every three days to help stave off our (my) suicidal impulses.

"What about the guy Valentine dated three years ago?"

For the first time in weeks, Valentine cracks a smile. "Michael would be great."

"I don't remember him," Bethany says. She tugs at her elf's hat. "This hat itches, but it's too cute to take off. Do you like it, Jenny?"

"Love it. I'm also loving the matching shoes, although I'm amazed you can walk with the toes curled up." I turn to Valentine. "Who's Michael? I don't remember him either."

"He's the real estate broker who had a weird toenail fungus. During our supposedly exclusive relationship, he joined a dating service and a singles' tennis league. Then he vacationed alone at ClubMed Antigua and brought home genital warts."

"Sounds like a real prince," I say, then turn to Bethany. "What about that guy you went out with?"

"The guy who ditched me in the movie theater?"

"No, the one who called you ten times a day until you bumped into him with his wife and two kids at Ikea."

"Oh. Harvey. He moved."

The Weaver looks nervously at her watch. "I can't stay long. I have to get Ginger from day care."

"You have time," Laura tells her. "Pick someone."

"I really don't want to do this."

"Don't be a wimp, Suzanna. Just say a name."

"If she doesn't want to do it, Laura," Valentine insists, "she doesn't have to."

"Aren't we all in this together?" I ask.

The Weaver thinks for a second. "Well, I hired a sitter once who walked Ginger in the rain without a hat."

"That's not exactly a heinous crime," Laura points out.

"Maybe not to *you*," the Weaver says, sniffing.

Laura sits up. "My turn. I have three—Bruce, Langston, and Shelby. I met Bruce at the beach, Langston at a bar, and Shelby at a party."

"Crimes?" Ivy asks.

"They fucked me, then ran."

"As Ah understand it, Laura, honey, the fuck and run is not necessarily a crime if yew are a willin' participant."

"I didn't participate in the *running.*"

Eventually it's my turn. "Well," I say. "There was a guy who came up in Group when we were still with Dr. Hensen, but I doubt any of you would remember."

"*I* remember," Laura says and proceeds to tell the girls about Tobias, the stairwell, and Debby Dupont. Curiously, though, when she tells my sad tale, the Weaver appears the most pained. She turns to me, her eyes widened in what looks like genuine empathy. It must've really affected her, I think, because after that night she never returns to Group. That is, until I call to tell her that Tobias is the guy we've elected to go after.

12

The executive boardroom at Municipal Life Insurance was created in 1893 as a symbol of the company's wealth and influence. Its elaborate gold ceiling, leather walls, intricately hand-worked chairs, and detailed parquet floor reflected the elegance of design and superb craftsmanship of the era. When MuniLife's home office was rebuilt in 1958, the room was re-created on the eleventh floor in the company's new building on Madison Avenue and Park Avenue South.

Today Municipal Life's boardroom is forty-five feet long, twenty-five feet wide, and twenty-seven feet high. Its ceiling is faced with nine-, twelve-, and eighteen-carat gold. A twenty-five-foot-long table, the center of which is made of Honduras mahogany with Primavera mahogany trim, fills the room.

Only the board of directors has access to the room; however, the company does give tours to special-interest groups. And when senior executives and their staff are invited to make presentations to the board, they are allowed to use the room to practice. "It's very intimidating," the tour guide will tell you, "even for the most seasoned businessmen."

When I was at MuniLife, I used to steal upstairs and join the tour groups. I was dutifully impressed and visited as often as I could. Tobias also loved the boardroom. He vowed to one day sit at the head of the twenty-five-foot-long mahogany table. Funny how life comes full circle: The boardroom at Municipal Life is where I want to take Tobias down.

Finding Tobias will be easy," I tell the girls. We're all assembled at T.G.I. Friday's, even the Weaver, who still hasn't decided if she'll help. "I know where he works and where he lives. I also know his daily routine." To my dismay, they find this very disturbing.

"You're still following this guy?" Bethany asks. "After all this time? You're almost as crazy as she is." She points to Natasha, who is wearing a down parka zipped to the neck, which she refuses to take off even though the restaurant is overheated.

"Honey," Ivy drawls, "that's just insane. Yew need to get yourself some help."

"It's not insane," Laura says. "It's an obsession. We can help her. But, Janey, if we're going to help you, you have to help us, which means it's time to start telling the truth."

"I've *told* you the truth! I told you everything he did to me."

"You didn't tell us you were still stalking him. And not-telling—"

"—is the same thing as lying," Bethany finishes.

"Can you get a skin disease from your own sweat?" Natasha asks apropos of nothing. Her forehead is bathed in perspiration. She's lost in her parka, as though it's a live animal swallowing her whole.

"What's bothering you?" I ask her.

"Janey, I'm talking to you," Laura says.

"Okay. I don't want to lie anymore, but I can't stop myself. Sometimes my words come out before I have time to think, and without even meaning to, I've created a story that's so big I don't know where to start breaking it down."

Laura peers at me over her glasses. "Lying is a coping mechanism you use to protect yourself from whatever bad feelings the truth might otherwise reveal. And"—she turns to Ivy—"her obsession with Tobias isn't about Tobias. I don't know what it's about, but we'll get to that—*if* she's willing to talk about it."

"I told you what happened," I insist, unsure of what else she wants.

"But there are still parts of your life we know nothing about and we're tired of having to fill in the gaps." She smacks a roll out of Valentine's hands. "That makes five!"

"Who made you roll monitor?" Valentine snaps.

I lean toward Laura and lower my voice. "I've never told you this before . . ." Everyone's silent, awaiting my startling revelation. "Your glasses make you look cross-eyed." I stand up and put on my coat.

Laura grabs my arm. "Where are you going?" she demands, and I'm reminded of Bethany asking the very same question when Group first began. I wonder what the girls would do if I dropped out. Would they miss me? Would they call me? Would they let me fend for myself?

The restaurant fills with the sulfurous stink of the pulp, a smell I haven't been around in a very long time. I begin to drift, remembering the day I came home from school and found my mother crouched on her haunches, her head stuck inside our small oven. At first I thought she was finally giving it a good cleaning, but she didn't respond when I called. Then I thought she'd fallen asleep in that position. Her decapitated body was bent like a shelf; her knuckles scraped the floor; and the bottoms of her feet were black with dirt. Her nightgown was hiked up and her underwear was showing. Embarrassed, I turned away.

It didn't dawn on me that she was dead, even as my eyes watered from the metallic gas. Mothers don't die. They may disappear without a trace, leave you and your father in a dirty old trailer, but they don't die. Not when you're thirteen.

"She died when I was young. She had cancer." Light-headed and woozy, I slip back into my chair.

"Drink this." Laura pushes a glass of water into my hands. Tears stream from my eyes, which burn as if they're melting into my skull. "You can't leave us. And we won't leave you."

"That's what my mother said," I tell her, not angrily, merely pointing out the irony.

"That's what they all say," Ivy says, whose own mother, I remember, is dead.

"But how do you live with that?"

"Painfully. But yew live."

"I'm not sure I can." I fight my desire to race out of the restaurant and run into traffic. I imagine a bus hitting me with such force I'm flung into space. I want to hear the sound of screeching brakes, feel the smack of the vehicle as it makes contact. My need to escape is as palpable as the stench of gas in the air is heavy. I hold on to the table for dear life. That's what it is, isn't it? Dear life? But by whose definition, I wonder. Certainly not my mother's. I force myself to stop drifting, to stay put. I'm bound to my seat, where every detail of her suicide unfolds before me. I recall that day with such precision, memory alone threatens to kill me.

As Operation Saggy Tits consumes our Thursday-night sessions, no one mentions my mother again. For the moment, the subject appears to be closed. One night Bethany shows up in full militia gear: camouflage pants, black boots, olive-green T-shirt, black beret.

"You've got to be kidding." Laura grabs Bethany's walking stick and raps her head. "This isn't Desert Storm. It's a prank."

"I'm the only one taking this seriously. It's been three weeks already and we don't even have a plan yet."

"We do have a plan." Laura turns to me. "Did you call the Weaver?"

"What's the plan?" Bethany barks.

I nod. "But she hasn't called me back."

"Call her again. We need Ginger."

"I'll call her," Valentine says. "Just tell us the plan already."

I clear my throat. "It's very simple. Ivy, we're using you as bait. I realize you have issues about your looks, but the fact is, you're gorgeous. More important, you're Tobias's type. He likes tall, lanky blondes, pin-up girls—all legs and cleavage and smoldering indifference."

"You sound like you want to fuck her yourself," Valentine says.

Bethany raps Valentine with her stick. "Be nice!"

"What do Ah have to do?" Ivy asks.

"First you use your temping skills to get an assignment at Municipal Life. Once you're inside, you use your feminine wiles to get Tobias interested. After he's thoroughly hooked, you tell him you want to have sex in a very special place." I pause. "MuniLife gives tours of their boardroom to the public. It has an enormous twenty-five-foot-long table in the middle. Ivy, your job is to convince Tobias to have sex with you on that table."

"Ah can't do that! Ah can't have relations in a public place."

"Relax," I reassure her. "It's a ruse. You won't really have sex with him. You just have to get him up there. While you're doing that, the rest of us will be taking a tour of the boardroom. The tour starts with a stroll through the executive offices. As we walk down the hall, we'll let Ginger go and she'll take off. When the tour guide races after her, we run away, sneak into the boardroom, and hide under the long table. Once we're situated, we call Ivy and tell her to bring Tobias up. He'll think he's gonna have sex so he'll tell the security guard he's practicing a presentation and lock the door. But when he lunges for Ivy, we jump out from under the table and grab him. Then we strip off his clothes and take pictures of him wearing ladies' lingerie, which we post on the Internet and send to the Groton Alumni Association, the chairman of Municipal Life, and Mr. and Mrs. Teague." I hold out my hands and beam.

There's a long beat of silence.

"That's the most stupid plan I ever heard," Valentine finally says.

"That's because it wasn't your idea," Laura retorts. "You can leave anytime you want, Valentine. This is a voluntary decision. No one's putting a gun to anyone's head."

"Except Tobias's." I smile. "I believe you're all familiar with our secret weapon."

One of the great things about Municipal Life's size is that they always hire temps. Ivy makes a few calls, finds out which agencies MuniLife uses, and goes down to register. While we wait for her first assignment, I go to St. Vincent's to talk to the Weaver.

When I get to the hospital, the Weaver makes me wait in the lobby for a half hour. She doesn't hug me when she sees me nor does she ask how I've been. "I'm extremely busy," is the first thing she says, glancing at the clock on the wall. "And Valentine already called to tell me the plan."

"Then I'll make it quick. We need Ginger to go on the tour, jump out of your arms, and race down the hall. While the tour guide is chasing her, everyone but you will sneak into the boardroom. You stay behind to help the tour guide and thank him for his time, et cetera, et cetera. Then you can leave or you can sneak into the boardroom with us, whichever you prefer."

"Valentine was right. Your plan is stupid. Janey, I have to go back to work." She pulls her hair into a ponytail. Her dangly silver earrings shine in the fluorescent white light of the hospital lobby. "You can't come by here anymore."

"Okay. Our plan is stupid. If you can come up with a better one, we'll consider it. In the meantime, this is what we're doing. Oh! We also need a knockout drug to immobilize Tobias so we can strip him. Nothing too strong. We need to be able to wake him up."

"Are you out of your mind? I could go to *jail* for giving you a narcotic." Her overarched eyebrows mock me.

"So we'll nix the drugs. But what about Ginger?"

"Well . . ." She plays with her earrings. I want to rip them off her fucking head for acting so self-righteous. "Ginger and I will be there for the action, but we don't want any other contact. I'm not coming to Group anymore, and I don't want anyone to call me. I'm only doing this because—well, I can't say why I'm doing this. If you need my help, I'll be there, but I think the six of you are acting like a bunch of hostile, bitter shrews."

"I'm sorry you feel that way—"

"I'm not like you," she continues. "I have dignity. I don't feel the need to get revenge just because some idiot doesn't call me back. I have other interests in my life."

"I have other interests, too, Suzanna."

She sighs. "Like what, Janey? Pulling pranks on old boyfriends?"

"No, I've mastered the art of feng shui."

"That's great," she says, but her oddball eyebrows make her look bewildered instead of impressed.

"I've been studying with Van Loo Getrude Hamma. He's a

famous feng shuiologist. He wrote *Benevolent Chi in Five Easy Steps*. Perhaps you've read it?"

The Weaver keeps checking her watch. It's obvious my mastery of ancient Chinese artistry isn't winning her over, but I refuse to give up. "Van Loo has done quite a bit of work with the canine population. Instead of the elements traditionally applied to people—fire, earth, water, metal, and wood—he works with stick, bowl, bone, ball, and biscuit. Looie and I could feng shui Ginger's work and play area. We could activate her chi—"

"Ginger doesn't have a work area and she doesn't need her chi activated."

"We all need our chi activated!" I screech. "Let me do this for you. Let me feng shui your life!" *Oh, sweet Jesus. I am out of control.*

The Weaver starts to walk away. "I told you I'd participate in your idiotic scheme. Just stay away from Ginger and me." She gives me a look of pity, then, head held high, she sashays down the hall, her nurse shoes squeaking against the linoleum floor.

For a second, I'm stumped. "Dignity is overrated!" I sputter, but she's too far away to hear me.

The temp agency finally calls Ivy. "Ah start on Monday," she says, "but Ah have some minor concerns. What if Tobias finds me repulsive? What if he thinks Ah'm a scrawny old woman with crow's-feet and bat wings?"

I promise her it won't matter. "He'll still fuck you."

Laura's worried about the plan. "How was the dry run?"

A few days ago, posing as the director of a historical-site preservation society, I took a tour of the boardroom. After the tour, the guide gave me a brochure, which I spread on the table to show the girls how Municipal Life is laid out. "This is the boardroom. It's on the eleventh floor, adjacent to the executive offices. Tours are given by a security guard named Moe. He rarely gives tours to the public anymore, so we may be the only ones up there. If we tell him we're reporters doing a story on historic boardrooms, he won't suspect anything."

"I don't want to be a reporter," Bethany cuts in. "I want to be a talk-show host."

"Fine. You can be a talk-show host. So Moe led me through—"

"And I want everyone to call me Ricki."

"Whatever, Bethany. Just let me finish. Moe led me through the executive corridors first, which are right outside the boardroom. It takes about twenty minutes to see all the offices and listen to his spiel about the artwork. Then we went into the boardroom. As I told you, the table in the boardroom—"

Natasha interrupts me. "You keep saying 'boardroom.' One of the symptoms of early-stage Alzheimer's is a tendency to repeat yourself."

"I'm trying to get you acquainted with the plan, Natasha. Please stay focused." I point to the brochure again. "The table is huge, so we'll have plenty of room to hide while Moe's chasing Ginger down the hall. Once we're situated, we'll call Ivy and tell her to bring Tobias upstairs."

"I'm not getting under that table," Bethany says. "I have bad knees."

"This is the plan. Take it or leave it. Okay, to recap. We go on the tour. The Weaver lets go of Ginger. Ginger takes off. Moe races after her. While he's chasing Ginger, everyone runs to the boardroom. The Weaver stays behind and thanks Moe for his help. She tells him someone got sick and we took her home. In the meantime, we're in the boardroom, under the table. We call Ivy and she brings Tobias upstairs. Tobias locks the door and we lunge. Mayhem ensues."

"What do you think he'll be wearing?" Bethany asks.

"If we do this on Friday, he'll be wearing khakis. What's the difference, Bethany?"

"No difference, and the name's Ricki."

I glare at her. "Why are you making this so difficult?"

"Because I don't want to be under that table."

"I'll tell you what. You can hide behind the door. How's that?"

She brightens immediately. "I'll let the Weaver into the boardroom. If she waits for What's-His-Name to catch Ginger, she'll come in after us, but if we're under the table, there won't be anyone to open the door."

"You're right," I say. "I didn't think of that. Damn, this is getting complicated."

"I told you it was a stupid plan," Valentine says.

"I think it's great!" Bethany exclaims. "And I can't wait. It's the best thing we've ever done." She pounds the table. "We're here! We're queer! We will not disappear!"

Laura stares at her. "Are you high?"

"No, I'm excited. We're sticking up for ourselves. We're finally saying, 'Don't fuck with us' to anyone who thinks girls in their late thirties—"

"Early forties," Ivy croaks.

"—should be put out to pasture. We're heroes, Ivy. Say we are!"

"Wail, Ah guess."

"Say yes like you mean it. We are here! We are queer! We will not disappear!" Bethany is trying to rouse us into a chorus when the restaurant manager leans over our table.

"Excuse me, ladies. Could you keep it down? We have other diners—"

"Go away! We're heroes." Bethany pinches his "Randall" name tag. "You can't put us out to pasture. Randall, you suck. Come on, girls. Say it with me. We're here! We're queer! We will not disappear!"

The rest of us are silent.

"Stop chanting, Bethany!" Laura says.

"I can't hear you because my name's Ricki." Bethany continues to chant and Laura glances at me as if to say: *This isn't going quite as I expected.*

True to her word, the Weaver keeps her distance, which casts an unfortunate pall on our enthusiasm. To be fair, though, the Weaver's ambivalence isn't the only reason for our discomfort. The girls and I possess an infinite source of histrionic behavior to draw from and Operation Sagging Tits provides us with the perfect opportunity to exhibit each of our unique neuroses in all its stunning glory.

In the first week of February, a mere ten days after Ivy assumed her duties as alpha seductress, I glare at her across the table. "Shut up, Ivy. I can't stand to listen to you anymore."

"Then don't listen. Ah'm just followin' orders."

"You knew what was going to happen, Janey," Laura says coolly. "In fact, it was your idea. So sit up, stop complaining, and give Ivy some credit."

Laura's right. It was my idea for Ivy to hook up with Tobias. But that doesn't make it any easier to hear a recitation of their mutual seduction, however contrived on her part. Last Friday, she positioned herself next to Tobias in the elevator and "mistakenly" walked into his office three times. Then on Monday, she dropped a sheaf of papers and bent over to pick them up, offering him a shot of her liposuctioned ass in full eclipse. When he finally asked her name, our plan was set in motion, which sparked within me a violent conflict.

As much as I want Ivy to seek out Tobias, as much as our plan hinges on his attraction to her, I become increasingly anxious as she recounts everything that transpires between them. He buys her coffee, sends her E-mails, and brushes up against her every time she passes. By using Ivy to lure Tobias, I've devised my own mental horror show, an endless loop that plays in my head and in which my deepest wishes and wildest fears are simultaneously realized.

"Guess what?" Ivy shakes a pair of silver hoop earrings. "Tobias gave me these."

I spit out my chardonnay. "You're gloating!"

Ivy won't look at me. "Laura, will yew handle this please?"

"Janey," Laura says firmly. "Tobias is a snake, a pitiful excuse for a man, which is why we all agreed to go through with this. You don't want him. Ivy doesn't want him—"

"He can be quite charmin', however," Ivy interjects.

"What's *that* supposed to mean?" I snap.

"All Ah'm sayin' is that Ah can see why yew developed a crush on him."

"It wasn't a *crush*." I bite off each word. "He said he *loved* me!"

Ivy smiles, as if remembering something pleasant. "Ah just can't believe how much fun this is turnin' out to be."

"You're the only one having fun."

Ivy gazes beyond me, looking like a girl who knows she's beautiful. "Your turn will come, Miss Jane," she tells me, but doesn't sound the least bit convincing.

I call her after Group.

"Hello?" she says breathlessly.

"I'm concerned about you, Ivy. Tobias *can* be charming. But he's also evil and heartless and . . . and . . . he has no manners."

"Ah'll take that under advisement. Send me the papers and Ah'll look them over."

"What are you talking about?" Then it hits me. "Tobias is there, isn't he? Ivy, please listen. He's a bad, bad man."

"Ah realize that, but now's not the best time to discuss it."

"Remember what he did to me? Remember how I walked into the bar and he was kissing that girl? He'll do the same to you. What's he doing at your house? You're not really supposed to have sex with him, Ivy. It's a setup." I start to cry. "How can you do this to me?"

"Don't go borrowin' trouble, honey. You'll only make yourself unhappy."

"You're not sticking with the plan!"

Ivy lowers her voice. "Janey, listen up. Just cause Ah'm supposed to get a hateful man aroused doesn't mean Ah'm not allowed to enjoy it."

"You're such a bitch!" I scream. "A low-rent, trailer-park, scheming var-mi-ent!"

"No, honey," she retorts. "That's yew." And slams down the phone.

I'm so upset I stay up all night. In the morning, I walk to Laura's apartment on East Fourth Street. She's supposed to be home all day writing an article, so I'm surprised when she doesn't answer the bell. I buzz several times, but she won't answer.

I'm determined to get into Laura's building even if it takes a bulldozer to plow through the vestibule. Finally an elderly woman appears lugging four bags of groceries. I offer to help and follow her inside when she unlocks the door. Then I trudge up the six flights to Laura's place.

"It's me!" I bang on the door. She doesn't answer, so I bang harder. "Laura! I know you're in there."

Finally she peeks through the crack. "Why aren't you at work?"

"We never should've sent Ivy in first. She's screwing up everything. She's already having sex with Tobias. She's gonna ruin the plan. The plan, Laura! She's gonna ruin the plan. What? Why are you looking at me like that?"

"I'm working, Janey. I'd rather not be disturbed." She tries to close the door, but I block it with my foot.

"You're wearing a towel!" I exclaim.

"I'm working naked."

I push the door open. Her apartment's a mess, but it's not a mad-writer mess. It's a boozy, late-night, shacking-up-and-shagging mess. I kick an empty wine bottle.

"Have you been drinking?" I look at her face. Her lips are swollen and her cheeks are flushed. "You've been with a guy, haven't you?"

"Of course not."

The toilet flushes. "You slut! Who is he?"

"My new boyfriend," Laura says. "I was going to tell you about him."

The bathroom door swings open. A guy pads into the room wearing nothing but boxers. Laura prances over to him and drapes her arms around his neck. "This is Todd."

"Ted." He nudges her aside so he can pull on a white Oxford.

"I said Ted." Laura lights a cigarette. "Ted, this is Janey. Perhaps, Janey, you'd like to tell me and my boyfriend Ted—who I love—why you're acting so insane this morning?"

I watch Ted button his shirt, pull a sweater over his head, and zip his jacket. "Well," he says. "Gotta go. Guess I'll call you." He steps into the hall and closes the door behind him.

"Isn't he dreamy?" Laura sighs, her face hazy behind a plume of smoke.

I sit down at her desk. "Laura," I say sternly. "I'm very disappointed in you. You promised to quit smoking." We both stare at each other, then crack up.

When we assemble on Thursday night, Ivy announces that Tobias reserved the boardroom for the following Friday. "He told the receptionist he had a board meetin' to prepare for and doesn't want to be disturbed." She smiles sweetly at me. "But he thinks we're gonna do it."

"Have you gained weight?" I ask her.

Natasha is wheezing. "I have a bad feeling the Weaver will bail at the last minute."

"You have bad feelings about everything," Bethany says. "You know why? Because you're crazy!" She shakes her hands in Natasha's face. "Crazy as a loon."

"Back off, Bethany," I say. "You're the one acting crazy. In fact, it seems like we're all having a few personal problems lately. Maybe it's stress, maybe we've been too focused on Tobias, but I've been hearing rumors about . . . I don't know . . . one-night stands. Would anyone, perhaps Laura, care to share?"

"It's interesting you would bring up that issue, Janey," Laura replies. "Because we're wondering why you're wearing sunglasses inside the restaurant. We know you tend to do this when you want to be invisible. Or dead. Is something—perhaps Ivy's flirtation with a guy who dumped you—bothering you?"

"I'm still worried about the Weaver," Natasha interjects. "She said we're acting like a bunch of shrews, didn't she? And victims. We're all acting like victims."

"I'm no victim," Valentine tells us. "I'm a strong, sensitive woman."

"Not to mention big," Bethany says.

"Oh my God. Did you just call me fat?"

"Not fat. Big. And maybe if you kept your pie hole shut, you'd lose a few pounds."

Ivy rushes to Valentine's defense. "Bethany, yew have no right to talk to Valentine like that, especially since yew let *your mother* move back into your home."

"Barbara's back? No wonder you've been such a bitch lately."

"She's my mother, Jenny, and she needs me." Bethany turns to Valentine. "I didn't mean to say you were big. It just came out." She snickers. "I'm sorry. I know I shouldn't laugh." But she can't stop and soon the noises she makes sound less like laughter and more like hysteria. Natasha makes similar noises when she gets panic attacks. She'll laugh, then cry, then gasp for air. Watching her was the first time I ever associated laughter with a cry for help.

Laura pats Bethany's shoulder. "It's obvious we're all a little freaked out about going after Tobias, so let's just relax. This was supposed to be fun, remember?"

"There's been a slight change," Ivy says, giggling stupidly. "Tobias and Ah are havin' lunch together on Friday, sort of like foreplay before the big event."

"This is how it starts!" I shout. "All it takes is *one person* to miss her mark, *one person* to follow her own agenda, and the entire plan is ruined."

"We're not supposed to get there until four-thirty," Laura reminds me. "If they're just having lunch, they'll be back way before then."

"Then why did she tell me? She's just trying to make me feel bad." I lean toward Ivy. "I'll tell you something, Missy." *Missy? Who says "Missy" other than prune-faced, swampy-crotched spinsters?* "You better stick to the plan. All it takes is one person to screw up everything."

Oh, I had no idea.

13

Operation Sagging Tits starts out exactly as planned. While Ivy and Tobias are having lunch in preparation for their boardroom rendezvous, the rest of us wait for the Weaver outside T.G.I. Friday's. We're all wearing black leather trench coats, black turtlenecks, and black leggings (it was Bethany's idea to dress like storm troopers, a look she accents with a powder-blue Pashmina shawl).

Natasha stomps her combat boots. "Why are we doing this in February? It's freezing out here." She peers down the street. "The Weaver's not coming. Something's wrong."

"She's coming," I insist. "The Weaver knows the meaning of loyalty, which apparently Ivy never learned in Appalachia."

"Ivy's from Alabama," Laura points out. "And you're being too hard on her."

I'm about to defend myself when the Weaver turns the corner carrying Ginger in a baby Snugli. In her black doggie trench coat, black thermal cap, and silver eye patch, Ginger looks like a mini canine terrorist.

The Weaver adjusts Ginger's patch. "Ginger scratched her cornea," she coos. "Her eye hurts very, very much." She turns to us. "I'm here. It's late. Let's go."

"I want a cup of coffee," Bethany announces, knotting her Pashmina. She takes it off and reknots it as if practicing her technique for tying up Tobias. (We've replaced the knockout drug with bungee cords and bedsheets—not as dramatic but equally effective.)

"We don't have time," Laura says.

"I'm getting coffee. And you can't stop me." Having her mother back home has resurrected Bethany's teenage hostility, from which she isn't sparing any of us.

"Let Bethany get coffee." Valentine's strangely docile. I attribute this to anxiety, which all of us are feeling. Surprisingly, only Natasha appears composed as she arranges our supplies in two oversize duffel bags, counts, then recounts the bungee cords, and folds lingerie into perfect squares. Granted, none of us knows what horrific visions are flashing through her overly active mind, but only Natasha seems prepared to begin Phase III (Phase I was seducing Tobias and Phase II was hunting and gathering supplies).

"We need a Group shot," she says when Bethany comes out of the restaurant.

"This isn't a family reunion," Laura snaps, but Natasha holds up the Polaroid.

"We should make sure the camera works." She asks a passerby to take a picture, and as we wait for it to develop, we admire each other's swank trench coats and jaunty thermal caps.

I study the shot in the cab on the way to Municipal Life. In it, Laura and Natasha peer straight at the camera and Bethany holds her coffee cup in the air like a trophy, her red lips pursed in an insane clown storm trooper smile. I'm on one side of her, hidden behind my sunglasses. Valentine is on the other, her coat buttons straining against the girth of her stomach, and she's glancing at the Weaver as if trying to catch her eye. But the Weaver is looking away and the effect is one of isolation, as if she's purposely avoiding Valentine, and as though she's unconnected to any of us or to the act of the picture taking itself.

When he greets us in the reception area, the security guard pumps our hands. "My name's Moe. I'll be your tour guide for the boardroom and the adjacent executive offices, which is where we'll begin." As predicted, we're the only people taking the tour, and if Moe notices we're dressed in spy outfits, it certainly doesn't thwart his enthusiasm for leading us through MuniLife's hallowed corridors.

Before we leave reception, Moe gestures to the thick oak doors that seal off the sacred boardroom. "One of our senior executives will be coming up to the boardroom to practice a speech he's preparing for the board members for a board meeting, so we may have to cut our tour of the boardroom a little short."

"He just said the word 'board' four times in one sentence," Natasha hisses. "Janey, what if he has—"

"Alzheimer's? A brain lesion? Ebola? He has nothing. Keep walking."

Off we go. The executive suite is composed of four long corridors configured in a square. The halls are dimly lit, with large pieces of expensive artwork on the walls. We pass each painting slowly, dragging the duffel bags behind us like bags of dirty laundry.

Just as Moe begins his speech, Bethany announces she has to use the ladies' room. "Is that okay?" she asks Moe, ignoring Laura's obvious displeasure. We aren't supposed to go anywhere until the Weaver releases Ginger.

Moe bobs his head. "Sure it is, miss. You can find the washroom right down the hall."

"You can't go to the ladies' room," Laura says sweetly. *"It's not time yet!"*

"I have to go. I just had a twelve-ounce cup of coffee. And this coat is making me sweat."

"You had to have the coffee, didn't you? And *you* wanted to wear the coats. Why we didn't wear normal clothes like normal people is beyond me."

"Because we're not normal people," Bethany retorts and bounds toward the ladies' room with Laura in full pursuit.

The rest of us trudge on. Moe describes every single inch of the executive floor in excruciating detail, all of which I'd heard just one week before. He explains the history of the boardroom, when the board meets, who the board members are, how the board members are chosen, how long their term as board member lasts, what their duties as board members entail, and "Look!" he says, pointing to the wall. "Here are oil paintings of each board member—"

I glance at Natasha, who shakes her head. "I lost count," she says. "At least ten. And now 'board' is the only word I can hear."

As we inch down the corridor, I ask Moe how long he's been leading tours.

"Six years, give or take. I'm a retired postman who couldn't stand being home all day." He chuckles. "Actually, it was my wife who couldn't stand it. So I came to MuniLife looking for a summer job, and I've been here ever since."

Waving a white-gloved hand, Moe points out each senior executive's office, and I can imagine him strolling with his mail cart greeting his customers. He's a big man, thick and muscular, with the same body type my father had pre-stroke: biceps that bulge when he flexes, massive thighs, cords of veins like telephone wiring under his skin. Seeing Moe's reverence for Municipal Life reminds me of the way Zack used to talk about the pulp. Then it strikes me, how horrible it must've been for Zack to give up his work. And how he still must suffer, his great limbs immobile, unable to spend his every waking day inside that stinking mill.

"Thank you for the tour," I say to Moe, remembering the way I blamed Zack for my mother's death. He must hate me now. "Thank you, Moe," I repeat, my eyes misty.

"Pleasure's mine. They don't pay me much, but I don't do it for the money."

"I used to work here. My name's Janey Fabre."

"I thought you looked familiar."

I don't want to remind him that I took his tour only seven days before. "It was a long time ago, when I was first starting out. I'm an actuary."

"An actuary! How about that, a young gal like you. We have a lot of actuaries around here. It takes a lot of education to be an actuary. Good for you!"

With that, I burst into tears. I'd waited forever for my father to acknowledge the scholarship to MIT, the fellowship to Harvard—full disclosure: I did my graduate work at Harvard, but didn't like to tell people for fear they'd think me arrogant—and the subsequent years of actuarial exams, but he never did. So I shouldn't be so shocked to find myself bawling like a baby when a stranger says, "Good for you," as casually as if he's pointing out the exits.

"Did I offend you?" he asks, startled by my reaction. He reaches into his pocket and pulls out a handkerchief.

"You know what an actuary is!" Tears cling to my eyelashes. I blink them away and blow my nose. "No one knows what an actuary is."

He looks confused. "Are you all right to continue?"

"She's fine," Natasha cuts in, pointing to the wall. "She always gets like this around portraits of famous people."

Moe glances at me. I nod and wipe my eyes. "Okay, then," he says. "Let's move on. Actually, these portraits here aren't of famous people. They're of previous board . . ."

As Moe resumes his speech, Natasha grabs my arm. "What is wrong with you?"

"I got all choked up talking to Moe. He reminds me so much of my father. Do you know what I said the last time I saw him? I told him that it was his fault my mother's—"

"You want to talk about your father *now*? In the middle of a job?"

"It's not a 'job,' Natasha. It's a prank. And I want to share my feelings—"

At that moment (right on cue) Ginger leaps out of the Weaver's arms and races down the corridor. What happens next can only be described as a doggie ballet gone horribly awry. Ginger shoots off like an oversize furry bullet. She's either on some kind of stimulant or she's sick of being held, because that pooch moves as fast as a rat. Unfortunately, her eye patch hampers her vision, so in the course of her mad dash, she slams into the wall with such force that her little body is lifted, literally, into the air. Coming down, she lands on a nail sticking out of the carpet (!), and after an ear-piercing howl, she limps forward, leaving bloody paw prints in her wake. Still yapping like mad, Ginger wobbles down the hall, but because of her eye patch and crippling injury, she bangs into—and bounces off of—every wall, door, and person that stands in her path. Eventually she starts dragging her paw, her shrieking *YAP YAP YAPS* fade to sad *yip yip yips*, and finally, finally, after ramming into her last sharp-edged corner, poor little Ginger curls into a ball to lick her wounds and keen in pain.

This entire episode occurs in a shorter time than it's taking to recount, but it's at least a minute before anyone reacts. Moe moves first, lumbering to Ginger's final resting spot. The Weaver snaps out of what must be mental paralysis because she doesn't yell "Ginger!" until Moe has the poor dog in his arms and is walking back toward us.

At this point, everyone but the Weaver is supposed to sneak off to the boardroom, leaving Moe running to catch Ginger. Then when Moe returned, the Weaver was supposed to tell him that Bethany got sick and we took her home. But neither Bethany nor Laura has come back from the ladies' room, Moe has already caught Ginger, and the one-eyed pooch is cuddled so sweetly in his arms, it seems unfitting for us to abandon her. My entire plan, however stupid, is foiled.

Moe hands Ginger to the sobbing Weaver as gently as he would relinquish an infant.

"Thank you," she chokes out, her green eyes wide and shiny, her eyebrows arched as if to say WOW! HOW DID WE GET HERE?

"Perhaps we should go to the boardroom," Moe says softly, stroking Ginger's hatless head.

As we retrace our steps through the executive hallways, I pick up Ginger's thermal cap and hand it to the Weaver, who won't look at me. As Moe sings to Ginger, I'm reminded (again) of my father and again (much to Natasha's dismay), I start to cry. Thoroughly incapacitated by thoughts of Zack, I can't even begin to consider how we'll execute our plan.

We do have a stroke of good luck when we reach the boardroom. The receptionist who sits outside tells Moe that Tobias Teague called five minutes before to say he's running late, but he *is* coming up to practice his speech so could Moe please make sure the room is empty?

"You should expect him in half an hour," she says in a monotone reminiscent of Charlie Brown's teacher. "But I have to leave at five on the nose. My sister Betty had her hip replaced Tuesday and is expecting me for supper, so you'll have to do all the locking up yourself."

Behind Moe's back, I give Natasha a high-five. If nothing else, Tobias's tardiness has given us some time.

"Sure, Martha," Moe tells her. "Leave when you want to." He points to Ginger. "This little critter had a bit of an accident. Caught her paw on a nail. We're gonna lay her down for a few minutes in the boardroom so she can get her bearings."

Martha looks at Ginger, but doesn't respond. Apparently, she doesn't care if the dog imploded and splattered the executive corridor with its internal organs. She's gonna be out of that office at five on the nose to have supper with her sister.

"Is that all right with you?" Moe asks the Weaver. "We can lay your puppy down in the boardroom so she can rest. Or, if you'd rather, we can end our tour here."

"She'd like to stay," Natasha interjects. "We've gone this far; we may as well see the super-duper boardroom."

Bent over Ginger, the Weaver's voice is muffled. "We'll be fine. We'll both be fine."

I touch Moe's arm. "We're ready to see the boardroom now."

"Then, ladies, step this way." With a flourish of his gloved hand, Moe opens the thick oak doors. I hear the girls' collective gasp as we step into the cavernous space. Inside, the amber light heightens the opulence and drama of the gold-gilded walls and large fireplace. The twenty-five-foot-long table fills the room almost to capacity. It's like stepping into a room at Versailles.

To Moe's surprise (but not ours), Laura and Bethany are lounging in the intricately hand-carved chairs. Bethany has her feet up on the long table, which almost causes Moe to go into convulsions. A Pekingese on amphetamines bounding through the executive suite leaving bloody prints on the carpet doesn't faze him, but a pair of Manolo Blahnik boots on the twenty-five-foot-long Honduras mahogany table is more than he can bear.

"Get those boots off that table!" he booms.

Startled, Bethany puts her feet on the floor. "Oh my God, Moe. I didn't—"

Moe clears his throat. "Sorry, miss. Didn't mean to yell. It's just that this is the boardroom and we can't have folks putting their feet on the boardroom table. The board members expect the table to be perfectly waxed so that when they conduct their board meetings—"

"Moe, sweetie," Natasha interrupts him, opening the duffel bags and pulling out bungee cord. "Please stop saying the word 'board.' It's making me crazy." She hands me a bunch of cord. "You tie up Moe. And you, Valentine, lock the door."

"Oh no," I yelp. "Not Moe!"

Natasha grabs Moe from behind, catching him by surprise. "We don't have a choice. Tobias will be here any second."

"What are you doing, miss?" Moe struggles to free himself, but Laura jumps up and, together, she and Natasha lower him into a chair. I can't believe I'm watching Natasha. The one person I assumed would crack under pressure and fret about invisible lead particles in the air has turned out to be the coolest of us all. She also looks the coolest with her ankle-length leather coat, big combat boots, long braids, and fabulous cheekbones.

When I tell her this, Natasha laughs. "It's the anticipation that kills me. I'm fine once I'm in motion. Here's some cord, Laura. Tie him to the chair."

Laura wraps the cord across Moe's chest. "What took you all so long? We've been waiting here forever. That woman outside tried to stop us, but Bethany and I blew right past her."

Valentine locks the huge oak doors. "We were detained." She points to Ginger's paw. "Ginger had an accident."

"Is she okay?" Laura asks the teary-eyed Weaver, who nods miserably.

"I'll report you!" Moe yells as Laura holds him down. "You won't get away with this—" But Laura pulls out her gun (our secret weapon), which immediately shuts him up.

"Okay," Natasha says. "The plan has changed. Since Tobias isn't here yet, we still have time to make this work. We'll tie up Moe—sorry, Moe, but we don't have a choice—then tie up Tobias the second he steps in this room."

"Now wait a second, miss. We have rules here in the board—"

"Moe? What did I say about that word?" She slaps a piece of masking tape on his mouth and finishes wrapping bungee cord around his body.

Seeing that there's no way to deter her, I kneel by his chair. "We're not going to hurt you," I promise. "You're the nicest man I ever met. We're really here for Tobias Teague. So please let us do this and we won't ask you for anything else."

There's a knock on the door. We all tense up but it turns out to be Ivy.

"Yoo-hoo. Anyone home?" When she walks into the room and sees Moe tied to the chair, Ginger lying in the Weaver's lap with a swollen, bloody paw, and Laura holding a gun to Moe's head, her eyes widen. "What the hell is goin' on?"

"It's a long story," Natasha answers. "Where's Tobias?"

"He'll be here any minute. Who's *he*?"

"This is Moe." I pat his shoulder with daughterly love.

"Ivy," Natasha orders, "wait for Tobias in the reception area. When he shows up, knock three times so we know it's you."

As we close the door behind Ivy, Bethany waves the Pashmina like a cape and puts her arms around Laura. "Take me to the cas-bah, dahling."

"Stop acting like an ass!" Laura yanks the Pashmina out of her hands.

"Give that back!" Bethany wrests the shawl out of Laura's fist, then wraps and wraps and wraps it around her neck so tightly, it looks like a surgical collar.

Their argument is interrupted by three knocks. I break out in a cold sweat. *This is it,* I think, pulling on a black hood. I bought the hood at an S&M shop in the West Village, figuring it would heighten the afternoon's drama. But given the way our plan is unfolding, the hood is superfluous. "Open the door!" I whisper to Laura, who starts when she sees my head.

"I'm scared, Janey. You look like an executioner."

"Unbelievable." Natasha shoves Laura out of the way. She takes a deep breath, counts one-Mississippi, two-Mississippi, and clicks the lock open.

"We got you, Tobias!" I yell. My hood is on cockeyed, so it takes a second for me to see Martha the receptionist, not Tobias the dickhead, standing in the doorway.

"*Ivy,*" I screech. "You were supposed to wait for Tobias."

"Ah couldn't help it. Martha was gettin' suspicious."

Martha pushes past Ivy and cranes her neck to see into the room. "Moe, are you all right?"

"A-OK." Moe has chewed through his gag. "Are you leaving for your sister's?"

"I'd like to . . . dear!" she says to Natasha. "Please take your hands off me." She steps inside. "Look at you, Moe! You're all tied up."

"Yes, Martha, it seems that I am. Just do what these ladies say and you won't get hurt."

She starts to tremble. "I'm going to call security." But Natasha catches her around the waist and lowers her into a chair.

"Gently," I snap. "And don't gag her." I hold up my bungee cord. "This is all we have left. If we use it on her, we won't have enough for Tobias."

Natasha looks at Bethany. "Give Janey your Pashmina."

She grabs her neck. "No fucking way. It was three hundred bucks."

"Bethany," I snap. "Watch your language." I turn to Martha. "Sorry about this. I know you have plans with your sister, so we'll try to get you out of here quickly. In the meantime, though, please bear with us."

Laura and Bethany struggle over the Pashmina until Natasha steps in and grabs Bethany's hands. "Get it off her," she tells Laura, who unwinds (and unwinds and unwinds) the shawl from Bethany's neck, and helps me wrap (and wrap and wrap and wrap) it around Martha.

Just as we finish tying up Martha, I hear Ivy scream, "Don't go in there yet!"

Tobias steps into the room. "Why?" he asks, looking around. At the sound of his voice, Ginger leaps off the table. "Look at you, poochie," he exclaims, crouching on his haunches. "What happened to your paw?"

I watch him stroke Ginger's ears, stunned that he's actually *here*, in the boardroom, less than ten feet away. Then Natasha yells, "Get him!" and we all rush forward in a blur of black leather.

What the hell is going on?" Tobias roars. "Who are you people?" After a long, hard struggle we finally have him tied to a chair, lined up next to Moe and Martha in a corner of the huge room. Natasha, Ivy, Bethany, and I are at one end of the table. Valentine and the Weaver are at the other. The Weaver strokes Ginger, who's asleep in her lap.

"Laura," Ivy wails, "do something, would yew? Ah'm about to pee mah pants."

"Do you need to use the powder room, dear? It's down the hall, to the left." This is from Martha who, harnessed to her chair with the Pashmina wrapped around her torso in a tight X, resembles a marionette.

Laura stands in front of Tobias. She's sweating so much, the gun slips out of her hand. "Tobias Teague," she says, bending over to pick it up, "we're here to . . . to . . ." She looks at me. "It wouldn't kill you to step in. This was your idea, you know."

I mutter, "Oh, please," and stand up. Laura's supposed to tell Tobias that we're avenging his shabby treatment of an old girlfriend, at which point I plan to rip off my hood and yell, "Voilà, Tits! It's me." But with Moe and Martha watching (not to mention Laura's glandular emissions and sudden lack of composure), the timing just doesn't feel right.

That's when Natasha steps in again. She snatches the gun from Laura, hops into Tobias's lap, and rips a lock of hair from his head.

"That hurt!" Tobias yells, but stops when Natasha holds the gun up to his face.

"You know what's gonna hurt worse? If I blow your fucking head off—excuse my language, Martha. So shut up and sit still while we explain why you're here."

"Dear," Martha asks, "may I have a glass of water? I'm parched."

Natasha points the gun at Bethany. "Get Martha some water. She's parched."

"You are not the boss of me," Bethany says, but scrambles out the door.

Natasha turns back to Tobias. "This is the deal, Tits. You're an elitist, self-absorbed guy—"

"Who has no manners," I add.

"—who has no manners," Natasha agrees. "You treat women like objects, with no regard for their feelings, and behave as if basic rules of conduct don't apply to you."

"I do not! And why are you calling me Tits? I don't know you!"

As soon as the words are out of his mouth, Natasha clocks him with the butt of the gun. "I said *shut up*! We're going to show you how it feels to be treated like an object, and you will comply with our wishes or we will kill you. Do you understand?"

Rubbing his skull, Tobias smiles. And there it is: the charismatic grin, the arrogant lift of his chin, the sparkling blue eyes, all of which make my chest constrict. I adjust my hood to look at Ivy, and see that she's gazing at Tobias with the same longing I feel.

"Here's your water." Bethany holds up the cup so Martha can sip from it. "Watch the Pashmina. I just had it cleaned."

"Can we hurry this up?" the Weaver asks. "Ginger's really hurt." We all know she wants to give up and go home, but we're too far along to back out now.

When Tobias begins to struggle, Natasha clocks him again. "I said sit still!"

"Tobias, do what she says," Ivy implores.

Afraid she might be compelled to save him, I rip off my hood. The room is dark, and I can barely see through my sunglasses. "Hi, Tobias. Remember me? Wait! Before you answer, I need to know one thing. Are you in love with her?"

Tobias refuses to answer, so I reach into the pocket of my coat and pull out a gun (my double-secret weapon), which I point at his face.

"Where did that gun come from?" Laura shrieks. "I took it away from you in Group!"

"I took it back the morning after your one-night stand with Todd."

"His name was Ted and it wasn't a one-night stand."

"Laura! I thought you weren't sleeping around anymore." This comes from Valentine, who's shouting from the other end of the long table.

"He said he'd call me. It's a *relationship.*"

"Okay," I cut in. "It was a one-night relationship. But this is my moment." I turn to Tobias. "Answer me, Tits. Are you in love with her?" I point the gun at Ivy.

"Don't yew point that gun at me!" Ivy yells, to which I almost blurt out, *It doesn't work, you mongrel,* but hold my tongue.

"You tied me up just to ask if I'm in love with her? The temp? I don't even know her." Tobias is truly amazed, and I have to admit, he's truly gorgeous. *I love you,* I want to say. *Just because I tied you up in bungee cord and plan to post naked pictures of you on the Internet doesn't mean I don't have very deep feelings for you.*

"So you're not in love with her!" I yelp, almost adding, AHA!

"We really need to hurry this up," the Weaver says.

"Suzanna, I realize you have things to do, but could you give me a moment here?"

"Ah never said he was in love with me, Janey," Ivy insists.

"But you admit to having sex with her?"

"I didn't have sex with the temp." Tobias laughs. "Not yet, anyway."

Suddenly Moe speaks up. "He was going to do that here." Everyone turns to look at him.

"Excuse me?" Laura asks.

"This isn't the first time he's brought a gal up here to have . . . uh . . . relations. But this is the first time, Lord knows, that six other gals showed up to watch. Isn't that true, Martha?"

Martha nods. There's silence until Ivy wails, "Yew said this was your first time." Then she walks over to Tobias, rears back, and smacks him.

Moe flinches. "Not to add salt to your wounds, miss, but I would bet he says that to everyone he brings up here."

I look at the red handprint on Tobias's cheek. "I'm sorry he lied to you, Ivy. But you didn't have to lie to *me* about sleeping with him. That was an awful thing to do."

"Just say it, Janey. Say, 'I told you so.' "

"Janey Fabre!" Tobias calls. "I thought it was you. Jesus, how long has it been?"

"Three and a half years. Close to four."

Having regained her composure, Laura steps in. "This is the deal, Tobias. We're gonna take off your clothes and dress you in skimpy lingerie. Then we're going to take pictures of you in unsavory positions, which will be used as we see fit. You will comply or, like Natasha said, we will kill you." She pauses. "And your whole family," she adds.

"I'm still thirsty, dear," Martha pipes up, looking at Bethany.

"This isn't Denny's, for God's sake," Bethany snaps, but runs out again to get more water.

Natasha points the gun at him. "We're gonna make you pay for what you've done."

Tobias looks confused. "So you're tying me up because I planned to have sex with the temp? She asked *me* to come up here. I didn't force her to do anything."

"Stop calling me 'the temp'!" Ivy yells. "Mah name is Ivana."

"I didn't know your name was Ivana," Natasha says, still holding the gun to Tobias's head. "Did anyone else know her name was Ivana?"

"Wait a second," I say. "Just hold on. Tobias, we are *not* tying you up because of Ivy." I turn to Natasha. "No, come to think of it. I thought it was just Ivy." Then back to Tobias. "We're doing this because you're an *asshole*. Remember the night you were kissing Debby Dupont at O'Malley's?"

"Which night? I kissed Debby a lot. Have you spoken to her recently?"

"Why the hell would I speak to Debby Dupont?"

"Didn't you and I go to Groton together?"

"No, Tobias. We didn't." The gun is slippery in my hand. I'm developing Laura's glandular problem, which doesn't bode well for our plan's execution. Moreover, the fact that Tobias thinks he and I went to prep school together isn't a good sign, either. "I didn't go to Groton. I went to Welter. This must sound familiar, because only recently, you were chasing me through midtown."

Tobias is staring at me intently. Then he glances at Ivy, who's hunched in her chair with her head in her hands. She isn't making any noise, but I suspect she is crying.

"Say something." I shove my face two inches from his. "Say you're sorry, say you never meant to hurt me, say you didn't give a shit. Just say *something*!"

There's a long pause.

"If we didn't go to Groton together," Tobias asks, still studying me, "then who the hell are you?"

14

When I imagined our belated reunion, I figured Tobias would be surprised or hostile or even regretful. But it never occurred to me, not even once, that he'd have no idea who I was. I'm so taken aback, my legs begin to wobble, and Laura has to lower me into an intricately hand-carved chair.

It takes a few minutes, but I'm finally able to speak. "You're lying, Tobias." I'm back on my feet (albeit shaking and sweating) and standing over him. "I *know* you remember me."

He stares at the gun in my hand but doesn't say anything.

"We worked here together. You bought me presents. You fucked me in the stairwell."

"Janey," Ivy says. "Your *language*." She cocks her head toward Martha, who sits with her hands folded primly in her lap but stares at me with her eyes wide, as if she's watching a movie unfold.

"Excuse me, Martha. Just trying to make a point."

"Now that you mention it," Tobias says slowly. "I do remember seeing you here a long time ago." He shakes his head. "Still. I don't remember us having sex. But if you say so . . ." He cracks a smile. "Was it any good?"

"Actually, no. You had impotence issues."

"Then you've definitely got the wrong guy. I've never had that problem. So what do we do now?" He looks at the Weaver across the long table. "Why don't you let me go?"

"Why are you looking at *her*?" I shriek. "She can't help you."

"Maybe we should let him go," Natasha suggests. "If, of course, what he's saying is true." She glances at Laura, who seems to be contemplating the situation.

I stare at her, then at everyone else. Everyone else stares back at me. No one utters a sound. I break the silence with a pitiful cry. "It's true! We were lovers. He insulted me in front of all his friends. How can you not believe me?"

"It's not that we don't believe you," Laura starts to say.

"We *don't* believe you, Jenny. You always lie. Even Hensen said so." This is from Bethany, who's eyeing Martha. "I want that Pashmina back, you know."

"Fred didn't say she lied," Laura says. "He said she didn't tell the whole truth."

"I wish Dr. Hensen were here," Natasha says wistfully. "He'd know what to do."

"We should thank God he's not. He'd cart us off to Bellevue."

"You're wrong, Laura," the Weaver pipes up. "I think he'd understand everything."

"Who cares about Dr. Hensen? I'm telling the truth!" How can this be happening after all we've been through? Then I'm struck by a thought: Maybe Tobias and I never were together. Maybe I imagined the whole affair. Could I be that demented? "Can't you see what he's doing? He remembers me. He just wants you to believe I'm crazy."

"Janey, sit down, okay? Let's relax." Laura points to the fireplace. "That's beautiful," she tells Moe. "Does it work?"

Moe tries to sit up, but the bungee cord makes it impossible, so he points with his chin. "That's an exact replica of a fireplace an original MuniLife founder saw in the Chateau de Villeroi in France. It's carved from dark Santo Domingo mahogany, just like the doors, window frames, table, and chairs you see in this room."

"Interesting."

"And if you study the rug," he continues, "you'll see it features beige and green tones that echo the colors and design motif of the wall covering. The walls above the wainscot—"

"Stop it, Moe!" I yell. "Laura, everything I told you about Tobias is true."

"I hear you, Janey. And I believe *you* believe that. But what if over the years you embellished? In your own mind, I mean? Let's say you had a crush on Tobias and you imagined all the things that could happen if the two of you got together. And what if, as you struggled with one loser guy after another, you coped with your disappointment by continually revisiting this imagined relationship. Then as time passed and your memory got distorted—as everyone's does—you began to believe that your relationship with Tobias actually happened. So the past you remember is real in your memory but it's not real as it actually occurred. It was Proust, I believe, who said that memory is not ours to command. Maybe that happened to you?"

"If that were true, you pretentious, cat's-eyed bitch, I should be locked up in an institution doing papier-mâché."

"You said it," Bethany pipes up. "Not us."

I turn to her. "Where the hell do you get off? You're married to your mother. And you!" I whirl back to Laura. "You're so afraid of getting involved with men, you recklessly fuck them to ensure that the relationship will fail. How dare you comment on my life!"

"Ah think she made an interestin' observation," Ivy says.

"What the hell do you know? You are so insecure, you spend thousands of dollars on plastic surgery to stave off the aging process. Well, you're gonna get old, Ivy. And you better find a way to accept it before you end up a booze hound like your mother, who had so many face-lifts she practically had eyes in the back of her head."

"Yew are out of line, Miss Jane," Ivy says, "speakin' of the dead with such disrespect."

"Speaking of mothers," Natasha chimes in, "why don't you tell us what really happened to yours? Did she disappear or did she die? It's time to come clean, Janey. Tell us the truth."

"Yeah, Janey," Tobias agrees, "tell us the truth."

I stare at him. If my gun actually worked and had bullets, I would blow his brains out. I close my eyes and envision my mother: head in the oven, back flat as a table, nightgown hiked up, dirty feet exposed. My chest grows hard, as if a piece of fake paneling is lodged in my rib cage. I've never betrayed her memory before, but I know if I don't, Tobias will go free and I'll be back where I started almost four years ago.

"My mother was a saint," I begin, feeling as though offering her up in this way is the worst kind of sacrilege.

"They're *all* saints," Natasha says. "Now tell us what happened."

I put my hood back on and brace myself for a crack of thunder, a torrent of blood, or a deluge of frogs. "My mother killed herself. She sealed off the house, turned on the gas, and stuck her head in the oven. I was the one who found her. I was thirteen years old."

The boardroom is silent. Bethany lets out a long, low whistle. "Wow," she whispers. "No wonder you don't cook."

My confession leaves me spent. I rest my hooded head on the table and try to drift away. I hear Martha crying and I want to comfort her but can't get up. I'm as incapacitated by sadness as my father is crippled. I finally understand the catatonia he suffered when my mother killed herself, why he just lay in their bed day after day. How can you move when the woman you love is willing to die? What activity could possibly follow such an absurdity? Sometimes the most you can do is lay yourself down and hold yourself still.

"Janey?" Laura asks, stroking my hood. "You all right?"

"I'm sorry," I whisper. "I'm sorry I said those awful things to you and Bethany."

"And to me," Ivy interjects.

"And to you," I agree. "I didn't mean them. But what I told you about my mom was true." I point to Tobias. "And what I told you about him. I admit I lied about things when we first met, but I've changed. We've all changed."

"But has it been for the better?" This comes from the Weaver. "Is this"— she holds up Ginger's paw—"a meaningful change?"

"It's only one part of it."

"Take off the hood," Laura instructs. I do as she says and she hugs me. "We believe you."

"No, you don't. But that's okay. *I* know the truth, and that's what's important." I look at Tobias. "So what do we do now?"

He smirks. "Let me go."

"Did anyone consider," Ivy asks, "that he was plannin' to dupe me? He told me this was the first time he brought a woman up here and Ah believed him. Maybe Ah'm a fool, but why would yew get him for Janey and not for me? And what about all the other girls he brought up here thinkin' this was his first time? What about them?"

"She's right." Laura turns to Natasha. "Get the camera. Let's teach this asshole a lesson."

To say that Tobias struggles is an understatement. "I don't remember her!" he keeps swearing. "Let me go."

"The only person we're letting go is Martha." Natasha stands over Martha's chair and unwinds (and unwinds and unwinds) the Pashmina. "Her sister needs her. Martha, would you like another glass of water?"

"No, dear. I'm fine." But when Natasha finishes unwrapping her, Martha won't let go of the shawl. "I want this," she says quietly.

"Oh no!" Bethany exclaims. She's sitting on Tobias's lap so he can't get up. "No way. You are *not* taking my Pashmina. Laura, tell her she can't have that."

"If we give you the shawl," Laura says slowly, "you'll never tell a soul what you saw here. You'll go home to your sister, have a nice dinner, and come back to work as if nothing happened."

Martha nods and turns to the door. But before she leaves, she hugs me. "I'm so sorry for your loss."

"Thank you, Martha, but it happened a long time ago."

"It doesn't matter when it happened. You never stop missing your mother. No matter how long ago. My own mother passed away when I was sixteen, but there isn't a day that goes by when I don't think of her. You *must* let yourself remember your mother. You must. That way she lives on as long as you do. And just so you know, even if these girls don't believe you about him"—she points to Tobias—"*I* do. He's a goddamn menace!"

"Martha!" Moe calls. "Your language!"

"Well, he is!"

"We believe her!" Laura shouts as Martha walks out. "We believe you, Janey," she insists.

"It's all right. Everything's all right." And for some reason, it is.

Telling the truth about my mother—and about myself, I suppose—has finally afforded me peace of mind. Admittedly, I feel tremendous sorrow, but I'm also suddenly clearheaded, as if for all these years, my head has been filled with static. It's an awakening of sorts, which I put to good use. "Strip him," I order. "We'll start with his shoes and work our way up."

Laura and Natasha take off his loafers and toss one to me. I hold it in my hand, amazed by its size. "Tobias, I never realized your feet were so big."

"Big feet are a sign of a big dick."

"You are a big dick. But you don't have one. Remember, I've seen it."

"Sure you did." The girls remove his shirt and Tobias sits barechested in the chair.

I put my hand on Moe's shoulder. "I know you have a responsibility to Municipal Life. But I hope you can see that we're not bad people. All we want is a few minutes alone with Tobias. We promise not to hurt him."

Moe considers this. "I have a responsibility to the firm."

"We'll be gone in a half hour," Laura promises.

Moe looks at Tobias. "Like Martha said, Mr. Teague is a menace. He's rude and disrespectful and I've looked away far too many times when he's brought unsuspecting gals up here. I'll give you a half hour and not one second more." He turns to Bethany. "You keep your feet off the table, young lady."

After I untie Moe, I hug him. "Thanks for everything."

He gets up and stretches his legs. Then he looks at Tobias again, walks out of the boardroom, and closes the heavy door behind him.

As soon as Moe is gone, Natasha and I try to take off Tobias's pants. He squirms in the chair, which makes it impossible for us to unbutton them, so we decide to stand him up. "We need everyone's help," I say. "Laura, grab one arm. Bethany, you grab the other."

Laura and Bethany do as they're told. Valentine pulls a sheet out of the duffel bag and spreads it on the table. Tobias tries to wrench himself out of our grasp, but there are seven of us and only one of him, and working together we're able to lay him down and pull off his pants.

"Bethany," Laura says, "grab the camera and underwear. We don't have much time."

I hike myself onto the table, crouch on my haunches, and hold the gun to Tobias's head. He tries to sit up, but I push him back down.

"You're really gonna do this?" he asks, no longer smirking or smiling or cracking wise. He's scared and I know it, which fills me with a feeling of Herculean power.

"We're gonna ruin you."

Tobias struggles to sit up again. This time, he manages to get up on his side, bracing himself with a stiff right arm. He tries to lift himself all the way, but his palm suddenly skids on the newly waxed table, forcing his arm to give out and his upper body to collapse. When he falls backward, there's a loud *crack* as his skull hits the table's thick mahogany edge. His head bounces once, twice, and then he is silent.

I flinch when I hear the crack, but it happens so fast, I'm not sure what's going on. My first thought is that he's purposely fallen, so I shake him really hard. "Tobias," I yell. "Get up!"

The Weaver pushes me aside. "Get out of the way! He hit his head." She jumps onto the table and straddles him. "Move back, Janey. Now."

I get down and stand behind her, too stunned to speak. Then I see the blood, which seeps from the back of his head and pools by his ear. "He's bleeding," I say stupidly, watching it stain the sheet.

"I'm a nurse," the Weaver reminds me, instantly calm. "I'll take care of this. Valentine, grab another sheet from the duffel bag."

I take a step forward. "Is he breathing?" I ask, mesmerized by the blood.

"Barely." The Weaver takes a sheet from Valentine, which she bunches under Tobias's head. The second sheet is quickly soaked.

"That's a lot of blood," I observe. "Do people always have so much blood in their heads?"

The Weaver is in complete control. I've never seen her do anything remotely nurselike before and she responds to our crisis with stunning precision. She's much more capable than I ever imagined, certainly more capable than I am, since all I can do is stand in the one spot, look as dumb as I feel, and ask distracting questions. But the Weaver moves with single-minded purpose and intimidating efficiency. She presses the back of Tobias's neck and instructs Valentine to hold his head so she can administer CPR. "Hold the sheet against his skull. Just like that. Press hard."

Tobias's eyes are closed and his face is drained of color. The Weaver opens his lips and breathes into his mouth. She looks at her watch, then breathes again. "Press harder, Valentine," she demands, then turns to the rest of us. "Listen to me. We don't have many options, so I need you to do as I say. Harder, Valentine, press harder! There's too much blood leaking out." She thumps on Tobias's chest with her fingers, then listens to his heart.

Still crouched on the table, the Weaver turns to me. "He's lost a lot of blood," she says, then trails off.

"What does that mean?" I search her face but it's void of expression.

"It's not good."

"What does that mean?"

She turns her attention back to Tobias. "I can't staunch this bleeding and he's not responding to CPR. I'll keep trying, but if it doesn't work, we need a plan to get him out of here."

"A plan?" I can't stop looking at Tobias. His cheeks are very pale and his lips are a weird pink color, with a bluish tint.

Rivulets of sweat run down the Weaver's face. Her red hair is matted. She's breathing hard. "We have to get him to St. Vincent's. One person can stay behind, but the rest of you have to leave."

Laura offers first. "I'll stay."

The Weaver gives her a long, measured look. "You sure about that?"

Laura nods. "You'll need a hand cleaning up."

"One person won't be enough," Valentine insists. "I'll stay, too."

"Does he have a concussion?" I ask. "Can you stitch him up?"

"I have friends at the hospital who can help us." The Weaver wipes her forehead with the back of her hand. She looks really tired. "We can dress Tobias up and walk him down the stairs—"

"The stairwell is probably locked," I tell her.

"So we'll hide in the bathroom until everyone's gone, then take the elevator down and get him into a cab. A guy I know in the morgue will register him as a homeless John Doe without asking questions. But if we do this, none of you can tell a soul—"

"The morgue?" Bethany interrupts.

"Look at all this blood!" the Weaver yells, still thumping Tobias's chest. Her voice booms through the silent boardroom. Who knew such a big voice could come from such a dreamy person? But she isn't dreamy anymore. She's heroic as she kneels on the table and tends to a guy whose head is cracked open. "But we have to get him out of here before Moe gets back, and if all of you stay, it'll be chaos. So go—get out of here. Valentine, Laura, and I will deal with this."

"But why the morgue?" Bethany repeats.

The Weaver looks at her in an expression that says, WE'RE IN BIG TROUBLE, YOU IDIOTS. Tobias's blood streaks her face like war paint. "Bethany." She speaks as if addressing a child. "We're taking him to the morgue because"—she breathes deeply—"Bethany, I can't revive him. I'm trying, you see how hard I'm trying, but his head hit the table in such a way . . . he hit it at a weird angle, right above his ear. Bethany, I'm sorry."

"Why are you sorry?"

"Bethany, Tobias is dead."

When I hear her say Tobias is dead, I picture my mother crouched on all fours with her head in the oven. My mother was dead and now Tobias is dead. I gave her up and the blood came after all.

THE FORCE OF MORTALITY

15

Although actuarial science is a highly complex discipline, its foundations are not so esoteric that the average layperson can't understand them. The science itself is grounded in mathematical calculations, which are based on one or more actuarial assumptions. The calculations are often the answer to a "What if?" question, and the assumptions, although based on experiences of the past, are usually about the uncertain future.

For example, what is the likelihood that the girls and I will get caught for having killed Tobias (we'll call that *u* for us) if none of the girls (*g*) goes to the police? In this case, the likelihood is $u \times g = 0$. However, this answer is valid only if *g* remains zero, meaning no girl confesses.

As a junior actuary, I learned to make "What if"–type calculations. To solve these calculations, all I needed was actuarial mathematics and the provision that any assumption I used was treated as a given. Now the problems I encounter have a much higher degree of mathematical complexity, as well as multiple assumptions. And seeing that Tobias is dead, nothing, especially the assumption that the girls will keep quiet, can be treated as a given. So to return to the original example—

What is the likelihood that the girls and I will get caught if:

- None of the girls (*g*) goes to the police?
- The boardroom rug was stained by Tobias's blood, which Moe sees on his next tour?
- Someone spotted the girls and Tobias and tells the police?

- Someone from the morgue at St. Vincent's rats out the Weaver?
- My sunglasses, which I left in the boardroom, are discovered?

The list of assumptions is endless, given the data I have at my disposal, and more important, the data I don't. Thus it's clear to any actuary that the likelihood of the girls and me getting caught cannot be determined by applying standard actuarial science.

But God knows that doesn't stop me from trying.

It's been almost ten days since we killed Tobias. I try to convince myself I don't feel guilty about it, but I do for many reasons, the least of which is that it was my crazy plan to begin with. I want to believe that the seven of us would rush to each other's rescue should the police come calling, but after all that's happened, I'm no longer confident in our ability to save each other.

Group has taught me that to live in the world, I must remain present. I can't envision my mother sailing the high seas with a Greek fishing magnate, nor can I pretend that having my cousin in New York for the weekend was amusing for me. Because of prearranged plans, Billy, my mother's sister's son, came in from Welter the day after we killed Tobias. Part of me loved staying up late, drinking beer and watching world wrestling, but the other part, the part I'm having trouble hiding, was so uncomfortable I couldn't bear looking at him.

On Saturday I took Billy to the top of the Empire State Building, where he gazed down at the buildings. "I'm moving here," he said emphatically. "When I turn eighteen, I'm coming to New York."

"To do what?" I stood beside him, wishing I could climb the heavy wiring and hurl myself over.

"I'll do anything. I just want to get out of Welter."

My response to this was, "You know my mother killed herself, don't you?"

I didn't think he heard me, so I said it again.

"I heard you the first time." Billy paused. "My mom told me Aunt Sally was stung by bees. She said she got an allergic reaction and died in her sleep."

"And you believed her?" I asked incredulously. "It was suicide, Billy. She sealed off the windows, stuck her head in the oven, and turned on the gas."

We were both so distraught we had to go home—Billy because he felt duped and me because my aunt had trivialized my mother's covert and complex planning to a single bee sting. Although I regretted telling my cousin the truth, I could no more keep myself from saying the words aloud than I could stop seeing Tobias's skull cracked at the base and the Weaver straddling his body, her hands red with his blood. The truth festered like the itch of dry skin, which I scratched again and again, even at the most inopportune moments.

During a meeting on Monday with Graham, Audrey, and a client from Blue Cross and Blue Shield, I explained that the Blues's high loss ratio stemmed from their reinsurance practice and could be corrected through contract negotiation. When I finished, I cleared my throat. "My mother killed herself," I announced. "She stuck her head in the oven and turned on the gas."

"I'm so sorry." The client glanced at Graham, then back at me. "Should you be here today?"

"Oh, she's been dead twenty-two years." I gathered my papers. "We'll have the proposal ready next week, which will include a work plan, a feasibility study, and our fees. Should I call you Tuesday to follow up?"

Graham shot me a look. *What?* I wanted to say. *I'm just telling the truth. We should all tell the truth. Graham, you haven't slept with your own wife in two years. You'd feel so good if you said it out loud.* Unfortunately, Graham didn't see it that way and in his office after the meeting, he said that I seemed distracted and I should take a week of vacation, or longer if necessary.

"I'm going through changes," I explained, wondering if I should tell him about Tobias. *My friends and I killed an old boyfriend,* I could state in my new matter-of-fact way. *Do you know how much blood is in a person's head? It's staggering.* "Maybe I could use some time off."

I quickly learn that being away from the office does more harm than good, especially since I have nothing to do all day but wait for a SWAT team to kick open my door and haul me downtown. With all this free time, my thoughts drift to suicide, my mother's as well as my own. If this is her legacy, I decide, then I need to accept it. If this is my destiny, then I should embrace it. I pull out my death list and study it carefully, weighing my options.

What most people don't understand is that in the mind of a potential suicide, there are no assumptions to ponder, no "What ifs?" to analyze. The assumptions, as it were, become a foregone conclusion. Instead there are only options, each of which becomes equally plausible. And not just options for self-destruction, I mean all options. Should I get my morning coffee or slash my wrists? Take the train to the Cloisters or hang myself? Order Chinese or jump off a building? When you have two concepts in your head, both of which feel equally plausible, the question is not "What if?" but "Which?" And if you don't share these equally plausible, and equally seductive, options with anyone else, there's no one to tell you which of the two might actually be the more intelligent choice.

Although the girls and I are talking, our conversations sound different. We speak in platitudes: *He deserved what he got, his time had come, he asked for it,* which dilute any emotion we may otherwise feel. I continue to announce that my mother committed suicide; so many times, in fact, that Laura finally says, "Heard you loud and clear, Janey. Let's give it a rest."

But I can't stop. I say it to my doorman, to fellow video renters at Blockbuster, and to deeply uninterested check-out girls at the Food Emporium. Unfortunately, the effect of telling the world about my mother doesn't connect me to anyone or anything. On the contrary, I feel a profound sense of detachment. I hear the literalness of the words, but over time their meaning becomes lost. I suppose the same thing is happening in Group's conversations. Our clichéd speech has an anesthetizing effect, which enables us to create distance between the magnitude of Tobias's death and our horror at actually having caused it.

We got together a few days after that fateful Friday. I spoke to the girls over the weekend, when Billy was taking a nap, but no one had seen or heard from the Weaver, and she didn't show up at Ivy's apartment, where we met instead of T.G.I. Friday's.

"It's not a good idea to go back there," Laura told me on the phone. "In fact, none of us should be seen together." But she agreed to come to Ivy's and tell us what she and Valentine did with Tobias after we left.

Ivy took me on a tour of her apartment, off Fifty-seventh Street, which is a gorgeous two-story duplex with a panoramic view of the city. She and Jackson were in the midst of divorce proceedings and, apparently, the var-mi-ent had millions squirreled away.

"He's tryin' to hide his assets," Ivy said as she showed me the master bedroom, "but mah lawyer is a pit bull. He's gonna get me everything Ah deserve." She smiled, although she didn't seem happy. "Ah badgered Jackson until he admitted he was with more women than just Ole Miss during our marriage."

"Sounds like you're the pit bull," I said, to which she replied, "I learned a lot in Group." But neither of us laughed. She continued her tour and I admired the high ceilings. The apartment had two working fireplaces, one in the master bedroom and one in the living room where the girls were waiting. "You have a lovely place," I said, feeling uncomfortable being alone with her.

"Thank yew. Unfortunately, Jackson's tryin' to move me out."

"Where does he expect you to go?"

"Back home. To Alabama." I had started down the stairs when she grabbed my arm. "Ah'm real sorry, Janey, about Tobias."

"I'm sorry, too. I never meant for him to die. A prank's a prank, but I never thought—"

"Ah meant Ah'm sorry about how Ah acted, teasin' yew and all. Ah behaved badly and Ah'm real ashamed. Yew didn't deserve that. But Ah hadn't had a man's attention in such a long time and it felt so good—"

"You don't have to explain," I reassured her. "We all behaved badly. The guy's dead."

She nodded solemnly. "Ah also want yew to know that Ah believe the things yew said. Ah hate to speak ill of the dead, but that man—well, let's just say he got what he deserved."

"No one deserves to die like that, Ivy. But thank you for saying you believe me. I don't think anyone else does."

I didn't. Although no one said so explicitly, there was a tension in the air that I attributed to the girls' feeling that not only had I lied about being with Tobias, I'd led them into a situation from which there was no escape.

"Before we start," Laura said, taking a seat on Ivy's red leather couch, "I want to say that we're in this together. If one of us gets caught, we all get caught. Agreed?"

No one looked at me. Finally Bethany said, "Just turn yourself in, Jenny."

"Why should I?"

"You said he was your boyfriend and he wasn't. You said nothing would go wrong and it did. It was *your* plan."

"So what? His hand slipped, and he hit his head. It was an accident."

"But why should we all have to worry? If one of us confesses, the rest of us can move on. Look, I'll visit you in jail. I'll bring books, gum, cigarettes, whatever you want."

"Have you ever heard the word 'accessory,' you idiot?" Natasha interrupted. "We're *all* accountable. We aided and abetted, then covered up the whole thing. And if you think you can make some deal with the police and not go to jail, you're insane."

"You'd really blame this on me, Bethany?" I asked. "After all we've been through?"

"Wait," Valentine cut in. "No one's going to jail. Laura, Suzanna, and I took care of everything." She explained that the three of them got rid of the blood, cleaned the room, and packed up the supplies. Then they dressed Tobias and walked him down the stairs, which, luckily, were propped open. "We were frantic because we weren't sure when Moe would get back, but we finished around seven. The stairwell was empty, so no one saw us, although it wouldn't have mattered if they had. We put a thermal cap on Tobias's head and Ginger's patch over his eye. He looked like he'd had too much to drink, which was what we told the cab-driver who took us to St. Vincent's." It was at St. Vincent's, she said, where the Weaver presented the situation to a friend in the morgue.

"Can we trust this guy?" Natasha asked.

Valentine nodded. "He logged Tobias in as a homeless John Doe, just like Suzanna said. She answered all his questions and gave him some cash. She trusts him. We should, too."

"What about when Tobias turns up missing?" Natasha pressed. "What about when his parents start looking for him? The police will get involved."

"They'll never connect Tobias to the John Doe at St. Vincent's."

"You can't know that for sure. If they do, they'll be led to Moe, who'll lead them to us. Oh my God, we're going to jail!" Natasha flung her head between her knees and started panting.

"Calm down, Natasha. I trust Suzanna. Besides, in the unlikely event that someone's led to us, all we have to say is that it was an accident, which we all know it was."

"But we covered it up!" Natasha screeched. "They'll do an investigation. They'll ask all kinds of questions. They have DNA testing. No one will get away. We're totally busted."

"Let me finish. The guy at the morgue promised us that if the police do come around, they won't get any answers. Apparently, corpses get lost all the time and—"

"There's something else you're not telling us, isn't there?" I interrupted. "Otherwise, you'd be freaking out just like we are."

"I think," Valentine replied slowly, as if calculating how much she wanted us to know, "the guy in the morgue may have had a crush on Suzanna—"

"What is it with men? This guy's so in love with her, he'll cover up a murder?"

"It's reckless endangerment, Janey, not murder. I looked it up. It wouldn't even be that if we'd called an ambulance. But we didn't . . ." She trailed off.

"Then it's the Weaver's fault!" Bethany said. "She and that dumb dog should be in the pokey."

"Does she cast a spell on these guys?" I asked. "She's not even pretty."

"It's the red hair," Laura said. "I told you. Men *love* red hair."

"No," Ivy cut in. "It's the damsel-in-distress syndrome. Ah know Jackson loves that about me. Loved," she said, catching herself. "He *used to* love that about me." I reached for her hand and squeezed it, not only in a gesture of comfort, but also one of forgiveness.

"Is the Weaver seeing this guy?" I asked. "The morguetician? Is she sleeping with him?"

Valentine shrugged. "She didn't say, and at this point, it's none of our business. But she wanted me to make it clear that no one should worry. The situation is under control. She doesn't want any calls, and under no circumstances should anyone stop by the hospital. She also said it's best if we don't speak to each other. Nor should we meet in public. Given all she's done for us, I think we should respect her wishes and leave her alone."

"She really hates us, doesn't she?" I asked Valentine.

"She doesn't *hate* any of you. She just wants to make sure no one gets caught."

"What about my sunglasses? They're still in the boardroom."

"We checked the place ten times before we left and didn't find any sunglasses. You must've lost them somewhere else."

Natasha looked around the room. "It's going to be very hard. I need you guys. You're my only friends. Valentine, who will I talk to?"

Valentine got up. "That's not for me to decide," she said firmly. "Just don't be stupid."

Natasha called that same night. "You'll talk to me, Janey, won't you?"

"Of course. I need you as much as you need me." We made plans to see each other in a few days. "Go back to work," I told her. "And act as if everything's the same."

"But it's not. Nothing's the same."

"And nothing's different except that Tobias is dead. His being alive didn't have any more impact on your life than his death should. Besides, it wasn't our fault. It was an accident. An accident," I repeated.

Ivy and Natasha called the next day. Even Bethany called, promising she wouldn't go to the police. "I'd never do that to you,

Jenny. All for one and one for all, right?" Then she said she'd tried to reach the Weaver. "She wouldn't answer her phone at home and her cell-phone message says she's out of town, but I'm gonna keep trying."

"Leave her alone," I said, not wanting to tell Bethany that I'd also been calling the Weaver and hadn't had any luck. *Where was she? South America? Didn't people on the lam go to Argentina?* "I'm serious, Bethany. Don't call her. She didn't want to be involved in the first place." *And don't call me, you traitor. I'm heading out to Argentina.* Hasta la vista, *baby!*

"But I have to talk to her. I have to know for sure that nothing bad will happen."

"Nothing bad will happen. If you act like everything's normal, soon it'll feel that way. You'll see. That night with Tobias will be a bad dream. Nothing more, nothing less."

Despite my many doubts, and the nervous way I watch *America's Most Wanted,* waiting for my picture to appear under their 1-800-Tips Line, I want to believe this. And soon, as the days pass and the police don't lynch me, I begin to relax.

I develop a routine. I have breakfast at the diner on Sheridan Square where Tobias used to get his morning coffee. Then I walk to St. Vincent's to say hello to the Weaver. The personnel lady tells me she's away on vacation, but I sit in the waiting room anyway. I figure the vacation is her cover story and she'll appear any minute in her pretty pink nurse suit.

At noon I begin my meandering stroll down Bank Street, hoping to bump into the Weaver out walking Ginger. I peer into Tobias's window, but his apartment is dark, and there's no movement inside. My afternoons are spent watching back-to-back talk shows and calling the Weaver. I never leave a message but continue to hit Redial and hang up when her machine clicks on. I even call Tobias, but he doesn't answer either. I scour the paper and watch the news, but I don't see any reference to a missing frat boy, certainly not a dead one. Then at night I read books about war criminals and how to beat polygraph tests. Overall it's not such a bad way to spend my time, although my feet hurt from walking all day in bad shoes.

I can't stop thinking about suicide. Dr. Hensen used to say that my suicide ideation is its own pathology, that I derive pleasure from the planning, the way other people dream about leaving their wives or embezzling money. In fact, during Group he persuaded me to keep fantasizing. I'd only be in danger, he said, if I ran out of options.

Back then, though, with Dr. Hensen, I had other fantasies to distract me. The prospect of running into Tobias, of hearing his apology, of us being buried together on a hillside overlooking the Atlantic in the Teague Family Cemetery gave me the strength I needed to keep moving forward. But with Tobias gone, I'm growing splintered and defeated. I've become hyperaware of my actions and thoughts, watching myself as if through someone else's eyes. I also feel lost, as if I've let go of the cord that yoked what it means to live with how it feels to be alive. My mortality has become intermingled with Tobias's and can only be salvaged if the Weaver appears. If she lets me apologize, I think, then I would feel better. I could do something good. I could cleanse my guilt. I could hope for redemption.

I begin to dream about her. In my dreams, the Weaver looks like my mother, but she has her own facial features, especially the arched eyebrows. I know she's the Weaver, but I'm also sure she's my mother and their simultaneous presence unsettles and confuses me. The Weaver/my mother stands over my bed, but when she leans in to kiss me, she shakes her head back and forth, losing her dangly silver earrings in her wild red hair. In these dreams, unlike those of the past, I feel no comfort. I also have the sensation of needing to say something important, something meaningful, but can't quite reach the words to say them aloud. Then just as I have them, I wake up and all my words are lost.

After a week or so, I take off my babushka-style scarf and I stop looking over my shoulder, but I haven't stopped wondering what will happen next. I continue to call the Weaver, although there's never any answer, and I still check the paper, but there's never any news. Ever since that evening with Tobias, I've had a nagging feeling that something's amiss, that I've overlooked an important aspect concerning his death. It's not the sunglasses. It's not the blood. It's something vague and distant, like the words on the tip of my tongue in my dream.

I tirelessly revisit that night, studying each moment again and again, and for some inexplicable reason, I keep returning to Ginger. I focus on her swollen paw, then see Tobias's cracked head, but can't come up with the detail that links the two images.

And so I press on. My days pass without incident. No burly men holding guns push me into unmarked vehicles. I'm not called down to the station to take part in a lineup. And the Weaver doesn't return from South America or some town in Utah where she's been placed under witness protection in exchange for her testimony.

I continue to ponder my uncertain future. (See a movie or blow my brains out? Have a tuna sandwich or swallow rat poison?) And I continue to wait for the Weaver to call and my knot of uncertainty to worry itself out. Whatever we did that night to incriminate ourselves (hair left behind for DNA testing, fingerprints on the mahogany table) will eventually be exposed. Then I'll have all the data I need to forecast the "When?" proposition. It's only a matter of time. Like my long-lost mother who shows up in my dreams, the answer will appear. In the end, whether I'm ready or not, the truth will come to me.

16

Bethany peers into my face. "What's wrong, Jenny? You look awful."

I take in her ballroom skirt, peach twin set, and lizard-skin ankle boots. "You, on the other hand, look outstanding."

We're back at T.G.I. Friday's for our second Group session since Tobias got hurt. Last week, the six of us spent the entire time speculating about the news (or absence thereof) and trying to guess where the Weaver might be. At the end of the night, we promised to refrain from mentioning Tobias again. It was time, we agreed, to return to us.

"So where's Ivy?" Laura asks, glancing at the door. "She's a half hour late."

A minute later, Ivy strolls into the restaurant wearing an oversize floppy hat and black wraparound sunglasses. She mumbles hello and sits down.

"Take off the hat," Bethany says. "We don't have to be incognito anymore."

"Ah'm not in-cog-nito. Ah just like the hat." Ivy rests her chin on her hand, using the hat's floppy brim to hide the left side of her face.

"Why are you sitting like that?" Laura wants to know.

"Why am Ah sitting like what?"

"With your hand covering your cheek. What are you hiding?"

I can't keep quiet any longer. "I think we should get Tobias's body out of the morgue, take him to his apartment, and make the whole thing look like a suicide. This way, we won't be scouring the news all day."

Laura's voice is calm. "I'm not scouring the news." She looks at Valentine. "Are you?"

Valentine shakes her head. "We're finished with Tobias."

"Think about it. We put a gun in his hand and write a note. Someone writing a fake suicide note to conceal a murder—"

"It was reckless endangerment, Janey," Valentine reminds me. "Not murder."

"—usually imitates the dead person's handwriting exactly, which is why they get caught. So all we have to do is write the note in block letters. Or type it into his computer."

Laura stares at me over her glasses. "What's the preoccupation with suicide?"

"Janey has a point," Ivy says. "We should at least agree on a story in case his body is found. It's been three weeks. Somethin's bound to happen anytime now."

"It's over, Ivy," Laura says, "just like Valentine said. Now show us your face or I'll rip that hat off your head myself."

I'm unsettled by Laura's and Valentine's composure. The waiter appears, but Laura doesn't even look up. When she doesn't offer him a tit shot, it occurs to me that Tobias's death may have quashed her need to act out in public. But the longer I study her, the more certain I am something else is going on.

"Ivy!" Bethany cries. "What happened to you? Jenny, look at her!"

I turn. Ivy's face is handless and hatless and completely exposed. Her left eyelid droops, making the rest of her face look palsied. "Ivy," I ask, sucking in a gasp, "is that from Botox?"

She nods and puts her sunglasses back on.

"I thought you were feeling better."

"Ah was. Then Ah got a call from my lawyer and Ah realized Ah'm gonna be a forty-two-year-old divorcée. Who's gonna want to date me? Ah'm gonna live alone in that big ole apartment like some broken-down mule."

"So Jackson's letting you keep the apartment!" Bethany claps. "We should celebrate."

Laura points to Ivy. "Does she look like she wants to celebrate, you dope?"

"Yes, look at me. Ah'm a broken-down mule with ptosis."

"Is that what it's called?" Natasha pushes up her cheeks as if her face is made of clay and she can shape it with her fingers. "Is it just from the Botox or is it an aging thing? Do you think I'll get it? Are there herbs I can take? Should I stop drinking red wine?"

"No, Natasha," Laura snaps. "You should take a tranquilizer and shut the fuck up. Ivy, it can be fixed, right?"

She nods. "Dr. Vaughn said it happens sometimes when the Botox accidentally spreads to the eyelid muscles. He said Ah should look normal in a month. He gave me eyedrops, but they aren't helping. Ah just have to wait and see." She sighs sadly. "Ah may need more surgery." For the first time since I've met her, the prospect of additional surgery doesn't excite her.

Natasha's still pinching her cheeks. "Can Botox spread into your brain?"

"Dr. Vaughn said Ah'd be fine. Ah just have to give it time."

"I'm going to find this Dr. Vaughn," Bethany vows, "and tell him that if he ever lays a hand on you again, I'm gonna shove a Botox needle up his ass." She whips her head around. "I know! We should all go to his office. We'll scare the hell out of him. We can—"

"Bethany," Laura says, "our last attempt to make a point didn't prove so successful. Let's sit this one out."

"Has anyone spoken to the Weaver's mother?" I ask. "Maybe she knows something."

"I doubt it," Laura says. "And if we call, she'll just get suspicious." She turns to Valentine and a look passes between them. But I'm too caught up in thinking about the Weaver to contemplate its meaning or even if there's meaning at all to be contemplated.

You're back!" Audrey exclaims as she walks into my office.

I motion for her to sit down. "I've been back for almost two weeks."

"I know, but I've been with a client in Nashville. Did you miss me?" She leans over to hug me.

I instantly recoil. *Did I miss her? Was she my child?*

"I missed you," she continues. "You want to go over the Blue

Cross deal? Graham let me meet with the client myself. It was so exciting!"

"That's great." I push my glasses up the bridge of my nose. "But I'm really busy. Can you come back later?" She nods, obviously deflated. "Shut the door behind you!" I call out.

She sticks her head back in. "Want to go to lunch today? My treat?"

I shake my head and turn back to my computer, grateful for the silence. But as I start to work, I become increasingly uncomfortable. When did I become someone who could watch a man die and not confess? Was it when my mother left me to wait for her unlikely return? When I had no one to tell when my period came, no one to help me fill out college applications, no one to watch me graduate? Did being motherless also make me merciless?

I call Audrey back to my office. When she sits down, her short skirt hikes up, exposing her thigh. "I knew something was different!" she exclaims. "You're not wearing sunglasses. I never realized your eyes were so pretty."

I blink back sudden tears. "I did a horrible thing," I whisper.

She waves. "Oh, it wasn't so bad. You just said something personal about your mom to the Blue Cross guy. We still got the business."

"That's not what I meant." I study Audrey carefully. She isn't a dope. She's just a girl on the brink of womanhood facing an uncertain future. I was a girl like her once, not nearly as pretty, but as helpful and as dedicated. If I try, I can show her how business works, hold her hand when she worries, encourage her to take risks. I can do that for her. I can be a good mentor—and a good mother, too, if that's what she needs. Just because I don't have one doesn't mean I can't be one. And maybe I can save her from ending up like me.

I choose my words carefully. "Graham wouldn't have put you on the Blue Cross engagement if he didn't think you were up to it, Audrey. It's a big step. I hope you'll ask for my help if you need it."

"Of course, Janey. I thought we were a team."

"We are. But when I was first starting out, I made a lot of mistakes. I don't want you to make those same mistakes. If you still need a mentor, I can help you."

She rises to hug me. "Of course I do. Thank you, thank you, thank you!"

"First, your enthusiasm is one of your best qualities, but people in business don't hug and they don't sign their E-mails with 'Love.' "

"Okay," she says sheepishly, sitting back down.

"You're a stunning woman. But to be taken seriously, you have to dress appropriately." I point to her suit. "Your skirts are too short and your heels are too high. If you want, I'll take you shopping for suits. And I don't mean old-lady suits, but"—I roll my eyes—"groovy outfits that show off your figure without exposing it."

She bites her lip as if fighting back tears.

"I'm sorry if I've offended you, Audrey. I'm not very good at this, but I'll get better."

"I'm not offended. I just don't know what to say."

"You don't have to say anything. All you need to do is listen. You should go to Women's Initiative meetings where you can network. It's important to have friends in this business. I should've cultivated friendships long ago. But it's not too late for you."

"It's not too late for you either, Janey. Lots of people change their ways, even at your age."

I blanch but stand up. "Come here. Give me a hug."

"Really?"

"I'm different already," I say.

I need your help," Natasha whispers into the phone two nights later.

"I don't do tax returns," I remind her, yawning and rolling over to look at the clock. "Why are you whispering?"

"There's a man in my house and I want him to leave."

Envisioning a thug wielding a knife, I sit up and snap on the light. Is he there to avenge Tobias's death? Who had betrayed us? Was it one of the girls? "Are you in danger, Natasha? Should I call the police? *Answer me: Are you in danger?*"

"Not yet. But I think he wants to have sex." Her voice rises in panic. "What if he doesn't floss? Imagine the bacteria lodged in his gums! You have to come over and make him leave."

Everything becomes clear. "You woke me up at midnight to talk about a *date*? Are you crazy?" When she whimpers, I backpedal. "I didn't mean crazy. You're not crazy. All of us are a little on edge lately. You like this guy, right?"

"Sure I like him. I like him *a lot*. Do you know how few eligible black men there are?"

"Yes, Natasha. You've told me many times, but there's probably a better time to discuss the implications of race and gender on the ever-shrinking dating pool. Maybe you're anxious because you *do* like him. Maybe you're worried that having sex will lead to intimacy, which—"

"Please come over and make him leave. Please, Janey? I'm down on Broome. It'll take you five minutes, maybe less, and I'll pay for the cab."

I pull on my clothes and head downtown. If she needs me, I'll rescue her. The same way, when the police show up and I agree to take the fall, she'll find a way to rescue me.

I've never been to Natasha's loft before and I'm surprised by how spare it is. She has a baby-grand piano, a hand-painted screen separating the bedroom from the foyer, and a few pieces of furniture. The walls are filled with paintings. I suspect Natasha did most of them. They're abstracts in vibrant colors, which make the empty apartment feel opulent.

Natasha hugs me, then turns to a tall man seated on her leather couch. "Blake's an architect," she says by way of introduction. "Janey's an accountant."

I hold out my hand. "I'm an actuary, Blake, and I'm sorry to barge in on you like this."

"She's pregnant," Natasha goes on, "but she's not sure who the father is."

I glare at her. "That's right. I'm pregnant and I don't know who the father is, but Natasha offered to help me figure it out tonight."

"I see." Blake glances at my stomach, an affable grin on his face.

His deep voice is sexy, and when he shakes my hand, his grip is firm. "I was just leaving."

"That's too bad." He's gorgeous: almond-shaped eyes flecked with gold, luscious brown skin, and a muscular body clad in cashmere and suede. "Natasha," I blurt out, "Blake is the most handsome man I've ever seen. This close, I mean."

"Thank you," he replies, still staring at my stomach, still grinning.

Seated at the piano, Natasha's fingers dance over the keys without touching them. "He is." But instead of looking at Blake, moon-faced and misty-eyed (like me), she stares at her hands and continues to play without making a sound.

"Aren't you going to say good-bye, Natasha?" I pull her up from the bench and push her toward him. Blake raises her hand to his lips. I don't know how she feels, but I'm swooning.

I move behind the screen, hoping to see them kiss if only for the vicarious thrill. "I'll be back here," I call. "Go about your business."

"I had fun tonight," I hear Natasha tell him. I also hear her pacing back and forth in her small foyer. *Stand still!* I silently shout. *Don't let this one go.*

"I had fun tonight, too," Blake replies. "We always have fun. And if you're not ready to make love"—he says "make love" in a deep baritone. Behind the screen, I swoon again—"just say so. I don't want you to feel pressured into anything you don't want to do."

I'm ready! You won't be pressuring me. I scratch the screen with my fingers and it starts to wobble. "Oh no!" I yelp. "Sorry about that, young lovers."

"I think I'm ready," Natasha says. But when I hear her unlock, relock, then unlock the door, I know she's spinning into anxiety's orbit. *Keep going, Natasha. Say good night.* "Blake, I really like you." *That's it. Stay focused.* "But I have to tell you—" *No! You have nothing to tell him.* "—I worry about plaque. People who neglect their gums risk all kinds of cancer."

There's a long silence. Finally Blake says, in sheer amazement, "You don't want to kiss me because you think I have plaque?"

"Oh no, Blake . . ." And she's off. "Not just plaque. There's tar-

tar and bacteria and God knows what other types of organisms growing in the deep cavities of your mouth—"

"She's just kidding," I cut in. "She's trying to tell you that she's afraid to kiss you because she's shy. Don't listen to her."

"Janey, you know how I feel about germs, and I don't know what his brushing regimen entails. Blake, do you brush three times a day and after snacks?"

"I gotta go," he says quickly. "Good luck with the baby, Janey." Then he mutters, "I'll call you," which echoes through the loft like a death toll.

"What a jerk!" Natasha pulls me onto the piano bench. I listen to her rant about how rude Blake is and why didn't she see the signs and when will she meet a guy who isn't fucked up. "He was probably just using me for sex," she concludes.

"But you didn't have sex. How could he be using you?"

"He was *going* to use me. I know guys like him. Thank you so much for coming over. You really saved me. Can you believe that asshole?"

I look into her eyes. "He's not an asshole. He's a nice guy."

"Are you saying it's me?" She turns her back to me and pings a piano key.

"Yes, Natasha. It's you." I get up to go. "Maybe it's never been them—the men, I mean." I think of the girls: Bethany, Laura, Valentine, the Weaver, Ivy, and me, especially me. I also think about Tobias, now dead. "Maybe it's us. Maybe it's been us all along."

I'm at Tobias's diner on Sheridan Square, ordering coffee during my ritual Saturday constitutional when I hear a man behind me say, "I believe I was ahead of you."

Turning back, I see a dark-haired man eyeing me. I tell him I'm sorry and step out of the line so he can move ahead.

He chuckles. "I'm teasing. Stay where you are." He squints. "I feel as if I know you from somewhere. Do you work around here?"

I shake my head. I want to speak, but I'm too flustered. Despite his very large head (a head that rises from his neck like a beach ball with eyes), he's tall and handsome and wearing a suit, just like the D/L/CEO from my fantasies. And he's using *my* lines, my infamous "I believe I was ahead of you" and "Boy, you look familiar." This has to be destiny. "Do you work here?" I ask finally.

"In this diner?"

Ha ha ha, Big Head. "No, you're wearing a suit and it's Saturday."

"I'm a cop. I stopped in for a doughnut." He holds out his hand. "Lawrence Hilton."

"Janey Fabre." I drop my purse and all its contents fall out. A cop? Is he here to nab me? I scramble to pick up my keys.

Lawrence crouches by my side. "Let me help you."

"Oh no. I'm fine." As I stand, I bump up against him. Is that a gun in his jacket? I try to get past his body, but he's blocking my path. He's not a big man, but the size of his head gives him enormous dimensions. His forehead slopes like a dinosaur egg, his eyes have the radii of tires, and his nose—Jesus, that nose is an Egyptian pyramid lodged on his face. I picture thousands of Israelites scaling it with ropes.

"I really have to go," I squeak. *Just cock your head, Lawrence, and give me some room.*

"I was just kidding about being a detective. It's a residual boyhood fantasy. I'm actually a lawyer for St. Vincent's. I have to go into the office today."

"You're a lawyer?" An L of the D/L/CEO variety. At long last I found one! "At St. Vincent's? Any corpses appearing unexpectedly?"

"Lady!" The counter guy calls. "Toasted poppy today or just coffee?"

When I say, "Just coffee," Lawrence asks me if I'd like to have coffee with him.

I turn to say I'd love to have coffee with you, Mr. Lawrence the L with your cute colossal head, but something furry rubs against my ankle. It's a dog, a Pekingese just like Ginger, wearing a pink doggy sweater and tiny knit cap. I kneel to read her tags. Lawrence kneels, too, and lifts her paw in greeting. "Hello, pooch," he says, rubbing her ears.

As I watch him, the missing detail about Tobias comes to me suddenly, as if it's always been there, as if I've never not known.

That night in the boardroom when Tobias walked in, Ginger leapt at the sound of his voice. He called her "poochie" and asked what had happened to her paw. There was a familiarity between them, an intimacy that suggested they'd already met.

"No dogs in here!" The counter guy shouts.

As Ginger scurries away, I start to tremble.

Lawrence catches my arm. "You okay?"

"I'm fine," I reply, not fine at all. "I have to go to the ladies' room."

I follow Ginger to the back of the diner where she jumps into a booth holding a man and a woman. I approach the table on rubbery legs, losing myself in the space that exists between fantasy and reality, seeing and not seeing the couple before me. It's the Weaver and Tobias looking tanned and rested. Her hair is pulled off her face and he's wearing my sunglasses on top of his head. Neither of them is aware of my presence, but both are alive and well—and together.

17

A fact every actuary learns: Regardless of how many "What if" scenarios you design or assumptions you make, reality is always an ambush.

Neither Tobias nor the Weaver glances up as I approach the booth. Tobias's hair is bleached white, his teeth gleam against his bronzed skin, and his eyes are as blue as Bahamian water. Then I look at the Weaver and have a stunning revelation, which has nothing at all to do with my being duped.

She's been on the beach, too. There's a spray of freckles across her sunburned nose. Her red hair is woven with strands of gold. A sliver of sun filters through the window, illuminating her face as if she is radiating light from within. Her dangly earrings act like a prism, casting snatches of color across her face, causing her green eyes to sparkle. The overall effect is one of great beauty, enhanced by the loving way Tobias gazes at her. I feel as if I'm seeing the Weaver for the very first time and, in doing so, she's alive in a way I never considered before. This is how men see her, I think, amazed by the way her attractiveness quotient grew by a simple change in perspective. It's not just the red hair or her vulnerability or the way she loves Ginger. It's the whole woman who sits here, self-possessed and dignified, glowing in the sunlight.

"You're gorgeous," I blurt out. "I never realized, Suzanna. I never noticed."

That's when the two of them see me, although I have to admit that among the three of us, Tobias is clearly the most stunned.

"Janey," he says, practically choking on his juice. "What are you doing here?"

I pluck my sunglasses from his head. "These are mine. How can you see out of them?"

"We have the same prescription." He laughs shrilly, like a girl. "What a coincidence!"

I turn to the Weaver. "I don't believe in coincidence anymore."

"Janey." She speaks softly, avoiding my eyes. "This is not what you think."

"You don't know what I think. *I* don't even know what I think."

"Tobias and I are just friends. We met on the street once, months ago. I didn't realize until later in Group that he was the same guy—your guy."

"How many Tobias Teagues can there be in the world?"

"He told me his name was Toby. I didn't make the connection. When I did, I tried to discourage you from going after him—you know I did—but you were so adamant, I decided to back off and rearrange things so no one would get hurt. Your rage, all the girls' rage, scared me. I thought that by intervening, I could diffuse your anger and in the end we'd all have a laugh."

"At my expense. It was at my expense. Isn't that right, Toby?"

"Listen," he starts, "I didn't—"

"Shut up." I turn to the Weaver. "You betrayed me." Then I remember Laura and Valentine's uncharacteristic calm the previous Thursday. "All of you."

She shakes her head. When I see her dangly silver earrings swing back and forth, I feel the urge to throw up. "Natasha, Bethany, and Ivy didn't know a thing until yesterday. The whole plan, the boardroom, the blood—that was me. Just me."

"And Valentine." I pause. "And Laura." Of all the girls, Laura's betrayal cuts the deepest.

"Valentine didn't want to go along with it. I had to convince her. And Laura figured it out as it was happening. That's why she stayed. She was going to tell you. We all planned to tell you."

"When?"

The Weaver doesn't answer.

"Suzanna, I've been looking for *you* so *I* could apologize. I thought it was me. All this time, I thought it had to be me." I turn and walk away quickly, wanting to run.

"I never meant to hurt you," she calls.

"Yes, you did. Or else I wouldn't have found out like this."

On my way out the door, Lawrence Hilton catches my arm. "What's wrong?"

"Nothing," I answer, but I can hear my voice sounding dreamy and faraway. "I'm perfectly fine."

"Are you still up for coffee?"

"I don't think so, Lawrence Hilton. My life has suddenly changed." I nudge him aside and race out of the diner. I swear I hear Tobias laughing behind me. The sound rings in my ears all the way home.

My phone starts to ring two hours later. All the girls call, one after the other, but I don't pick up or listen to the messages. Eventually I turn off the machine and spend the rest of the weekend in bed, the only place, it seems, where I truly am safe.

I keep thinking about the Weaver. Tobias chose her. She saves people's lives. She has vibrant red hair. And men, Laura said, *love* red hair. In the end, the girls were willing to stand behind her and cast me aside. Just like my father. To him I was an inferior replacement for my dead mother, a constant reminder of the one woman he would always love more.

Dr. Hensen used to tell me that I am entitled to live just like anyone else, that my life—the *me*—is of equal value. I always agreed because I couldn't bear his scrutiny, and if I agreed, he'd leave me alone. But I've never believed in my own value, in the entitlement of me. I believe that every act of self-assertion is conceited and shameful, every instance of self-love narcissistic and dirty. I don't deserve to love myself or other people. And I certainly don't deserve to feel love in return. I asserted myself with the girls. I said, I am here. I said, I exist. I even said, I love you. But instead of feeling entitled, I feel ashamed. In so many ways, I feel dirty.

I'm in my office on Wednesday when Graham shows up. "Got a minute?"

I wave to a chair.

"Why are you wearing sunglasses?"

"I can't find my regular glasses." I lean forward. "What can I do for you?"

"Remember the proposal you sent to Chrysler a year and a half ago?"

I nod. "They turned us down. Said they were going with Buck."

"They weren't happy with the team Buck put together. I don't know the whole story, but Brad Pierce called and asked if we'd meet him. It's tomorrow, which is Thursday, I think."

I look at my calendar. There's a big black X through Thursday. No more Group. It's been four days since I ran into Tobias and the Weaver. Four days spent dodging the girls. They've called and stopped by my house, but I won't answer the phone or open the door. They've even come to my office, but I had Audrey tell them I wasn't in. I throw out their letters and delete their E-mails. I can't bear hearing their fake apologies and lame excuses. The Weaver, Valentine, and Laura betrayed me. Natasha, Bethany, and Ivy hid the truth. All six of them humiliated me. Nothing they could say would undo this.

I look up. "To be honest, Graham, I can't meet with Brad. I know Chrysler could mean big money, but I have too much on my mind right now."

"You want to tell me what's going on?" Graham's face is grave. His sudden concern makes me burst into tears.

"I don't know how this happened." I wipe my nose on my sleeve and Graham offers me a handkerchief, which reminds me of Moe, who reminds me of my father. "I used to be so composed and now I have snot everywhere." I blow into the handkerchief.

"You might have been composed," Graham replies, "but you weren't much fun." He closes my door. "Janey, I've never told anyone this except my wife, but the year I was up for partner, the stress almost killed me. I worked day and night. I drank too much and was belligerent and hostile. I even had an affair—"

"You told your wife *that*?"

"I left that part out, but the point is—"

"That's a big part. You had an affair. And apparently it wasn't the first time—or the last." I say this as if it's me, not his wife, whom he betrayed.

He narrows his eyes. "There were mitigating circumstances." His voice is no longer warm, nor is it kind. "You don't know the whole story and, frankly, it's none of your business."

"*You* came in here, Graham. I didn't come to you. And I think what you did was unforgivable. I would've kicked you out."

"I was trying to tell you how stressful it is to make partner. I see the toll it's taking on you. I came in here as your boss and your mentor, and in some sense, your friend. I didn't come for absolution." He gets up. "Watch yourself, Janey. You should know when to quit."

Graham doesn't know me that well. I won't quit until I've destroyed everything. But when he starts to leave, I panic. "Wait! I'm sorry. I was out of line. Please accept my apology."

He considers it. After a few long seconds he says, "Apology accepted," then he sits down and picks up where he left off. "The year I was up for partner was the worst of my life. But it doesn't have to be that way for you. I know you're having a rough time. I see how hard you work. But don't let the job get the better of you. I have no doubt you'll make partner. But you've got to let up. Find a boyfriend, get married, have a kid. Find a life outside the office."

"You think it's so easy to get married? You think I can just go get a boyfriend? I'm not exactly the ingenue I was at twenty-three."

"I only meant there's a world beyond this." He smacks my computer.

"I know. And I appreciate it. But to tell you the truth, I'm not sure I want to make partner. I'm not sure what I want."

"It's a big decision, and you're right to question it. But don't throw away all your years of hard work. You're a brilliant actuary, Janey. More important, you have a hell of a lot of integrity. You'd be making a big mistake not to consider the option. And if you do decide to lobby for partner, I promise I'll be here to help you every step of the way."

I smile. "I never knew you cared."

"You never asked, which is your biggest flaw. You have to learn to ask for help. And," he adds, "my wife *did* kick me out. For two years. It was my first and only affair." He pauses. "People are fallible. You can't forget that. Especially when you make partner."

"*If* I make partner," I say.

"I'm your boss," he retorts. "Don't correct me."

Audrey peers into my office after Graham walks out. "Is everything okay?"

"Go back to your desk." I swallow hard, refusing to cry in front of her.

"You seem so sad lately. Do you want to talk?" I shake my head, but she won't stop. "Are you sure? I'm happy to listen."

"I said *no*! Just leave me alone."

She scurries away. Hit with a pang of guilt, I call her on the phone. "Audrey, I'm sorry. I didn't mean to yell. I know you're trying to be helpful. Please forgive me. I'm acting like an ass."

"I understand," she says, still sounding hurt.

"I'm having a personal crisis, a crisis of faith."

"Oh, Janey, I didn't know you were religious."

I sigh. "That's a figure of speech. I've had a disagreement with some friends. I shouldn't take my problems out on you. I'm sorry."

"I forgive you. We're a team. You can always talk to me."

"I appreciate that. We'll have lunch tomorrow. Tomorrow will be a better day."

But the next day is no better. Neither is the one after that. My head is heavy. My throat burns. My chest feels cracked open, carved out, and stripped for parts. I lie on my bed, seeping into the sheets like water into sand. I don't want to die as much as I want to drift, but I want to drift away and never return.

My nights are long and restless and I wake up every morning in a drugless stupor. At the office, I try to get lost in my financial models, but they don't give me any relief. I can't step inside the work. I can't get displaced. I keep thinking about the girls, wondering how they could deceive me. I know Ivy was equally tricked;

and Bethany and Natasha aren't nearly as culpable as the Weaver, Valentine, and Laura, but they all mass together in my mind, the same way they did when I first started Group and couldn't distinguish one girl from the other.

Loneliness has no past and no future. I feel so profoundly alone I find it hard to believe that I'd ever had friends. Nor can I imagine what my life would be like if they were to come back. It's as though I've always existed, will always exist, in a singular state. My loneliness cannot be altered by willpower or reason. I'm painfully self-conscious, the embarrassment of the girls' deception endlessly compounded, making me that much more visible, that much more freakish. I sense people staring at me, seeing my shame and my dirtiness, clucking at how foolish I was to feel so entitled. As the me in the world contracts, the me in my head expands and both feel awkward and clumsy. But I can't muster the resolve to change my situation. I can't distance myself from my own mental minefield any more than I can give in to my distress and call someone for help.

I consider talking to Dr. Hensen, but don't know how to explain all that has happened. One moment I was moving securely through time, in sync with the girls, with the world, with my life. Then a split second later, with no warning at all, I'm totally out of step. This is what happens when you court yourself too well, when you fail to watch the signs. It's easy to become complacent when you connect with someone else. I had connected six times so I became six times more smug, six times more careless.

"This should teach you a lesson, Janey," my father told me after my mother killed herself. "Don't ever love nobody more'n they love you." He was right. But what he should've said was, "Better you shouldn't love anyone at all."

I thought that might be you!" Moe exclaims as I get off the elevator. "I got a call from downstairs that Janey Fabre was here, but couldn't place the name. You here for another tour of the boardroom?"

Forcing a smile, I shake his hand. "I've seen enough of that room to last me the rest of my life. Actually, I'm not sure I know why I came by. I just had the urge to see you. Where's Martha?"

"Took some time off to care for her sister. There are no tours today, so I'm all by my lonesome." He motions for me to sit. "What can I do you for?"

"Well," I begin, then falter. "That night with my friends was a setup. But not for Tobias. It was a setup for me. Did the girls tell you that?"

Moe shakes his head. "I got back to the boardroom just as they were leaving. You were already gone. I don't know what I was thinking when I told you ladies to go ahead. Musta had my head screwed on wrong. I went back to stop you, but the three gals who were still here were packed up and ready to go. The place was real neat. Nothing out of whack. Mr. Teague was laughing, so I figured something funny musta happened, but no one told me what."

"Were the girls laughing, too?"

"Just Mr. Teague. He said, 'Moe, I oughta pop you,' but that was it. Didn't seem angry, but he hasn't brought any women up since. I felt real bad for not doing my job. I saw the guns—"

"The guns weren't loaded." I touch Moe's big arm. "But you couldn't know that. And you did do your job. You protected Martha and yourself from a bunch of crazy women. Anyway, it's not worth getting into now. It's over."

"Is it?"

I nod but can't look at him. "Seems that way. I haven't spoken to my friends." I shrug. "Too angry, I guess."

"I'm sure it'll all work out in the end." He takes my hand. "Let's go for a walk."

Moe leads me through the executive suite. We stop in front of the oil portraits of all the board members. "I bet you end up on this wall someday," he says.

"Me? I'm just a poor girl from the sticks." We continue to walk down the long hallway and I tell him he reminds me of my father. "Before his strokes, he worked in a paper mill. He loved his work. I haven't seen him in a long time."

Moe peers down the hall. "It's a funny thing, fathers and

daughters. When my youngest went to law school, it was one of my proudest moments. We didn't have any lawyers in my family." He chuckles. "I was a mailman and she's off in Washington clerking for a judge. Crazy world, huh? I don't see her much, but boy do I miss her."

"My father was just relieved to get rid of me."

"What would make you say that?"

I resume walking. "I didn't come here to burden you with my problems."

"No burden. It's just conversation."

"My father broke down when my mother killed herself. He went back to work, but he was never the same. He treated me as if I was a stranger. He stayed as far away as possible."

Moe's still holding my hand. "Maybe in his own way, he was trying to protect you."

"That's a reach." I love the feel of his hand wrapped around mine. He has hands that could crush a rock with one squeeze.

"Fathers do anything to make their girls happy. Sometimes it even means saying good-bye." Moe speaks wistfully, as if thinking about his own daughter in Washington, preoccupied with her life, too busy to visit, forgetting to call.

"If you were my father," I blurt out, "I'd come by to see you every day."

"But I'm not," he says softly. "Although I would appreciate a visit now and then." He releases my hand. "Maybe you should go see your pop."

"And say what? He doesn't speak to me."

"He has his ways. All men have their ways and their reasons, however foolish they may seem." He propels me gently toward the elevators. "Tell him you think about him even though you're far away. Tell him you miss him."

"And if he doesn't respond?"

"Tell him again."

I'm on the highway, driving north, when I remember that I didn't call Graham to let him know I'd be out of the office for a few days.

I jerk around, afraid I also forgot my bag, but it's on the backseat where I dumped it with a stack of unread mail.

After leaving Moe, I wandered down Twenty-third Street. I passed the school for the blind, the residence for the deaf, the halfway house for the mentally ill, and United Cerebral Palsy. It was late in the day and the buses were being loaded in front of the UCP building. I stopped to help the drivers roll the wheelchairs into the vans and buckle them to the floor. Then I went into a bar and ordered a Coke.

I sat in the back, where a boy and girl were shooting pool. They were young (kids from the School of Visual Arts, probably) and appeared happy, too happy to watch for long. On a napkin, I began a letter. "Dear Dr. Hensen, you were right when you said we were moving too fast. We had a bit of trouble, or rather, I think I'm in trouble. I'd like to see you—"

The boy dropped his cue stick, which clattered as it hit the floor. He pulled the girl to his chest and hugged her hard. After watching them for a minute, I decided I couldn't stay in the city with all these kids around, so I stuck the letter in my pocket, stopped off at my apartment, went to Hertz, and got on the road.

I hit a patch of ice and the rented Taurus starts to skid. It's the end of March and the roads are slick, but I hold on to the wheel. It'll take me six hours to get to my father. A week ago, I told Natasha that it wasn't them, the men, who were always to blame. "Maybe it's us," I'd said. "Maybe it's been us all along." If this was true, then I needed to see Zack. I needed to better understand his relationship with my mother, his relationship with me. *It's all your fault!* I'd screamed at him. But whose fault was it really? He wasn't the only person she left.

Although I'd gotten used to my mother's untenable sadness, I was actually surprised when she killed herself. I suppose I shouldn't have been. For her, for me, suicide is a hunger. It's not the hunger you get right before dinner; it's the hunger you get when you haven't eaten for days, when you're starved, when you're hollow. You stave off that hunger as long as you can but, like all unsatisfied cravings, it always returns.

A truck cuts me off. I swerve, barely missing his fender. But the near collision doesn't startle me. On the contrary, as I watch myself realign the Taurus, I'm filled with a sense of well-being. I look at the cars traveling in the opposite direction, then inch to the left where there's no divider between me and the oncoming traffic. I blink from the glare of the headlights. All it takes is a turn of the wheel and I can shatter the long line of lights headed toward me.

It's really so simple. Forget the plans and the schemes. Forget the death list. I just have to be willing to die. But haven't I always known how simple it is? Didn't I know how easily she sealed off the trailer and turned on the gas? Didn't I know that when she got down on her knees, her mind was already at rest, her heart no longer aflutter? And when she lay her head on the small oven door, didn't she finally satisfy her bottomless appetite? Wasn't her first breath of the sick smell in the air as reassuring as her own mother's voice? Don't I deserve to feel equally satisfied? I'm her, aren't I? Reborn in her image, fated to follow the path she laid out? *Dr. Hensen, I think I'm in trouble.* There are no decisions to make. The truth is so simple. I am my mother. I am willing to die.

I watch the cars speed by, their tires spitting up snow and ice. *Dr. Hensen?* I close my eyes. *I didn't call. But you'll forgive me?* And because it's so simple, because it's my destiny, because I have absolutely nothing else, I turn the wheel an inch to the left, step on the gas, and accelerate into space.

LIFE CONTINGENCIES

18

To an actuary, when the word "risk" is used as a noun, it expresses the possibility of loss or injury. As a verb, the same word denotes the exposing of one's person or property to loss or injury. Thus within the common meaning of "risk," there are two related but distinct elements: (1) the idea of loss or injury and (2) that of uncertainty.

Within an economic setting, the actuary expresses loss in terms of monetary units. Whether it is economic loss (theft), income loss (death and disability), or the loss of property value, the actuary refers to this as "economic loss." If the probability of economic loss is greater than zero but less than one, some party is exposed to the possibility of economic loss. Actuaries define this exposure as economic risk.

It is almost axiomatic that human beings have an aversion to economic loss, and hence to economic risk. Some persons are more risk averse than others, but very few expose themselves or their belongings needlessly. There are those individuals who seem to thrive on taking chances even though there seems to be no possibility of gain; but even these people find some satisfaction that compensates for the possibility of negative economic consequences.

Consider the Suicide ("Suicide" expressed as a noun, not a verb). The Suicide finds satisfaction in the act of dying or, rather, comfort in the probability of no longer living. The actuary refers to the Suicide, collectively, as an anomaly because suicide (expressed as a verb, not a noun) is a disruption of the natural course of life over a standard amount of time, a period generally assumed to be fifty years or more.

The actuary accounts for this anomaly using complex techniques that adjust actual experience to that of conjecture. When these techniques work well, deviations of experience from what was initially assumed are taken care of in an orderly fashion. The Suicide becomes a statistic (instead of a demented woman in a rental car following in her dead mother's footsteps), the continuance of present trends is rationally adjusted, and the concept of economic risk as it relates to economic loss remains universally (though not absolutely) true.

But how does the actuary refer to the Suicide who finds comfort in the act of ending her life, yet fails miserably at the attempt?

I call myself a spineless fool.

Needless to say, I arrive at the outskirts of Welter alive and intact. At the very last second, just as I veered into oncoming traffic, I jerked the wheel to the right. To be honest, I didn't realign the car because I was struck by Life's very preciousness. Nor did I have a cinematic epiphany wherein I realized I could transform my despair into ecstasy by forgiving the girls, returning to my office, and spending the rest of my days doing good works. The truth is, I jerked the wheel because I wanted to spare myself the humiliation of causing a multicar pileup and the indignity of dying in a rented Ford Taurus that smelled faintly of urine.

I took a deep breath, put both hands on the wheel, and decided that the car-on-the-highway death scenario was (in a word) dopey. Better I should set myself on fire, jump off the Brooklyn Bridge, and end my days in a blaze of glory that could be misconstrued as a protest against human-rights violations. Why deny myself the possibility of martyrdom, much less a shot at continuing coverage on *CNN Headline News*?

As a concession to my first real suicide attempt (albeit uninspired and unsuccessful), I got off at the next exit. I spent the night at a Days Inn outside Woodstock, where I left a message for Graham saying I had a family emergency and I'd be out of the office for a few days but would check in as soon as I could. Then I took a bath and watched HBO. In the morning, sated by a movie in which Sean Connery has sex with a woman less than half his age (which some people would consider as painful as a multicar pileup), I got back on the road and made my way into Welter. I couldn't die without seeing my father again. After that, I promised myself, my time would come.

Welter, New York, was established in the late 1800s at the foothills of the Adirondack Mountains about one hundred miles northeast of Syracuse. When you approach it from the south, bypassing Albany and Schenectady, Little Falls and Utica, the view from the car is breathtaking. Clapboard houses line the highway. Lush fields hold grazing cattle. Snow-capped mountains rise majestically against the horizon. From miles away, the entire scene is a blaze of color: endless blue sky, bleached clouds, acres of green hills.

At half that distance, the scene shifts. You take a right onto a two-lane highway that twists and turns. Along the road, now dark and less inviting, are broken-down trailers, particleboard shacks, and A-frame houses with asphalt siding hidden among snags of fallen, decaying trees. Occasionally you pass a collapsing porch roof propped up with long pieces of raw lumber and a concrete slab that had once been the foundation for Smith & Son's Hardware. Beverly's Academy of Dance is boarded up, and a mile farther, on the left, past thick patches of trees and muddy trucks parked on gravel lawns, are the burned-out remains of the First Baptist Church. A sign announcing a long-ago flea market is still stuck in the ground.

To get to Welter, you have to go through Lynden Falls, where there's a reprieve from the surrounding poverty. Lynden Falls is a quaint village with rows of houses that are scrupulously maintained, several well-attended churches, and an annual Christmas tree lighting ceremony where the entire town gathers for hot chocolate. The pulp is in Lynden Falls, situated at the spot where the Black River meets the Wild Moose. I always dreamed of living in Lynden Falls when I was growing up. The kids there were no more wealthy than I was, some were even poorer, but they all seemed to possess an air of community, which was absent from Welter, a town you sometimes admitted you came from, but never had any reason to go to.

Welter is located twelve miles north. It exists mainly as someplace between other towns, and you can pass through without even realizing it. Welter has no town square, no banks or movie theaters. There's a Mini Mart, once a 7-Eleven, where you can get gas, cigarettes, and frozen burritos; a locksmith/gun supply, which opens according to hunting season; and Jungle Jim's, a miserable little bar housed in a cinder-block bunker.

Two things characterize Welter: aluminum-sided trailers set off from the road, way back in the woods where the sun never shines; and the stink of the pulp, which fills the air like fog twenty-four hours a day, seven days a week. In the winter the trailers are closed up, and except for an occasional dim light in the front window, they appear uninhabited. The cold months last much longer up here than they do in New York City. It takes a lot to endure a winter in Lewis County. Everything in this part of the state is forest, deer warnings, and endless banks of snow.

I drive slowly, waiting for the break in the trees right after the second turn, about five hundred yards up from the old Hostess outlet. The snow is packed almost four feet high, and the roads are wet and slippery. I feel the ice crunching under my tires as I cut the wheel and turn into a driveway hidden from the road by a thick patch of trees.

I pull up to the trailer. Years ago, my father nailed siding to the trailer to build an extension, but he never finished the project, and now the siding is warped, destroyed after too many winters and too much neglect. He also cleared away the debris in front in a vain attempt to grow a lawn, but new trees had fallen and the walkway is cluttered.

As far as I know, no one has been inside since Willy and Rufus took him to the Shepherd Center. I expect to find the trailer gutted, like the torched hulls of abandoned cars, but surprisingly, it's intact. The front steps are gone, but they've been replaced by stacked cinder blocks. All the windows have glass in the panes.

Inside the car, I put on my hat and gloves and knot my scarf.

When I get out, the freezing air numbs my lips, fogs my glasses, and stings my eyes. I hold my scarf against my mouth and climb up to the trailer door, which I fling open with one hand.

The air inside is as cold as the air outside. I snap on a lamp. Amazingly, it works. The trailer is exactly as I last saw it. There's no hospital bed or TV, but my father's chair still faces the empty console, the seat imprinted with the shape of his ass, as if he only got up an hour ago.

I go into the kitchen and turn on the faucet, which sputters, then spews chunks of filth. I hold my hand under the water until it finally runs clear, then shut it off and take a step toward the oven. The door is wide open, its outsides streaked with black soot and its insides splattered with grease and charred with burnt clumps that look like muddy divots. She must have been really desperate, I think, to stick her head in there.

As I survey the trailer, I begin to get vertigo. It amazes me that I'd lived in this house for so many years with my parents, but can't sustain a single memory of the three of us together. It's a strange mutation of time, the way my growing up had lasted for years but I can remember it only in split-second images, and how altogether different it is from the day I found my mother dead. I can recall each detail of that afternoon with stunning precision: her beige cotton nightgown, the black grit on her feet bottoms, my father's blank stare, the way he doubled over when they lifted her into the ambulance. The event passed so quickly, but in my mind it lasted for hours. I still hang on to the memory, analyzing everything we did, everything we said. I often wonder what I would think about if someone other than me had found her. Would I have anything else to remember her by?

Who's there?"

I can hear my cousin Billy shouting, but I'm lost in the twilight of sleep and can't be sure if he's actually there or calling to me from inside a dream. He yells again and I slowly wake up. When I'm finally able to orient myself, I realize I'm in my old bed, shivering from the cold.

"Who's in here?" Billy demands. "I saw your car parked outside. Who are you?"

"It's Janey." My voice is just a whisper. How long was I asleep? I look out the window. It's dark already. "It's me, Billy," I say, gaining strength.

My cousin stands in the middle of the trailer, his gangly body swaddled in a down jacket. He wears a thermal cap and hunting boots and holds a six-pack of Rolling Rock. He has his arm around a girl who's also swaddled in down, her stringy blond hair peeking out of a hat. All I can see of their faces are two pairs of watery eyes and two red-tipped noses.

"Janey! What are you doing here?" Billy flips on a space heater. "You're shaking!" He throws a blanket around me. "You could've froze to death."

I put my hands inside my armpits to help heat my body and let him rub my shoulders. I introduce myself to the girl, who smiles shyly but doesn't respond.

"This is Martine," Billy says. "Sometimes we come here after school to . . . you know . . ." Grinning, he nuzzles Martine's neck. She giggles, crooks a finger through his belt loop, and pulls him toward her. I'm reminded of the two kids I saw together in the bar before I left New York. I can't seem to escape young, happy couples.

"Does your mother know you come here?" I ask, realizing that he must've replaced the lightbulbs and windows.

"Are you gonna tell her?"

I shake my head. "But come on. Of all places."

Martine pulls her scarf off her mouth. "Billy came to stay with you in the city, right? I'd give anything to live down there. It's great, I bet. Anything's gotta be better than Welter."

Her voice, shrill and childlike, grates on me. I move to the door. The afternoon has assumed a surreal quality. I need to escape, to check in with Audrey, to normalize.

Billy catches my hand. "Where are you going?" His brows are knitted in concern, which catches me off guard. He's a good kid, I think. Always has been. "Are you going to Mom's?"

"I guess I should," I tell him. "It'd be kind of rude if I didn't, right?"

"Are you okay? I didn't mean to scare you before. And when I asked what you were doing here, I didn't mean to sound like you shouldn't be here, like you're trespassing or something. Sometimes I'm a real jerk. This is your house and all—"

"Don't worry." I squeeze his upper arm, which is thick with muscle. When did he get so strong? And why didn't I notice when he was visiting me? "I just wanted to see the place. Besides, this used to be my house." I take the blanket off my shoulders and hand it to him. "But now it's just a dirty, run-down trailer. It doesn't belong to anyone."

Aunt Honey, my mother's younger sister, lives in Lynden Falls, about a mile from the pulp. She married a trucker after high school. Uncle Jerry isn't home very often but he makes enough money to keep them afloat.

I never saw much of Aunt Honey growing up. She and my uncle bought a place in Lynden Falls, down the street from my grandparents, who lived in the same house until they died—Grandpa when I was four and Nana six months later. Grandpa Langston owned a general store where the entire family worked. Unlike my father's parents, they weren't pulpers and held anyone who worked at the mill in disdain. Lynden Fall's social hierarchy is as self-conscious as Manhattan's, albeit on a much smaller scale. In upstate New York, the slightest financial disparity will foster the most egregious arrogance, which is passed down from generation to generation.

My mother claimed Aunt Honey carried on the Langston superiority complex long after their parents died, which made me dislike my aunt intensely, although I always had a soft spot for Billy, who was adopted when I was in college. Over the years, I caught snippets of my aunt's life from my parents' conversations. My mother whipped information like daggers of accusations at my father, who responded with self-righteous silence. *Honey said Jerry would be happy to introduce you to his boss if you want to leave the pulp. Honey's redecorating her kitchen. Honey's going to Jamaica. Honey's going to Florida. Honey's going to the Grand Canyon, Zack! The Grand Canyon!*

Each time I heard the name "Honey," I tensed up. Even when Aunt Honey came by to check up on me after my mother died, I was rude and bratty and impossible to talk to. Like I said, I was my mother's girl and my loyalty runs deep; so deep, in fact, I still feel angry with my aunt as I drive the twelve miles between Welter and Lynden Falls.

I stand outside her A-frame house and take a deep breath. I haven't seen her since my father's second stroke, and I hadn't spoken to her until Billy called and asked if he could visit for the weekend. Our conversation was stilted but polite. I got the impression that Aunt Honey didn't think much of me for abandoning my dad, but I told myself she didn't know the entire story and had no right to judge. Still, I tremble as I bend my head against the bitter wind and trudge up her lawn.

"Jane? Oh my God! What are you doing here?" Aunt Honey is holding a broom. She steps back to open the storm door. "Come inside! Get out of the cold."

I force a smile. "I was in the neighborhood."

"Is something wrong?" We stand facing each other, unsure if we should hug. Like me, my aunt has big glasses, which make her eyes appear small behind the thick lenses.

"I'm up here visiting my father and thought I'd stop by."

"When was the last time you saw Zack?"

"When was the last time *you* saw Zack?" I counter, forgetting my promise to remain charming and pleasant. I stomp my boots on her mat to shake off the snow.

"Let's not get into that, dear." Aunt Honey sweeps the floor by my feet as if she can sweep away my unpleasantness. "Tell me all about New York. How's your job? Do you have a boyfriend? Gosh, it's been a long time." She's doing a terrible job of hiding her discomfort with my sudden and unexplained appearance. "Billy told me you had a beautiful apartment in New York. You must be very successful. You're an accountant, right? You always were a math whiz."

"I'm still an accountant." We glance at each other at the same time, then quickly turn away. Aunt Honey was born ten years after my mother, but they share the same icy blue eyes, patrician nose, and delicate chin. Aunt Honey looks older and softer than I remember. Her hair's piled on top of her head, and the few strands that escaped curl around her ears and frame her face. She wears pink sweatpants with a matching sweatshirt that has a green mallard embroidered across the chest.

"Cute outfit," I tell her. Just as I step into her living room, she catches my arm and points to my feet.

"Your boots. I just cleaned the carpet. It picks up everything."

"Oh sure. Sorry." Feeling like a poor relation, I kneel down to take off my shoes, then pad to the couch in my socks. We both sit. "Well," I say finally, "where does one begin?"

"You look good," she tells me.

"You do, too." I play with the doily that's on the arm of the couch. "Does this have a purpose?" I wonder if she'd laugh if I put it on my head.

"Keeps the fabric from wearing down."

"I always thought they were just decoration." There's a long beat of silence. I can hear myself breathe. I hold my breath as long as I can, ticking off the seconds. "Actually"—I gasp as I expel the air from my lungs—"I wonder . . ."

My aunt glances up expectantly.

"Forget it."

"No, tell me. What do you wonder?"

I look into her eyes. I want to ask what my mother was like when she was in high school, if there was ever a time she was happy to have me, why she left when I was so young. Instead I blurt out, "I wonder how you can live with yourself for blowing me off when my mother died. I'm your fucking niece. Didn't you feel any responsibility at all?" It takes me a second to realize what I've said, but my aunt answers before I can take it back.

"I tried my best, Jane. I came around to see you, but you didn't speak to me. You wouldn't even look at me."

"What did you want from me? I was only thirteen. My mother was dead."

"I meant after," she says softly, reaching out to me. Instinctively, I jerk away. "All the years after. I tried. I know it was hard for you with Sally being so sick—"

"You should have tried harder. Everyone should've tried a little goddamn harder." Now that the words are out, I can't stop them. "You didn't do shit! You came around a few times, pitied me a little, and went right back to your perfect fucking life and your stupid fucking doilies. You left me to rot with Zack. So don't tell me how hard you tried because you don't even know about trying!" I stand. "I have to get out of here."

I'm out the door and walking to my car when I hear my aunt call, "Jane, don't leave. Please don't leave. Let's talk awhile."

I stand in the wind and watch her beckon from the house. With nowhere else to go, I hike back up the path to the porch. When I reach her, I see tears glistening in her lashes, behind her big glasses. "I'm sorry," I tell her quietly. "What I said was awful. I'm nasty when I'm nervous. It's a defense mechanism. I don't mean anything by it."

"When I get nervous, I clean." She leads me into the house and we both sit on the couch. "You probably think I'm crazy."

"God no. I have a friend who gets liposuction when she gets nervous. And another friend who obsesses about arsenic levels in tap water. And another friend who eats everything in sight." I grin. "She loves the rolls they have at T.G.I. Friday's—" I stop. I *had* these friends, I correct myself, *had* them.

"I'm glad all those clichés about neurotic New Yorkers aren't true." Aunt Honey laughs, but a sob escapes her. "You're right, though." She dabs her eyes with the hem of her duck sweatshirt. "I should've tried harder. My therapist says I couldn't deal with the pain. It was all so much, so quick. And I was so angry—not with you, Jane, never with you. Although I suppose it didn't feel that way." She looks up at me and I see my mother's blue eyes.

"Your *therapist*?" I search her for more signs of my mother. "You see a therapist?"

"Now you sound like Zack. Yes, I'm in counseling. I also have indoor plumbing and, from time to time, take in a moving-picture show."

"I didn't mean it like that. I've been in therapy, too."

We sit for a while, not speaking, then I jump up from the couch, go outside, and knock on the door. "Hi," I say softly when Aunt

Honey opens it. "It's been a long time since we've seen each other, and I wanted to stop by. I know I haven't been easy to reach, literally or figuratively. But I have so many questions about my mother and didn't know where else to go." I pause. "Can I come in?"

She stares at me. "You're all grown up." She exhales. "You look so much like Sally. I got spooked when I saw your face, but it's you. It's really you." She holds out her hand and I take it.

So when was the last time you saw my father?" I ask, picking off imaginary lint from my sweater. "I'm not passing judgment. I just want to know because I haven't seen him myself in a long time and I'm not sure what to expect."

"I haven't seen him in a long time either, not since he went to Shepherd. I do see Willy and Rufus occasionally, and I ask about Zack. They're both retired now, so I suppose they don't have much else to do but visit with him. Apparently, he's made lots of progress. He's in a wheelchair, but his speech is better. It's terrible, I know, that I haven't gone to see him, but—"

"Please don't apologize. No one's gonna crown me daughter of the year anytime soon."

Aunt Honey pushes her glasses up the bridge of her nose. "Jane, I've known your dad almost all my life. He's a difficult man. I also know how hard it was for you when Sally died. I wish I could've helped you, but I was grieving myself and didn't know how. It's no excuse, but it's the truth. Anyways, you've done right by Zack. Don't you ever think different. I only wish Billy had your sense of responsibility. He's running around, drinking, staying out all night. I feel like I don't know him anymore."

"He's a good kid. He'll come around." I pause. "You said my mother was sick. Was it cancer?" I ask this hopefully. If my mother had sacrificed herself to spare me the pain of a fatal illness, then she was a martyr. If she was perfect and holy, I'd have all my answers.

Behind her glasses, Aunt Honey's eyes widen. "Zack never talked to you about Sally?"

I shake my head. "Was it breast cancer? A brain tumor?" I reel off Alzheimer's, leukemia, multiple sclerosis, and blood clots until Aunt Honey asks me to please stop.

"Sally was diagnosed with manic depression. She had terrible mood swings but refused to take her medication. You don't remember?" Aunt Honey answers her own question. "How could you know? You were just a little girl."

I'm quiet awhile. "I knew. I just didn't want to know. It was better not to know."

"Maybe back then. But now you're all grown up."

"All the more reason to deny it. Part of me still believes she killed herself because she hated Welter. Or my dad. Or me." I look up. "She didn't hate my father, did she?"

"She loved him. And she loved you. Zack didn't want to believe she was sick. He thought psychiatry was nonsense. He made excuses for her. Said she was tired and overworked. He couldn't see that no matter how much he did for her, how hard he loved her, she wasn't gonna get better." She shakes her head. "He was so ashamed."

"How do you know?"

"He told me after the funeral. But once he admitted it, he didn't come around anymore. Zack wasn't one to look weak."

"Which is why he refused your help when he had his stroke. It just seems so crazy to carry around all that guilt for so long."

"Whose guilt are you referring to?" Aunt Honey asks. "His or yours?"

My eyes water. "Why do you think she did it?"

"It's an evil illness. Gets you in its clutches and won't shake you loose. Unless you're in the thick of it yourself, you can't imagine how awful it is."

"I can," I tell her softly, wanting and not wanting to talk about my mother; wanting and not wanting to talk about myself.

"You suffer from manic-depression?"

"She left me the depression," I say wryly. "She took the manic with her." And then the tears come. "How could she leave me? I was her daughter! How does a person do that?"

"I don't know. I really don't know."

I fight the impulse to touch her as long as I can, but the urge is unbearable. I lunge forward. Nestle my nose in her neck. Breathe in her unfamiliar smell. Speak into the strands of her hair. "I was hoping enough time had passed and my dad would tell me about her. It's why I'm here, I guess."

"Don't expect too much from him." Aunt Honey strokes my head. I love the feel of her hand, the tender way she brushes my hair with her fingers. It's been so long since I've been touched by a mother and it amazes me how much I can miss something I barely had. "In many ways, Zack's become just like her—tormented, troubled, terribly unhappy. Maybe you shouldn't go right now."

I sit up. "I have to know her, Aunt Honey. I have to find out."

Aunt Honey nods. Her big glasses reflect the glow of the lamp and in them I see my mother's face. Then I realize that it's myself I am seeing mirrored in her lenses as they wink in the light.

19

The decision to see my father was a mistake, I decide, pulling out of the parking lot at the Shepherd Center. When the receptionist called his room and announced that I was in the lobby, he told her he didn't have a daughter and under no circumstances should I be let in. At first I got weepy and begged her to tell me his room number. But she was as big as a bull and equally stubborn and told me that "long-term residents don't gotta see anyone they don't want to. Specially," she added, "when they lie about who they are."

I tried to reason with her. "Dorothy," I said politely, glancing at her name tag, "why would I lie about being his daughter? Who else would I be?"

When she wouldn't budge, I demanded to see the director. "*I* pay Mr. Fabre's bills. I came all the way from New York City to see him and I'll be damned if I'll let you stop me." She raised an eyebrow but didn't move. "Do it! Get your boss out here right now."

Dorothy gave me a fuck-you eye roll but lifted the phone in her chubby hand. "At least," she said as she dialed, "say *please*. Mr. Reilly, where you at? We have an uninvited visitor who wants to see Mr. Fabre."

But when Mr. Reilly appeared and pumped my hand in greeting, he reiterated what Dorothy had said. "While I appreciate your desire to see your father—"

"If he *is* her father," Dorothy interrupted. "Mr. Fabre claims he don't got a daughter."

"He *doesn't have* a daughter," I chimed in, correcting her grammar. "I mean, he has a daughter, and I'm her. Why won't you just let me see him?"

"Ms. Fabre." Mr. Reilly was calm, but his voice belied an effeminate haughtiness, which was compounded by his exaggerated gestures. "The center's philosophy is to give our long-term residents as much autonomy as possible. Most residents are dependent on caregivers for mobility and other bodily functions that you and I take for granted. Thus, when it comes to visitation, we try to afford them as much say as possible over who visits and when. We don't want them to feel they are at the mercy of a relative's whim to visit whenever the mood strikes."

I reminded him that I paid Zack's bills.

"I can give you a tour of the facilities," he said, dramatically stroking his woolly mustache. "But I can't admit you to Mr. Fabre's room without his consent."

Dorothy glanced at me with a look of triumph. "I told her the very same thing."

"This isn't some drunk tank in Beverly Hills," I spat out. "It's not as if you're housing Bette Davis back there."

"Nor is it a zoo, Ms. Fabre, where you can be admitted at your leisure to throw peanuts. Perhaps if you came back tomorrow, we could have a word with your father in the meantime. You'll need to call ahead, of course, but I'll see if some type of arrangement can be made."

"But I pay his bills," I repeated, my boldness waning.

"Be that as it may, your financial support does not entitle you to unscheduled visitation."

"I doubt Zack is fit to determine who he wants to see. If you don't let me see him, I'll stop sending checks."

Mr. Reilly chuckled. "Mr. Fabre may be taciturn, but he certainly knows his own mind. And if you do decide to withdraw your funding, your father will be out on the street without appropriate care. But if that's what you want . . ." He trailed off with a wave.

"I'll be back tomorrow, but I suggest you tell my dad that I expect to see him. If he refuses, tell him I'll toss his ass back in the trailer he came from. You can also thank him"—I threw my scarf over my shoulder—"for making my visit so pleasant."

As I turn onto the highway, the Taurus hits a patch of ice and I start to skid. I immediately panic and want to slam on the brakes.

Instead, I suck in my breath, stay with the skid, and ease off the gas. The wheels eventually hit gravel, which slows the car down. I tap the brake with my toe, hold the car steady, and exhale in relief.

My vehicular triumph revives my mood. I'm determined to go back to the center the next day and force Zack to talk about my mother. I have to do this, not for me but for her. She deserves to be remembered, to have not died in vain even if that's how it seems she lived.

Back in my motel room, I call Aunt Honey. "He won't see me," I tell her, trying to hide my disappointment. "He even said he doesn't have a daughter."

"He's just a sad old fool, Jane. I told you not to trouble yourself with him. Some people can't deal with the past."

"Is that why you didn't tell Billy the truth? You could've done better than a bee sting, Aunt Honey."

"Wow," she replies, "you go right for the jugular, don't you? That wasn't necessary. You were already ahead."

"*Ahead?* What the hell do I have?"

"You got out of Welter. You're a professional. You make a nice living."

"But I don't have a family. I don't have anyone." I'm silent, overwhelmed by the reality of my situation. I am a family of one. I'm alone in the world.

"Jane? You still there? I'm sorry you found out I lied to Billy. I was afraid he wouldn't understand. Frankly, at the time, I didn't understand myself. I know you came up here hoping to get answers, but I don't think Zack can give you what you need. He wasn't capable of giving Sally what she needed. He—"

"He's my *father*. I have to give him a chance."

She waits before asking how she can help.

"Just be there when he fails me."

I try calling my father, but the operator at the Shepherd Center tells me his phone is off the hook. I retrieve my messages from my apartment. The girls have called. At first I don't want to listen, but quickly relent. They're worried, they tell me. Please call. They sound frantic.

"I'm really sorry," Laura says. "I know you don't believe this, but I have a reason for not telling you what the Weaver was up to. Please forgive me, Janey. Don't run away."

I don't erase any of the messages. I keep Ivy's promise of a two-for-one ass lift. "As soon as Ah found out, Ah called yew but yew wouldn't answer. We really got fooled, didn't we? Ah can't even look at the Weaver, Ah'm so spittin' mad. Anyway, yew and Ah deserve a treat. Dr. Vaughn promised to cut us a deal if we want to get our butts raised together. So call me soon and Ah'll set up a consultation." I also keep Valentine's threat to eat an entire black forest cake if I don't let her apologize, Bethany's offer to let me do her taxes, and Natasha's elaborate description of the new ventilation system she installed in her apartment.

I thumb through a J. Crew catalog, debating whether or not to pick up the phone. A letter slips from the pages. It's from Dr. Hensen and dated a few weeks before I caught the Weaver with Tobias.

Dear Janey, Laura, Bethany, Natasha, Ivy, Suzanna, and Valentine:

It's been a while since our last session, and I wanted to let you know that I regret how abruptly our Group ended. Although a few of you have kept me abreast of what's been happening in your lives, I felt compelled to tell you that I am still very invested in your well-being. I would be remiss if I didn't say how proud I am of all seven of you for the steps you've taken toward achieving mental health, and how pleased I am at the way you've come together to nurture and protect one another. You are all, each in your own way, very brave women. I don't say this to patronize you, but rather to applaud your ability to reach out to one another with dignity and empathy. I believe love begins when you cast aside your fears and expose yourself—your very true self—to another person. And look at you, Janey and Laura and Bethany and Natasha and Ivy and Suzanna and Valentine. Look at all of you! What love you have wrought. What a rare and generous gift you have given each other. I've never had a Group develop such an enduring connection, and while I don't take responsibility for

that connection, I will say I hope we may all meet again to continue our work together. Be well and remain in contact, not only with each other, but also with me.
Yours very truly,
Frederick W. Hensen
Harvard, B.A., M.A., Ph.D.

I stare at the letter a long time. If love begins when you expose yourself, when does it end? When my mother died and my father shut down, didn't he begin the long, slow process of love's termination? And didn't the girls destroy any love we had when they chose to betray me? I replay their messages a few more times because it feels so good to know that they're out there. Then I check out my butt in the mirror and consider Ivy's ass-lift proposal.

The next morning, I don't fare any better. Dorothy is waiting for me when I show up at reception. "Mr. Fabre has requested that we do not admit you into the Shepherd Center at all."

"I demand to see him."

"And he demands you don't."

"Call Mr. Reilly. Actually"—I lean over the desk—"I'll call him myself."

Despite her heft, Dorothy is quick. She snatches the phone away. "Mr. Reilly ain't here. But he told me that if you were to come in and make a ruckus, I was to call security."

I look over Dorothy's shoulder at the swinging double doors. White-coated doctors, physical therapists, and patients in wheelchairs glide through unchecked. "I want to see the facilities. I'm paying for them."

"Mr. Reilly will be back this afternoon. He's the only one who can give you a tour."

I'm about to leave when I see Willy stroll through the double doors. "Janey Fabre? Is that you? What are you doing here?"

I've known Bertram Williams since the day I was born. He's a short, hairy man with a powerful upper body and the bow-legged, arm-swinging gait of an ape. Willy is smaller than I remember and his gait's less cocksure and steady, but his hug is still breathtaking.

"I came to see Zack," I say when he lets me go. "But he won't see me."

"I wouldn't feel too terrible about that. He's been in a bitch of a mood lately. Jeez, you're all grown up." He turns to Dorothy. "Are you stonewalling this young lady?"

"Mr. Fabre doesn't want to see her, so I can't admit her. Besides, this young lady has been very rude."

"*Zack,*" Willy retorts, "doesn't know what the hell he wants. Who are you to come between a father and his daughter? Zack hasn't seen his little girl for a long time."

"Apparently, Bertram," old Dorothy spits, "Zack doesn't want to see his little girl."

Tears sting my eyes. "Forget it, Willy. I'll come back later and talk to the director."

Behind Dorothy, a nurse pushes a man in a wheelchair through the double doors. He's shouting, and his voice echoes through the lobby. Dorothy doesn't look back—she doesn't even glance up—to see who the resident is or why he's yelling.

"You sure you want to leave?" Willy asks. "I'm happy to take you back there. Rufus and Joe are coming by later. I know Zack will act decent once he sees you." He takes my hand. "Come with me. I don't give a crap what Dotty here has to say about it."

"I'll just call security, Bertram," Dorothy pipes up, "and have you thrown out with her."

"Would you shut up? This is important." Willy swings my hand. "God*damn,* you look good. How's New York City? I don't see a ring. You got a boyfriend?"

I study the double doors. "Everything's great. And if my dad doesn't want to see me, I'll just go back to New York. But you tell him I came, okay? You tell him I wanted to see him. Make sure he knows I was here."

"Will do." He eyes me. "It ain't like you to give up."

"Don't worry." I crack a smile. "Everything's under control."

My first and only call is to the Weaver. "Tell me when you first started talking to Dr. Hensen," I demand when she picks up the phone.

"Janey? Is that you? Oh my God, it's good to hear your voice. We're all so worried. Are you okay?"

"Just tell me when you first went to Dr. Hensen. Alone, I mean."

"I've been talking to him from the very beginning. Why does it matter?"

"From the first day?" I ask, incredulous. "Why did you talk to him and not to us?"

"I didn't know if I should stay in Group, so I went to talk to him about it. I didn't feel like I belonged. No one seemed to like me much and I felt excluded from your outings."

"You were always invited, Suzanna."

"No, I wasn't. Not really." I start to argue, but she cuts me off.

"I know what you call me. I'm the Weaver. The Dream Weaver. Did you think I wouldn't find out?"

"So you humiliated me because of a nickname? It wasn't even my idea. It was Laura's."

"I wasn't trying to humiliate you. I was worried things would get out of hand."

"I don't believe you. Let's start over. Who are you and what's the deal with your dog?"

"I'm nobody really. I feel like a nobody, or I did before Group. I always felt isolated, which Dr. Hensen says is a common problem for children of alcoholics. He helped me with that."

"Was it Dr. Hensen's idea that you hook up with Tobias and tell him about our plan?"

"Of course not. You know he'd never suggest that. I met Tobias a few months ago, when I was out walking Ginger by my apartment. He lives two doors down. Then I slept with him—"

I imagine them in the diner, two lovers together, laughing at me. "So you fell in love."

"We did not! Janey, you have such a selective memory. Remember how upset I was when I slept with a guy who didn't call me back? That guy was Tobias. In fact, the whole idiotic scheme you guys cooked up started with *my* distress."

"I remember you being upset about someone, but I didn't know it was Tobias."

"At the time, he was just a random guy, so I didn't tell you his name. But when I heard what you were planning to do to him, I got nervous. I was afraid something terrible would happen. Dr. Hensen told me to reason with you; to point out that nothing good would come of revenge. I talked it over with Valentine and we decided to show you how foolish you were acting. We had Tobias respond to Ivy when she flirted with him. He let her think it was her idea they were going to the boardroom—"

"How could you do that to Ivy? She never did anything to you."

"I don't know. I really don't. I didn't think she'd actually fall for him. I thought she'd be able to keep an objective distance."

"Would you have been able to?"

"Probably not," she admits. "But I didn't think about it that way. I got caught up—"

"Think about it now. Think about how bad Ivy must have felt. Think about how bad you would've felt."

"It's all I've *been* thinking about. I've apologized to Ivy a million times. Today was the first day she's spoken to me since I told her the truth. The whole thing was supposed to be a joke. Once we were in the boardroom, Tobias was supposed to hit his head against something, turned out the table was as good a place as any, which was why I brought all that blood from the hospital. We had every intention of explaining the next day, but—"

"I knew people didn't have that much blood in their heads!"

"Duh, Janey. I brought three bags from the blood bank."

"Okay, Suzanna. You had a plan. You're the double-secret agent. But I don't understand why Tobias agreed to go along with it. I thought he blew you off."

"I called him again. We started to see each other. After he supposedly died, we went to the Bahamas—"

"So he went along with it because he loved you." She doesn't answer. "Why did he love you?" I whisper. "Why did he love you and not me?"

"Why does anyone do anything? You can't choose who you love. But I don't love him. You have to believe me."

"Then why did you go on vacation with him?"

"I had a crush on him," she answers slowly. "When he didn't call me back, I got obsessed. I wasn't used to being rejected. I *thought* I was in love with him. But it wasn't love. Dr. Hensen helped me with that, too. You know what it's like to be obsessed, especially with someone who doesn't respond, someone who's not even that likable. Instead of running away, you chase him and chase him, but you can't ever catch him. Janey, you were invested in him for years, but not in Tobias the person he is now. You were invested in the memory of a guy who hurt you, a guy you were furious with."

I suddenly think about Zack. She could be talking about my father, I realize. Zack had hurt me and is still hurting me. And I'm still chasing him. Is my obsession with Tobias a sick incest thing? Am I headed for portrayal in a Lifetime movie: *Double Indemnity—Sex with My Father via a Frat Boy Proxy?* Is there a support group for this kind of thing?

"I can accept that you had a crush on Tobias," I say. "But still, you lied to us. You betrayed us. And you did it because you felt left out and talked about. You didn't want to protect us, Suzanna. You wanted to hurt us."

She doesn't answer.

"But you know what? I can forgive you. I'm your friend, and friends love each other, not for their perfection but for their flaws, because it's their flaws that make them human."

Suzanna perks up. "A few months after Group started, you and I bumped into each other on Bank Street. Remember? I was walking Ginger? She was wearing her purple beret? You acted as if you were ashamed to be seen with me. It made me angry. And the more you and the girls got along, the angrier I got. Valentine was angry, too. She was tired of Laura always telling her what to do. Every time Valentine picked up a roll, Laura smacked it out of her hands. So we came up with the plan. We had every intention of telling you the next day, but Laura figured out what was going on and suggested we wait. She said if we did, you'd realize how awful it is to lie to the people who trust you the most. She truly believed the exercise had therapeutic value even though it sounds ridiculous now that I'm saying it myself. You still there?"

"Uh-huh."

"Anyway, when Tobias and I got back from the Bahamas, we told Ivy, Natasha, and Bethany. They wanted to tell you immediately, but Laura said we should give it a few more days. She had this theory that if you found out we were all in on it, you'd be so shocked, you'd never lie again. She can be very persuasive, especially when she's wrong. After that, everything happened so quickly. You bumped into me and Tobias, then you took off." She exhales. "That's it. That's the whole plan. We were jealous and spiteful and now we're sorry. I feel so much better telling you. I knew you'd understand. You do understand, don't you? Janey? Hello?"

"ARE YOU OUT OF YOUR FUCKING MIND? How could you do that to me? Especially when you knew how I felt about Tobias?"

"Why are you yelling? You said we were friends. You said you loved my flaws."

"Are you *mental*? Did you tell Dr. Hensen what you did?"

"Yes. After you saw me in the diner with Tobias. He freaked. He wanted to call you. I promised I'd tell you myself, but I couldn't get in touch with you. Janey, I'm so sorry. It was my idea. All of it." She starts to wail. "How can you ever forgive me?"

I let her cry. "There is something you can do," I say finally, and tell her about my father. She immediately agrees to drive up.

"I'll be there by ten tonight," she promises. "And tomorrow I'll get you inside. I know exactly what to do. I'll take care of everything."

There's an awkward moment.

"So what's happening now?" I ask. "Between you and Tobias?"

"Nothing. We went away together because it was part of the plan—"

"—and because you liked him."

"That, too. But when we were away together, he disgusted me—"

"—because you're commitment-phobic and can't stand to have someone like you."

"That, too. But I also saw Tobias for what he really is—an insecure, pathetic guy. That morning in the diner, I was telling him it was over between us. But then you showed up."

"But then I showed up," I repeat. "You know what's so ironic? I always thought you were such an enigma. But you're not. You're just a regular woman. Although I never suspected you'd be capable of such pettiness. Bethany, yes. Laura, maybe. But you, never."

"Yeah, well," she replies. "No one's perfect."

I spend the rest of the day shopping with Aunt Honey for duck sweatshirts, then we go to a movie. When I get back to the Days Inn, I spot a St. Vincent's van in the parking lot. The Weaver is in the lobby waiting for me. In her arms, she holds Ginger, who's dressed in a red doggie sweater and black earmuffs. I look around for the girls, but they didn't come.

"I'm sorry," is the first thing the Weaver says when she steps outside. Her breath comes out of her mouth like a plume of smoke.

"I know." I try to quell my disappointment at the absence of the other girls. "It's freezing out here." I pick up Ginger and start walking to my room.

"Wait. I can't go inside until I say I'm sorry. And Valentine's sorry, too."

"I get it, Suzanna. You're sorry. Valentine's sorry. Come on. It's freezing."

"And the girls are sorry, too, for not telling you the truth as soon as they found out."

Then why aren't they here? And what the hell will she and I talk about for the rest of the night? Suzanna is squinting at me as if awaiting an answer. The wind whips through her red hair and blows it around her head like an overpicked Afro. With the light from the lobby shining on her face, I see her beauty again, vulnerable and sweet, and I can understand why Tobias loves her and not me. And yet she's just like me. She has the same longings and insecurities that I have, and I didn't treat her nicely. I feel shame and remorse. "You should've worn a hat," I tell her. "And a scarf."

"Do you think you can forgive us?" She blows on her hands to warm them.

"When I'm able to feel my fingers and toes, I'll consider it."

"Do you miss the girls?" she asks. "The pussy posse?"

I nod. "You guys are the first real friends I ever had. But do we have to talk about this out here?" I hold up her dog. "Ginger's face is covered in frost."

"She'll be fine." The Weaver's nonchalance toward her precious Pekingese shocks me. "I thought about asking everyone to come up with me, but I wanted to spend time alone with you. We could call them. I know they'd come if you asked."

I wrap my scarf around her neck. "I really want to see my father, and they wouldn't get here until tomorrow, which means we'd have to wait another day."

"But we could use their help getting you in and out of his place."

"I'm really cold. If you want to call them, fine, we'll call them. But can we go inside? Look at Ginger! Suzanna, I think your dog is dead."

"So you want me to call them?"

"Do what you want. I'm going inside."

I'm starting to walk away when she yells, "It's okay!" She slides the van door open and Laura and Ivy and Natasha and Bethany and Valentine pile out.

"It's about goddamn time, Jenny," Bethany declares. "My ass is chapped from sitting on the floor for six fucking hours. That van doesn't have any seats!"

"You came," is all I can think to say.

"We did." Laura takes my hand. "We all took the day off from work. But we weren't getting out of that van until we were sure you'd forgive us."

"You really came." I turn to Suzanna. "Thanks for this."

She smiles.

The seven of us stay up most of the night, just talking. "I'm sorry your dad's being such a jerk," Laura whispers just before morning. "But we'll get you in there to see him."

"I know you will. I'm so glad you're here." I feel myself flush, which I hope is the stirring of love and not, as I fear, my first menopausal hot flash. "Laura, you know this theory you had about me being so shocked, I'd never lie again?"

"It sounds crazy when you say it like that."

"What other way is there to say it?"

"You have to believe that when I first came up with the idea, it made perfect sense. I thought you'd have a visceral reaction that would—"

"Laura," I interrupt, "when did you get your Ph.D. in psychology?"

"I don't have a Ph.D. in psychology."

"And I don't wear a triple-D bra, which means you'll never see me dancing naked for money."

She considers this. "Good point," she finally says.

20

Operation Father-Daughter Reunion starts off brilliantly. The girls worked out the details during their drive upstate. All I have to do is sit—literally *sit* in the wheelchair they brought—and go along for the ride. We eat breakfast at a roadside diner. Valentine has two scrambled eggs and a slice of dry toast and doesn't touch the hash browns.

"You've lost weight," I tell her. "You look great."

She nods proudly until Bethany says, "So I won't mention the Big Mac with fries she inhaled in the van yesterday. Or the chocolate shake she sucked down. Or the two apple pies."

"Yew are so rude, Bethany," Ivy exclaims. (*And you're acting lahk some kinda var-mi-ent.*) "Valentine was just nervous. Actually, Janey, we were all nervous. Poor Natasha was carryin' on about the engine fumes! She hung her head out the window like some kinda dog."

"The van smelled like smoke, Fatso," Natasha retorts. "What's so funny about that?"

Ivy immediately shuts up and, after breakfast, sidles up to me. "Do Ah look fat?"

"Not exactly *fat*," I reply thoughtfully, spinning her around. "Your ass droops, but it's nothing a little cosmetic surgery wouldn't help."

"Ah only suggested the ass lift because it was something yew and Ah could do together."

"Let's try a movie first, how's that?"

When we get to the Shepherd Center, I take off my coat and put on a surgical gown Suzanna brought from the hospital and a black wig Bethany filched from her mother.

"How did you get this van from St. Vincent's?" I ask, tucking my hair into the wig. "Let me guess. Another poor schmuck at the hospital is in love with you."

"Actually, he's not. I had to give him a deposit. But I got the wheelchair from an orderly who asked me to dinner—"

I hold up my hand. "Save it."

"It's the red hair," Laura says, tugging on Suzanna's hair, gently and with affection. "I told you. Men *love* red hair." She hands me a pair of oversize wraparound sunglasses. "Put these on." Then she slathers white powder on my face and a pale matte lipstick on my mouth.

Ivy sticks a straw hat on my head. "Now yew look real sick but still stylish."

Suzanna is dressed in a doctor's white coat and has a stethoscope draped around her neck.

Bethany blows into the end. "Can you hear me? Can you hear me now? Can you—"

"Yes, Bethany! I can hear you." She yanks the stethoscope away. "Why are you acting like such a baby?"

"Because she still lives with her mother," I say.

"Barbara's shipping out in May." Bethany sighs. "She's in love with some wacko she met on the Internet. Can you believe it? She hooks up with some retired millionaire who's, like, a hundred years old—he's got a goiter on his neck the size of a golf ball—and now *she's* giving *me* dating tips. Like I *really* want some guy with a goiter."

"The millionaire part isn't so bad," Ivy says, suddenly interested. "What kind of dating tips?"

The rest of us tilt toward Bethany, but Laura interrupts. "Can we get this show on the road? Valentine, do you want to push the wheelchair?"

Valentine shakes her head. "But thanks for asking."

"Just want to prevent any miscommunication down the line." Laura throws a blanket around my shoulders and rolls me up the ramp that leads to the center's front door. Just before we enter, she tells me to hunch over. "You just had a stroke," she explains. I let my head flop to the side. "You aren't dead, Janey. Much to your chagrin, I'm sure."

"I don't want to be dead. I just like knowing it's an option."

"It's always an option, but we're here to make sure it doesn't happen for a very long time."

Inside, Suzanna marches up to Dorothy. "I'd like to see the director. I called earlier to schedule an appointment for Mrs. Teague and her daughters."

"Who're you?" Dorothy asks.

Suzanna glances at us. "My name is Weaver. Dr. Dee Ream Weaver."

Bethany cracks up. Laura kicks her.

"Where's Valentine?" I ask, trying to look around.

Laura pushes my head down. "She forgot something in the van."

"A Mars Bar most likely," Bethany says.

"Shut up, Bethany," the rest of us hiss.

"What time was your appointment, Dr. Weaver?"

"It's now. So would you tell Mr. Reilly to come out? Mrs. Teague needs to be admitted immediately. Her daughters brought her and, as you can see, she isn't feeling well."

I make hacking noises until Laura smacks me. "Stop it," she says, smacking me again.

"That woman just hit her mother!" Dorothy yelps.

"It's circulatory compression," Suzanna assures her. "It helps facilitate breathing."

Mr. Reilly comes out to greet us. "It's so nice to meet you, Doctor. This must be Mrs. Teague. How are we feeling today?" He bends over to look at my face and I groan like a dying cow, which makes him jump back in alarm. "Dr. Weaver, perhaps Mrs. Teague should be in a hospital. We can't admit her if she isn't well."

"She'll be fine. She just needs to lie down."

I continue to make bovine noises until Mr. Reilly steps away from my chair. "She seems to be in terrible pain. We can't be held liable if she should"—he lowers his voice—"*expire* on our premises before she's been examined by our own physicians."

"She's not in pain. The sounds you hear are caused by involuntary contractions in her bronchial passages. Now could you please show us the facilities so we can get her settled?" Suzanna also lowers her voice. "Mrs. Teague's daughters plan to pay full freight. They will also make a sizable donation to your center if you admit her within the next two hours."

"Step right this way, ladies!" Mr. Reilly gestures forward with a flourish and the seven of us troop behind, right past Dorothy, through the swinging double doors.

"Stop scratching!" Laura whispers. "You're not supposed to be able to move."

"The wig itches. And I can't see with this hat on." I take it off just as Mr. Reilly turns around. Laura grabs my hands and makes windmill movements with my arms.

"Is it okay for Mrs. Teague to be flailing like that?"

"Overhead gesticulation helps coordination and flexibility," Suzanna tells him. "Why don't you concentrate on showing us your facilities and I'll worry about Mrs. Teague."

He resumes the tour but not before glancing at me one more time. I stick my tongue out and his eyes widen. "Muscle spasm," Suzanna explains, directing him on.

Mr. Reilly leads us through the center, pointing out the two dining rooms, physical therapy machines, swimming pool, sauna, whirlpool, library, and small auditorium. The place is lovely. The walls are freshly painted and the rooms are large and bright. There's a screened solarium where residents sit in the sun and read, and a day room with a wide-screen TV. It's sunny and clean and the residents we see, while in various stages of illness, seem well cared for. Every corridor has a nurse's station where there are signs announcing bingo, movies, and shopping excursions to Syracuse.

"Wow," Bethany says. "I want to move in here. What's the average age of the men in this place? Do you encourage your residents to fraternize?"

"We have a fair ratio of men to women," Mr. Reilly answers.

"We're very proud of our facilities. We're funded by the state, as well as private contributions like yours."

"We're interested in the living areas," Laura says. "Could you show us those?"

We round a corner and walk down a long corridor. Most of the residents' doors are closed, but Laura opens each one as we pass, repeating, "Do you see your father? Do you see him? Do you see him?" until I snap, "I'll let you know, okay?"

"Did you say something, Mrs. Teague?" Mr. Reilly drops back to touch my arm.

"She doesn't speak," Suzanna replies. "The aphasia, you know."

"But she can hear," Laura says. "You sure are cranky today, Mom!"

"Stop yellin' at her," Ivy says. She turns to Mr. Reilly. "She's anxious. She's going to see her father for the first time in years."

"She's going to see *whom*?"

Realizing her mistake, Ivy bows her head. "Her father," she mouths, and points to the ceiling. "Our Lord."

"Dr. Weaver!" Mr. Reilly exclaims. "We really should have our specialists examine her."

"I *am* a specialist. So please shut your trap."

He scurries to point out the recently renovated fire-alarm system. For each step the girls take forward, Laura wheels me five steps back. I peer inside each room we pass. In one, an old man is sitting up in bed, propped against the pillows, watching television. He lifts his eyes to me, then returns to the TV.

"It's my dad! He's in there."

Laura starts to wheel me into the room, but I grab her arm. "Stop, Laura! I don't know what to say to him. I can't do this."

"Calm down."

"Come with me." I try to get out of the wheelchair, but she won't let me.

"You need to go alone. You'll be fine, I promise." Laura pushes me forward and I roll into the room and along the polished floor until I smack into Zack's bed.

I jump out of the wheelchair and lock the door. Then I pull off my wig and turn to face him. "Hiya, Daddy," I say brightly. "Long time no see."

"How did you get in this place?" is the first thing he wants to know.

"I accepted your engraved invitation," I reply, watching his face. When he speaks, his mouth pulls to the side and his lips pucker as if wanting a kiss. What he said actually sounded like, "Ow iddd eww geh nnn hiss pace?" He drags his *D*s and drops his *T*s, and his *S*s are a disaster, but if I listen carefully I'm able to interpret what he's saying.

I can't stop staring at him. Gone is the brawny father I grew up with. In his place is a frail and shrunken man with hooded eyes that are milky and soft. He's aged immeasurably since I last saw him and is now unfamiliar to me—this pale, wheezing man whose body seems fashioned for two separate people. His left side is sturdy and in motion; his right is limp and immobile. This is the man who terrorized me? This is the man I've been so afraid to visit? In a span of mere seconds, I experience the entire aging process. I escaped seeing my mother grow old, so to see my father suddenly looking elderly and enfeebled is breathtaking and cruel; maybe even more so because I was spared my mother.

As an actuary, when I consider the force of mortality, I calculate life span at a professional distance. But as a person, as a daughter, to see my father dwarfed by his bed, drooling on his pillow fills me with sudden desperation. There must be a way to exchange my own working limbs for his useless ones, to return to our trailer and restart the clock. Only this time, I swear I'll get it right; this time, I'll know what to do. I want to run away from this old man and his soft, milky eyes. Instead I use the edge of the sheet to wipe off his mouth. As I touch his face, I blink away tears.

"You look good, Daddy. But you could use some color. Don't they take you out?"

"Iss col oussie," he says, slurping his *S*s. I can't figure out what it means, but I catch the edge in his tone. *You're foolish and stupid,* I hear him say, *for showing up where you're not wanted.*

"You won't take my calls, and when I come here, you turn me away." As I speak, I purposely tower over his bed, over his body.

"Why would you do that?" I'm closer to him than I know he can tolerate. Had he not had a stroke, he would push me away or turn toward the wall, but his limp right side has rendered him helpless. Still, Zack, being Zack, won't be deterred. He slumps against his pillows and closes his eyes.

"You can pretend you don't see me," I tell him, "but I'm here. I exist. And I'm not going away this time."

He mumbles something under his breath.

"What?" I move close to his mouth. He doesn't even smell like the man I remember. Instead of beer and pulp, he smells of antiseptic and bleach. In a gesture of deference, I step back to give him room. "Please, Dad, say something."

He exhales but doesn't speak. A string of saliva clings to his chin, which makes my anger yield to a choking sadness. TALK TO ME! I silently scream. WHAT DID I DO TO MAKE YOU HATE ME?

"Look," I say, forcing myself to expose my weaknesses regardless of the consequences. "I've changed a lot in the past four years."

"Five," he mutters. "It's been five years." He speaks in a monotone, which is startling at first, but from what I've read about stroke victims—and trust me, I've read—it's not unusual.

"Okay, five." I pick up the tempo. "During that time, I learned a lot. I've been in thera . . . I've made friends, good friends, and I realize now that you and I fucked up. Well, you fucked up first and I followed. But it doesn't have to be this way forever. We can get to know each other. We can be a family." My voice cracks. "I was wrong to stop visiting. But you were wrong to think you could make Mom go away by not talking about her. I miss her so much. I want to know who she was, what her life was like before me. You can't deny me this, nor can you deny me a father. I need you, Daddy, and I think you need me, too."

He mumbles once more.

"Say it again, but this time louder and slower."

"I'm an old man," he chokes out, licking his lips. "All busted up and dying." He opens his eyes, stares into mine. "What's done is done. Let it lie."

"You're not dying." I look around the room, take in the clean white walls, the walker in the corner, the hospital bed with its metal rails. I'm struck by an idea. "Let's get out of here." I'm starting to help him up when I hear a rap on the door.

"Who's there?" I wonder if Mr. Reilly noticed I disappeared. When Valentine responds, I open the door. "Where have you been?" I ask. "And how did you get in here?"

"I was calling my office from the van and by the time I finished you guys were already inside. So I went around the back, waited for someone to leave, then slipped in as they went out. A nurse gave me your dad's room number. Where's everyone else?"

"No one stopped you? You could've been a murderer! My father can't protect himself. I'm gonna give Reilly a piece of my mind—"

"You do that. But right now we have more important things to worry about." She glances at my father. "Did you talk to him? Is that why you're so keyed up?"

"I'm not keyed up. I'm annoyed. I couldn't enter this place without government clearance and you waltzed right in to hack him to death. He's a defenseless man. Look at him!"

"He can hear you, Janey. You've gotta calm down." Valentine pats my father's shoulder. "She gets a little anxious, Mr. Fabre, but she'll be okay. How are you?" When he closes his eyes, she turns to me. "What now?"

"I want to get him out of here."

"For good?" Valentine asks in alarm.

"For a few hours. Help me load him into the wheelchair."

"Where we going?" My dad demands. "I ain't going nowhere until you tell me."

"What did he say?" Valentine whispers. "I can't understand him."

"He wants to know where I'm taking him. Give me a hand. No, wait! Find the girls and pull the van around back. I'll meet you there."

"You sure about this?"

I nod. After she leaves, I pull back my father's blankets, exposing his frail legs. He moves to cover himself and under his arm's lean covering of skin, I can see the stringy fibers of his atrophied muscles. "I'll help you get dressed so we can go for a ride."

"Not till you tell me where to."

"We're going to the pulp, Dad. Your turf. Where we can talk man-to-man without you feeling weaker or smaller than me. But I need you to shift your weight so I can lift you up."

At first I don't think I can touch him, not because he's sickly but because he's my father and I haven't touched him in thirty years. There's an instant when his sagging, mottled flesh touches mine that I feel myself recoil. But I shrug off my discomfort and help him out of his bed and into a pair of jeans, one leg at a time. His right side, his limp side, is hard to maneuver, but I hold him from behind and inch up his jeans, then pull a sweater over his head and nudge his arm into a sleeve.

It's not our most graceful moment. We stumble a lot, fall back onto the bed, struggle to get upright. But there's an intimacy we share as we work together to dress him, and despite the energy we expend, I don't want it to end. Although he says nothing, he holds on to my arm, and throws his weight against my body, surrendering his will to mine, allowing me for once to be his daughter, to let me love him.

Afraid of skidding, I drive the van slowly, keeping both hands on the wheel. My father and I slipped out unnoticed through the center's back door, but apparently the girls had a harder time getting out.

"You should've seen that Reilly guy's face when Laura showed up without you," Bethany calls from the back. "He couldn't believe you just rolled away."

"What did you tell him?" I ask, watching the road.

Natasha laughs. "She said you wanted to take a look around. So Reilly goes, 'But she can't move her arms!' So Suzanna tells him some bullshit about muscle contraction, and he starts screaming, 'Mrs. Teague! Where are you? Where did you go?' Then Valentine shows up and says there's an emergency and we have to leave. He's all atwitter, thinking we left you somewhere in the building without paying your entrance fee and refuses to let us go until we find you. So Laura tells him to check the pool because you always go for a swim around two, and he lets out a yelp and runs away. I'm sure he envisioned you floating facedown in the water."

"I bet he thought we planned to dump you in the pool all along," Laura says. "So when he ran off, we slipped out the back. He's probably putting out an all-points bulletin over the intercom right now: 'Seal off the exits. There is a stroke victim wheeling herself—I repeat, wheeling herself—through the building!' "

Smiling, I glance in the rearview mirror to check on my father. The girls used the floor harnesses to lock his wheelchair into place and are kneeling at his feet to make sure he's comfortable.

"Mr. Fabre, your hands are freezing!" I hear Laura exclaim. "Bethany, take off your coat."

"Why do I always have to give up my clothing?" She lays her mink across my father's legs. "That coat cost five grand, Daddio. I want it back."

I ask Valentine for her cell phone, then dial Willy and Rufus and tell them to meet me at the pulp. Valentine stares out the window. "It's beautiful up here."

"I want to show you guys something." I drive past Lynden Falls and into Welter. When we get to the old trailer, I stop the car. Bethany asks where we are.

"This is the house I grew up in. I wanted you to see it."

"*This* is your house?"

I stiffen. "What's wrong with it?"

"Nothing's wrong with it, Jenny. The way you described it, I thought it would be a shack. But it's a cute little place stuck back in the woods. It's so . . . I don't know . . . cute."

"Bethany's right," Laura says. "You really did this house an injustice. It's small, but it's hardly a shit hole. Excuse the expression, Mr. Fabre, but Janey has a way of embellishing. We thought she grew up in a cardboard box."

"Don't tell him that!" I say as we get back on the road. "Dad, I never said anything like that." When I catch his eye in the rearview mirror, I see what I think is an expression of anger. I look again, this time remembering what Dr. Hensen told us about anger and sorrow and how, for some people, they're bound together in one single emotion. And I suddenly understand that my father isn't a brute who hates the world. He's a crippled old man the world has undone. Dr. Hensen was right. My father had been crippled all my life, long before my mother killed herself, long before he suffered the strokes that finally felled him.

"I'm sorry," I mouth in the mirror, but he's turned away and his sad, milky eyes aren't seeing me. They're focused instead on the scenery passing him by outside the window.

I was foolish to think my father and I would be able to talk at the pulp. I thought I could park him in the shift manager's office and have a sentimental heart-to-heart. But when we get there, Rufus, a big-bellied man who resembles a bearded Buddha—and who when I was sixteen was a prominent fixture in my sexual fantasies—grabs the wheelchair. He gives me a quick hug, then pushes Zack through the plant so he can see what's been done to the decades-old press.

I'd also forgotten how loud it was inside the old mill. Willy hands us goggles and earplugs. "Tom Brisbane's kid is shift manager now," Willy calls to me. "He said we could have fifteen minutes on the floor." He waves the girls to the Fourdrinier wire where the pulp, having been bleached, blended, refined, and drained into stock, flows out in one uniformly thin slice.

"That's pulp?" Laura shouts. "This is so unbelievably cool!"

Even though I'd seen it before, I had to admit it *was* cool. The Fourdrinier wire, which is an endless moving screen, drains water from the stock to form a self-supporting web of paper. Willy shows the girls how the paper web is moved off the wire and into the press section, which is about a quarter mile long and two stories high.

"Why didn't you ever bring us here before?" Laura asks. I shrug but don't answer. As we walk the length of the presses, Willy explains the process. I know the girls can't hear him, but they nod enthusiastically, wide-eyed and humbled by the awesome machinery. As we watch, the press is squeezing more water out of the stock between two felts. Then the stock moves into the first drier section, where more water evaporates as the paper web winds forward among an array of steam-heated drums.

I look up. On the wall beside a huge American flag is a sign that says "360 Days Without a Lost-Time Accident. Keep Up the Good Work!" The sign makes me think of the days before the machines were computerized. My father hand-fed the stock into the driers and stood right beside the steam-heated drums as the paper web wound forward. By then, things had changed since the 1920s, when men stripped down to short pants and bare feet to stave off the heat, but my father still risked his fingers, eyes, skin, and lungs every time he showed up for work.

I glance at my dad, who's no longer sullen but is sitting up in his wheelchair, his eyes bright and alert, waving his good hand at a cluster of men. Rufus kneels by his side, his legs as thick as cut lumber, and listens intently.

"What's he talking about?" I ask Willy, who sidles next to me as we walk into an office. The roar of the machines is muted, but we can watch the floor through a large picture window.

"Probably telling the younger guys how he helped develop the machine guards."

I hop onto a desk and stretch my legs. "Talking shit, you mean."

Willy watches me. "It's true. Back in the seventies, when OSHA came around, Zack led a task force to get the pulp up to code. It was right after Rufus's brother, Ray, snagged his hand on a gear. You probably don't remember that."

"I didn't even know Ray worked here."

Willy nods. "Your dad made a huge stink about it to management, which was right around the time OSHA was threatening to shut us down. Because of Zack, they revamped the engineering controls and chemical-processing systems. They also put in fire-suppression mechanisms and eyewash stations. Your father helped save a lot of men from getting hurt."

"Yeah, right. Willy, you're so full of it."

"I'm telling you the truth. Your dad was a great man around here."

Through the window, my father is showing the girls the size

press where a water-resistant surface is added to the paper web in an immersion bath.

"See that second drier section?" Willy asks. "Where the sheet passes through the Measurex scanner? That's where Ray caught his hand. Before OSHA, those gears were exposed. If you didn't watch—POW! Kiss your hand good-bye. Zack came up with a way to encase those gears. Now every gear is covered and there's a checks-and-balances system for protecting the guys when they're cleaning them."

I'm stunned. "Zack never told me he did anything like that."

"Know what else? Your dad wanted to be an engineer. Shit, he was smart enough, but he went right from high school to the pulp. That's why he's so proud of you. College, grad school, the whole damn thing. And then you revamp workers' comp. You're his hero."

"I didn't *revamp* workers' compensation. I design different types of plans." As annoyed as I am by my father's lie, I'm also surprised he told it. "How do you know he's proud of me?"

"I know what I know." Willy squeezes my leg. "It was a nice thing you did today, bringing him here. Look at him. The guy's actually smiling."

"I had ulterior motives. I hoped if I brought him here, he'd talk to me. Stupid, huh?"

"Not stupid. He's your dad. Then again, he's also Zack. What do you want to know?"

"About my mother." I speak slowly, watching my father through the big window. "What she was like." He's still talking to the guys crouched by his chair. He looks so happy. For a second, I catch a glimpse of the poor kid from Welter who wanted to be an engineer.

"Sally was a great lady," I hear Willy say. He's also watching Zack. "She loved you and she loved him. But she wasn't well."

"She could've seen doctors."

"She did, Jane. For years. Where did you think all Zack's money went?"

"I never thought about it. But after she died, why did he stay in Welter? He could've moved to Lynden Falls. Gotten a nice house. Maybe remarried. People do it."

"Some people. But for Zack, there was just one Sally. He did date some. In fact, there was this one gal—" he stops. "I shouldn't be telling you this."

"You have to, Willy. What was her name?"

"Sherilyn What'sit . . . Andrews! Sherilyn Andrews. She was a dainty thing. A schoolteacher. Not bad looking. They went out a few times, but nothing ever came of it. Zack tried, but you know how these things go."

"I can understand him not telling me about another woman, but why wouldn't he talk to me about my own mother?"

"I really don't know." Willy pauses. "I know you came up looking for answers, but you ain't gonna get more than you have, especially about Sally. Zack has sealed off that door and thrown out the key."

Rufus sticks his head in. "Brisbane's kid is about to have a fit. We need to go."

I meet up with the girls at the calendar stack where massive steel polishing rolls give the paper its final finish. The paper web is wound up in a single long reel, which is as big and as thick as a redwood's trunk. A mechanism slices the reel into rolls and rewinds them onto cores, which are taken to the finishing room to be weighed, wrapped, labeled, and shipped.

I watch the rolls being sliced and wound, marveling at the process, which is a continual exercise in refinement. Lumber is turned into pulp, pulp is treated and turned into stock, stock is dried and turned into paper. The process has gone on for almost a century, and, watching it, I feel proud of my father. And in a smaller way, I'm proud of myself.

Bethany's watching two men who stand by the slitter and lift off the paper rolls. I recognize one of them. His name's Luther. We went to high school together. I lift my hand to wave but he doesn't wave back. "How often do you do that?" Bethany asks.

" 'Bout every ten minutes. Watch out!" Luther rolls the core to the side.

"All he does is roll that thing off that other thing every ten minutes?" Bethany asks me.

"All day, every day."

"That's gotta be kind of boring."

"It pays the bills, Bethany." I tap Luther's shoulder. "I'm Janey Fabre. From Welter."

Luther grins. "I remember you, Janey Fabre." And when he shakes my hand, I feel very glad he does. I'm also relieved that he has all his fingers.

Outside, I take a deep breath, expecting to smell pulp. Surprisingly, the air is sweet. "The pulp doesn't smell anymore. What happened?"

Willy laughs. "It hasn't smelled for over a decade. Where you been?"

I look up at the mill, which rises above our heads and casts a long shadow across the parking lot. I realize then that the smell I carry isn't the phosphorous stink of the pulp, but the metallic smell of gas. When did I merge the two? More important, how do I eliminate the smell now that I've identified its source?

"I don't know how to thank you," I say to the girls. I call to Ginger, who'd stayed in the van all day and was now racing through the parking lot.

"Thank us for what?" Laura asks. "You called, we came. It's a pact."

"A pact," I repeat, thinking of my mother and her long blond hair.

"We also owed you," Suzanna says. "And Ivy. We owed you both."

"Don't worry, honey," Ivy pipes up. "Yew'll be payin' on that one for a long, long time."

We say our good-byes at the center. The girls are driving the van back to New York, and Willy's taking me to the motel where I can pick up my rented Taurus.

"You didn't tell us you went to Harvard, Jenny," Bethany says. "We had to hear it from Zack." She points to my father, who's inside the center with Willy, waiting for me.

"He also told us you revamped workers' comp," Laura chimes in. "You know how I feel about disclosure. Not-telling is the same thing—"

"As lying," I finish. "I feel as if we've had this conversation before."

"And I suspect we'll continue to have it."

"That's where you're wrong," I promise. "Just watch."

I see you had yourself an outing," Mr. Reilly says as I wheel my father past the reception desk. "I have to say, Ms. Fabre, I don't appreciate your little stunt. We have rules—"

"Shut up, Reilly," my father barks. Even though it comes out, "Hum up, Eimmy," I can hear the disdain in his tone, which makes me proud, for once, of his rudeness. "My daughter's paying your goddamn salary."

When we left the pulp, I promised myself I'd keep everything light. I wouldn't probe him for answers. I'd let things lie. But the minute we're alone in his room, I ask about Sherilyn Andrews. "Who was she?" I blurt out. "Why didn't you ever tell me about her?"

"Who the hell is Sherilyn Andrews? I don't know her."

"Willy told me you dated her. He also told me you did all that work at the pulp with OSHA. I didn't know that." He doesn't answer. "Dad? I'm trying to talk to you."

"What the hell do you want from me, Jane?" What he actually says is, "Wha heh ooh eww wan fom ee, ane?" His face is twisted, but I can't tell whether it's from the stroke or from the pain of having to speak to me. For the first time in my life, I see my father as a man to pity. It's an unbearable moment. I now understand that he is smaller than I am in so many ways, smaller and also more needy.

"I want to talk to you." I enunciate every word as if he were deaf. "I want to know you. And I want to talk about Mom."

"I did what I could." He presses his head against the window. Darkness falls early and the light from the courtyard reflects his face in the glass. "I loved her. Maybe too much." His words are less of a statement than a plea for me to understand the sacrifices that love had cost him, the life to which that love had condemned him. Hearing him, I realize why he told me to keep my own love in check. *Don't end up like this,* he was saying. *Live larger than me.*

I clear my throat, try to swallow my tears. "You can never love anyone too much. I'll always love her with all of myself. And believe it or not, I love you the same way. But that doesn't mean I'll become her—or you. It doesn't mean I'll stop living."

I watch his face in the window. His eyes are open. His cheeks are wet.

"Daddy, if I hadn't been born, would you have become an engineer? I know you can't say, but I hope you're happy that I'm your daughter. It's hard to know because you never tell me."

"You're my girl, Janey," he chokes out. He raises his good hand to hide his face.

"I didn't mean to upset you." I'm crying, huge wracking sobs that shake my body. "I want you to know I forgive you. I don't blame you, not for Mom, not for me. Not for anything. I've missed you, is all. I missed having a dad. But I'm glad I came to see you. And I'm happy that you're living in a clean, well-lit place. It's important to be in a clean, well-lit place. Where people talk to you. This place is so clean and . . . I don't know . . ." I'm crying so hard, I can barely speak. "So beautiful," I whisper, wiping my eyes.

He still has his hand over his face. A single tear drips through his fingers. He doesn't shake it away. Finally he tells me he needs to lie down. I help him out of the chair and into his bed. "You're a good girl," he says, clearly exhausted. "A smart, brave girl." And two minutes later, he's asleep.

I decide to write him a note and tell him I'm happy I saw him. I search his dresser for a pencil. In the bottom drawer, underneath a worn Bible, I find bundles of pictures wrapped in brown paper. I lift the pictures out of the drawer and rifle through them. My breath catches. They're pictures of my mother and me. Shots I've never seen, that I didn't know existed. Years and years of pictures just hidden away.

I quickly empty the drawer. He has my diplomas! Not just from high school, but from MIT and Harvard, still rolled in their original packaging and tied in ribbon. I hold them up, amazed he had saved them. A piece of plastic flutters to the floor. Inside the plastic is a note. The writing's unfamiliar, but instinctively I know it's my mother's.

Dear Zack and Dear Monkey,

I'm very tired this morning. More tired than I've been in a long time. I don't know if you understand, but if you were so tired it might all make sense.

P.S.—Monkey, you're a big girl now. Learn to be happy. Lots of kisses. No tears.

As I read, I feel the ground give way. I have the sensation of falling even though I'm still standing. I wave the paper in the air as if its weight can help me balance, but you can't plunge this far and still survive. I'm not merely falling off my feet but off the earth itself. I slowly lower my body into my father's wheelchair.

I study the note, unable to fathom why he kept it from me. I imagine him watching me read it, laughing *ha ha ha* at my surprise and despair, seeing me suffer this final indignity. His snoring is guttural and intense, righteous in his submission to sleep. I see him through my own eyes, see his bitterness and hurt, his beat-up body and wasted life. I see him and I hate him.

Watching Zack sleep, I can imagine him dead. Then it's me, not my father, who I want to die. I want to lie in the gutter and let a truck roll over me, break all my bones, shatter my spine. My anger surges through me like an electrical current. My breathing is labored. My head roars with blood.

I decide to call Tobias. At first it's a fleeting thought, but the more I consider it, the more sensible it seems. I want to know why he wants Suzanna and not me. I need to hear him say out loud that I'm simply unlovable. When he finally says this, I swear I'll move on once and for all.

I wheel myself over to my father's nightstand, and without hesitating I pick up the phone.

21

It's weird to be talking to you after so much time. But I wanted to see you. To set things straight." I wait a beat. "Don't you have anything to say?"

He doesn't answer immediately, so I take the time to orient myself. He looks the same, I decide. Which is a good thing. And I'm completely in control, which is also a good thing. So far, this is going better than I expected.

Dr. Hensen tilts. "Let's back up. You were about to call Tobias but—"

"I called you instead!" I am triumphant. "We had a pact. I was supposed to call you if I felt like hurting myself for real. You don't remember?"

"Of course I remember. You wanted to kill yourself." It is a question.

"I wanted to kill *something*."

"Or someone," he says. "But maybe not you. Tell me what happened before you called."

I start with my trip up to Welter in the rented Ford Taurus, knowing he doesn't mean I should go back that far. But I can't get to the diplomas or the pictures or the note without telling him that Zack had saved men's lives; that he loved my mother deeply; that in the end, he called me brave. At one point, I interject how sorry I am that I lied about my mother, but I hadn't been ready to confess to her suicide. "I don't mean 'confess' like I did it. I mean confess to the truth."

"Perhaps you do mean 'confess' as though you did it," Dr. Hensen says. "Or rather, feel responsible for it."

"Maybe." I didn't mean to lie, I continue, but sometimes stories came out of my mouth before I could stop them. Lying made me feel safe. It made me feel strong. But I wasn't going to do it anymore. "My mother committed suicide," I say, almost proudly, and glance at the clock.

"Don't worry about the time, Janey. Tell me about the phone call."

"My father fell asleep, so I decided to write him a note. I wanted to tell him how good it was to see him. That I'd come back to visit." I curl my hand into a fist, clenching and unclenching my ringless fingers. "I looked in his drawer for a pencil, but instead I found pictures." I reach into my briefcase and take out my Palm Pilot.

"Pictures of your mother?"

I nod. "And of me." I hold my Palm in my hand. "I also found my diplomas. I thought my dad threw them out years ago, but he didn't. He kept everything." I squint at the screen and realize I didn't tell Audrey about a meeting at two. The thought sends me spinning. "I need to make a call," I say in a voice that is frantic and crazy and not really mine.

"Not yet, Janey. What else did you find?"

"A note," I say bluntly. "From my mom." I take the note, still wrapped in plastic, out of my pocket. "You can read it." I hold it out to him tentatively, afraid to offer her up, to give away that part of myself to the world.

"Why don't you read it to me?"

I get up from the couch and slam it into his palm. "Because I want *you* to read it. Don't make this into a whole fucking thing."

He reads the note quickly, which pisses me off. I want him to read it slowly and deliberately so he can savor every word, commit it to memory. "You must be very angry," he says. "Your father saved all these things and never shared them with you." He waves the note in the air. DON'T BE SO CARELESS, I silently scream. IT'S ALL I HAVE LEFT! "But instead of being angry at him, you wanted to hurt yourself."

"Right now I want to hurt you."

"Did you ever consider that staying at arm's length was your father's way of making sure you'd be safe? Maybe *he* felt responsible for your mother's death, and didn't want to do to you what he'd done to her. And maybe, too, he forgot he had the pictures and the note. After two strokes, those things could've slipped his mind."

As I think about this, I begin to feel shame. Because I lie, all I see is deception where there may be innocence. *Of course* my dad planned to give me the note. I think of his face in the window. His soft, milky eyes. The tears on his fingers. *Of course.*

"Why are you crying, Janey?"

"You've got me all turned around." I wipe my face. "You tell me to be mad at my father for hoarding those personal things. Then you say I have no right to that anger because he meant to give them to me but got sick and forgot. I can't keep up with you, and I'm really smart!"

"I know how smart you are. I'm sorry if I confused you. I didn't say your father was going to give you the note. I have no way of knowing that. However, you began our discussion by listing his accomplishments to make sure I knew what a good man he was. But you *did* get angry with him. You were filled with rage. And because you can't tolerate that rage, you turned it against yourself. What I meant to say is this: Your father is a decent man, a flawed man, but decent. *And* he makes you very angry."

"So why can't you make your point in a more direct way? What happened to you, Dr. Hensen? Laura was right. You're all over the place."

He smiles and scribbles notes on the pad in his lap. "How is Laura?"

"Didn't Suzanna tell you?" I shoot back.

"You think all we did was talk about Laura?"

"You've been talking to Suzanna since Group started, and during that time, she came up with an elaborate scheme to humiliate me, so it's obvious you weren't delving too deeply into *her* goddamn issues."

"If I'd known about her plan, I would've called you immediately. You must believe that."

I shrug, not wanting to concede that yes, I do believe him. I have to believe him. He's where the buck stops, the end of the line. I didn't mean to call him from my father's room. I actually dialed Tobias first, but when I heard his voice, I panicked and hung up. My desire to hurt myself was overwhelming, but I couldn't stop thinking about the girls. Despite their foibles, despite my own, I love those six women and that love makes me responsible; it holds me accountable. If I disappear, I'd have to leave them behind and they'd worry forever that it was somehow their fault. So I pulled out Dr. Hensen's number. "Help me," was all I said. "Please help me."

"Look at me, Janey," he insists. "Your childhood was not easy, not by any stretch of the imagination. It must have been intolerable to live with a man who refused to discuss your mother's illness and subsequent suicide. I suspect it was lonely and frustrating and confusing. Your work is to explore these painful feelings in a way that doesn't necessitate your own self-destruction." He holds up my mother's note. "At the same time, you must acknowledge how angry you are with her. She abandoned you. She left you with a man who didn't have the emotional means to care for you. And in the end, your father's inability to connect with you came at a very high price, for you as well as for him. He could've lost you for good. But he didn't, which is a testament to your capacity for love and forgiveness."

"Or masochism." I reach for my mother's note. "What I don't get is how to reconcile my anger toward my father with my desire to have him *be* my father."

"One of the signs of mental health is to be able to hold two related but different ideas in your head. Your father makes you furious but he is still a good man. Your mother left you in a devastating way, but she was ill, and her illness had nothing to do with how deeply she loved you. Janey, you've made so much progress in the past two years, both inside Group and out. You have learned how to open yourself up, as well as how to love and receive love in return." He shifts in his seat. "How would you feel about continuing?"

"You think I'm crazy?"

"Please don't say 'crazy.' I don't like the term 'crazy.' But I think continuing with Group may help you work out your relationship with your mother."

"My mother's dead, Dr. Hensen."

"People die," he says, tilting so far to the left, I'm afraid he'll fall off his chair, "not your feelings for them. Group will be different. I'm making changes. But whether or not you decide to come back, you must resolve a significant issue: Can you allow yourself the success you deserve even if it means surpassing your mother?" He looks at me as if awaiting an answer.

I point to the clock. "I believe our time is up." I pause. "I want you to know how grateful I am that you answered my call. I was very conflicted about Suzanna talking to you, but the truth is, part of me felt protected, as though you were behind the scenes the whole time. I knew if I was really in trouble, you'd be there to save me."

"You were in trouble. You did call me." He says this emphatically.

"But *you* didn't save me." I wave my mother's note like a flag of surrender, wondering if Oprah would be interested in my life story. "It was the girls and me. We saved each other."

My mother died in the spring, the year I would've turned fourteen. We buried her in Welter, not Lynden Falls. When I smell freshly cut grass, hear church bells, or watch televised awards ceremonies, I am reminded of that day. Sensory perception notwithstanding, I'm often reminded of that day. Sometimes the memory filters through my head and I barely flinch. Other times my grief brings me to my knees. But the memory is there always, alive in my subconscious like a gas burner on low, ready to flare up at the slightest spark.

I don't remember who attended the funeral. When I try to conjure up my father, Aunt Honey, Willy, and Rufus, their faces are blurry and fluid. But what I do remember is the brown casket she lay in, the taste of salty tears, the thick smell of pulp, the sound of a shovel casting dirt in her plot. I suspect I've conflated the sights, smells, and sounds of other funerals I've attended into one *Uber*-funeral, one that may or may not be my mother's. So her casket might have been black, not brown and the smell in the air jasmine, not pulp. But in the absence of actual experience, I defer to my fantasy. Meaning I may not have experienced my past as much as I imagine it, but that doesn't make it any less real or any less true. Or, most important, any less petrifying.

When your mother dies, the world becomes a vast, uncontrollable place. Alive, she could scale it down to a more manageable size, but without her, all shape and meaning is lost. To acknowledge her absence is to acknowledge the black hole that exists as the rest of your life.

I wanted to believe that telling lies about her death would allow the truth to be overruled by her sudden reappearance. But deep down I knew a part of me, the part that was her, the part that made my life whole, was irretrievably lost. So I see myself at her funeral, a thirteen-year-old girl with oversize glasses, a girl with nothing left to lose. *She's not leaving without me,* I promised myself.

I really don't remember if her casket was brown or black, and I can't say for sure what I smelled in the air. But I do know that my need to fuse my destiny with hers did not, as I have claimed, begin with Tobias. It began long before that, the day my mom was put in the ground. *She's not leaving without me*, I vowed on that spring day in Welter. *Even if it means ending my own life as well.*

When people talk about loss, they speak of landscape and time. When you reach the other side, they say, the pain will go away. Give it a few weeks, they promise, you'll feel much better. But there is more to loss than expanses to cross and seasons to endure. In mathematics we accept that there is logic. We can solve for x, find the value of y. And just like in math, we look for logic in life. We expect the world to conform to a predetermined sequence. We want our mothers to know our daughters and their daughters to know us. But sometimes our lives don't conform in this way. Sometimes mothers leave before our daughters are born, before we say our good-byes. The premature losses cut us deepest, and keep cutting us no matter how far we travel or how long we wait.

But now there are times in my dreams, and in my waking life, too, when I'll feel my mother beside me. She's a voice I keep hearing, a shadow I keep seeing, a tear I keep tasting, lost but still alive and still very real. What I've learned and keep learning is that I don't have to disappear for my mother to comfort me. She can come to me in my dreams and I can feel her kiss on my cheek. I can reach out and touch her even though I'm asleep. I don't have to die to feel her presence, which is a kind of relief. It's not happiness, of course, but it is a relief.

I went to see Aunt Honey the morning after I found the pictures. I didn't tell her about them. Even in my rage, I needed to protect my dad from judgment, but I also needed to talk about my mother.

"When Sally killed herself," Aunt Honey told me, "I felt different from the way I did when Nana died. Nana was very old. She'd lived a long life. I felt lost, of course, but I had Billy and Uncle Jerry, and I couldn't stop missing my mother so much that I forgot how to be one. But when Sally died, I felt bitter and angry. It was an *event*, the likes of which none of us had ever experienced before. It was suicide, and I couldn't understand how, in the face of it, people kept moving, how things kept on going. Zack went back to work, Billy went to school, my car started, our clocks ticked. How can all this go on, I kept thinking, when my sister stopped living?"

We were walking along the riverbank, bundled up against the cold. The mud beneath the leaves pulled at our shoes and clogged the indented soles of our boots. From where we stood, I could see the back of the pulp, hidden in the mist that rose off the Wild Moose. The river was still coated with ice. I wondered how far I could tread before the ice cracked under my feet and opened up to receive me. I imagined my coat filling with water, billowing around my neck, binding me in a stranglehold. Would I try to swim? Would I call for help? Would I fight to live? Yes, I would, I thought. Yes. Yes. Yes.

"I sort of felt like that," I told Aunt Honey, still watching the river. "I thought if I died, I'd be acknowledging her, making people take notice. I also thought she could rest easier because she'd know we were paying attention."

"Jane, you don't have to die to honor your mother. You'll see that when you're a mother yourself. Children make you face certain realities. You can't disappear. You can't leave them to wonder."

"My mom didn't feel that way. She wanted to get out of Welter, consequences be damned."

"Sally was ill. She would've been unhappy anywhere. But she wanted you to get out of here because she wanted more for your life than the pulp. I feel the same way about Billy. I cringe when I think of him ending up here without seeing the world."

"It's not so bad here," I replied, thinking of my father. I couldn't stop thinking about my father. I missed him already and I hadn't even left.

"Of course not." Aunt Honey laughed. "It's my home. But look at you, Jane. You've done more with your life than my sister ever could've hoped. You got out of Welter."

"I also came back." I had an idea. "Billy should come to New York when he graduates. He can stay with me, figure out what he wants to do, maybe take some classes. It would be good for him and I think it would be good for me."

My aunt didn't answer at first. "Let me give it some thought, okay? I hate to impose."

"You're not imposing. I suggested it."

As we headed back to the street, chunks of riverbank broke loose and fell into the water. I grabbed Aunt Honey's arm and helped her maneuver through the slush. The pulp loomed in the mist like a distant mirage. "You never know," I said thoughtfully. "He might decide to settle down here." I looked at Aunt Honey. "And that wouldn't be such a terrible thing."

"You'll come again, won't you? To visit, I mean?"

"Of course," I said, touching her face, my mother's face, my own face. "You're my family."

Eventually I meet up with Tobias. Two months after I see Dr. Hensen, I decide to call him. Not out of anger or desperation or the need to hurt myself, but because I am curious. We agree to meet at a bar near my apartment, around the corner from Municipal Life.

He isn't as handsome as I remember. He looks the same, his eyes are still blue, his jaw is still chiseled, but his face lacks something. The boyish charm and insouciance are gone. He's just an average guy with the same black suit, the same tan raincoat, and the same blank stare as a hundred other guys. He could be anyone, I realize. He could be no one.

"You look different," I tell him.

"I am different." We stand at the bar, sipping our drinks, both of us still wearing our coats. "After that day you saw me with Suzanna, I was going to call you."

"To say what?"

"To apologize, I guess." He steps from side to side, like a kid waiting to be punished. "To tell you not to be mad at Suzanna."

"*You guess* you want to apologize?" I snap. "You're not sure?"

Tobias shrugs. At that moment, he does remind me of Zack, not in looks, but in size and in gesture. He's no longer the mythic character I carried in my head. He's just a guy who thinks he's in love with a girl. But Tobias doesn't understand love and the myriad ways in which it fills you. I know this because of how small he seems. The love he feels for Suzanna—the love I felt for him—isn't love. It's a vacuum that sucks up the last fragments of self, leaving us desperate and depleted and alone.

"What Suzanna and I did was wrong," he says, raising his head to meet my eyes. We stare at each other in a contest of wills. He blinks first. "But we had good intentions."

"What about *you*, Tobias? Don't you feel remorse?" I decide I've seen enough. I'm afraid that the more he holds out, I'll start to beg for things I don't want anymore, at least not from him. "This was a mistake," I tell him.

He follows me out of the bar. "I do feel remorse. Please—" He grabs my arm. "Stop."

I shake off his hand and whirl around. "You humiliated me! I thought you loved me. You said you did. Then I walked into O'Malley's and saw you kissing that girl. And you laughed at me in front of your friends, as if I didn't matter. As if I wasn't even there."

"Janey, I was young and stupid. I did stupid things. I still do."

"Then you pretended not to know me in front of *my* friends. Imagine how awful that felt."

"Suzanna said it was a prank, that we'd all have a laugh. I thought we loved each other, Suzanna and me. But she doesn't love me. She never did."

"I'm asking about you and me." I look into his eyes, which used to glint like jewels. Now they're as dull as dirty water.

"I didn't realize how you felt. I didn't think it was that big a deal."

"It was a big deal to me." *Tell me you're sorry, Tobias. Tell me you're sorry so I can forgive you. I want to forgive you, but you have to want to be forgiven.*

"After you left Muni," he says, "I used to see you at the diner on Sheridan Square." His Everyman's face is blank. "I should've talked to you—I wanted to talk to you—but it seemed like you wanted to be left alone." He shrugs. "You're not invisible, Janey. I saw you every time. And you did matter," he adds. "You do matter."

"I'm not invisible," I echo. "I matter." *Maybe it's never been them, I'd told Natasha. Maybe it's us. Maybe it's been us all along.* "I understand things now," I tell him. "I know myself." I crack a smile. "I even like myself. When we were together, I wasn't a whole person. I was so afraid of my own needs and desires, I pretended not to have any. I've learned only recently how to express myself, and I'm sorry for both of us that I've been so furious with you for such a long time, especially since in the end my anger was about so many other things. But still, Tobias"—I raise my hand to hail a cab—"you acted like a goddamn jerk." I look at him. "That's all I really wanted to say."

I get in the cab even though I'm only a few blocks from my apartment. As I speed away, I look at Tobias through the back window, expecting to feel victorious. Instead I feel sad. He stands on the curb with his raincoat flapping open, hands clenched together and head hanging low. To a random passerby, he might appear to be bent in prayer.

I tell the driver to go uptown. I need to be in motion, to feel myself travel. I'm ready to move away from Twenty-third Street. I'm ready to start living large.

A few weeks later, I take Audrey out for lunch to celebrate my return, explain her part in our meeting with HBO, and remind her that she shouldn't show up at the office unless she's wearing a bra. "Don't get me wrong," I tell her. "You have very nice breasts. But you should leave a little to the imagination."

I also have a meeting with Graham in which I tell him that despite my anxiety, I do want to make partner. "I'll do what it takes." The words come out easily because I come from a mill town. I know how important my work is for men like my father who need benefit plans that are fair and equitable.

I'm a good actuary, but it's not just because I'm adept at financial modeling. I realize that to be proficient at my craft, I have to be alive outside my head. Actuaries understand that there are limits to everything: time, work, money, life. For example, when I calculate a period reduced to the infinitesimal, I apply a related analysis that involves conditional momentary probability densities, or "forces" of termination. In the actuary's world, nothing lasts forever, and even if it does, we can force the perception of its inevitable conclusion.

Outside the actuary's world, too, there are limits to our consciousness, of our understanding. I may never learn what my father said to my mother the first time they met or when he knew for sure he had fallen in love. Nor will I ever know how my mother felt when she realized she was pregnant or why she chose to name me Jane, questions I didn't ask when she was alive because it never occurred to me that she was going to die.

But what I do know is that you can't stave off mortality or resurrect the people you love, not even by telling tales. And every time I remember my mother, I die a little. But inside that death is a reminder that I am still alive. My mother was tormented, and with her torment came a terrible isolation. I know this because I have my own torment and my own lonely days, but I don't have to let them destroy the life I've worked hard to create. I may never understand why she gave up her life on that particular day in that particular way, but unlike my mother, who never learned otherwise, I have ways to assuage my loneliness, to sustain in myself the will to live. To do the one thing she couldn't. I can rise from the floor, dust myself off, and pick up the phone.

"I remember you!"

I jerk up to see a man studying me. His face is vaguely familiar. Then again, I'm at the diner on Sheridan Square where, after so many visits, everyone looks familiar.

"But you don't remember me. My name's Lawrence Hilton. We met a few months ago."

Zeppelin Head! "You're the lawyer from St. Vincent's. What are you doing here?"

"Reading." He holds up his book so I can see the spine, which says *Mars Attack: Avenging the Red Planet.*

"You like books about Mars," I say stupidly.

"Love 'em." He grins. "You, too?"

Instead of answering, I blush.

"I wondered if I'd ever see you again." His head is as big as a satellite dish. I bet he can pick up signals from Pluto on that thing. "The last time we met, you rushed out of here so fast I was afraid I did something to offend you."

"It wasn't you. I just saw some friends . . . forget it. It's a boring story."

Lawrence glances at his watch.

What? Are you so busy with your investment portfolio and hair transplants and Viagra consultations that you don't have time for my story? "I guess you have to go, huh?"

"Actually, I do have some time, Janey."

"You remembered my name!" I swoon.

"Of course I remembered." He searches my face with his killer brown eyes. I can't stand the attention, so I look at his feet.

"You're not wearing any shoes!"

"They're back in the booth. I've been here awhile." He holds up *Mars Attack.*

It wouldn't kill me, I decide, to read up on Mars. Or to see an episode of *Star Trek*. Or—I can't believe I'm even thinking this—to discuss the possibility of a parallel universe. A girl must branch out if she wants to live large.

"Hey, Janey, how would you like to have . . . uh . . . I could go for some . . . hmm . . . I'm really thirsty." His face reddens, which takes a long time because his forehead is so expansive.

Seeing him flush makes me suddenly self-conscious. I take off my glasses. "I only need these for reading," I tell him. I put them back on. "Actually, I need them for everything."

"I like your glasses," he says shyly. "They make you look like a sexy librarian."

Come again, Mars Man?

The counter man interrupts us. "Hello, lady. Coffee for here or to go today?"

Lawrence Hilton looks at his watch again.

Why are you rushing me? Don't you see I need time? I have to decide if I want a baby. I have to consult fertility experts. I have to find a baby broker. I have to fly to China with a pediatrician and a child psychologist. Give me time, goddamnit!

"Lady, make a decision already! Coffee for here or to go?"

"So . . . can I buy you coffee?" Lawrence checks his watch one more time.

"If you're busy, just say so. We can have coffee another time. I'm busy myself. I'm a very popular person."

He holds his wrist up to his ear and shakes it. "I think my watch is broken. The second hand won't move. But if you have things to do, we can meet some other time. I have a deposition late this afternoon, but I can cancel it."

"You'd cancel your deposition for me?"

The counter man is screaming. "Lady, you're holding up the line! Coffee for here or to go?"

"Give me a minute!" I scream back and spy Larry's sneakers under a table. They rest on their sides, toe to toe, heel to heel. Given the size of his head, his sneakers are relatively small, but they look worn in and comfortable. They're the kind of shoes you reach for on a Sunday afternoon when you're strolling with your girl, holding a ring in your pocket (two-carat brilliant-cut Tiffany diamond in a six-prong setting), preparing to propose (on your knees by a lake), so you can have a family (I work after the baby is born, minimum two children, three max) and live happily ever after (retirement in Boca, early bird dinners, condo on a golf course, adjacent plots on a craggy hillside overlooking the Atlantic).

"I'd love to have coffee with you, Larry." I pause. There are limits to everything, I know, but why always capitulate? "Only today's not so great. Why don't I give you my number and we'll get together some other time?"

As I say this, I feel young and impetuous, like a sexy librarian or a sexy actuary (if there were such a thing). Forced termination be damned. I suddenly have all the time in the world.

22

"This is Kathryn Falco," Dr. Hensen tells us. "She's going to help me lead Group from now on."

"You didn't say she was a woman," Laura says. I can see she's sizing up Kathryn Falco, wondering what she's made of, if she can go the distance.

"Did you go to Harvard?" I ask.

Kathryn Falco shakes her head and her glossy bob shines in the dim Group light. She's prim and proper, wearing pearls and a headband and clean white pumps. She holds the handles of her purse, which rests squarely in her lap. "I went to Princeton."

"Princeton," Bethany mutters, nudging me. "Figures."

"Yew sure are pretty, Miz Falco," Ivy says.

Laura glances at Ivy. "But you're the prettiest."

"That's not what Ah meant," Ivy protests, but Laura tells her that of course it was what she meant. The rest of us nod, knowing Ivy.

"It's Dr. Falco," Dr. Hensen informs us. "Not Ms."

"But you can call me Kathryn." Her eyes travel around the circle slowly. I suspect she's sizing us up, too.

"Are you married?" Natasha asks, and Kathryn Falco says yes. "Four years," she adds.

"How old are you?" This is from Valentine, who has her own purse nestled in her lap, something she does when her body feels big.

"Thirty-one."

"Thirty-one," Valentine repeats, hunching over. Laura gives me a shrewd look behind her glasses. *Happy marriage,* she is saying. *Thirty-one years old. We'll eat her alive.* But she gives Kathryn Falco another chance. "You have kids?" she asks politely, hiding her scorn.

Kathryn Falco nods again. "Two. A boy and a girl."

Laura rolls her eyes. The girls and I are silent, miserable, wanting to tell Dr. Hensen that he's made a mistake. "But I hate them," Kathryn Falco adds, a hint of a smile on her prim pink lips.

Ivy's confused. "Yew hate them?"

"It's a joke," Laura tells her. "She was trying to be funny."

There's an audible sigh in the room. Kathryn releases her grip on her purse. Valentine puts hers on the floor.

"Who wants to begin?" Dr. Hensen asks.

"I had a dream last night," Suzanna starts in. She looks at Laura.

"Go on," Laura urges her. "Who was in this dream?"

"There was Ginger of course and a doctor from the hospital . . ."

As Suzanna recounts her dream, I look at the girls. All seven of us are here, assembled again to finish what we started more than two years before. We didn't meet at T.G.I. Friday's to hold a pre-Group summit. We simply called each other and agreed to show up. We'll give Dr. Hensen another chance, we said. Let the old boy show us what he's got. And we didn't say it, but we knew that this time, we'd keep him informed.

It wasn't easy to come back. To excavate the truth, to examine it from seven sides, to bear witness were all tasks none of us relished. But there are thresholds we cross when we love. We remind Ivy that she's the most beautiful, we encourage Suzanna to weave her dreams, we touch our father's mottled flesh. We let our mothers rest in peace.

I came back to talk, not just about my mother, but about myself. On my own time, I reconstruct her with the pictures I took from my father's room. In one she's wearing a sleeveless shift, her belly big with me. In another we're sitting on our trailer steps, her long blond hair draped like a shawl over my shoulders. In a third we're asleep on my bed, her body curled around mine. I have fifty or so shots of us captured at different times in different places, but when I study each one I can tell that the man who took them—the father, the husband—is peering through the camera with unyielding affection. Occasionally I call Aunt Honey to help me fill in the gaps, to explain what it is that I'm actually seeing. But more often than not I conjure up the memories, real or imagined, all by myself.

Suzanna continues to talk about Ginger and the doctor and the taxi they were driving through the streets of San Francisco. Kathryn glances at me and I lift my head slightly, signaling that when Suzanna is done, it will be my turn to share, to come clean, to confess.

"Ginger was driving the cab like a maniac!" Suzanna exclaims. "Then this truck was headed right for us but Ginger veered out of its path, drove up on the sidewalk, and saved the day."

"I'll be damned," Laura replies. "Ginger saved the day." She touches Suzanna's shoulder and waves her cat's-eye glasses. "So who's the guy? The doctor in the cab? The one you're not talking about?"

"He's just a guy." Suzanna's face turns pink all the way to the roots of her electric-red hair. "I'm gonna save him for next week." Her arched eyebrows shout YOU WON'T BELIEVE WHAT HAPPENED TO ME.

None of us presses her for more information. We've learned to take our time and allow each other to reveal ourselves slowly. But Suzanna won't be let off the hook. Next week, we'll ask about the man again. If she avoids our questions, we'll hold them for the following week or the one after that. We'll wait as long as it takes. That's what we do for each other. We wait. And we keep coming back.

Mental health is a process. I see now that I'll never fully understand myself unless I understand my mother and father. But I'm ready now to be a whole person, to take responsibility, to be part of a healthy relationship. No one, not even men who behave badly, are completely at fault. I look around the circle. There are no victims here.

"I'd like to share," I announce.

Kathryn looks me over. "Your name's Janey, isn't it?"

I nod. "But you can call me Jenny." I grin at Bethany. "We like it better."

Kathryn nods her approval, which I think is presumptuous since she's just met me, but I let it go. I can be a bigger person now. I can give her a chance.

"I'll be damned," Laura repeats, tilting her head. "You'd like to share." She pushes her glasses up the bridge of her nose. I decide that even though I love her, I still hate those glasses. I resolve to take her shopping for a new pair. Bethany is wearing camouflage capri pants and zebra-skin mules. She'll have to come shopping, too.

I want to tell the girls about my mother and how it feels to be left behind. It will be easier now because before, the two of us were so tightly wedded we weren't separate people; we were one lonely mother, one little girl. But it's not that way anymore. I am me. My mother is someone else entirely. I've also learned that I am more than just her daughter, which makes loving her—and forgiving her—a whole lot easier. At the same time, she is an inextricable part of me, a good part, not deadly. And if I should get the urge to vault from a rooftop (Full disclosure: Therapy is not an exact science), there are six pairs of hands pulling me back, six heads tilted in concern, six urgent voices screaming STAY.

I have the girls. The girls have me. I am living so large.

"Listen to this," I begin.

acknowledgments

For generous gifts of time and space, thanks to Aon Consulting, Deloitte & Touche LLP, the MacDowell Colony, the Virginia Center for the Creative Arts, and the Writer's Room.

For insight, encouragement, and due diligence, thanks to Lyons Falls Pulp & Paper, Bill Contardi, Dr. Karen Hopenwasser, Stephanie Finman, Ellen Geist, Jennifer Civiletto, Emilie Dyer, my parents and sisters, and the brilliant actuaries who vetted this book.

For wisdom, patience, and faith, my love and gratitude to Carolyn Marino.

For all this and so much more, my heart to Keith Dawson.